AN

"It is sad for anyone to be so totally _____ na said softly.

"I am not alone." Red Fox took her hand and caressed it softly. "I have you. What more could a man ask for?"

Had there been a husky note of longing in his voice? Brynna wondered. Or was it merely her imagination that caused her to think so? Was he remembering their last night together, and did he want her again?

Her heart beat with anticipation. "Red Fox," she said softly, looking at him beneath the fringe of her lashes. "Do you want me?"

He cupped her chin in his palm and lifted her face slightly. "Look at me, Brynna," he urged gently. "Can you not see the wanting in my eyes? Can you not hear it in the sound of my voice?"

"Yes," she whispered huskily.

"I need to be wanted. I must be."

She felt a flush rise to her cheeks before she spoke. "You are."

The Paperback Trade
843-2947

WARRIOR'S DESTINY
BETTY BROOKS

**ZEBRA BOOKS
KENSINGTON PUBLISHING CORP.**

ZEBRA BOOKS are published by

Kensington Publishing Corp.
850 Third Avenue
New York, NY 10022

First Printing: July, 1995

Printed in the United States of America

To Kate Nowak,
my spit-and-polish friend.

To Jim Martin.
We shared the box of Ex-Lax you found when you were
three. And we shared the motor oil to cover a childhood
foe. We shared the boat you made out of an old truck
top. And we shared the dugout you labored all day
to create. We shared the fort we built across the creek,
and we even shared our best friends . . . I married
yours, you married mine.

And now, Brother, we share something else . . .

Chapter One

Spring, 1214 A.D.

The golden sun was hot overhead and the ocean breeze, barely strong enough to stir the flaming red curls tumbling carelessly across Brynna Nordstrom's shoulders, was sullen, chafing.

Lifting a lock of sweat-dampened hair from her neck, Brynna turned her back to the ship's rail, allowing the breeze to reach that portion of her skin for a moment.

Such heat was unheard of in Brynna's homeland. Winters were severe in Norway, with a bone-chilling cold that required several layers of clothing to keep warm. Spring, when it came, was little better, though the air seemed almost reluctant to release its icy chill. But here! Here, heat appeared more an enemy than a friend. As each passing mile brought her closer to her destination, Brynna felt the need to peel away still more and more of her outer garments. All had been discarded now save one . . . the silken knee-length shift worn next to her skin.

"I never expected it to be so hot here, lass," said a male voice nearby.

"Nor did I, Timothy," she answered, turning to meet the gray-haired man's faded blue eyes while at the same time releasing her tousled hair and allowing it to fall across her shoulders again.

"Mayhap it will be cooler once we are inland," Timothy Riley remarked, joining her beside the ship's railing.

"I pray so," she muttered, turning her attention once again to the dark, vine-choked forest growing along the shoreline.

"Do you suppose we might have passed the mouth of the river without noticing it?" Timothy queried, his voice edged with concern.

"No." She shook her head in denial, feeling the brush of sweat-dampened hair against her cheeks. "One of us would have seen it." Brynna had no doubt about that fact. They could not have missed it, not with seventeen pairs of eyes searching the shoreline. If there had been an opening wide enough to sail the *langskip* through, then they *would* have seen it. "The river cannot be much farther," she muttered, narrowing her eyes to probe the dense growth of trees. "It has to be. We passed that large peninsula yesterday, and according to Nama, it was only a day's travel to the river from that point."

Another male voice suddenly intruded on their conversation. "Was she measuring the distance traveled with a brisk wind billowing the sails, or by the strength of the crew who manned the oars?" The speaker was Lacey, her second-in-command.

"She did not say," Brynna admitted. "And I did not think to ask. My every thought was concentrated on leaving Norway before my father discovered my plans." She searched her memory carefully, going over her conversation with the woman from the Eagle Clan.

What had she said about the wind?

Unable to recall the exact words, Brynna said, "I think there were strong winds. She spoke of Wind Woman being angry, her breath harsh."

"Wind Woman?" Lacey asked.

"Yes. Nama always spoke of inanimate objects, growing things, as though they were living beings. It was the way of her people."

"If there was a brisk wind, then the *langskip* must have been powered by sails."

"And there has been no wind to speak of since we sailed around the last landmark."

"True," Lacey agreed. "But we have more crew than your brother had when he sailed with the *skraeling* woman, Nama. More hands to man the oars."

"I suppose you are right," Brynna allowed, the words expelled with a heavy sigh. "I only wish I had taken the time for more detailed questioning. What must I have been thinking, to believe we could actually hope to face no deterrents in this strange, new land when we have such scanty information of which to avail ourselves? I must have been mad to ask no more questions of Nama than I did."

"No use blamin' yourself now, lass," Lacey growled. "I, for one, would much rather be searchin' for a lost river in this new land with a madwoman like yourself than sleepin', as I was, on that cold dungeon floor your father was so kind to provide for me." Though his tone was stern, a smile fluttered across his lips and humor showed in the depths of his dark Irish eyes.

Brynna cast a quick sidelong glance toward the man beside her, a withering response forming on her tongue. She would not have Lacey, nor any other man here, for that matter, thinking she'd been in any way responsible for their incarceration while in Norway.

No, that had been entirely her father's doing. Indeed, had it not been for her own desire to break free of her homeland and her father's domination, these men might yet be chilling their bones upon the dungeon floor.

Yet even as the words of rebuke threatened to burst from her lips, her eyes noted the traces of humor that lingered within his eyes, softening the features of his weatherbeaten face, and her voice stilled. It was obvious the man bore her no personal animosity, his comments having been directed by jest. And as fleeting as his smile had been was the one she returned him.

She continued to study him, wondering, as she oft had done before, about his past. An overheard conversation made her aware that he had acquired his nickname because of the network of scars that marred his back—evidence of the years of physical abuse suffered at the hands of various dungeon masters. What his real name was, she had no idea, for he spoke no word about his past, and it was not in her nature to pry. His hunched shoulders, coupled with his nearly skeletal frame, gave him the appearance of being shorter than his full height of six feet.

Brynna doubted the man would have survived much longer in the damp cell where she'd found him, but if Lacey felt even the smallest measure of gratitude for her intervention, aside from the chiding comments, he managed to keep it well hidden. The same was not true for Patrick Douglass, however. Though he had occupied the cell adjoining Lacey's, Patrick had not shared the other's apparent lack of gratefulness.

Indeed, Patrick had shown over and over again—both in word and deed—just how deeply he felt indebted to her for his freedom.

Though in truth, he should not feel so, Brynna quickly realized. Her motives for setting them free had been entirely selfish. Had she not wanted—nay, needed—desperately to escape the marriage her father, the jarl, had so callously arranged, then the men would still be within the confines of the jarl's dungeon, and she would at this very moment be wed to Angus Sigurdson.

Not that she believed those men she'd released deserved confinement in cells any more than she deserved an imprisoning marriage to a man she loathed. But still her motives in freeing them had not been altruistic by any means.

So Patrick had no need to be grateful, though she most certainly appreciated those frequent expressions of gratitude, she must admit, and to have received like expressions from the one called Lacey would not have been entirely loathsome to her.

Her thoughts drifted to her father and Brynna wondered fleetingly what the jarl might do should he find them. His wrath would, of course, come down hard against those men who'd escaped his dungeon, but would he harm her as well? The men would most likely be taken back, but as his only daughter, Brynna surely would not be imprisoned. But then again, Fergus Nordstrom could be extraordinarily cruel when crossed.

And she *had* crossed him, she reminded herself.

Twinges of guilt gnawed at the edges of her thoughts as she realized how improbable total escape from her father truly was.

Even now, a *langskip* might be sailing in pursuit with Fergus Nordstrom at the helm, his fury growing as vast as the seas he crossed. The mere thought caused icy fingers of fear to clutch her spine and she shivered.

Brynna swept her gaze around the *langskip,* reassuring herself the fourteen men she had recruited in England were still aboard. All were fighting men selected for that purpose, but the long journey had taken its toll and they were weary, too tired to endure long in hand-to-hand combat, should it become necessary.

"Something worries you, lass." Though formed with a question, the words were spoken with knowing certainty. Poor Timothy, Brynna thought fleetingly, casting her eyes toward him. He was totally unaware of the danger she had placed him in by recruiting him for this journey.

"Yes," she said huskily. "I was wondering about my father. He will leave no stone unturned until he finds me. Of that I am certain."

"Would the woman from the Eagle Clan be likely to tell him your destination?" Lacey asked.

"No," Brynna replied. "Nama would keep her knowledge to herself."

"Then the jarl would have no way of knowing where you went."

"I said Nama would keep the knowledge to herself," Brynna replied. "I fear the same cannot be said of my brother, Garrick. He will most certainly guess that I have come to find Eric and will not hesitate to tell my father. No time will be spared before my father comes after us. I should have warned you all of my father's wrath sooner, I suppose, but I believe in my heart you each knew the risks involved." She paused and looked at Lacey. "At least, those of you who have known his wrath before."

A sigh escaped her lips. "Oh, well, perhaps we can find Eric soon. Unlike Garrick, my eldest brother will find it in his heart to protect me. I am certain he will."

"To need protection from one's own father is foul, lass," Timothy said sorrowfully. "How could the jarl . . . or any man . . . do harm to an innocent girl such as yourself?"

"He would not harm me physically," she replied. "At least, not intentionally. Yet he would wed me to a despicable man who might do so."

He nodded sagely. "That has always been a woman's lot in life. You cannot change the way of the world, lass."

"No. Not the way of the world. But I intend to have a say in my own life. I bow to *no* man's will."

His faded eyes sparkled with something like admiration. "Aye. You make that clear. You have spirit, girl, and I warrant you will need every bit of it before we leave this wild, unexplored land."

"This land is not completely unexplored," she corrected. "My brother has been here before us, and Lief Erickson before him."

Her thoughts turned inward to the last time she'd seen her brother Eric. He'd been standing at the helm of his longboat, waving goodbye to her while the sun turned his hair into a golden halo. That had been almost two years ago, and Eric had still not returned from his journey.

He had always been an explorer. And when Eric heard about Lief Erickson's journey to the New World, he had decided to explore it himself. With an eleven-man crew, he had sailed up a big muddy river leading into the interior. When the longboat became stuck on a gravel shoal, Eric and five other men had followed one of the tributaries west. Brynna was to learn later that it was the last time they'd been seen by the crew that remained on board.

Although the crew waited past the agreed-upon time, they finally gave up hope and sailed for home. A few months later a second expedition, manned by the other two Nordstrom brothers, Garrick and Olaf, was launched. Finding no sign of their brother and believing him dead, the two men had returned home again, accompanied by Walks with Thunder of the Desert Clan, and Nama, woman of the Eagle Clan.

From their first meeting, it seemed a bond had formed between Brynna and Nama. That bond, and Brynna's deep sadness at the loss of her older brother, had apparently worked on Nama's sympathies until she'd finally revealed the true facts concerning Eric's fate, a truth the Eagle Clan woman had not seen fit to divulge even to Garrick, the man she had come to love.

It was upon learning from Nama that Eric was still alive and living in the New World that Brynna realized she had no choice except to find him. He alone could save her from a hateful marriage she could not abide. And it was then, too, the plan was borne to help those convicts in her father's charge escape, so the crew she badly needed for the *langskip* she would steal from her father's fleet could be had. It had been a daring and reckless plan, and one she often feared would go asunder. But so far it had not. So far they had escaped the jarl's grasp. And now, if they could simply find the lost river entrance to this new land, her chances of finding her brother would be greatly increased.

"And I will find him," Brynna muttered aloud.

"Did you say something, lass?" inquired Timothy.

"Only that I would find my brother."

"Of course you will. And if that river is anywhere along this shoreline, then we—" He broke off suddenly, staring fixedly at the verdant land ahead of them where the trees grew in such abundance.

"What do you see?" she questioned sharply.

"Look!" he exclaimed.

She followed his pointing finger to a spot where the green foliage seemed to change colors. Moments later, Brynna realized they were looking at a wide gap in the shoreline.

Her heart jerked with anticipation. "The river!" she exclaimed. "It must be the river of which Nama spoke! Oh, it just has to be!"

"Take it easy, lass," a deep, gravelly voice said. "A

river is there, but it may not be the one for which we
search.''

"It is," Brynna said, her voice filled with excitement
as she turned to the man who had spoken. "Patrick! Do
you realize what this means? We found the river. Soon
we shall find Eric."

Patrick Douglass's face remained calm and showed not
even a trace of enthusiasm for their find; but that made
no difference to Brynna's mood. She was certain they
had found the river described by Nama, and if the river
was there, then so was the mesa where her brother now
made his home.

"We *will* find Eric," Brynna repeated firmly. "The river
is where Nama said it would be. And so were the other
landmarks. Soon we will reach the tributary my brother
followed. It will lead us straight to the mesa. And Eric."

"I hope for your sake we do find him, lass," Patrick
said gently before turning back to his crew.

Patrick Douglass was a big man, over six feet tall, and
his shoulders were broad and muscular. Though it was
undeserved to some extent, Brynna had earned his undy-
ing gratitude by aiding in his escape. For that act, he had
sworn to protect her, and she had every confidence that
he would not rest until she was safe with her brother
again. The thought gave her comfort.

A smile widened her lips as Brynna felt the *langskip*
turn toward the mouth of the river, and as they entered
the watery passage, she strained her ears, eager to hear
the same sounds her brothers had heard before her—
the high-pitched howling that revealed the presence of
wolves, or the flutelike tones of birdsong—yet she heard
nothing save the gentle lapping of water against the sides
of the boat as it slid smoothly through the river that was
swollen from the spring rains.

As the longboat drifted slowly up the river, moving cautiously inland, a certain tone of melancholia fell across the occupants of the vessel, as if the tangled forest that grew so copiously along the river's edge were closing itself off to them, forming an impenetrable barrier they should not, could not, pass.

The very air around them seemed charged with warning. Yet, heedless of danger, the longboat crept further inland, making its way up the river that wound sinuously, like some gigantic serpent, past still bayous and moss-covered oaks, past the shimmer of white magnolia blossoms glistening in shadowed light against a backdrop of dark green and luxuriant foliage.

Brynna spared a brief glance at the brawny crew who manned the oars, dipping them into the water, pulling them back, leaning forward, dipping again, then moving with a backward motion. Although they seemed to row with effortless ease, she realized from their bulging biceps and rippling muscles the effort they were expending to move the longboat relentlessly against a current that must be incredibly strong. She knew that if they were able to master that current, they would certainly be able to handle anything that came their way in this wild, beautiful land.

Before many days had passed, Brynna would discover how badly she had underestimated the danger awaiting them.

Red Fox slept, his body thrumming with the dream he was experiencing while sweat poured from his body, like an instinctive reflex washing away the dark memories that coursed through him. In his dream, he saw the glow of embers. . . .

. . . The only light in the sweathouse came from the heated coals supplying the heat needed to cleanse him before the wedding ceremony that would bind him to Sweet Willow—a fact which caused him great happiness. He was contemplating their life together and basking in the glow of her love when suddenly he felt a change in the atmosphere . . . a deep sense of foreboding, of danger lurking somewhere nearby.

He crawled across the sweathouse, pushed open the elkhide flap, and peered out at the tangled growth of vine-covered trees around him.

There was nothing there to cause him worry, but still his heart thudded with dread of what was to come.

His gaze traveled higher, took in the stars glittering in the darkened sky. Again, all appeared normal—but he sensed it was not. Something was out there, waiting for him, approaching.

Fear of the unknown throbbed within him, beating heavily in his chest as he continued to probe the forest for the unknown danger that lurked ever closer.

Then, suddenly, strange though it seemed, the stars appeared to jump erratically before winking out completely. An inhuman roar bellowed out of nowhere and Red Fox stiffened in uncontrollable fear. It swept over him like layers of suffocating mud and a lump formed in his throat, making breathing difficult.

The deafening growl surrounded him, held him captive, refused to allow him thought. A vibration shook the ground beneath him and something heavy crunched across the dry leaves nearby.

Then he saw it: a bear! Larger than any he had ever seen before. And the sight of a feathered arrow penetrating its neck told him the beast was obviously

in great pain, angry enough to vent its rage on anything that chanced to get in its way.

Realizing he must escape the enraged beast, Red
Fox attempted to rise. But all his movements seemed
to take place in slow motion.

Crunch, crunch!

Red Fox shivered as the bear came closer. He
could feel the weight and bulk and the black presence
of the beast, could feel its hot breath as it glared at
him with burning eyes.

He attempted to flee in the face of its wrath, but
as though guessing his thoughts, the bear rose on
its hind legs and raked its sharp claws through the
air. Their hardened fury scratched brutally over his
face.

Pain slashed through Red Fox's cheek, stabbing
into his flesh with intense heat, as though a flaming
torch had been held against his face. But the warrior
had no time to wonder at the damage the beast had
wrought. His only thought was escape.

Escape!

The beast struck again as Red Fox stumbled back-
wards. Had the warrior not lost his balance and
tumbled to the ground, the bear certainly would have
decapitated him. But it was only a short reprieve,
Red Fox quickly realized. He was surely a dead man
refusing to accept that fact.

As the bear growled again, Red Fox looked into
its eyes and cried out in fear. The beast's eyes were
on fire. It was not of this world, but from that other
place which was meant to keep such evil from them.

Realizing he could never escape such a monstros-
ity, that he was already as good as dead, Red Fox
opened his mouth in a silent scream. . . .

. . . And woke abruptly.

He lay rigid on his bed of leaves, his body soaked with sweat, his eyes staring up into the darkened sky above him. How long would the recurring dreams of the bear's attack continue to plague him, he wondered bitterly, recalling the pain of long ago.

He fingered the long, puckered scar that seared the right side of his face from brow to lower jaw. It seemed to throb beneath his touch as it so often did after he'd had the nightmare which had become his nightly companion.

Once, long ago, before the bear's attack, Red Fox had smugly believed he'd held the world in his hands. He'd been preparing for his marriage to Sweet Willow then, secure in her love. But the bear had changed everything for him. Unable to summon the courage to fight the bear on his own, he had been dependent upon a childhood friend to intervene and save him from certain death. And so it was because of his friend Black Wing's help that he had escaped with his body, if not his courage, intact. Now the scar marring his features as it cut its jagged swath across his cheekbone and eye—such an ugly sight— served as little more than a constant reminder of his cowardice. And it had been enough to drive Sweet Willow away. Sickened by the sight of him, she had abandoned their pledge of betrothal, leaving him instead to be the object of pity for all whose path he crossed.

Perhaps it would have been better, Red Fox considered now, as he had so often done in the past, if the bear had killed him. At least then he would not have been forced to suffer the condemnation of his own people. Oh, how well he could remember the looks he'd been given when first he had recovered from the deadly assault. Some had gazed openly with pity, while others had cringed with revulsion at the sight of his horrid scars. But it was those whose look was doubting, as if wondering how such a coward had been born into their midst, that bothered him most. At last, unable to bear the incriminating eyes of his own people any longer, he had left them, willing to make his way alone. He had become a wanderer, a man without a people.

It was a lonely life, but what else could he expect, when it was his own face that caused others to draw back and pull away? But the loneliness had been hard to take, too—at least at first. Finally, though, the spirits were kind to him, leading him to find the wolf cub—a newborn— left alone when the mother's life had been claimed by a hunter's arrow. He had cared for the weak and helpless cub, grateful at last to have even this poor bundle of living flesh on which to lavish his attentions. And the cub had repaid his efforts by growing into a strong, beautiful animal, sleek with health and vitality. He had grown into a steadfast friend as well, paying no heed at all to the scars upon his master's face.

Wolf, who had been sleeping nearby, seemed to sense the warrior's thoughts. Lifting its head from its paws, it met its master's eyes with a patient yellow gaze.

"Go back to sleep, old friend," Red Fox told the wolf. "There is nothing you can do for me. I have a demon on my back and no one can shake it loose but me."

As though reassured by the warrior's words, the animal lowered its head and closed its eyes again.

But sleep did not come so easily for Red Fox. If he so much as closed his eyes, he feared the nightmare might return. And though he knew that to stay awake, facing the night with wide-eyed deliberation, was in its own way a cowardly act, he did not try to force himself to sleep. After all, who was left to know, or even care?

No one . . .

Except himself.

Chapter Two

The tributary Nama had so clearly marked on the crudely drawn map she had given Brynna lay just ahead, but even as the longboat drifted toward it, the sun was slipping low on the horizon and would soon be gone, leaving behind a blazing sky which would soon be swallowed up by night. It would be best to wait for first light, it was quickly decided, before venturing even further into unknown terrain. Thus the anchor was dropped to hold the longboat secure against the river's current. Tomorrow would be time enough to dock and go ashore.

Later, when the evening meal was ended and the hum of activity had died down to no more than a whisper in the darkness, Brynna stood at the ship's railing, her eyes probing the depths of the shadowy oaks that clung to the river's edge. She hoped to spot at least the shining glimmer of some wary animal's eyes as it came to the river to drink. Garrick had told her much about the strange animals in this new land, and she was eager to see them for herself.

But alas, none peered back at her through the darkness; no shadowy forms could be seen moving along the bank.

Brynna gained great satisfaction in knowing her journey was almost at an end. Soon, if fortune smiled on her, she would find her dear brother, Eric. Soon, she would see his dear face once more. The mere thought set her heart to pounding with eager anticipation.

She looked up at the sky, rippled with pale blue ridges of moonlit clouds. Was Eric, even now, looking up at that same sky? Was he wondering when another longship would sail up the muddy river he himself had traversed?

Brynna heard the ripple of laughter behind her and turned to see one of the crewmen breaking open a cask of ale to celebrate the success of their journey. But although they laughed and talked among themselves, their voices were subdued, their eyes watchful, each man obviously knowing there could be dangers in this unknown land.

Suddenly, Brynna heard a high-pitched howl in the distance. The howl was taken up by other voices echoing around them, and she realized it must be the wolves calling to each other. Were they announcing the arrival of intruders? she wondered.

The canine chorus obviously disturbed the horses that were stabled midship, for they began to shudder and stamp their hooves against the oak beam floor, bumping their flanks against the poles that corraled them.

Realizing they would soon break free if they were not calmed, Brynna hurried toward them and met Patrick Douglass halfway there, his intent obviously the same as hers. He was a good man, she thought again. She had been fortunate in her choice of men the day she'd set him free from her father's dungeon. In fact, were truth told, every aspect of her journey thus far had been good. She could only pray that it continued so.

But for some reason she couldn't understand, she feared it would not.

The late afternoon sun was hot overhead and the breeze tugged at Red Fox's hair, blowing loose tendrils across his lower jaw, teasing at the quiver of arrows, fletched with owl feathers and tipped with flint warheads, hanging from his back by a leather thong.

He was a powerfully built man, and the fringed buckskin he wore, designed to hide his scars, could hardly hide his strength.

The beaded headband he wore kept his hair from blocking his vision while he loped through the forest, following the deer that carried his arrow in its side, knowing he must be there when it fell so that the animal's suffering might not be prolonged.

He ran swiftly, breathing evenly and without strain, for as a child he had trained at long-distance running, traversing great distances through rugged country.

Part of his training had involved carrying a mouthful of water through rough terrain without swallowing it or spitting it out. And during that same training period he had been made to stay awake for long periods of time to learn how to deal with exhaustion. Now, he could run all day and all night in the most forbidding terrain without stopping to rest, using only a small rock in his mouth to hold his thirst at bay.

Disappointment flowed through Red Fox when he suddenly lost the trail he followed near the edge of a shallow creek. Quite obviously, the animal had entered the water.

Although Red Fox searched both sides of the stream, he found no sign of the deer and had no way of knowing whether it had gone downstream or up.

Intent on finding the animal, if for no other reason

than to deliver it from its misery, he turned his footsteps downstream, searching eagerly for signs of where the animal had left the water. He had gone only a short distance when he saw the smoke drifting skyward.

Three days had passed since Brynna and the six men who'd accompanied her began following the tributary on its winding path north. On that particular day her mount, Shadow, had stumbled in a rabbit hole. Fearing further travel might cause the animal to go lame, they'd decided to make an early camp to allow the strained tendon to heal.

She stood beside the stallion, currying his mane and breathing in the not unpleasant smell of horseflesh that mingled with the clean fragrance of pine and the tangy scent of moist earth.

"What do you think of this new land, Shadow?" she asked the stallion, who pricked his ears forward at the sound of her voice.

"I allow that were he able to speak, the stallion would say he'd rather be home, lass," Patrick said from behind her. "Animals have no sense of adventure."

"What a thing to say, Patrick. How could you possibly know that?"

"Shadow is used to cooler temperatures," he answered gruffly. "The heat can drain a man's strength. Just think what it must be like for an animal wearing hide fit for a colder climate."

"Shadow will adapt," she said, "as the other horses will."

"Perhaps. If they were staying. But I thought you intended to leave here as soon as you find your brother."

"And so I shall," she replied, feeling a sense of regret

that it was so. "But meanwhile, I plan to enjoy this wild, beautiful land while it is still possible."

"If the *skraelings* keep their distance," Lacey muttered from his place beside the fire, where he had been watching Timothy and one of the other men prepare their evening meal.

"Do you really think they'll attack us?" Brynna asked anxiously, putting aside her curry comb and releasing Shadow so he could graze on the long grass beside the narrow stream that fed into the tributary they were following.

"Who knows what they'll do?" Lacey asked, his gaze lifting to probe the shadowy forest that surrounded them on three sides. "We might have been better served had we camped in the open."

"No," Patrick disagreed. "The cliff wall behind us will protect us from attack in that direction. And we can set a guard to watch the other directions while we sleep. He can sound the alarm if anyone approaches."

"This meat has cooked long enough," Timothy announced, interrupting their conversation as he stuck his knife into the roasting carcass. "Here, you," he said to the nearest man. "See the Lady Brynna has the best portion."

"You spoil her," Patrick said gruffly. "I'll wager her teeth are as strong as mine."

"Stronger, perhaps," Timothy agreed. "But the strength of her teeth is not in question here. Her ladyship has paid well for our services. That should warrant the best we have, even if her title did not. Which it does."

"My title is of no consequence here, Timothy," Brynna protested. "Neither is the fact that I happen to be a female."

"That is a fact," Patrick said. "If we take into account

that you are the only woman among us, you would be delegated to cook all our meals."

"And your belly would be crying out for some decent food," Brynna responded with a smile. "Cooking is not one of my accomplishments."

"I warrant you sew a fine seam, though, lass," Lacey said.

"I fear not," Brynna returned with a shudder. "I am woefully inept at that, too."

"I thought all ladies were taught to sew when they were only children," one of the other men said, joining the teasing.

"Mother tried teaching me," Brynna said. "On those rare occasions when she could find me."

"I gather you were usually in hiding, then." Patrick said.

"Usually," she answered.

There was a ripple of laughter as the men continued with their teasing banter. None was aware of the eyes peering out from beyond the cover of the dense forest. None knew how closely they were being watched.

Red Fox's heart thudded against his ribcage as he slipped from tree to tree, working his way closer to the campfire where the strangers laughed and talked together, obviously unaware of being observed. But although the strangers were not of the People, they were not the sole focus of his attention. It was the four four-legged creatures grazing near the stream that caught and held his interest.

What were they? he wondered. And what purpose did they serve? He had never seen their like before, had never even heard of their existence.

One of the beasts, its black hide gleaming beneath the rays of Father Sun, seemed to sense the warrior's presence,

for it stopped grazing and turned its head in his direction,
at the same time uttering a snuffling snort and shuddering
slightly.

Red Fox froze. Sliding behind the nearest tree, he was
keenly aware of the quiet that descended upon the group
around the fire. A moment later he heard footsteps crunch-
ing over fallen leaves, and instinctively he dropped to his
belly, sliding under the nearest bush. Just in time, he
thought, as he saw the feet and legs of one of the strangers
pass by his hiding place. He lay there quietly, waiting for
the shout of discovery, but none came. A moment later
the man passed him again, obviously having satisfied
himself there was no one about.

Red Fox felt immediate contempt for the strangers.
They obviously had no knowledge of the ways of the
People, for the man, in his ignorance, had not once even
glanced toward the ground.

Waiting only until he heard the conversation resume,
Red Fox scurried from his hiding place, circling away
from the strange animals until the campfire was between
himself and the four-legged beasts.

Red Fox took up a position behind a tree so he might
study them a moment longer to gain some insight into
their presence.

His gaze swept the group, stopping suddenly on the
figure seated on the fallen log. It was a woman, but a
woman such as he had never before seen. Long hair, as
bright and golden as Father Sun, framed her delicate
features, while eyes as blue as a summer sky peeked out
from beneath thick lashes. Her skin, as pale and creamy
as mother's milk, looked flawless in the afternoon light.

As he watched, one of the men who had obviously
been cooking the meal, cut off the tenderest portion of
meat and carried it to her as though she were someone
of great importance.

That in itself was surprising. For even though she was beautiful, other women were good to look upon. She laughed and spoke with them as though she were an equal, quite unlike the women of his clan, who were properly silent around men, shy and unassuming even as children while they trained in the duties they would perform all their lives.

He tried to put the golden-haired woman in the place of the women of the clan. It was obviously a much different life than what she was used to. The clan women were kept constantly busy in their search for food—berries, nuts, tubers, small animals and fish—and the preparation and storage of provender for the People as a whole. Those things were what women did; there could be no other life for them. Yet this woman appeared to lead no such life.

Red Fox frowned heavily. What use was such a woman? he wondered. What was her purpose, if not to work providing food? Was she there for no reason but to satisfy the lust of the men around her?

His gaze swept across the faces of the men. Lust did not gleam in their eyes. None looked at her with eager wanting. Hunger for her marked no expression. No, he decided, she was not in the company of these men for that reason. But what *was* her purpose in being there?

Finding no good answer, he decided to follow the band of strangers for a while. They were an odd people. He felt the need to study further the men who treated a mere woman with such reverence, if for no reason than to learn the motivation behind such odd behavior.

At last his gaze returned to the woman seated in their midst. It might not be such a bad thing to own her, he decided at last. Properly trained, she might be worth having. She was fair to look at, and her manner seemed easy enough. With that final thought, he turned from his place in the shadows, retreating to the place where Wolf waited for him.

Several days of traveling passed without incident. At last, however, the tributary Brynna and her men were following so faithfully began to narrow, its waters squeezed between bluestone cliffs. The travelers paused to consider an alternate route.

Pulling her mount to a halt, Brynna wiped beads of sweat from her forehead, trying to ignore the pain of her chafed inner thighs, which were rubbed raw by constant friction, by summoning up thoughts of her homeland.

What had her mother thought when she'd been told her only daughter had fled Norway? Brynna wondered briefly, pushing back the twinge of guilt that nudged her heart. She was almost certain Gilda Nordstrom had accepted the news with stoic calm. But what had she felt inside? Had her heart been burdened? Had she sought out solitude in order to shed tears of pain away from the notice and pity of others?

Brynna had no such concerns for her father's reaction, she realized ruefully. In typical fashion, Fergus Nordstrom, the jarl, had most likely roared his rage toward the poor servant left with the task of delivering the news to him. And he most certainly felt betrayed. She had thwarted his plans for her marriage, destroying his chance to profit from the alliance. He would be furious.

A smile pulled at Brynna's lips at the thought of her father's rage. It served the pompous old goat right. Surely he had known she would never allow herself to be wed to a man she did not want. She was not chattel to be sold at her father's merest whim—especially not to such a pig as Angus Sigurdson, whom she most heartily despised. Let Fergus go live with the man, if he felt Angus in such need of a Nordstrom mate. Let him stare each day at the balding pate and red nose and bulging belly and know it would be a lifelong task. Angus was ugly and horrid, and an idiot, besides. And she would never be his wife!

Yet Fergus Nordstrom would not easily tolerate such defiance as she had shown. Eventually she would have to face his wrath. Her only hope was that when she did, Eric would be at her side, staunchly defending her against their father's rage.

Once more Brynna felt a pang of guilt for having left her mother without so much as bidding her farewell. But it had been a risk she could not take, though even this realization did not lessen her remorse. She loved her mother dearly and would have given anything not to have to cause her pain.

Anything, that is, except marry Angus Sigurdson.

Still, she had no true regrets about leaving. And she had no intention of returning to Norway until Eric was by her side.

No matter what happened.

Not even if Fergus himself stormed down this very tributary and demanded her immediate return to Norway. She would not go. Not without Eric.

Nor would she allow herself to consider that her eldest brother might not want to return to Norway with her. It was too repugnant a thought.

Suddenly Patrick spoke, pulling her out of her reverie. "We cannot follow the stream any longer," he said. "We have no choice now except to go up . . . over the ridge and hope we can find a way down the other side."

Realizing the truth of his statement, Brynna urged her mount forward into the dense forest of pines. As the forest closed in around the tiny band, the air grew still and quiet, with only the sound of their own horses to break the silence.

Without prelude, apprehension fell across Brynna like a heavy cloak as they traversed farther into the shrouded woods.

Goosebumps raised on her arms suddenly, and without actually seeing any signs of human presence, she felt as though a thousand pair of eyes were trained on her.

Though she longed to stay astride her mount and dig her heels into his sides, urging him into a gallop, she knew she could not. Whether she was being watched or not, the pines grew so thick, so close together to afford an avenue of escape. In fact, farther travel meant leading her horse on foot.

No sooner had the thought occurred when she realized the others were already dismounting. She followed suit, shivering as she did, keeping reins in hand in case Shadow sensed her unease and decided to bolt.

Her heart hammered in her breast as Brynna followed a long, arduous trail that finally reached the top. Even then, she could not mount again, for it appeared the easiest way down the ridge was a dry creek bed whose bottom was covered with many-colored round pebbles.

Urging the horses into the dry wash, they followed its twisting path as it wound down the mountain.

Brynna's sense of being watched grew ever stronger as they neared a bend in the dry creek bed where the tree branches spread across the dry wash with such thickness they formed a canopy of leaves overhead.

Again she shivered and a sense of foreboding overcame her. "Patrick," she called, her gaze searching the over-hanging branches. "Wait a moment, please."

Instead of calling a halt to the procession, Patrick slowed his steps until he walked beside her. "What is it, Brynna?" he asked. "Are you in need of rest?"

"No more than the rest of you," she said. "But there is something about those branches ... I feel something ..." Her voice trailed away uncertainly.

"What about those branches?" he asked, studying the thick overhanging foliage. "Do you see something there, lass?"

"No. But—" She shivered again. "I feel as though someone is watching us."

"There is no one," he replied, with a patient voice. "Otherwise, Lacey would have found them and raised the alarm."

As Brynna watched, Timothy entered the area beneath the heavy canopy of leaves and directly behind him went several other men of their party. Patrick was right, she told herself. She was just tired. There was really no cause for alarm.

Then, suddenly, even as Brynna had her mouth open to speak, to tell Patrick her imagination must be working overtime, she heard the hideous cry.

"Aaiieeee!"

Something dropped out of the branches and knocked Timothy to the ground. He cried out horribly, but the sound died as quickly as it had begun.

"Skraelings!" Patrick shouted, snatching her off her feet and swinging her up on the saddle. "Ride, Brynna! Ride as fast as you can! Flee this place!"

"No!" she protested. "I cannot leave you alone!"

"Be gone!" he shouted, reaching out a hand to smack her mount on the rump. "We will find you later!"

Shadow rolled eyes dark with alarm and reared high into the air, pawing at the air with his forelegs, whinnying with fear. Although Brynna tried to control him, the horse had caught the scent of blood and could not be controlled.

Wheeling around, it kicked up its heels and fled the place of death.

Chapter Three

The thudding of Brynna's heart eclipsed the pounding of hooves as her mount raced away from the sound of the battle. Although she fought hard to control Shadow, her strength was puny in the face of the stallion's fear. It took every ounce of her concentration to cling to the bolting animal.

The shouts of battle became increasingly distant as the horse raced away, its hooves thudding along the dry creek bed until they reached a place where the trees grew so thick that Shadow was forced, of necessity, to slow his pace.

The stallion finally stopped, his sides heaving with the exertion expended by his fear-ridden flight.

"Easy, boy, easy," Brynna murmured, shivering as she searched the forest from which they had just emerged for sign of pursuit.

Coward! her heart cried. *How could you run away and leave the others to fight?*

Not my fault! her mind reasoned. *I would have stayed and fought with them but Patrick . . .*

Did you try to dissuade him? her heart asked.

There was no time! her mind argued. *He acted too fast! There was no stopping Shadow!*

"I must go back," she muttered, but in her heart she knew it was already too late. What had happened had happened. She had no idea how many savages there had been; she only knew their numbers had seemed overwhelming in that fleeting moment before Patrick had smacked her mount on the rump.

"I must go back," she said again. "I cannot leave them alone." But a moment later she was still there, weighted with indecision. At last a movement somewhere in her peripheral vision made her turn her head.

Her gaze swept the thick growth of pines, taking in the darker green of dense leaves covering the copious bushes clustered along the forest floor. The feeling of being watched had returned, stronger than ever, now that she had experienced its consequences, and she struggled to cut free the threads of fear that wound their way up her spine, but to no avail. By now, the fear within her had become so strong she could taste it, strong and bitter, on her tongue.

Setting her jaw at a defiant angle, she admonished her cowardly heart, commanding it to see her through the battle that was sure to come at any moment. For it would be a battle, she decided grimly, drawing her sword from the sheath fastened to her saddle. The broadsword was thin and lightweight, especially designed for Brynna's hand, a gift from her father years before. The blue and red jewels encrusted on the hilt sparkled beneath the rays of the sun as she lifted it and waited for the yet unseen enemy to advance.

She did not wait long. Almost instantly, three *skraelings* erupted from the dense forest and raced toward her, howling their fiendish warcries, their tomahawks raised in a vicious threat.

Shadow snorted with alarm and would have run from the howling savages had Brynna not dug her knees into his sides, silently admonishing him to hold his position.

Strangely, a calm had washed over her in those precious seconds before the *skraeling*'s attack. She had no doubt that she would die within the course of battle, for one against so many had no chance, and perhaps it was the certainty of death that brought about the calm. But of one thing more she was certain, too: she would not die alone.

One of the savages, a man with black and yellow paint zigzagged across his forehead and cheeks, drew back his arm and flung his war ax.

Time ceased to have meaning as Brynna's eyes caught a glance of the blade streaking toward her, and she was instantly mesmerized by the lofty way it fell end over end as it arced its way through space. But then, with reflex taking charge where thought had failed her, she slumped easily down to the left side of the saddle in that split fraction of time before blade was to meet with flesh and she felt, rather than heard, the whistle of wind as the air was displaced where, an instant before, her head had been.

There was no time to contemplate how close she had come to decapitation, though, because Shadow, frightened beyond endurance by the fracas going on around him, chose that moment to bolt upward, rearing high into the air, his forehooves clawing at the empty space before him. It was all Brynna could manage to stay astride the great stallion's back.

At once the *skraelings* scuttled back, their fear of the

strange animal in their midst overriding all semblance of bravery. But only for a fleeting moment did the horse succeed in driving them all away.

One of the savages, either bolder than the rest or more ignorant of the danger presented by the flashing hooves, returned, flinging his body's entire weight against the horse's right flank, his hand reaching up toward Brynna's leg.

Reacting swiftly, more from instinct than training, Brynna swung her sword in an arc, the blade granting no mercy as it split open the savage's skull.

Blood gushed from the gaping wound as Brynna attempted to right herself in the saddle and regain control of her steed. But even as her body straightened, she felt a savage arm slide around her waist, another's hand reaching out to clasp her sword and wrench it free, while yet another managed to drag her down from her mount, flinging her to the ground, where she landed with a hard thud. The breath whooshed out audibly, robbing her of what little strength she possessed and filling the emptiness in her lungs with pain.

Rolling quickly onto her back, Brynna stared up into flat, black eyes that glittered with barbarous intent as with his eyes alone the savage promised to avenge his fallen comrade. She had no weapon within grasp save instinct and intellect, and for the moment, even these seemed destined to fail her.

But hope would not be so easily destroyed.

With the warrior's stalwart frame bent over her, his hand guiding the knife into a high arch before beginning the downward thrust that would culminate only as the blade plunged into her heart, Brynna felt death settling over her, lightly at first, almost tenderly, the way grass might feel the kiss of the morning dew. And in that final moment she welcomed death's touch, calmly resigned to her fate, only eager for whatever pain was forthcoming to be swiftly gone.

But even as the sun's rays fell against the polished stone blade as it began its downward thrust, her mind screamed out against such resignation, demanding that she fight.

Jerking back her leg, then, she kicked out, every ounce of her waning strength contained within the thrust, and knew only intense satisfaction when she felt the ball of her foot connect with the man's scrotum.

"Aaiiieee!" the warrior screamed, falling away from her, his hands clutching his manhood as he fell to the ground in writhing pain. Yet even before he was fully away from her, another had come to take his place, and for an instant, Brynna once more felt all was lost.

Mary, Mother of God, her mind silently beseeched, *If I am to live through this, then give me back my sword so I might fight!*

Her gaze skittering across the ground, she caught a glimmer of the jewel-encrusted handle lying in the dirt, but even as her hand reached out to claim it, she knew it was beyond her grasp.

She glanced quickly back to see one of the *skraelings* bending toward her, his hands arched out before him, the fingers splayed, hatred shining in the depths of his dark, savage eyes.

And then, as suddenly as his attack began, the warrior's body gave a jerk, and his mouth opened wide to let out a fearful shriek.

"Aaiiieee!" he cried, but no threat was caught within the sound. It was more the high-pitched, liquid sound of death. And even before he began to fall, she was aware of the others retreating.

Only then, with his legs giving way beneath him, his body crumpling backward like an article of clothing cast aside, only then, did Brynna notice the arrow piercing the warrior's chest.

By then he was dead.

Before her mind could deal with that fact, she saw another warrior turn toward her.

Move, move! her mind screamed. *Retrieve your blade!*

With heart thudding out her terror, Brynna leapt toward her sword and bent to grasp it. But the warrior was there before her, kicking the sword away, turning and reaching for her.

That decided her: there was nothing left to do except run.

And so she did. She ran as fast as her legs would carry her, through the forest, crashing over matted leaves, fallen branches, and anything else that lay in her path.

Brynna had no idea how long she ran, stopping for breathless moments of time, barely long enough to catch her breath before continuing her mindless flight. Finally, she broke through the forest into a clearing. She paused then, clinging to the slender trunk of a sapling while trying to ease the pain of a stitch in her side.

When her heartbeat finally slowed, the pain in her side had eased, and the fire in her lungs had been quenched, she started across the clearing, mindful of putting as much distance as possible between her and the savages. She was halfway across the clearing when she halted in midstride, staring fearfully at the lioness she had surprised. It was feeding on a newly killed deer.

Red Fox was vaguely aware of the girl racing toward the forest as he faced the one remaining warrior—like the girl, all the others had fled at the sight of his arrow— and though it was his intent to possess the strange female, he was not disturbed by her flight. He could find her easily enough, when he chose. Right now, though, there were more pressing matters . . . like the warrior from the desert clan who had remained behind to fight.

Red Fox studied the enemy before him. The desert clan warrior was poised for combat, his feet spread wide, his body crouched, each muscle tensed. He was taller by a foot's length than those comrades who had fled into the forest, and the expanse of his shoulders was broader. In his right hand he gripped a knife, the long blade sharp and deadly. Gently he swayed back and forth, the weight of his body balanced first on one foot and then the other, his eyes alert to any movement.

Warily, Red Fox began to circle his opponent, moving slowly, he dropped the sling of arrows and his bow from his shoulder, casting it aside without so much as a glance while at the same moment pulling a knife from the sheathe at his waist.

With the knife then gripped securely in his hand, he took note of his opponent's every movement, even to the rise and fall of the other's chest as he drew and expelled breath.

Several moments passed as the two warriors faced each other, and the air grew heavy with the tension radiating from their bodies like heat from a noonday sun.

"Do not interfere with me," the desert clan warrior warned at last, his voice low and mean. "The woman killed my kinsmen. She, too, must die."

"Did you not expect her to fight for her life when it was you and your clansmen who attacked first?" Red Fox inquired.

"Still, she is mine to do with as I please. By right of conquest."

"Conquest?" Red Fox sneered. "You have not conquered me. As you can plainly see, it is not I, but your kinsmen, who lay dead upon the forest floor."

"But you will soon join them," the desert clan warrior countered.

Red Fox laughed aloud. "You place more confidence in your strength than is wise. You should join your companions hiding in the forest while you have the chance."

"I do not scare as easily as they do," the other man jeered, flicking a couple of jabs with the point of his knife. With agile movements, Red Fox avoided the blade as he continued circling his foe.

"It was the sight of your scarred face rather than your arrow that drove the others into the forest. I do not doubt they mistook you for a demon," the desert clansman taunted. "Tell me, was it carelessness that caused such scarring, or were you a coward, running away and caught?"

Rage boiled like bile in Red Fox's throat, and for a moment the memory of his scar burned white-hot against his skin as pain and humiliation flickered in his eyes. And for the most fleeting instant, pain-wracked recollections caused his bravery to vanish and his body slumped.

His enemy caught the moment and with a short ripple of haughty laughter escaping from his lips he lunged, the slender blade slashing the tender skin of Red Fox's belly.

But even as he felt the knife's sting, Red Fox danced backward, dodging the next swipe of the blade, his own knife held ready, his body tensed and waiting for the opportunity to strike back.

And in the next instant it came. The warrior from the desert clan, now cocky with newfound nerve, leapt forward, his knife arcing toward his adversary's chest. But Red Fox was the swifter of the two, jumping aside, swinging one foot upward to catch the other's hand and send the knife spinning harmlessly into the brush.

Then Red Fox struck, sending his own blade into the man's chest, feeling it rip through muscle and sinew and bone, knowing the exact moment when it pierced his opponent's fragile heart.

For a second the desert clan warrior's eyes widened with surprise, but then they glazed over as death's pallor robbed the color from his face. His jaw slackened, his breath mixing with blood to rattle momentarily in his throat, and he crumpled to the ground, his spirit escaping from the shell that had been his form. He would fight no more adversaries in this world.

Red Fox watched the warrior die, then looked down at his own belly, noting the thin line where the other's knife had grazed his flesh. The cut was shallow and would heal quickly, he supposed. He wiped the blood away with his hand. Stepping with callous disregard past the slaughter surrounding him, Red Fox bent down to pick up the jewel-encrusted long-blade he had seen wrenched from the girl's grasp. She had used it to fight valiantly, the way a man, a warrior, would fight. Such a strange female, he thought again, and if he was to know her better, he must once again find her. Soon. Before those remaining desert clansmen did. Without her long-bladed knife, she would have no chance against them.

Taking only a moment to retrieve his bow and arrows, he moved swiftly from that place of death, careful to move along the same path of retreat the girl had used.

Terror blurred her vision as Brynna stumbled backward into the tangle of bushes, her eyes never leaving the lioness for one moment. The tawny cat stalked closer, its body fluid and graceful, its eyes locked with the girl's.

Run! Brynna's mind screamed. *Run! Get away while you can!*

Her breath rasped harshly and her fear was a hard knot in her throat. God! Would she never escape this forest alive? Had her escape from the *skraelings* been no more than a moment's reprieve?

No! Every instinct she possessed, every fiber of her being, cried out against acceptance of her fate. She must not give up, could not give up! A vision of her body, shredded beneath teeth and claws, spun her around, sent her dashing through the forest again, determined to escape the lioness, or die in the effort.

Branches whipped at her face while thick masses of leaves obscured her vision and made her lose all sense of direction.

Brynna had no idea whether she was running back toward the savages she had so recently fled, or away from them, though at the moment she did not care. The threat of the lioness was far nearer, far more real.

With her heart pounding and her breath burning like fire in her chest, she ran onward. Thin streaks of blood bloomed across her cheeks where the protruding branches scored her skin like knives.

Sparing a quick glance over her shoulder, Brynna half expected the lioness to explode through the trees and drag her down. But instead, she saw nothing. Even so, the sound she heard told her the animal had given chase.

"Eeeuuuuoouuwwww . . ." the cat growled, from what sounded like just inches behind her.

Brynna realized she had no hope of outdistancing the animal, and her gaze skittered over the densely covered area, searching for a hiding place . . . a cave . . . a hole . . . something large enough to provide shelter. Anyplace that would offer even the most meager protection.

But her search was in vain. There was nothing . . . nothing but bushes and trees and vines. Nothing to offer her refuge from the danger that followed so closely at her heels.

"Eeeuurroouuwww . . ." the cat screamed again.

Hide! Hide! Hide! her mind cried out, keeping time with the frantic beating of her heart. *You must hide!*

Where? Brynna frantically questioned. There was nowhere she could conceal herself.

"Eeeuurroouuwww!"

Mary, Mother of God, please help me!

Tossing another look over her shoulder, Brynna saw that the cat was almost upon her. She screamed and raced toward the nearest tree—a sapling that still had enough lower branches to allow her handholds.

Desperation lent her strength as she wrapped her fingers around the warm bark of the lowest branch and swung her legs upward, wrapping them securely around the branch.

The cat's piercing cry filled the forest as she leapt toward the girl, who was fast escaping in the tree. Brynna's breath rasped harshly as she climbed higher and higher, not daring to look down until she was wedged in the fork of a limb fifteen feet off the ground.

But the tawny feline would not be so easily deterred. With fluid grace the lioness bunched her muscles and exploded upward, her huge claws flashing out as she scrabbled for purchase in the lower branches.

No, no, no, Brynna's mind screamed in terror.

Frantically, she continued to climb higher and higher until the tree trunk measured no more than three inches around. The tree began to bend beneath her weight and she realized she could climb no higher. There would be no further retreat.

Patrick Douglass stood among the dead and dying, blood oozing from the many cuts that crisscrossed his flesh. Grimly he surveyed the bloody scene around him.

There were at least twenty *skraelings* dead in the dry creek bottom and a quick count showed him that five of their own party had perished. Only he, Lacey, and Michael O'Leary remained on their feet.

"Where is Lady Brynna?" Michael asked.

"I sent her away when they attacked," Patrick replied. He started for the nearest horse, knowing he must find her before the escaping savages did. "Lacey," he added, "See to our people. I will return when I find the lass."

Brynna's heart hammered savagely within her breast as fear threatened to overcome her. She closed her eyes and concentrated on the feel of the rough bark as it pressed against her fingers. Taking a long, deep breath, she slowly exhaled, feeling the tremors leave her hand and arm.

Slightly calmer, she looked back down the tree to assess the situation with more composure, and immediately the sight of the lioness creeping closer set her shivering again.

"God, help me," she whispered, knowing only divine intervention could save her.

Even so, she could not allow herself to give up. Even now, her mind was searching for ways of escape. She wondered if she could drop to the ground and flee, momentarily confusing the feline. It just might work, she realized. The slender sapling, released from her weight, could very well act as a catapult, hurling the cat through the air.

Hope, like spring, was born anew. It flared brightly as she looked toward the ground and estimated the distance.

Perhaps she could drop free. While the cat was recovering from its fall, she could—

A growl soon interrupted her plans, jerking her eyes toward the sound, and her spirits dropped again.

For now, on the ground below her, a large gray wolf was circling. If it was mindful of the cat's presence, it gave no sign.

Instead, Brynna noted with a new surge of alarm, the

wolf seemed intent on focusing his cold, yellow gaze on her alone, his mouth held slightly open to expose long, sharp teeth.

After a moment, as Brynna clung helplessly to the slender tree trunk, praying for deliverance while knowing none would come, the wolf sat back on its haunches and gazed up at her. In time, the wolf's expression seemed to say, its quarry would come to it, and then it would have nothing to do but eat its fill and thank the lioness for the provision of a lovely meal.

The wolf continued to sit on its haunches, its tongue lolling, saliva dripping from its point. Its eyes remained hungrily fastened on her.

Nearby, the cat growled and hissed, spitting out its anger toward the newest interloper, but the wolf still did not move.

With terror clutching at her heart, Brynna heard the first bone-chilling sound of green wood breaking. The slender sapling trunk creaked and moaned and splintered free, no longer able to bear the weight of the girl who clung to it so tenaciously.

Chapter Four

Red Fox followed the girl's trail through the forest, taking note of the fact that she had made no effort to hide the trail of broken branches that so easily marked her way. As if any who cared to look for her were welcome to follow.

But then, he reminded himself, perhaps she had no knowledge of such things; perhaps she was unaware a trail could be covered.

He loped through the dense growth of trees, knowing she could not have gone far. And wherever she was, he told himself, he would find her. There was no way he would allow her to escape. A woman such as she, with hair of burnished gold, should be worth many pelts if he chose to use her for barter. If not . . .

Suddenly, he heard a faint noise somewhere in the distance. He froze, becoming so still that he could hear the soft sigh of Wind Woman through the trees. But it was more than Wind Woman's song he had heard before. Straining, he listened for the other sound.

Silence.

No! There it was again. A soft ping. Almost like flint striking against rock. Distant, yet close enough to hear.

Wondering what could have caused such a noise, Red Fox abandoned the trail he was following—he could always return to it—and crept silently toward the sound.

The thick mat of leaves carpeting the forest floor became thinner . . . small rocks bulged upward from the ground as though attempting to escape from Mother Earth's embrace. The saplings were thinner, too, the trees growing farther and farther apart, until at last they gave way completely to the larger rocks that covered the earth.

At the edge of the clearing he saw it, immediately recognizing it for what it was.

The four-legged beast the girl had ridden.

It stood with bowed head, its sides heaving from its flight—or perhaps fear caused it to blow through its nose and shiver as it did. No matter; the animal would soon be calm and rested enough.

Red Fox knew his spirit guide must have led him to the beast, and that could mean only one thing: he was meant to possess it.

His! he exulted. The beast was his! And soon the girl would be his as well, for without the animal, where could she go? She would not travel far on foot; of that he was certain.

Murmuring softly, Red Fox approached the great black beast slowly, careful lest he frighten the skittish animal. ''Do not be afraid,'' he soothed, hoping the mere sound of his voice would gentle the beast. But as he drew closer, the animal sidestepped skittishly, bobbing its head, its large brown eyes rolling with distrust.

Still holding out his hand, Red Fox moved nearer, whispering soothing phrases as he went, his hand tingling with the anticipation of touching the great beast's flesh.

At last, his fingers grazed the horse's muzzle and both man and animal jerked back from the touch, but Red Fox persisted, patiently waiting for the horse to become used to the sight of him, to know he meant no harm. Only then, when he was certain of the great beast's trust, did he dare to touch the flesh again.

The muzzle was warm and soft—so very soft, he thought with amazement, very much like a mink's pelt.

The animal snorted and rolled its eyes again, pawing the ground nervously. It was all Red Fox could do to remain still, for he had already taken note of the harm its deadly hooves could do to a man.

Warily, Red Fox lifted his hand, sliding it up the length of the animal's head, from eye to jaw to nose, his fingers lightly brushing against the fine, soft hide. The horse did not move.

Red Fox had seen the girl sitting upon the animal's back. Even now, the strange contraption she'd sat upon was fastened to the beast. Could he mount the animal? he wondered. Could he sit atop the back of this four-legged giant as she had done?

"Uuuurrrooooo!"

The distant howl chilled Red Fox's blood. It was Wolf. His cry was unmistakable.

"Uuuurrrooooo!" The cry came again, rising in volume, beckoning the warrior to come.

Red Fox looked toward the sound. Something was wrong. Wolf could not call without reason. He looked at the animal beside him. What should he do? He could not leave the beast, now that he had found it, yet neither could he ignore Wolf's cry for help!

Brynna's fear was almost overwhelming, so certain was she that she was living the last few moments of her life.

The sapling trunk snapped and cracked, unable to bear the burden of her weight. Only inches from where her foot rested in the fork of the two limbs the great cat clung, its sharpened claws allowing it to edge closer to her flesh, and beneath the lion waited the wolf, like a lord waiting to be served his meal.

It was a miracle the combined weight of woman and lioness had not already proved too great a burden for the sapling's strength. But it would break free soon enough, Brynna considered, sending both herself and the cat hurtling to the ground, where each would be forced to contend with the wolf as best they could. She feared the cat would fare much better in the encounter than she would.

Why did she cling so stubbornly to life? she wondered. Surely her friends were already dead, overcome by the sheer number of *skraelings* who had attacked them. Why could she not simply give up the fight? It would be so easy to let go of the slender trunk and fall. The wolf would most likely go for her throat, making death almost instantaneous! Her life would be over in a flash . . .

And yet, to die in such a way—alone, away from family, in this strange and untamed land . . . and to be so very close to Eric, yet to never have seen him, her entire trip for naught—was unthinkable.

Tears stung her eyes as she thought of Eric. He would never know how much she loved him, how desperately she had need of him. He would never know how close she had come to finding him.

"Eeuurroouuww!" the cat growled, and the big gray wolf responded with its howl beginning low and rising higher and higher in volume until even the sound of Brynna's thumping heart beating rapidly against her eardrums was at last drowned out.

Cra-ack!

The sound came just as the canine solo ended, sending

a new lump of fear to join the one already lodged in her throat. The limb had obviously bent as far as it could. And now—

Cra-ack!

Oh, God!

The sapling dropped several inches, then broke beneath the strain, sending her plunging down . . . into the jaws of the slathering wolf waiting below.

Red Fox ran fleetly through the forest, his senses attuned to his surroundings. The creatures who occupied the dense growth of trees were silent, disturbed by the howling wolf.

Or was it something else that disturbed them?

His question was answered when he broke from the forest into a clearing and saw the wolf gazing upward into a sapling bent low above the ground.

Red Fox's searching gaze soon found the lioness in the tree, moving farther along the trunk. And then, at last, the warrior's eyes fell upon the girl.

Cra-ack!

Red Fox heard the sound of wood splintering, saw the limb drop several inches.

Cra-ack! The sound came again, then the sapling broke. He raced forward, his arms spreading and lifting . . . and the girl plunged down . . .

The weight of her drop as he caught her in his arms almost sent him to the ground.

Red Fox was conscious of her weight against him, of the softness of her skin, the sweet scent of her hair, but there was no time to consider these things, no time for anything, because Wolf was beside him, whining anxiously, warning him the lioness was still a danger.

Opening his arms, Red Fox dropped the girl on the

rocky ground and turned to face the cat who had been thrown across the clearing when the limb had snapped.

Wolf's whine turned into a low growl, but the warning was unnecessary, for Red Fox was already alerted to the mountain lion's actions. His fingers gripped the handle of the knife sheathed at his waist and jerked it free as he faced the cat, even now preparing to lunge for him.

There was hardly time to react before the weight of the huge lion struck him, the force knocking him to the ground.

Finding himself pinned beneath her, Red Fox struggled desperately to free the hand that gripped the knife, but at first it seemed impossible.

The lioness's foreleg fell against his arm, as heavy as a log, and even as he struggled, he could feel his fingers growing numb as the weight of the animal pressed against a vital artery cutting off the flow of blood.

But even as it seemed all was lost, the tawny cat moved ever so slightly and the warrior felt his hand jerk free, the knife still gripped tightly by numbing fingers.

Raising his arm only to slam it downward immediately, Red Fox feared for a moment she would sink her vicious teeth into the flesh of his forearm, so close was her mouth to where his hand and arm pulled free. Even with the thought, he could almost feel the pain of skin and bone being torn asunder.

But instead, the cat let out a plaintive scream as the first thrust of the knife blade sank into her flesh, and one large paw.

The claws were extended, raking across his shoulder, sending fire surging through his flesh. It was as if he had been seared by hot coals.

Again and again the cat screamed and again and again Red Fox plunged the knife deep into her side, striking no vital organs as it tore through her flesh over and over again.

Brynna, who had been momentarily stunned by her fall, regained her senses slowly. She was aware of a heavy thudding sound somewhere nearby and thought, at first, that it was only the fearful beating of her heart.

A low whine beside her chased the cobwebs from her mind and sent a new fear surging through her. Swiveling her head on the stem of her neck, she saw the big gray wolf beside her, its yellow eyes meeting hers, then moving to a spot somewhere beyond her right shoulder.

Her breath rasped harshly as she pushed herself to her elbows and scrambled away from the animal.

It whined again, an anxious sound, not the least bit threatening, as though it were trying to tell her something. She chanced a quick look behind her and her heart skipped a beat, then picked up speed at the sight that met her eyes.

A battle ensued only a short distance away. The mountain lion was attacking the *skraeling* who had caught her in his arms.

He would be killed, she realized, watching the animal claw viciously at the man though he stabbed it repeatedly with his crude knife.

Brynna knew she should run, should get away while she could, but she could not. She could never be the coward her fear so easily demanded. She could not allow the man, *skraeling* though he was, to be killed when he had stepped in so willingly to save her life.

Her eyes scanned the ground for a weapon, but she found no stone or stick large enough to be of use. Then, just as she was about to turn her search in another direction, she saw the glitter of bright color peek from beneath a scattering of leaves.

It was her sword!

There was no time to consider how it had come to be there. Only time to react. She wrapped her fingers around the jeweled handle, and uttering a shrill battle cry, swung the sword down toward the animal's head.

As she struck, man and beast rolled aside, and only the flat of her blade struck the great head. But it was enough to get the cat's attention.

Snarling, baring its sharp teeth, it rolled away from the man and faced her.

Brynna's blood turned to ice.

"*Eeeuurrooww!*" the lioness growled, slashing its tail against the ground and glaring at her with yellow eyes.

Brynna's sword felt incredibly heavy as she raised it, preparing to meet the fury of the cat, but she already knew the outcome. The moment the lioness sprang toward her she knew.

Chapter Five

Red Fox could hardly believe what his senses told him. The lioness was gone . . . and he was alive! Half-blinded by the sweat of exertion mingled with the red haze created by the blood seeping from many facial wounds, he looked, and found, the source of his reprieve.

The girl.

She stood there, legs planted apart in a fighting stance, gripping the jeweled handle of her strange blade in a threatening manner as she faced the tawny cat that only moments before had been so intent on eating him.

Such bravery! he marveled. Why had she not run while she'd had the chance? He had little time to think about that, however, because the lioness was bunching her muscles, preparing to leap, and Red Fox knew the girl would have no chance at all against the cat's strength.

Even as the thought occurred, Red Fox lurched to his feet, and gripping the handle of his knife, launched himself at the lioness, raising the knife and arcing it down into the heavy flesh of the mountain cat, feeling his blade cut through sinew and muscle before he jerked the blade out and sent it streaking downward again, repeating the action over and over, seeking to end the life of the savage beast before it succeeded in its attempt to end theirs.

He was aware of white-hot pain as sharp claws raked his flesh over and over again, gouging deeply. Yet even as he felt pain from the wounds he knew he could not give in to the blackness which threatened. Not when he knew the outcome of the act, the life of the girl with sunset hair.

Visions of the bear's attack and the way it had mutilated him filled his mind as he stabbed into the flesh of the lioness, and perhaps it was that memory that kept his strength from flowing away, the knowledge that this time, he would not lose. This time, he would defeat the savage beast, would kill his enemy.

He had no idea when the lioness stopped breathing; he only became aware that it was no longer moving. Then he realized it was silent, that the only sound he heard was the beating of his own heart, the harsh rasping of his breath as it heaved in and out of his tortured lungs.

Brynna, even as she wondered if the man who sought to conquer the savage beast still lived, commanded her shaky legs to move, forcing them to hold her weight as she scrambled upward, gaining her feet and leaping toward man and beast, her sword arm lifting, readying itself for the downward stroke that would surely get the beast's attention again and perhaps give the *skraeling* a chance to roll out from beneath its heavy bulk.

She had completely forgotten the wolf until it streaked into her path, tripping her up and tumbling her to the ground with such force that her breath whooshed from her lungs and she lost her grip on the jeweled handle.

Scrabbling desperately for her weapon, she felt the hot breath of the wolf against her face, knew without a doubt that its sharp teeth would sink into her throat in that next moment and closed her eyes against the attack!

Surprisingly, it did not come.

Instead, she became vaguely aware of the dust that filled her nostrils and slowly she opened her eyes, wondering if, by some miracle, the wolf had fled the scene.

It had not!

It stood over her, watching with those yellow eyes that seemed to hold a warning.

She could not move, could do nothing except stare, mesmerized, at the animal that waited so quietly, yet so warningly.

The lioness was dead!

Elation mingled with triumph as Red Fox slowly became aware of that fact. Unlike his battle with the bear, this time, as with the desert clan warrior, he had been successful in dispatching his enemy. Twice in one day he had refused to let cowardice rule him.

The animal was dead!

But at the moment, its weight was almost crushing him. Struggling against the heavy bulk that threatened to smother him, he crawled slowly from beneath the slain beast.

Then he searched for the girl.

His search did not lead him far; she was only a short distance away, obviously kept there by the threat of the wolf standing guard over her, giving her no chance to move.

Red Fox gathered his strength about him and pushed himself to his feet. Then, limping slowly toward her, he made his way to where the girl lay prone, her eyes warily watching the wolf.

At the sound of his moccasins thudding against the ground, she looked up. Her eyes widened, becoming round blue circles. Was it surprise or fear that caused the reaction? he wondered.

Feeling a slow, warmth trickling down his face, he wiped at it with his right arm. Blood. Obviously from one or more of the many gouges the cat had inflicted.

He spared little thought for the girl, however, knowing they could not stay where they were. Someone was certainly searching for them at this very moment—whoever had survived the attack, though whether it would be the warriors from the desert clan or her own people, he had no way of knowing. But he did know without a doubt that he was in no shape to challenge either group.

She found her tongue as his fingers wrapped around her forearm, pulling her to her feet.

Although she must have been frightened both by him and by the presence of the wolf who stood guard, she found that her voice seemed strangely calm when she spoke in the language that was unknown to his ears.

"Where are you taking me?" she asked, tugging her arm from his grasp as she waited for his reply.

"Come along, woman!" he growled in his own language, grabbing her arm once more and jerking her forward.

Perhaps it was the harshness in his voice, or the roughness he displayed as he grabbed her arm. Or perhaps it was merely reaction from all that had happened on this day that made her dig in her heels and pull against his grip. Whatever the reason, she refused to follow the *skraeling,* refused even to allow his touch.

Impatiently, he chastised her, grabbing her wrist once more. "Stop this foolishness, woman! It only causes delay! You have no choice except to go with me!"

But instead of complying, as any other woman would have surely done, the fiery-haired Brynna yanked her wrist from his grasp with such force that he spun around to gape at her, his mouth dropping open, his utter shock evident. Although he could not understand her words, he knew she was refusing him. Twice, in fact, she'd defied him. Never had he known a woman to do such as that! For a moment he could only stare at her, too stunned to do more. And she returned his stare, fury blazing in her summer eyes, her hands placed defiantly at her hips. But her anger only served to make her more of an enigma to him . . .

And to make him want her more. How he longed to possess a woman of such fire.

Realizing that he was wasting precious time he could ill afford, he bent swiftly and grasped her behind the knees, slinging her over his shoulder before she had time barely to wail a protest. But even as she kicked and screamed and sputtered her anger, he ignored her, loping into the forest with her instead, the gray wolf close at his heels.

"Let me go " Brynna cried, beating her hands on the back of the savage who carried her as though she were no more than a sack of coal.

She cursed herself soundly for not escaping while he was battling the mountain lion, even though reason told her she could not have done so.

At least, not while the wolf stood ready to devour her at the first move.

And that same wolf trotted along behind them now,

ignoring her completely as it followed its master like a
dog.

He shall not be my master! she silently vowed, kicking
her feet inward, hoping to injure the man who carried
her. But except for an occasional hard slap on her rump,
he ignored her actions. "Release me!" she cried, grunting
with pain as the *skraeling* trotted even faster through the
forest.

Where were they going? she wondered frantically. It
was obvious by now that he had a particular destination
in mind. But what? And how could he carry her so easily
when he must be exhausted from his battle with the mountain lion? What sort of superior strength did this *skraeling*
possess?

Her mind was assaulted by these questions and many
others, but they were suddenly swept away like leaves
before a brisk wind when her captor loped into a clearing
and callously dropped her on the ground.

Thud! The force of her fall left her breathless, her rump
smarting from its swift impact with the hard ground. But
fury allowed her to ignore the pain as she sprang to her
feet, whirling around to face the savage who had dropped
her.

And when she saw him, her eyes widened.

He stood beside a horse that was tied to a sapling.

Shadow!

Elation filled her.

With Shadow beneath her, she would escape from the
grasp of this barbarous fool. There would be no way he
could catch her while she was astride the animal. Brynna
almost laughed aloud as she envisioned him running after
her, the distance between horse and man ever widening.
Soon there would be nothing but dust clouds to show she
had been there. And he deserved no more!

As she watched, Shadow side-stepped skittishly, calming instantly though, when the *skraeling* spoke in soothing tones and held out a gentling hand. As feelings of being somehow betrayed tickled at her insides, Brynna stared with open-eyed amazement at both man and beast.

Never before had she seen Shadow so easily subdued. What kind of power did the savage have, anyway? There must be something unique in his makeup, something that both wolf and horse recognized; otherwise, they could never be so compliant, so trustful, so easily commanded.

Suddenly she remembered Mick O'Halloran, the old man who for years had been their stablehand. He, too, had possessed that strange affinity with animals—especially horses. Once, when questioned, Mick had told her it was a special gift, that there were others like him, others who, like himself, could walk up to a wild animal and instantly calm its fears.

Was it the same with the *skraeling?* she wondered. Did he, like Mick O'Halloran, possess that special gift?

At last, mindful that precious time was being wasted as she contemplated the *skraeling*'s talents, Brynna pushed herself to her feet. If she was to ever escape this man, the time to do so was now. But her movement toward the horse was soon halted, for the wolf acted quickly, positioning itself in her path, a low growl of warning rumbling in its throat, making it obvious to any who cared to listen that it intended to guard her well.

It seemed she had no choice except to use her wits against both master and beast. She searched her mind for the words she would need if she were to have any hope for freedom.

Yet to her utter amazement and chagrin, she could only remember one of the words Nama had taught her before she'd left Norway. "Friend," she said haltingly, hoping the savage could understand the word uttered in such an unpracticed tongue.

Betty Brooks

As she said it, the warrior froze and turned toward her, speaking quickly in that same guttural language she had just used. However, it was not his words—they were spoken too swiftly for her to grant them meaning—but his appearance that caused her to start and shrink away. Until now, the shadows of the forest had successfully hidden the scars that marked his face. But as he turned to her, sunlight streamed through an opening in the leaves and fell across his countenance, granting a full view to the horrid scar seared across his cheek and eye as jagged as a lightning bolt.

Yet even though the white and puckered flesh was hideous to behold, it was not for this reason that she cringed.

She was no weak-kneed female prone to easy swooning; it would take far more than an unsightly face. But what she saw before her now was a face as savage and untamed as any beastly predator ever encountered by man, and she cringed not from repugnance but from sheer terror.

Realizing at once, however, that he had mistaken her actions, she tried her best to cover up her feelings. She could not run—not now, he was too near—and so must allay his suspicion as he had allayed Shadow's fear.

"F-friend," she stuttered again, her tongue stumbling over the unfamiliar language even as she held her hand, palm outward, in the manner Nama had once shown her.

"Friend?" he repeated harshly. "You call yourself friend—?"

Although he continued to speak, she could not understand the rest of his words, but she assumed, seeing the anger and distrust glittering in his eyes, that he was disputing her right to call him "friend."

She searched for words to reassure him but could find

none. "Friend," she repeated softly, keeping her eyes away from the scar that made him appear so sinister.

Something flickered deep in his dark eyes then, and he surprised her by nodding his head.

"Friend," he agreed, then surprised her by adding, "Friend, come!"

He beckoned her closer and she glanced quickly at the wolf standing guard. He looked at the wolf, too, and at once, to Brynna's astonishment, the animal visibly relaxed as though a signal had passed between beast and master.

Then the *skraeling* spoke to her again, a single word, and yet it spoke volumes. "Come!"

She did not hesitate to obey, for even that small action would bring her closer to Shadow. And if she could somehow manage to take him unawares—

The thought had barely formed before he leapt into the saddle and extended his long arms toward her. Hands gripped her waist and swung her into the air. Before she had time to wonder how he had accomplished this, she was lying belly down across her own mount.

The indignity, as well as the ease with which he had accomplished the move, coupled to gnaw away at her insides. Her stomach muscles clenched into a tense, coiled knot.

Twisting around, she grabbed the saddlehorn with her fingers, seeking to right herself on the horse, but he would not allow her to do so. His fist came down and struck her hands with enough force to break her hold.

"Ouch!" she grunted, turning to glare at him. "I will not ride in this position." Realizing he could not understand her, since she spoke in the Viking language, she tried again, shaking her head and adding another word to her protest. "Friend. No."

He rewarded her with a hard slap on her rump.

Shadow, having been agreeable to everything else the savage had done, seemed to take offense at the slap. The stallion snorted, shaking his mane and rearing high, almost unseating the warrior.

Tightening his thighs, the savage managed to retain his seat, but Brynna would not have been so lucky had he not locked one arm around her waist to keep her there.

When Shadow dropped to the ground again, the stallion stamped his forelegs against the hard-packed ground and shook his head as though he disapproved highly of the warrior's actions.

The *skraeling* looked at the stallion's rolling eyes for a long moment. Then, to Brynna's astonishment, the warrior circled her waist and lifted her upright, settling her on the horse before him.

"Friend," he said, his lips twitching as though he were amused. Then, "We go, friend."

Brynna came very near to grinning as she realized they were actually conversing. Well, not really, she silently amended; four words did not make a conversation. But it would do for now. Perhaps the foreign tongue Nama had so painstakingly taught her would make sense once she heard them spoken often enough. At least, if the words were spoken slowly enough.

Red Fox, having no way of knowing what had brought the faint smile to the woman's lips, took it as a sign of compliance and nodded agreeably, reining the horse around until it faced north.

"We go," he said again.

Then, as though Shadow were responding to some silent command, the stallion loped toward the distant mountain.

Chapter Six

Alarm streaked through Patrick Douglass as he knelt beside the dead *skraeling*. Not because the man was dead, but because of the arrow that pierced his chest.

The weapon that had killed the man was not one of their own. Therefore, he must have been killed by another savage, one of his own kind.

Which presented an enigma. Why would one of his own people kill him? Had there been a struggle over the Lady Brynna? Had the fellows who lay dead on the ground been the losers?

More than likely. For what other reason could there be except possession of a woman such as Brynna to cause the *skraelings* to turn on each other so quickly?

It was a fact that her grace and beauty were beyond compare. Even in Norway, a land where beauty was no stranger, she was considered a great prize to be won.

Patrick himself was not immune to her charms, but she would never know the feeling he carried for her deep within his heart, for a woman such as Lady Brynna, born

to wealth and title, would not welcome such affection—
common sense told him that much. Why risk building a
chasm between them that he could never cross? At least
now, serving as her protector, he was granted the privilege
of being at her side. Or he had been . . . until the *skraelings*
had attacked. Patrick wondered if he had sent her running
from one ambush straight into the center of another.

Leaving the dead savage where he lay, Patrick went to
examine the other two. One had been killed by a primitive
weapon, while the other's skull had been split open—by
Brynna's sword, from the looks of it.

Worry etched the creases in his forehead deeper and
he wondered if Brynna had been the one to deal the death
blow. If she had, she had probably put herself in even
more danger.

Fear coiled into a knot in the pit of his stomach, tightening painfully when Patrick thought of her lying dead
somewhere, discarded by the *skraelings* with no more
regard than a bundle of rags would have been given.

Or, even worse, was she caught up in a situation with
these New World savages that to a woman of her breeding
would seem a fate far worse than death?

Damn their souls to hell! If they harmed one hair on
her beautiful head, he would find them, if it took the rest
of his life; and then he would take great pleasure in flaying
every inch of skin from their bodies.

With frustration jerking his head about, Patrick caught
sight of a deep hoofprint left in the muddy soil and immediately recalled Brynna's steed. Surely she was safe.
Astride Shadow, Brynna would have been carried swiftly
away from this carnage.

Where did she go? a silent voice questioned.

"Fleeing from the *skraeling* who slew his fellows,"
he answered aloud.

It was the obvious answer.

He prayed it was so, for it would mean she still lived.

Brynna searched for words to communicate with the savage whose hide-clad body seared her flesh wherever it came in contact. If only there had been more time to learn his language, she thought. The few words of that language—so guttural, so strange to her tongue—that she had managed to retain in memory were not enough to convince him to turn around, to take her back to her men.

But then, she reminded herself, there might very well be no men to return to, for how could they have survived the attack?

But even as the question occurred, Brynna dismissed it from her mind. They must surely have survived. To die in such a way, beneath crude stone blades, was unthinkable. And she knew that had Patrick Douglass survived the *skraelings'* assault, he would leave no stone unturned until she was found. Brynna was certain of that.

But still, she mused, she would be foolish to rely solely on Patrick's help. She must at least make the attempt to free herself, for what if he never came?

The man who sat behind her was a savage, she reminded herself, as if such a reminder were even necessary—totally unskilled in the use of modern weapons. Why, she was not even certain the crude knife he carried would be considered a weapon.

Although the blade was undoubtedly sharp, it was fashioned from some kind of primitive stone, possibly flint, certainly unequal to the tempered steel of her own weapon—the weapon she had lost—and the entire length of his blade was no longer than the span of his hand from wrist to fingertip. How could it be of but little use?

Feeling even more certain that she could escape from this *skraeling* before too much time had passed, Brynna searched for landmarks that would help guide her back to her men when the time came for her to retrace her path.

On her right was a sandstone cliff rising perhaps a hundred feet into the air. It would be a good marker.

And there, just a little beyond the cliff, was a large tree that had been split by lightning sometime in the distant past. Another good marker.

Surely she could remember those. And if she could not, well . . . at least the *skraeling* was taking her in a northerly direction. If—no! When!—When she *did* manage to escape from this savage, she would at least be that much closer to the big mesa where her brother, according to Nama, now made his home.

Oh, Eric, she silently cried. *Do you have any idea how much I miss you?*

The man behind her shifted in the saddle, bringing his body closer to hers, making her even more aware of his maleness.

A flush rose hotly up her neck and she hoped he remained unaware of it, because so far he had showed no awareness of her femininity.

Perhaps *skraeling* males did not hold the same thoughts regarding women as those men of her acquaintance, she considered. It was a fact that none of them so far encountered had taken notice of her feminine curves and flowing red tresses.

Suddenly another thought occurred. Why, to the *skraeling* brute who sat behind her, she might not appear the least bit comely! He could, in fact, think her red hair and fair skin—so unlike the dark features of *skraeling* women—quite ugly!

Then, recalling Nama's dark beauty, a sudden thought

occurred. Could the man who held her captive be one of
Nama's kinsman? Was it possible he was a member of
the Eagle Clan? And, if not, then could he be a kinsman
of Walks with Thunder? A Desert Clan warrior? If so,
then perhaps by speaking Nama's—or Walks with Thunder's—name, she might simplify her situation, make it
easier for him to think of her as a friend. Perhaps make
it easier for him to trust her. If she could make him
understand that she was a friend—

No, she reminded herself. She had already told him
that, and although he had understood her words well
enough, she was still a captive.

Yet, Brynna considered, it was worth another try. When
they stopped to rest, she would try again to talk with him.

Becoming aware of a painful ache where Shadow's
thick hide rubbed against the tender flesh of her inner
thighs, Brynna shifted in the saddle, trying to ease the
pain. She spent too much time aboard the longboat in
their journey across the sea, unable to ride. Now, flesh
once used to the rigors of the saddle was delicate and
easily bruised.

Immediately, the *skraeling*'s arm tightened around her
as though he feared she would leap to the ground and
race away.

When they came to a shallow stream, he stopped beside
it, and, clutching the reins in his right hand, slid from the
saddle and allowed the horse to lower his head and drink.

Brynna licked dry lips and looked longingly at the
water, imagining how it would taste.

What was the word for water? she wondered, searching
her memory.

Suddenly, as though it had only been waiting until it
was needed, the word came to her. She used it quickly,
her breath rasping harshly between her teeth as she tried
to convey her thirst to the man who had removed some

kind of portable vessel made of animal skin from his
waist and held it close to the stream.

"Water," she said in the guttural language he seemed
to understand, hoping she was pronouncing it right. He
looked up at her. "Water," she repeated, making scooping
movements with her hands and bringing them to her
mouth. Then, in her own language, she added, "I am
thirsty."

Brynna felt elated when he rose from the stream and
came to her. She shifted on her mount, preparatory to
sliding down, but he refused to allow the movement,
stopping her with a hand on her bared leg and handing
her the skin that, she saw, was now fuller than it had
been.

Surprised at how quickly it had filled with water, she
took it gratefully and tilted it to her mouth. The water
was cool and sweet as it flowed in her mouth, soothing
her parched throat on its way into her stomach. When
she had finished, she handed it back to him and used
another word that had somehow found its way into her
elusive memory.

"Stop," she said, pointing at the ground, hoping he
would understand her need to rest.

He shook his head, denying her request, making her
want to rail at him, to scream out her frustration and the
fear that had suddenly reared its ugly head.

Where was he taking her, anyway? And why did he
consider it necessary to continue traveling at such a pace?

That question suddenly raised another one: how long
before the sun set? If she was not mistaken, the sky had
already grown darker.

A quick glance toward the west sent a streak of alarm
through her. She had no idea how long before sunset,
could not know, since the sun had already disappeared,

either below the horizon, or covered by the storm clouds that were gathering swiftly in the west.

Why had she not already seen them?

The storm that was brewing could be a blessing in disguise. For if Patrick and her men were close, the rain might hide them while they made their approach. Or if they were nowhere nearby, it would make them lose their trail.

If only she could convince her captor to stop here!

She tried again. "Stop. I am tired." The last three words were spoken in her own language, and to make certain he understood, she placed her palms together, pressed them beneath her ear, tilted her head, and closed her eyes, miming sleep. When she opened her eyes again, she found him studying her with a mildly curious expression.

Hopefully, she used the word again. "Stop." But her efforts were to no avail. The savage gave no indication he understood her as he mounted Shadow and urged him into the water.

Thunder rumbled in the distance as they splashed across the shallow stream and the wind rose suddenly, blowing in short bursts, carrying the scent of rain with it.

Brynna threw an anxious look at her captor and managed to catch his gaze. "Look," she said, using the word Nama had taught her, then in her own language added, "Rain. A storm is coming. We must take shelter."

Although he had no way of knowing her language, he cast a quick look at the storm clouds and shrugged his shoulders and uttered a short indecipherable word. It could have meant, "Yes, I see the approaching storm and I share your concern." But she had an idea the sound meant nothing of the sort, that it might, in fact, have been a mere clearing of the throat.

Brynna eyed the storm clouds uneasily. Anything

greater than a light rain would wash away their tracks, hiding any trail they might be leaving behind for her men to follow.

"Please," she whispered aloud, knowing the man behind her could not possibly understand her words. "Intervene for me, Holy Mother. Hold back the storm so that Lacey can find our tracks."

Although the air remained dry, the storm clouds continued to blow in until they completely obscured the moon and obliterated what few stars the moon had allowed to shine.

When Shadow stumbled over some unseen object, she began to fear he would injure himself. Her anxiety manifested itself with an explosion of anger. "Stop!" After using the word from his language, she went on in hers, unable to stop the flow of words, unwilling even to try. "Ignorant swine! At least have a care for my horse!" she shouted, causing Shadow to sidestep skittishly, endangering him even further.

Realizing what she had done, Brynna lowered her voice and continued. "Are you are too stupid to see what you are doing?" she gritted, twisting awkwardly in the saddle in order to meet his dark gaze. "You are putting my horse in danger by continuing on in the dark." She pointed at the animal to better make her point.

She had no idea what made him respond this time, but respond he did. And wonder of wonders, he repeated the word for stop and used another word with it that sounded familiar.

She thought about the word, turning it over in her mind as she wondered if it was the one Nama had told her meant "soon."

It sounded like it, she thought, and that was enough to send hope flaring through her. If they were stopping soon, then—she frowned suddenly, feeling uncertain once again. Had he really said "soon," or had the word he used meant "later"?

Realizing she had no way of knowing, for he certainly could not tell her, she twisted around and faced forward again.

A moment later her captor dismounted and took Shadow's reins in hand. Immediately Brynna slid back to take full advantage of the saddle's broad seat in order to relieve her aching thighs.

With reins in hand, the *skraeling* led the animal through country that had become rugged in the extreme, circling around juniper and pine trees that clung stubbornly to the rough hillside.

If it hadn't been so dark, Brynna would probably have chosen that moment to escape from him, but she dared not try with the moon hidden the way it was and the few stars winking in and out the way they were. The *skraeling* obviously knew the country, for surely no human eyes could see through this shadowy darkness.

Brynna clung to the saddle horn with both hands, praying her mount would not step into a hole and injure his slender legs on the boulder-strewn hillside.

The warrior seemed to have a particular destination in mind, but she had no notion they had arrived until he stopped beside a rocky ledge and reached for her.

"We are sheltering here?" she asked, even though there was no thought of receiving an answer—how could the savage answer words he could not understand?

The warrior set her on her feet and pushed her toward the wall of rock facing them. She stumbled forward, feeling a new surge of alarm.

What was he about, anyway?

Her question was answered as her body failed to connect with the stone face of the cliff. Instead, she stepped into an even deeper darkness.

It was a split in the rocks, she realized suddenly. The savage had pushed her into a narrow crevice that split the sandstone cliff. She guessed it was his intention for them to shelter from the storm there.

Feeling his hand at her back, she moved farther into the crevice. How deep was it? she wondered, stepping carefully over a soft, spongy mass that gave with each step she took.

Leaves?

Or moss?

Brynna had little time to consider either choice, for it took all her concentration to traverse the darkness that seemed almost impenetrable until quite suddenly the ground beneath her feet became smooth and easy to walk upon and she could no longer feel the sides of the crevice.

Had they passed through it? she wondered. No sooner had the thought occurred than the *skraeling* broke his silence. "Stop."

Afraid of what lay directly ahead, Brynna immediately obeyed his command.

Although she was aware of movement, she could see nothing through the blackness surrounding them. Fearing the oppressive unknown, she stepped closer to him, near enough to feel his body heat.

Suddenly, unexpectedly, she was struck by a feeling of isolation, of intimacy, that was both disturbing and oddly exhilarating.

While she was still pondering that strange feeling, the savage bent over and fumbled in the darkness. She heard a sharp crack and saw a spark of light, gone as quickly as it had come.

What was he doing? she wondered.

Her question was answered as another sharp crack sent another spark shooting outward into the darkness. Another crack, quickly repeated, resulted in a flare that quickly turned into a crackle of flame.

He was building a fire in the crevice. She watched, fascinated, as he added tinder to leaves and the tiny flame grew until it caught the bigger pieces he added. Soon he had a small fire burning brightly enough to illuminate their surroundings.

It was then that Brynna realized they were in a cave. The walls were reddish-colored sandstone, and the cave was approximately twenty feet in circumference. The entrance wide enough to allow the horse to traverse the passage.

Brynna saw him near the entrance, tossing his head about, eyes rolling fearfully, his body wracked with shudders.

Intent on soothing her steed, Brynna started toward him. Immediately the warrior raised his head and pinned her with his dark gaze.

"No. Stop." His voice was harsh, almost threatening.

"Shadow is frightened," she protested, pointing to the stallion. "He is unused to being confined." That was not exactly true, she realized, as she uttered the protest. Shadow was used to being confined on the longboat. But this hole beneath the ground was not a ship; it was a cave, a dark place with no sky overhead. And her steed had no knowledge of such places—and apparently no liking for them.

The *skraeling* replied with a string of words that she had no hope of understanding, except for Shadow's name. Realizing he recognized the name for what it was, Brynna wondered at the man's intelligence, then immediately wondered as well why that should surprise her. After all, she had already met two women from this new land and both Nama and Walks with Thunder had exhibited keen intelligence.

Why then, had she supposed the *skraeling* would be otherwise?

Which posed a problem of some magnitude. How could she escape from a man who appeared to be as intelligent as she herself, and who was obviously much stronger, too?

She knew it would not be easy.

Chapter Seven

Lightning flashed overhead and thunder sounded, reverberating through the heavens. Patrick cursed loudly, knowing both he and his mount were at risk if he stayed in the open. He scowled at the darkening sky. He had already been subjected to one such storm and knew they could be severe.

Thunder growled and his mount snorted uneasily as Patrick searched for shelter. His gaze narrowed on a large oak tree with branches heavy enough that the lower ones almost touched the ground. He considered taking refuge there.

The idea was quickly dismissed as lightning streaked toward the ground. The tree's height would make it a likely target for the deadly lightning.

No; he would have to look elsewhere. Perhaps, he considered, the cliffs ahead might be a more useful place to seek shelter.

He urged his mount toward the cliff.

The wind picked up, blowing his hair across his face,

moaning and howling like a banshee, while overhead, the
thunder boomed and lighting split the sky.

His steed rolled its eyes in terror, fearful of the elements
and Patrick knew it was imperative to get them both to
safety. He urged his mount forward, scanning the cliff
until he caught sight of an overhang. He rode toward it,
knowing it was only high enough to shelter him. That
meant leaving his mount to take its chances in the elements.

While he was debating on looking for another place
to shelter, a resounding boom was followed by a loud
crack! Lightning struck the large oak tree, splitting it
down the middle.

Too close for comfort, he decided, leaping from the
saddle and crawling beneath the rocky overhang, reins
held tightly in his hand.

The noise of the falling oak, combined with the boom-
ing thunder and the scent of burning wood from the split
oak tree, served to frighten the horse to such an extreme
that the animal screamed in terror and jerked its head
back, rearing high, then thudding to the ground with
enough force to shake the earth around it.

Caught off guard, Patrick was unprepared when his
steed yanked the reins out of its master's hands, and before
he could react, the fear-ridden animal was racing away
as though chased by the hounds of hell.

As the storm moved across the land, it traveled in a
northerly direction, increasing in intensity as it passed,
until, by the time it reached the great mesa where the
Eagle Clan made their homes, it was a sight to behold.

One moment the late afternoon sun was there, the next
instant it was gone, swallowed in a world of churning

clouds that resembled—in color—an old yellowing bruise.

"The whirling wind comes," muttered Three Toes, one of the elders of the clan.

Nampeyo, the clan shaman, threw him a quick look, then stepped closer to the edge of the cliff city, feeling Wind Woman's fury as she tore at his garment, howling around him like a banshee.

Realizing he could not give in to her whims, he stood with head held high, hip-length hair streaming before the force of her breath, and sought the reason for the strange-looking clouds that gave off a curious light, illuminating both earth and sky.

"The whirling wind!" a voice cried, taking up the cry. "The whirling wind comes for us."

Nampeyo's gut tightened as he raised his right hand and grasped the sacred stone that hung safely in its medicine pouch around his neck. The weight was comforting to him as he raised his slender staff toward the sky with his left hand and began a prayer chant.

But Wind Woman refused to be calmed. She blew sharply, gusting around him, blowing from four different directions at once, seeming intent on pushing him off the cliff as she had done once before, long ago, when Nampeyo had been only a small child.

He had been afraid of her then, he remembered. But not now. Why should he be afraid now? Was he not shaman of the clan?

Was not his every thought for the good of the clan?

For that reason alone he stood steadily defiant, holding his position while Wind Woman moved around him, embracing him with her cold, invisible arms.

Although his eyes stung from windborn grit and dust, he ignored the pain and continued his chant, praying to the Star People, asking them to intercede for him, to ask the Creator—He who was above all else—to permit the people of the Eagle Clan to survive the storm that threatened to consume them.

"*Aaaiiieee!* The whirling wind comes!" More voices echoed the cry, over and over again, but Nampeyo tried to ignore the terror of those voices as he lowered his staff and opened his sacred pouch.

He must appease the Cloud Spirits, must make them leave without harming his people and their crops, which were ripening in the fields on the mesa above.

When the bag was opened, he dipped his fingers inside and dug out several grains of the sacred blue stones, tossing some over the cliff, then scattering more in each of the four sacred directions, hoping his actions would be looked upon with favor and his people and their crops would be spared.

Brynna woke to a feeling of incredible warmth.

Although her bed felt harder than usual, she luxuriated in the heat surrounding her, feeling very much like, she surmised, a butterfly might feel while wrapped tightly in its cocoon.

Breathing in deeply, she was aware of a slightly musty scent and below that, another one, less identifiable.

Curious, she let her lids flutter and lift; she opened her eyes and stared at the shadowy grayness overhead. And as she did, something clicked in her mind, as if a door had suddenly opened allowing light to filter through. And Brynna remembered.

She knew exactly where she was and how she'd come to be there.

The cave. The *skraeling* . . . he had brought her to a cave.

Where was he?

A swift turn of her head and she had the answer.

The *skraeling* lay beside her.

Goosebumps covered her body and she shuddered as she realized it was his body that was responsible for the feeling of delicious warmth she had been enjoying so much.

As her mind dealt with that fact, she realized something else as well: the extra scent, the one that had been so elusive, came from him. It was a musky scent, purely male, unfamiliar, yet not unpleasant.

Amazing though it seemed, she felt not the least bit threatened by his presence. Perhaps because he slept, she reasoned, stirring slightly, trying to move away from him without his knowing.

But such was impossible.

Although she had made no more sound than the rustle of a leaf in a warm breeze, it had obviously been enough to wake him.

He stirred and his eyes opened suddenly. With bated breath she watched him turn his head to stare at her and she found her gaze caught by his, held there by the most incredible black eyes she had ever before encountered.

Why had she not noticed their beauty before? she wondered. Even Nama's eyes, although beautiful, had not affected her in such a manner.

She continued to stare at him, unable to look away, barely breathing. Every sound—the wind outside, the rustling leaves—suddenly faded away in that timeless moment.

It seemed as though she and the man who was stretched out beside her were the last two people on the face of the earth.

Why did she not move away? Brynna wondered. How could she remain beside him when the feel of his warm flesh against her own caused a tightness in her throat, caused a sensuous tingling movement along her hips as though he had touched her there, as though he were stroking—?

Holy Mother of God! He *was* stroking her there! No! He must not! She must not allow him to take such liberties with her person.

Move away! an inner voice screamed. Stop this madness while you can!

But even as the voice screamed in denial, her limbs remained frozen, her body pressed firmly against the incredible warmth of him.

With his eyes fastened to hers, he began to lower his head, and as he did, his face turned slightly and she saw it . . . the long, jagged scar that made him appear so sinister, so menacing.

Despite herself, Brynna sucked in a sharp breath and shrank from him.

The *skraeling*'s dark eyes flickered deep within themselves, and his face hardened until it seemed carved from stone. As she watched, regretting that change in expression, his mouth twisted derisively.

It was that derisive twist that finally broke the spell, allowing Brynna to roll away from him quickly, leaving the warmth of his body—the body that had kept away the chill of the night—putting as much distance as possible between herself and him without actually running away.

He spoke harshly to her then, words she could not understand, and she knew, considering the fact that he had done her no harm—had indeed put his own life in jeopardy to save her from the mountain lion—her actions must have made her seem ungrateful.

Wishing that she could recall that moment, that she could have been prepared for the way he looked, she

searched for something to say, something that would ease
the tension that pulsated between them.

But she could think of nothing to say. The four words
they conversed with before were meaningless to her now.

Again he uttered harsh words, and Brynna realized he
must be waiting for her to reply.

Meeting his eyes again, she shook her head and said
in her own language, "I do not understand your words.
You must speak slowly."

He did not attempt to communicate again. Instead,
he turned away from her and reached for one of her
saddlebags—the one containing her foodstuff—and
reached into it as if it belonged to him.

She realized suddenly that he probably did believe it
belonged to him, by right of conquest. And so would she,
by that same right—and her mount and anything else she
might possess; and she had no words to dissuade him
from that belief.

The thought of her mount reminded her of the stallion's
fear of being underground. She turned her head, bent on
assuring herself of the horse's well-being.

It was then that she realized the animal was no longer
in the cave with them.

A distant howl woke Patrick and he opened his eyes
to a dull, gray morning. Although the rain had stopped,
the skies looked bleak, portending more of the same.

Hoping Brynna had taken refuge nearby, Patrick set
out walking in a northward direction, the way he'd been
traveling before the storm had descended upon him.

He heard the river before he saw it, and even though
he knew the waters must be in full flood, he quickened
his steps, hoping to find a way to cross.

His spirits, already at a low ebb, plunged to the depths as he stood on the riverbank, surveying the muddy water that rolled bank to bank.

The current rushed by mere feet away, and as Patrick watched, a cottonwood tree located close to the water slowly uprooted where the ground had become muddy and loose. The river tugged greedily at the tree as it tried to resist the pull of the surging water and failed.

With a loud crack the roots broke and the tree gave way with a groan, sliding into the river, caught by rushing water and a greedy current that grabbed and pulled, forcing it into the rapids to join the other trees and debris already floating there.

Patrick had no way of knowing how much the water had risen; he could only guess. Too much, he knew, to risk crossing. No man alive could swim in such a current and hope to live through it.

He viewed the river with a heavy scowl, realizing he must make a decision.

Should he wait beside the riverbank until its waters subsided enough to make crossing safe, or should he go upstream and search for a place to cross? The only other alternative was turning back.

Weighing each alternative carefully, he realized he might be better off turning back. Without a mount beneath him, his speed would be severely limited. But if he found his men, he could surely gain the use of a mount and the time he had lost could easily be made up . . . at least, he hoped it was so.

Having come to a decision, Patrick turned around and began to retrace his steps.

Brynna slowly chewed the dried venison the *skraeling* had provided for her breakfast, at the same time watching his expression while he drew pictures on the cavern floor. He seemed intent on what he was doing, almost oblivious to her presence, yet she sensed he was totally aware of her.

She wondered at her feelings, so totally unlike any she had known before. She felt compelled to touch him, to feel his bronzed skin against her own flesh. His hands were rough and callused, she knew, remembering the way they'd felt against her thigh.

If she leaned forward . . . ever so slightly, she would be able to feel the heat emanating from his body. If she just reached out—

The sound of his voice interrupted her thoughts and she started, feeling a rush of blood to her cheeks.

"What?" she asked, staring at him in utter confusion.

He spoke two words, then pointed to himself and uttered them again.

When she shook her head again, trying to make him understand that she had no idea what he wanted, he poked her with his index finger and spoke one word. Then, pointing to himself, he spoke two more words. Was he asking her a question? If so, what did he want to know?

Puzzled, she stopped chewing and watched him closely as he repeated his actions, again speaking the same two words. Could he be telling her his name? she wondered. It seemed possible.

Although the words made no sense to her, she repeated the words he had spoken and pointed to him as he had done. His lips pulled into a smile and he nodded his head as though he were pleased with her.

Apparently not yet satisfied, he pointed to the picture he had drawn on the earthen floor. She looked closely at it, wondering if it was supposed to represent a dog. Or perhaps, she considered, it might be the likeness of a wolf.

Seeming to realize she did not yet understand, he drew a picture of another animal, larger in size, yet very much like the animal he had used before. She studied it closely. It could be a dog. Or a wolf. Or one of the other creatures with canine features.

Perhaps a fox.

He said the name again. Then, using the two words he had said before, he jabbed his finger at his chest.

His name! He was trying to tell her his name.

Excitement flowed through her as Brynna bent closer to the picture, frowning down at it, intent on learning what the *skraeling* was called.

Repeating the two words he had used before, he pointed to the picture, then to himself, and finally to the cavern wall.

She looked curiously at the rock, wishing she could unravel the mystery. Rock Fox? No. Stone Fox? Was that his name? She touched the rocks nearby and repeated the word he had used. Immediately he shook his head, and, taking her hand in his, he brought it to the place he had touched before and repeated the word.

Brynna looked at the place where he held her hand. There was nothing different about it except the color, which was almost red.

Suddenly, she knew. The word meant "red." She looked at the picture again. Red Fox: it must be Red Fox. Certainly. That was his name. Named that way, more than likely, because of the copper glints in his dark hair.

Brynna smiled to show him she understood and repeated the word, over and over again, feeling a sense of excitement because they were actually communicating with each other.

Suddenly, he handed her the stick and jabbed his pointing finger at her and she realized it was her turn to give her name.

"Brynna," she said softly, then repeated. "Brynna."

He pointed to the stick, then to the ground, saying "Brynna, Brynna," and she realized with consternation that he intended for her to draw a picture of what it represented.

She shook her head, hoping he would understand. "Brynna," she said again, pointing at herself.

Again, he pointed to the ground, urging her to draw the picture.

Sighing, she bent over and drew the head of a girl with long, flowing hair and said, "Brynna."

"Good," he said in his own language, and she was glad he had spoken a word she could understand. "Brynna."

She laughed and nodded her head. "Yes," she agreed. "Brynna." After a moment, she pointed to him. "Red Fox."

His laughter echoed hers. And they continued in that vein, drawing pictures on the cavern floor and identifying them in each of their languages each one of them hoping that the lessons would enable them to understand each other better.

And Brynna could sense his deep interest when he drew a picture vaguely resembling the one representing his name. Then he added a saddle. "Shadow," he said, pointing to the animal.

"Yes," she said, nodding her head and smiling. "That is Shadow, my horse."

He pointed to the saddle on the animal's back and she realized he was asking her to give it a name.

"Saddle," she said immediately, touching the picture with her finger so he would know she understood the question. "That is a saddle."

"Where is Shadow?" she asked, in her own language, hoping he would understand. "Where did he go?"

He began to speak rapidly, too fast for her to understand,

and she reached out a hand to stop him, wanting—needing—an answer to her question.

"Shadow," she said again. "My . . ." She pointed to herself. "—My horse." She searched her memory for words to continue, but found only one that would express her concern. "Go," she said in his language. "Shadow go."

He nodded, looking quite pleased with himself, then spoke two words of his own. She turned them over in her mind. One of them was similar to "no," yet not exactly the same. Recognizing her confusion, he drew a line close to him and said a word that she recognized as near, then drew another line, farther away.

No farther? No. That made no sense. No far? No distance? Suddenly, something clicked in her mind: not far. She looked at the cave entrance and rose to her feet. "Shadow not far?" she questioned in his language.

He nodded his head, his lips stretching into a smile, pleased. Then, uttering a stream of words of which she could understand only that he wanted her to wait there for him, he left her alone.

Immediately he was out of sight. She hurried toward the exit. She had no intention of waiting there for him to return. Now was the time for her to leave him. She traversed the crevice carefully, mindful of the slippery floor that was covered with wet leaves that had blown in, headed for the exit.

When she reached it she found her way blocked.

The large gray wolf rested there on its haunches, just outside the entrance to the crevice. And when she attempted to step outside, the animal showed its large, sharp teeth and emitted a low warning growl; and she realized that he would not allow her to pass.

Chapter Eight

Patrick found his mount before he reached his men. The horse stood beneath the spreading branches of a large oak tree, its sides heaving as if it had recently been running.

Whether it had been chased by another animal or merely by its own fear of the storm was something Patrick supposed he would never learn.

Nor did he care. At least he had his mount again, and if he could find a suitable place to cross the river safely, then perhaps he would soon find Brynna.

He was on the point of mounting the horse when he heard a voice hailing him.

"Patrick!"

He turned to find Lacey trotting toward him.

"Where are the others?" Patrick inquired.

"A few miles behind me," Lacey replied. "And the lady Brynna? Have you not found her yet?"

Patrick had no need to ask Lacey how he knew he had been following Brynna's trail. The man had obviously read the sign on the ground before the rain had wiped out the tracks.

"No," Patrick replied, explaining what had occurred, ending with, ". . . and I have only just now found my mount. What about the rest of the horses. Are they still with you?"

"The other two, yes."

"Yet you are afoot?"

"We have two wounded among us," Lacey explained. "They needed the mounts more than me."

"Only two wounded?" Patrick asked with a frown. "I thought there were many more."

"There were," Lacey agreed. "But they have since passed on. The two left alive are seriously injured. Only Michael is strong enough to fight. I left him to look after the others."

Patrick expelled a heavy sigh. "The trip has already taken a heavy toll." He handed the reins of his mount to his friend. "Take my mount," he offered. Go ahead of me to the river's edge. You are more likely to find a place we can cross."

"The river is in flood?" Lacey questioned.

"Yes," Patrick nodded. "Too dangerous, I fear, for us to cross. And yet to delay is unthinkable."

"We might find somewhere to cross farther upstream," Lacey said, narrowing his eyes thoughtfully. "If not, maybe we could build rafts . . ."

"Perhaps," Patrick agreed. "But the construction of rafts would take time. Better, I think, to locate another crossing."

"If there *is* one," Lacey said, putting a foot into the stirrup and mounting easily. "Keep an eye open, Patty." A moment later he was riding away.

Patrick watched horse and man grow smaller as the

distance between them increased, just as the distance
between themselves and the Lady Brynna must be increasing with each passing moment. Yet he was helpless to do
anything about it, could only remain where he was and
wait for the rest of their party to reach him.

Red Fox loped along the rocky ground, stopping occa-
sionally to examine the ground for tracks. As he'd guessed
he would, the warrior found Brynna's steed a short distance from the cave, grazing where the grass grew long
and unchecked.

Murmuring soothing words, Red Fox slowly approached
the horse, and as before, Shadow remained passive,
unstartled, unworried by the warrior's approach.

When the warrior finally had the reins in his hand, he
relaxed, allowing his thoughts to return to the girl he had
left in the cave, guarded against harm by his faithful
companion, Wolf.

The girl.

"Brynna," he said softly, liking the sound of the name
that rolled so easily off his tongue.

He could still remember the feel of her body pressed
against his own, could remember as well the look in her
eyes when she had seen his scarred face.

Pain stabbed through him now, as it had then when
she'd recoiled from his ugliness.

He put the thought away, unwilling to dwell on it,
pulling from his memories instead that moment in time
before she'd seen his scarred features.

She had been docile then, submissive in his arms, had
even appeared yielding, willing to remain there as long
as he desired.

If only she had not seen his face!

But there was no use railing against fate. She had seen, and she had instantly recoiled. She had recovered quickly, though; he had to give her credit for that.

Where had she come from? he wondered. And what was her reason for coming? Was she the only one of her kind?

There was so much he wanted to know about her, but his questions would have to wait until they could communicate better.

His language, although strange to her tongue, was not completely unknown to her, and the learning of it should be accomplished with ease.

Which posed another question. How had she become so familiar with his language?

She could not have been long in his land, or the traders who traveled from shore to shore would certainly have spoken of her kind. Yet they had not done so. And yet ... yet ... something tugged at his memory. Something he had heard once about a people with golden hair.

Suddenly the memory was within his grasp. And he knew where he had heard it before: Shala. It was Shala, the woman from the Eagle Clan, who had mentioned golden hair. But she had spoken of only one man—her man. And he had come from a faraway place across the big salt water that he referred to as ''Norway.''

Could the girl who waited in the cavern be one of his people? he wondered, wishing he knew the answer.

Shala had called her man ''Eric.'' And his name had not meant anything except the man. It was the same with Brynna: her name meant nothing else. It was used only for her. Red Fox found it all very strange.

Yes, it must be true, he decided. Brynna must be from the same clan as Shala's man. For some unknown reason, Red Fox was displeased at that conclusion, and it only increased his determination to carry her far away from those who might follow after them.

Feeling a sudden need to hurry, Red Fox took Shadow's reins in hand and hurried back the way he'd come.

When Red Fox returned with Shadow, he lifted Brynna into the saddle, at the same time managing to keep a tight hold on the reins, making Brynna wonder if Wolf had somehow managed to communicate with the warrior.

Ridiculous, she told herself. There was no way Red Fox could possibly know she had tried to leave.

They covered many miles that day, putting more distance between her and her men. It was past dark when they stopped for the night, and after they had finished the evening meal, they sat around the campfire while Red Fox taught her more of his language. He pointed at rocks, then said a word for it, making her repeat it over and over until she had it right. Then he pointed to the grass and told her what it was called. He continued in that vein until he had told her the names of everything they could see. Only then did they retire for the night.

Although they slept together, as they had the night before, sharing Brynna's bedroll, Red Fox appeared to hold himself apart from her.

Brynna thought she would be unable to sleep beside him, but she was proved wrong. Her eyes had barely closed when she fell asleep.

Waking to the smell of roasting meat, Brynna crawled out of the bedroll and joined Red Fox beside the fire. "That smells good," she said, eyeing the carcass skewered over the fire. "Is it a rabbit?"

"Yes." He broke off a piece and handed it to her. "Eat now. We have much distance to travel."

Finding the meat too hot to hold, she handed it back
to him. "You hold it while I wash and freshen myself,"
she said. "The meat should be cooler by then."

When he made no reply, she turned toward the growth
of trees nearby where a shallow creek flowed strong and
clear. Her horse, Shadow, was hobbled there. Perhaps
now would be her chance to escape. If she could take the
rope from his forelegs before she was discovered, then—

"Go with her, Wolf." Red Fox's voice broke into her
thoughts, scattering her plans like leaves before a brisk
wind.

That set the pattern for their days and nights. Each
evening, after their meal, he concentrated on teaching her
to converse in his language. And she progressed well,
learning rapidly, as eager to speak with him as he was to
speak with her, until finally he asked her the question
that had obviously been preying on his mind.

"Where do you come from, Brynna?"

"I come from a place called Norway," she replied,
unaware that she was telling him something he'd already
guessed. Believing he had never heard of her home, she
continued. "It is a long way from here. You have heard
of the big salt water?"

He nodded his head. "Yes."

"You must travel across it to reach my homeland."
She waited for his reaction, but there was none. She
wondered then about his lack of reaction.

He reached for more wood and added it to their fire,
watching the flames catch hold and leap higher. What
was it about him, she wondered, that caused her to feel
this way? When they were close like this, his presence
wrapped around her like a soft cocoon, making it hard
for her to think of anything but him.

Realizing he had made no response whatsoever when

she'd spoken of Norway, she wondered again about his lack of response. It was almost as though he had heard of Norway before.

"Red Fox?" She waited until he looked at her before she went on. "Have you heard of my homeland?"

He nodded abruptly. "Yes."

"Where?" she asked eagerly. "Did someone speak of it to you, perhaps one of my people?"

He was glad he could deny that fact. "No."

"Then where did you learn about Norway?"

"From another," he said shortly. "Someone not of your clan."

"One of your own people, then?" she asked, wondering how that could be possible.

"No. She was not of my clan."

She. A woman. Disappointment swept over Brynna as she realized he had not been speaking of her brother, Eric. For a moment there, she had imagined that it might have been him.

"Who was she?" Brynna asked, wondering about the woman who had known of her home.

"Her name was Shala."

"Shala?" Brynna's heart gave a sudden leap. How many women would carry a name like that? "Shala from the Eagle Clan?"

He nodded his head slowly, his dark gaze never leaving hers. "The same," he admitted. "Do you have knowledge of her?"

She replied, "I have heard of her. From her friend, Nama, who is also my friend." Brynna could hardly control her excitement, yet she knew she must speak slowly to make herself understood. "Red Fox, did she—Shala—also speak of a man called Eric Nordstrom?"

Much as he wished to say no, Red Fox could not. It

was not in him to speak falsely. He admitted, "Shala
spoke the name. But not all of it."

"Not all?"

"She spoke only of Eric."

Leaning forward eagerly, Brynna placed her hands over
one of his and asked the question that was uppermost in
her mind. "Do you know where he is, Red Fox?"

He shrugged his shoulders and looked off into the
darkness. "I am told he lives on the great mesa with the
Eagle Clan," he replied.

"And you have been there, Red Fox?" she asked, her
voice reflecting her excitement.

"No."

Damn his one-word answers! Could he not see how
important this was to her? He seemed intent on giving
her as little information as possible. Forcing herself to
remain calm lest he refuse to answer at all, she said,
"Do you know how to find the great mesa where he
lives?"

"We have spoken enough on the subject," he said
abruptly. "It is time to sleep."

"Not yet!" she said sharply, curling her fingers around
his forearm to keep him beside her. "Red Fox, please,"
she begged in her own language, since she knew of no
such word in his. "Tell me if you know where to find
the mesa."

A muscle twitched in his jaw and she knew that he
was angry. "The man belongs to Shala! He is not for
you!"

Her tension erupted in a nervous giggle. "If Eric heard
you, he would be quick to deny that," she said. "He
belongs only to himself."

"He belongs to Shala," he repeated. "She would never
allow you to take him away from her."

"Take him away?" she asked faintly, realizing suddenly that he thought she had a romantic interest in Eric.

How could she explain they were brother and sister? she wondered, when there was still so much of his language that she had yet to learn. She had thought she could speak freely with him now, but apparently not. And yet she must make him understand.

Brynna searched her mind for words to explain, for words that would convey her meaning, but since he had given her no word for "brother," finally contented herself with saying, "The father and mother of Brynna are also the father and mother of the man called Eric."

Something flickered deep in his ebony eyes, making her feel he finally understood her relationship to Eric, and yet he remained silent for another moment . . . in the space of a heartbeat, his dark gaze locked on hers.

When he spoke again, his voice had not softened one iota. "Brynna came to this land to find Eric?"

"Yes," she said, nodding. "I am here to find Eric."

"After you have found him, you will go away again?"

Brynna wondered if he thought others of her kind would be coming. Perhaps that was what bothered him. "Yes," she said quickly. "We will go away from here. Will you take me to him?"

His eyes became shuttered and he turned away from her.

"You did not answer me, Red Fox!" she cried. "Will you take me to my brother? To Eric?"

"No!"

"But why?"

"Red Fox is Wolf Clan," he explained, his voice gruff, tension in every line of his body. "Shala is Eagle Clan." He seemed to think he had said enough.

"Why does that matter?" she asked, even as she realized

she already knew. Red Fox was from the clan that had taken Nama and Shala captive. Nama would have died in captivity had she not fallen from a cliff into a river.

"Our clans are enemies," he said, answering her question.

"You would not reconsider?" Even though she asked the question, she already knew the answer. If they were enemies, it would mean his life to travel to the mesa.

"Would you at least show me where the mesa is?" she asked. "You need not go there, Red Fox. If you would show me the way, then I could go alone."

"No." He denied even that request. "Our path lies in another direction."

"What do you mean?"

"We travel to my home, and it is far beyond the great mesa."

"I have no wish to go to your home," she said stiffly. "I came here to find Eric."

"And you found me," he said.

She nodded grimly. "Yes. I found you instead. But I have no intention of staying with you."

As soon as she said the words, she wished them unspoken, for even though she had spoken in her own language, he was learning incredibly fast and might have understood her meaning.

If so, if he thought for a moment she might try to escape him, he might take drastic measures to keep her with him, might even bind her hands and feet.

Brynna knew she must not allow that to happen. She would need every advantage to escape him. As she would, she determined. She would never remain under this man's domination when she had fled her home in Norway to escape another's rule.

For now, though, she would wait . . . and she would

watch, and there would come a time when he was not looking, not watching her as he was now.

And then she would leave him far behind.

Somehow, that thought troubled her. More than she cared to admit.

Chapter Nine

With head held high, Nampeyo moved among the ruins of the cornfield. His jaw clenched and he felt a terrible wave of inadequacy wash over him. He was too young, too unskilled in the ways of a shaman. He had no power to protect his people.

Wind Woman had bettered him once more, showing her power by destroying the People's crops, and sending the animals into flight.

What had he done—or not done—to bring the wrath of Sky Man down upon his people? he wondered. Perhaps, though, he considered, it was not he who had incurred that wrath. Perhaps, as old Three Toes had hinted, it was another who had done so. Perhaps, as the elder had hinted, Sky Man was angry because an intruder was among them, enjoying their bounty.

No, he chastised himself. It could not be. Eric had lived among them for several seasons now, and had it not been for him, the Desert Clan would have conquered them many times over, would now be enjoying the fruits of the Eagle Clan's bounty.

What bounty? a silent voice questioned. *The bounty is no longer. Nor is the fruit, for the service berries have been ripped away from Mother Earth by their roots.*

"The stranger among us caused this destruction," a voice murmured from somewhere nearby. "It is the man with golden hair who is responsible for all this devastation. Because of him there will be many empty bellies when the long cold is upon us."

Nampeyo spun as quickly as his crippled leg would allow, angrily facing the speaker. "You are a fool!" he told the man. "Eric works harder than any other man among us to make our crops plentiful. Since he came to live among us there have been none to know hunger."

"Evil has a way of sneaking in when your eyes look elsewhere," the man said belligerently. "Old Three Toes told me this."

"This shaman will not believe evil of a man who has brought nothing but good to our clan," Nampeyo snapped, reminding the man of his status in the clan. "And others of this clan should follow his lead lest they offend the spirits."

The man blanched at the thought of offending the spirits that saw to the clan's well-being. With eyes looking at his own feet, he hurried away from his shaman. But even as Nampeyo watched the man depart, he had a feeling he had not heard the last of the matter.

Eric Nordstrom, rising before the sun, saw the devastation the storm had wrought. Knowing the animals that provided the clan with meat would have fled, he paid a visit to Shateh, one of the few clan members he called friend, and more important, one of the best trackers left to the Eagle Clan.

Shateh, having been consulted, agreed with Eric's judgment that a hunting party must be formed immediately before another storm could form. If that should happen, both men felt the game would become fearful and flee the mesa altogether.

Shateh, a clan member, sent word to the hunters of the clan to assemble. Although they acted quickly, searching in places where game was usually found, it seemed they were too late. The animals had already gone.

Determined to check every nook and cranny of the mesa, Shateh gave the orders to continue the search. Still, they found no sign of game. The hunters directed ugly looks at Eric as though he were the one at fault, then began the long trek home.

Not so Eric and Shateh, who were both determined to find game while they could. While Shateh continued to search for tracks, the golden-haired Viking climbed up a hill to a rocky promontory.

Exultation swept through him as he looked down into a blind canyon. Scrambling out of sight, he slipped and slid down the hill until he reached the tracker who had stopped to watch him come.

Motioning the tracker to follow him, Eric returned to his vantage point and pointed into the canyon.

When Shateh looked into the canyon, his eyes widened. A wide grin spread across his face, for there, huddled together near a spring of fresh water, was a small herd of elk.

"*Aaaiieee,*" whispered Shateh. "There are more elk than I have fingers on both hands."

"Yes," Eric agreed, and although his voice was calm, he was silently jubilant. There must be more than thirty elk in that canyon. Too many for two men to kill. But if they could pen them up until the other hunters were summoned—

No sooner had the thought occurred than he began to work out a plan of action. Shateh nodded as Eric told him what they would do; then, when all was explained, he turned his face toward the village and loped off at a ground-eating pace.

Three days had passed since the storm and Brynna became increasingly uneasy as her companion learned more and more of her language and she learned more of his. Being able to communicate better should have made things easier for them, but instead, it served only to prove how different their cultures were.

She learned that, like Nama, he believed they lived in the fourth world, having come from a world beneath the earth. And, like Nama, he believed animals had spirits, that forgiveness must be asked for slaying them, before their souls departed from their body.

Much of his belief was still unknown to her, though, for there were many words that needed more explanation than he was able to provide with his small grasp of her language.

It was in an attempt to learn more that, when they stopped for the night after the fourth day of travel, she instigated a conversation, hoping to draw more information from him.

"You said the Eagle Clan and the Wolf Clan are enemies?" She made the statement a question.

"That is so."

"Then how could you speak with Shala, a woman of that clan?"

She already knew the answer, but it was her intention

to make him say the words. Why she needed to hear them she had no idea; she only knew that he must say them.

"The woman was not with her clan."

"Where was she?"

"In the village of the Wolf Clan?"

She waited for him to continue, but he did not, making it necessary for her to speak. "She went there alone? With no one to protect her?"

"Shala needed no protection from any man."

Brynna grimaced wryly. She had asked the wrong question again. Of course Shala needed no man to protect her. Nama had told her of Shala's prowess with a spear.

"She went alone to your village thinking to take on every warrior among you? She was indeed a brave woman."

Again there was silence.

She leaned closer to him, studying his face intently. "You did not reply, Red Fox."

"Your words did not require an answer, woman."

"Then let me ask again. She went among you of her own accord?"

"No," he said grudgingly. "And I will answer no more."

"You need not," she said sharply. "I already have the answer."

"Then why do you ask what you already have knowledge of?"

"Because it concerns me. Your clan took Shala and Nama captive. You were holding Shala against her will. Is that not so, Red Fox?"

"No."

"You lie!" she hissed.

"This tongue has never spoken falsely, woman! And it shall never do so. I have no reason to lie."

"Nama told me the whole of it. She had no reason to lie. She said your clan took them captive—she said—"

"They were taken captive," he admitted, obviously stung at being called a liar. "But Nama escaped when she fell from the cliff and Shala escaped at a later time."

"Then she is no longer captive?"

"No."

"And me, Red Fox?" she questioned. "Are you holding me captive? Will my men have to ransom me from your clan?" There. It was finally out in the open. All her suspicions had been spread out for him to see.

She waited breathlessly for him to reply.

Red Fox was unhappy with the unfolding events. He stared at the woman who sat with her arms around her drawn-up knees. Her hair was parted in the center, pulled back from her face, and secured at the nape of her neck with a piece of fabric torn from the bottom of her shift. Most of her hair fell loose down her back and over her shoulders and arms.

How beautiful she was, he thought, wanting nothing more at the moment than to stay where he was, drinking in the sight of her.

But there was more to this woman to admire than her beauty, he knew. She had compassion as well, had demonstrated it in her handling of her mount. The woman had strength beyond compare, and her resilience amazed him. Not once had she complained of weariness or hunger, as other women would surely have done when pushed as hard as he had pushed her. Not one word of complaint had been uttered. There had even been times when she had forgotten herself and smiled at him.

Not now, though. At the moment, her eyes glittered

like wildflowers laden with dew. And they glowed with inner knowledge as she waited for him to speak.

When he did, he chose his words carefully.

"It is not my wish for you to consider yourself a captive," he said.

"I will not . . . if you tell me it is not so," she said.

"It is not so."

She expelled a sigh of relief. Her plan had worked; he would not hold her captive. "Then I am free to go my own way."

"I did not say that."

"But you said I was not a captive."

"No," he denied. "I merely repeated the words you asked of me."

"Then you lied!" she cried, clenching her hands into fists, almost shaking with fury. "If I cannot go my own way, then I am a captive!"

"None of my clan can go their own way," he said quietly. "All are intertwined in some way or another, all dependent on their clansmen."

"Then why are you not there performing your duty?" she said sharply.

"The sight of me is no longer pleasing to my clansmen," he replied. "They turn their eyes away from me and shun my presence."

She felt appalled. "Because of your face?"

"Yes."

"How could they do such a thing?" she cried, feeling a curious pain inside. Leaning closer, she reached out a hand and traced a finger down the jagged scar. Even now, though the scratches left by the mountain cat's sharp claws were healing nicely, the newest assault to his flesh had left the old scar tissue red and angry looking, as if the bear's mark upon his face were new.

"It is not so bad," she said gently. "I hardly notice it anymore."

"I know," he said. "That has become apparent in many ways."

"You said it was a bear's attack that scarred you?"

"That is so."

"It left only the scar on your face?"

"There are other scars as well," he replied. "They are covered by my clothing."

"That is the reason you cover your body while the others of your kind wear only a loincloth?"

"That is the reason."

"It is also the cause of your bitterness," she said softly. "But, Red Fox, you must not mind others. You have no choice but to live with what you cannot change."

"I have no problem living with it," he replied. "It is others who have the problem. Until you came, there were none who did not show revulsion when they looked upon me."

"Only because they do not know Red Fox the man. If you would allow them to know the real you, then they would be unable to turn away."

"Perhaps," he said gruffly. "But I think not. Anyway, it no longer matters."

"But it should matter," she cried passionately. "No man can live alone in a place like this, Red Fox. Suppose you become ill, or are wounded. Such wounds as you have already sustained need proper care. And you could not do these things for yourself. No. You must return to your people. You cannot live alone forever."

"I am no longer alone," he reminded softly. "You are with me now."

Brynna heard the words and felt a sudden chill. By admitting her sympathy toward this man, had she doomed herself to remain at his side?

Chapter Ten

Patrick was dismayed when Lacey returned near sunset to say that he had found no way across the river. It seemed they had no recourse, but to wait for the water to recede enough so they could cross the river without risking life and limb.

That night, Patrick stared broodingly into the flames, his face set in hard lines as he remembered the night he had first met Lady Brynna.

Nama, the woman from the Eagle Clan, had enlisted his aid to flee Norway. His payment for that service was his freedom. Having only just been released from the dungeon where Brynna's father had sent him, Patrick was naturally suspicious of the jarl's daughter. But he had been wrong to suspect her. She had her own reasons for wanting to leave Norway. It was Brynna who distracted the sentry long enough for them to surprise him, and it was she who had selected the fastest *langskip* among the fleet.

The plan would have worked, too, had it not been for

her brother, Garrick. He had learned of their plan and come after them. Had it not been for his obsession with Nama, his need to keep her by his side, they might have escaped.

But they had not. Garrick had caught them and taken his woman and sent the two convicts, Lacey and Patrick, back to rot in the dungeon.

And Patrick had no doubt in his mind that they *would* have rotted there, had not Lady Brynna been so stubborn, so intent on keeping her own freedom.

His lips twitched slightly. It was his good luck that she *was* stubborn. For it was that same stubbornness that freed him. And it was that very same stubbornness that would carry her bravely through whatever fate had in store.

"The lass will be all right," Lacey said gruffly, intruding on Patrick's thoughts. "You need not worry overlong about her. She will never allow the *skraelings* to get the better of her."

Patrick's expression hardened and his eyes were alight with a burning need for vengeance. If a *skraeling* harmed one hair on her head, then he might as well already be dead, for nothing could stop Patrick from making it a fact.

Brynna waited until Red Fox was breathing evenly with sleep. Then, moving carefully, she slipped from the bed of pine needles and crept toward Shadow, praying the horse would not nicker and waken the sleeping man.

Shadow continued grazing without interruption, paying her no attention as she gathered up a bag of dried meat and hefted the saddle on her mount. Only moments later she was ready to flee.

But the man she had thought to be sound asleep was

craftier than she had imagined. She found that out when she attempted to mount.

A hand closed over hers and gripped hard, squeezing tightly, apparently in an attempt to make her release the saddle horn.

But she did not. Instead, she shouted at Shadow. *"Eeeouuw!"* she screamed, holding tight to the saddle horn so that when the horse reared into the air she did not lose her grip. Not so Red Fox, who was taken by surprise. The moment the horse reared into the air, he had released her and reached for her waist while he stepped back, attempting to drag her with him.

But he could not—not when her grip on the saddle was so tight. And in a totally unexpected move, she flung herself in the saddle and hurrahed the horse away from the camp.

Red Fox recovered with amazing swiftness. But even so, he could never hope to catch the horse and the woman who sat upon it.

His sides were heaving with exertion by the time he came to that realization. Then, sitting down on a fallen log, he struggled to figure out the best way to capture her again. He did not even consider failure, his desire to possess her was too great. No. He would find her, and when he did, he would do whatever was needed to keep her by his side.

There was no way he would let her go. Not now. Having found her, he would keep her.

He glanced up at the moon, then looked up the trail. There was enough light to enable her to travel, he supposed, but not enough to allow him to follow the trail.

Therefore, he must wait until daybreak. With any luck at all, he would catch up while she stopped to rest.

Having made that decision, he laid down and closed his eyes. Immediately, he fell asleep.

First light found Brynna near the foothills of a large mountain range. She was weary from riding all night, and worried about her steed, who had carried her without faltering over the rough, rugged terrain they had encountered.

She looked up the mountain. Its slopes were rugged, covered with gnarled trees and bushes, strewn with fallen rocks and uprooted shrubs. It would make a difficult climb for both Shadow and her if she chose that direction.

Her gaze dropped to her mount. Shadow stood patiently. His drooping head spoke of his weariness, yet he was willing to continue if it was his mistress's wishes.

Realizing she must allow him to rest, Brynna shifted in her seat and gripped the saddle horn, preparing to dismount. But in that moment, her eyes caught a glint of silver higher on the slope. At the same time the soft, rushing sound of water reached her ears.

A waterfall! Even as the thought occurred, she realized how thirsty she was. Her steed must be dry as well.

Reining Shadow around, she urged him forward, riding along the slope toward the waterfall, knowing there would have to be a creek somewhere ahead.

The morning sun burst over the eastern horizon, settling over the mountain junipers with a bright burst of color as Brynna reined Shadow up beneath a willow tree growing beside the shallow stream.

Dismounting, she allowed Shadow to drink his fill, then quenched her own thirst and splashed water on her face, hoping to ease her own weariness. Although the water was cooling, it was not enough to refresh her. Neither, she realized, would food and water be enough for her steed. They must have rest.

She looked back the way she had come, but saw no sign of pursuit.

Had Red Fox left her to her own fate?

Probably.

Somehow, that thought was unsettling.

Fool, she told herself. Is there no satisfying you? You ran away from him, left him alone. Why do you hope that he has followed you?

"I do not," she muttered aloud, but she knew that she was only lying to herself.

Red Fox would be a welcome sight, should he lope toward her. Even though he would be furious, as he had every right to be, she would welcome the warrior with open arms.

Despair clutched at her as she slumped down against the nearest tree trunk and sighed wearily. Would she ever see Red Fox again? she wondered. Not likely, she decided, immediately answering her own question, and somehow, that answer caused an aching hunger, a feeling that she quickly dismissed as her body's need for sustenance.

But curiously, even after she had eaten a piece of the jerked meat and washed it down with another long drink of water, the hunger still remained.

Feeling more alone than she had ever felt in her life, Brynna drew her knees up and rested her weary head against them.

Closing her eyes, she courted sleep, totally unaware that she was no longer alone.

Spreading Branches watched quietly from the cover of a gnarled juniper, hardly able to believe his luck. Instead of the game he sought in his early morning hunt, he had found a being that could only belong to the clan his people referred to as Monster Men. Yet this being was no man. Indeed, she could never be mistaken as such. Not when the garment she wore clung so tightly against straining breasts and rounded hips.

And although her hair was the same fiery color when touched by Father Sun as were the men they had fought with so many moons ago, she was much smaller in size, which would make her capture much easier.

Unlike his fellow clansmen, Spreading Branches had no fear of the woman. He did not share their belief that they were a clan who had escaped from the third world in order to wreak havoc on this one.

They must have come from a faraway land, he decided, a land yet unheard of by the traders who traveled this land from shore to shore. But where could such a place be? he wondered.

Finding no answer to the question, he looked away from the woman who had fallen asleep, his avid gaze glittering possessively over the sleek, dark animal grazing on the long grass growing beside the stream.

No. Neither she nor the animal came from the third world, for if there had been such creatures there, the elders would know of them.

Clutching his spear tightly in one hand, Spreading Branches crept closer to the sleeping woman.

Cra-a-ck!

Red Fox woke abruptly with a sense of being watched. Immediately alert, yet feigning sleep, he lifted his eyelids enough to see a bare slit of light and the watcher.

Wolf!

The animal, realizing its master was awake, settled

back on its haunches, obviously intent on resting after a long, weary night.

"I wondered when you would show up," Red Fox commented, sitting up and reaching for the weapons he had placed close at hand.

Wolf's yellow eyes watched closely as Red Fox looped his bow across his left shoulder and picked up his quiver of arrows, preparing to depart. Only then did the animal rise from his position.

Moments later, both man and beast had taken up the trail that Brynna had made no attempt to cover.

Crack!

Startled awake by the sharp sound, Brynna lifted her head and tried to shake the cobwebs from her mind. She could not have slept long, she thought, searching the area with sleep-dazed eyes.

Could the noise have been caused by Shadow? she wondered, her eyes darting toward the horse that stood in the long grass, his head lifted and his ears perked forward, as though he had been disturbed as well.

Her senses were attuned to her surroundings, her ears straining for sound, something out of the ordinary, but she heard nothing except the sound of water flowing downstream. That was surprising in itself. There should have been something . . . some sound . . . frogs croaking near the stream, perhaps, or birds singing as they flitted from branch to branch.

She looked around, focused on the branches of the sparsely growing trees.

How odd, she thought . . . not one bird could be seen.

Her nostrils flared as she breathed in the crisp, cool air around her. It carried a hint of moist earth, pungent near the shallow stream. And there was another scent, a harsh, musky scent that was slightly familiar, yet hard to identify. It assailed her nostrils, becoming stronger as the moments passed, as her ears waited for another sound and her eyes searched for what they could not see.

As the musky smell became steadily stronger, Brynna realized it came from somewhere behind her, somewhere behind the tree that had afforded her rest.

With muscles tensing, she eased away from the tree that was blocking her vision and slowly turned her head.

It happened so fast that her attacker was only a blur, a large wall of flesh converging on her, catching her unawares, snatching her from her sitting position and mashing her nose against the hard muscles of a bare chest, holding her head there so she could hardly draw a breath.

And although she flailed out with both hands, her attacker subdued her easily, circling her shoulders with bands of coiled strength, locking her arms to her sides so she could not use them to defend herself.

Red Fox! It was him, she felt certain. And although she felt a measure of relief that she was no longer alone, she felt a great deal of anger as well that he could treat her in such a manner.

"*Mmmppphh!*" she cried, her voice muffled by the hard flesh as she tried to spew out the fury that was slowly building, fed by the certain knowledge of his anger at being made to pursue her. "*Mmmppphh!*"

Brynna, unable to use her hands, kicked out with her feet, determined to free herself from his arms, yet feeling no real alarm, not until she threw her head back and set eyes on the man holding her captive.

He was a stranger! A *skraeling* whose face, although unscarred, struck terror into her very soul.

As realization set in, she reacted swiftly, opening her mouth and setting her teeth in the man's shoulder, while at the same time lashing out with her feet.

He howled with pain and reacted without thought, his hand lifting to deliver a hard blow across the side of her face.

Although the blow knocked her to the ground, she recovered quickly, leaping to her feet and running toward the cover of a thick growth of trees, racing toward it as fast as her legs would carry her.

A heavy thrashing noise behind her told Brynna her attacker had given chase. Her eyes darted wildly, searching for her mount, knowing that if she could reach Shadow, she could outdistance the man in a hurry.

Despair settled over her when she realized she was going the wrong way.

Her panic-stricken flight had sent her away from the stream where her steed was grazing. There was no possibility of reaching the stallion before the *skraeling* reached her.

She tried to run faster, knowing he had the greater advantage, since he was obviously used to chasing after prey.

Her breath came in short gasps and her heart drummed loudly in her ears as she silently cursed the time spent in leisure hours, the muscles too weak to sustain her through such an ordeal.

With a gnawing sense of fatality, she felt his hands on her once more, felt the moist earth beneath her as he threw her to the ground and pinned her down with his own body.

Brynna heard the sound of tearing cloth as her shift ripped beneath his rough handling and gritted her teeth as his callused hands slid over her breast, moving rapidly down her body.

The feel of his touch against her naked flesh sent bile rising into her throat. She swallowed it back, silently vowing she would never meekly submit to his will.

Clawing desperately at him, she fought in the only way she knew how, knowing all the while that his greater strength would eventually overcome her.

No! her mind screamed. You cannot let him take you!

At that thought, she went wild, her mind snapping like a dried twig.

Desperately, she lashed out at the savage, sinking her teeth into the tender flesh of his shoulder and neck as any animal might have done when caught by a hunter.

But her struggle was to no avail.

Seeming to realize he could no longer sustain her viciousness, the savage balled up one fist and struck her a hard blow to her chin.

Blinding lights exploded in Brynna's head, and her senses reeled. A soft whimper escaped from her throat just before descending darkness came on silent wings to claim her.

Chapter Eleven

Brynna smelled wood smoke.

The knowledge that a fire was somewhere nearby was followed by a fierce, agonizing pain stabbing through Brynna's right leg, a pain so intense that it jerked her into full wakefulness.

Then, whatever had caused the pain was suddenly repeated and she experienced a burning sensation in her right calf.

Brynna felt as if she were being stabbed with a sharp, heated knife blade.

That thought, as well as the pain, jerked her eyes wide open and she stared down at a large splotch of ocher color which would have been unidentifiable at such close range—a matter of mere inches—had it not been for her nostrils that quickly picked up the slightly musty scent of hard-packed earth.

Brynna looked up then and saw an old woman, her body twisted and gnarled by age. In her veined and knotted hand the woman clutched a stick, lifting it again and again as she jabbed the broken point of it into Brynna's tender flesh.

Already the skin of Brynna's leg had broken and she could see the dark stain of her own blood on the wooden point each time the woman lifted the makeshift spear into the air.

Something akin to satisfaction glimmered in the woman's eyes as she went about her task, as if she drew great joy from causing torment. Brynna tried to jerk her leg away but found that she could not.

Realizing that she had curled herself in the fetal position, Brynna attempted at once to pull her body straight, only to discover she could not.

Shock coursed through her as she realized her hands and feet were tightly bound.

That knowledge, coupled with a jabbing pain on her buttocks, jerked her head up. And as her head rose, so did her line of vision.

Panic such as she had never known before welled in her throat and she stifled a shriek, knowing she must not allow it to escape.

She must not allow the *skraelings*—who numbered at least three score—to realize how terribly frightened she was, how utterly terrified she felt on finding herself their captive.

The people of my land admire courage and despise cowards. Nama's words filled her mind. *The desert clan will torture the weak and delight in their fearful screams, but those who are able to laugh in the face of their enemies are sometimes allowed to live, to be adopted into the tribe, in order to make the clan stronger.*

Sound advice, Brynna realized, but easy to give when you were not confronted by a spectacle such as this.

How could she hold her fear at bay when a moving,

jabbering mass of ruddy naked skin and pale deer hide garments confronted her?

Mary, Mother of God, please help me! she silently cried.

The babble of voices seemed to roll over her in ever increasing waves. And their smell! Rank, but quite unlike the sour, rankling smell of Europeans who had been too long in their clothes.

That smell, accompanied with the heat of their closeness and their flat-black eyes that held no expression whatsoever, was almost unendurable, but she could do naught but suffer the torment.

Bound the way she was, Brynna could not escape their reaching, curled fingers that resembled talons, could not escape the pinching, the jabbing sticks that stabbed her flesh while their incomprehensible tongue, uttered by so many voices—shrill and deep, masculine and feminine— tormented her.

Fear warred with anger, knotting her stomach, and she swallowed back the taste of bile that rose in her throat. She would not disgrace herself. Whatever they had in store for her, she would somehow manage to endure.

Fearful of losing her senses, she lifted her eyes higher and stared beyond the savages, searching for one particular face among so many: the face of the man who had come to her rescue once before. But Red Fox was not among them.

Fool, an inner voice cried. *Why did you run away from him? He did nothing to cause you harm.*

A harsh voice sounded and the crowd drew back, parting enough for Brynna to see a dome-shaped mound made up of sticks and brush and put together with dabs of mud, obviously a dwelling.

As she watched, the hide flap that covered the entrance

of the brush hut was flung aside and a *skraeling* warrior emerged, pulling a man—obviously a captive, bound the way he was—behind him.

Brynna's attention was suddenly brought back to herself when she felt a sharp object pierce her right leg. Sucking in a sharp breath to keep from crying out, she turned her attention to her newest tormentor—this one a younger woman who, like the old crone, wore a shapeless hide dress. The woman's eyes were narrowed as she watched Brynna's reaction closely, while repeating the jabbing motion with the sharp stick she held in her right hand.

Trying to jerk her bound legs away to avoid the woman's torment only delayed the inevitable. When the stick connected with her leg again, it penetrated deeper than before and Brynna felt blood bubbling from the hole left behind.

Unable to keep a cry of pain from escaping, Brynna closed her eyes to hide her coward self from the faces in the crowd.

A loud voice, speaking in that harsh, guttural tone Brynna was coming to expect from the natives, caused the two woman to back away from their victim.

The *skraeling* warrior stopped before her and pointed a gnarled finger at her, speaking again in the language that Brynna was trying so hard to understand. Although she had learned to converse with Red Fox, the language these skraelings were using differed slightly, enough so Brynna could understand only a word now and then.

But she had no need to understand the words of the man before her. The moment he spoke, rough hands laid hold of Brynna's upper arms and dragged her to her feet. Her mind whirled with confusion, pain, and terror as she was thrust forward, almost falling, into a cleared and trampled space where four upright posts stood waiting.

Her hands were freed, then pulled apart, and although she struggled desperately, her efforts were puny against their strength. Moments later she was bound spread-eagled between two of the poles.

The crowd surged forward again and it seemed there were hundreds of the savages ... women and girls and boys whose hands were touching her, either to abuse her or to explore her pale body curiously.

Tanned hands snatched at her hair, pulling it sharply while others slapped her face, pinched her arms, ripped her garment, and intruded to the bared flesh beneath.

It seemed as though a veritable sea of faces loomed over her, laughing, hissing, baring their teeth, enjoying their captive's pain.

One old woman with snow-white hair spat into her face while a pretty young woman with saucy and derisive black eyes reached out a hand and twisted cruel fingers on the flesh of Brynna's upper arm.

Brynna thought she would faint with the horror of it all, but somehow she managed to hold onto her senses, fearing if she gave into the blackness that hovered ever nearer, she would never awaken again.

Above the babble of voices a drum sounded. It was echoed by others, a pulsating sound that reverberated through the air.

Suddenly the crowd parted and the male captive she had seen before was pushed forward. He landed on his knees in the dust. His hands were bound behind him and he seemed too weak to regain his feet. His clothes were no more than rags and his feet were bare.

Even through the blood covering much of his skin, Brynna was able to see it was as pale as her own and knew he must be one of her own crewmen. When he opened his eyes and looked at her, his light green eyes, almost translucent, revealed his identity.

Only one man among her crew had those eyes, recognizable even though they were now filled with fear, stark and vivid.

It was John Leverson.

"My lady," he rasped through cracked and bloodied lips. "I had hoped never to see you again. Had hoped you would be safe beside your brother by now."

John had barely uttered the words when the nearest warrior aimed a kick at his head and spoke loudly. "Silence, dog!" he said in his guttural language, then delivered another hard kick against John's nose.

Hearing the crack of bones as her crewman's nose broke, a sudden fury surged through Brynna, overpowering her fear. "You swine!" she shouted, knowing all the while the *skraeling* could not understand her, yet needing to vent her rage anyway.

Although the warrior sent a curious look in her direction, he did not cease his tormenting. Instead, he delivered another kick, this time aimed at John's back. As his foot thudded against John's flesh, the savage laughed, then turned to his companions who had stood by, silently watching.

He spoke to them in a commanding tone of voice, words uttered so quickly that Brynna was unable to follow them. But again she had no need. Two of the savages, obviously acting on his instructions, bent over and grasped John beneath his upper arms, hauling him upright much as they had done to her. Then, with John hanging limply between them, they bound him—spread-eagled—to the two remaining poles.

Her worry about John's condition made fear for herself less constant. With fresh blood seeping from the wound newly opened by the kicks, he would soon bleed to death—if, indeed, he had not already done so.

That thought caused a lump in her throat and she swallowed around it. Perhaps he would be better off dead, perhaps they both would, for they were unlikely to be rescued.

Red Fox, she silently cried, her gaze probing the forest around them. *Where are you? Have you left me to my fate and returned to your home?* Such an event seemed likely, for had he been searching for her, he would surely have found her by now.

The ache in her strained muscles made itself felt suddenly. Tied the way she was, there was no way she could ease the strain.

Although the *skraelings* had left her feet loose enough so she could stand, her weakened condition threatened to buckle her knees.

Tears of self-pity were threatening to fall when suddenly the drums began to sound. *Thrum, thrum, thrum, thrum. Thrum, thrum, thrum, thrum.*

The beat of the drums was accompanied by the crowd drawing back even farther, yet remaining in a circle perhaps ten feet distant from the captives.

Dark fear swept over Brynna as she waited to see what would happen.

The drumbeats picked up speed and the crowd fell silent, watching the captives avidly.

Becoming aware of movement in John's vicinity, Brynna turned her head to look at him. He was stirring from his stupor. His head lifted and he met her eyes. And what she saw reflected there made her aware that he obviously shared her fear . . . that the end was very near. And that whatever form it took, their fate would surely not be an easy one.

And now, when Brynna was certain she was near the point of death, she felt the true ecstasy of life. Faced with losing it, it throbbed and pulsated with a clarity she had never before experienced.

God help us, she silently beseeched, knowing no one else could.

Spreading Branches was unhappy with the turn of events. He had not captured the fiery-haired woman only to give her over to death. Such an end to a woman of her beauty would be a waste, but since he'd arrived at the village, things had gotten out of hand.

The People, knowing it was others of her clan that had caused the death of one of them and the disappearance of Walks with Thunder, and believing they were monsters who escaped from their own world into this fourth world where the desert people now made their home, had taken matters into their own hands.

Now, despite his every objection, the woman was staked beside her kinsman in the center of the village while their fate was being decided by the council.

Could he hope to sway the council's decision?

He looked at each of the elders of the tribe, but found no expression to give away their feelings on the matter.

Nevertheless, his gaze traveled around the circle, looking at each of the warriors and elders in turn, studying the faces of the chiefs and sub-chiefs and wondering again if he could sway their decision. As before, there was nothing to be learned from their expressions.

Although Spreading Branches feared the woman's fate was already decided, he refused to give up so easily.

He must at least try to save her life, must remind the council that the woman was his by right of conquest. And if he succeeded, he would not only save the woman from certain death, but would be allowed to keep the four-legged creature that had been with her.

The acquisition of such an animal would make Spreading Branches the envy of all men.

Yes. It was definitely to his advantage to convince the council of his rights.

He took a deep breath and prepared to plead his cause.

Red Fox's heart gave a jerk of fear as he frowned down at the tracks on the ground. The fear was not for himself, but for the girl, because the hoof prints that he followed were now entwined with those of moccasined feet.

Had the warrior who'd followed Brynna captured her already? He could not know for sure, but he was afraid it was so.

That thought sent him sprinting forward, racing through the stunted growth that soon gave way to a dense forest. He paused for mere moments when he lost the trail, then hurried on again.

As the hoof prints became more frequently indistinct, Red Fox realized that someone was taking great pains to cover them whenever possible. It was then Red Fox knew whoever was following Brynna had finally succeeded in overtaking her.

That knowledge spurred him onward, leaping obstacles as though he traveled on winged feet.

He must reach her without delay, Red Fox told himself, otherwise there would be nothing left of the fiery-haired woman with the courageous heart except her lifeless, broken body.

Patrick silently cursed himself for waiting too long, even though he knew there had been no alternative. That did little to console him now though as he bent over tracks that were even fainter than usual.

"These hoof prints look to be as much as a week old," Patrick said, frowning down at them. "Look at them,

Lacey. The lass must be way ahead of us, too far to catch anytime soon.''

Lacey stooped beside his friend. ''Time had nothing to do with fading these tracks,'' he growled. ''Somebody did that.'' He pointed to one side of the hoof print. ''Look. See how that edge is deeper? Someone has deliberately attempted to cover the prints.''

''Why should the *skraeling* do that?'' Patrick queried.

''Who knows?'' Lacey shrugged, rising to his feet again. ''Mayhap they are close to his village. Whatever the reason, someone has dragged brush behind the lady's mount to make the hoof prints less distinct. If we had been a day later through here, then the tracks would be gone completely. There would be nothing here to find.''

''You are sure she is still a captive? Is there not a chance she escaped and is dragging the brush herself''

''I think not. The moccasin prints are still with her.'' He shaded his eyes and searched the dry, barren land that lay ahead of them. ''I have a bad feeling about all this.''

Patrick had a bad feeling himself, but he kept it to himself, fearing to verbalize it, afraid that would make it a reality.

''The trail leads that way,'' Lacey said, pointing out the direction. ''We must make haste while there is time.''

Moving quickly along the trail, each of them hoped silently they would reach Brynna in time to save her.

Chapter Twelve

When Garrick Nordstrom's longship slipped around the bend and the vessel his sister and her convict helpers had commandeered came into full view, he felt his spirits take a downward plunge.

He said nothing, though—indeed, felt no need to, for Nama, his wife, stood by his side, and she, too, could see the devastation wrought by the *skraelings*.

"Others have been here before us," she said softly, her fingers gripping his right forearm as though she sought to offer him comfort. "The boat stands empty and deserted, my love."

"Perhaps not," he said harshly. "Brynna might have slipped over the side. She could have—"

"Brynna would not have done so," she reminded him. "She would have fought beside the others. It is not her nature to hide when danger is near."

"No," he agreed harshly. "But 'twould have been better were it not so."

Swallowing around the lump of fear in his throat, Garrick turned away from the siderail and gave the order to pull alongside the *langskip* even though he need not have done so, for the crew were already easing up beside the abandoned vessel.

It took only a matter of moments to determine there was no living soul aboard the craft. But Garrick had good reason to be hopeful; only a handful of the crew could be accounted for. That meant most of the others, unlike those poor souls whose bodies had been left on the *langskip* to rot, were still alive.

He voiced the thought aloud. "Brynna is not dead. Nor are most of her crewmen. They numbered many more than are here. They have obviously been taken captive by whatever clan populates this area."

Nama, who had been studying the arrow that pierced one crewman's throat, spoke up. "No, my love. Not the clan who make their home here. This arrow came from the bow of a desert warrior."

Garrick frowned down at her. "A desert warrior? One of Walks with Thunder's people?"

"Yes. And it is my thought that it would have been better to have been captive to this river clan than the desert tribe. They are dreaded by all other clans, hated for their cruelty, and shunned by all save their own kinsmen. If they captured your sister, then her life will not be an easy one."

"But she will live?" he questioned sharply.

"Perhaps. Most likely. But her fate will be decided by a council." She looked toward the distant mountains. "We must try to find her before the council members make their decision." She looked at him with sorrowful eyes. "They will connect her with you, and she may be made to pay the penalty for taking the life of their clansman."

"It was not Brynna who killed him," Garrick said bitterly. "He died at my hand."

"Only to save my life," she said, gripping his arm

tightly, hoping to ease some of his pain. "If you are to blame for his death, then so must I be. It was for my sake you took his life. He would have raped me had it not been for your intervention." She hung her head in shame. "My maidenhead is not worth your sister's life. You should have left me to suffer my fate."

"She will not die!" he said harshly, gathering her close against him. "Do not even think such thoughts, lest they become a fact." He caressed her dark hair. "You must not attempt to shoulder the blame when none of this is your doing." He squeezed her shoulders, then placed a soft kiss against her cheek. "Now, off with you, love. We must hurry to follow after those who have done this thing. Perhaps it is not too late to save my sister from those people you call the desert clan."

Nama watched the shore closely as Garrick gave orders to disembark, hoping for some sight of Brynna there . . . some sign that she might have escaped the clutches of those people she feared so much.

But there was nothing to see, nothing but verdant foliage and dense green forestland.

Staring into the shadowy forest, Nama was afraid, fearful of what they would find when Garrick finally caught up to the people who had abducted his sister and killed several of her crew. She had no doubt that he would find them, no matter how long it took.

Black Crow, a young warrior from the desert clan, had been standing sentry duty atop the tallest peak when a movement on a distant slope had caught his eye. He narrowed his vision and studied the slope for a long moment.

It was not an animal he saw. The creature walked upright. Someone was approaching.

He waited, knowing he must determine if one man came or many men. Then he saw it, another figure slightly smaller than the first one. And then another came behind that one.

Realizing he must sound the alarm, he raised his hand to his mouth and used the birdcall that would give warning to Broken Wing—the next sentry in line—that someone, as yet unidentified, approached their village.

An answering call told him his message had been received and he began his descent from his high mountain perch, traveling toward the slow-moving black specks in the distance, knowing Broken Wing would soon be standing where he had been a moment before, keeping watch until another warrior took his place.

" 'Tis a sorry state the two of us are in, Lady Brynna," said John Leverson, his eyes meeting hers. She read defeat there, and the knowledge that he had given up sent new fear surging through her.

"We are not beaten yet, John," she said. "We will find a way out of this mess."

"If you say so, lady."

Realizing she must get his mind off their plight, she said, "How did you come to be captured, John?"

"Shawn O'Malley found grapes in a grove offshore," the man explained. "Several of us decided to gather them. It was Jeremy, Gatsby, Malsby, and Shawn who went with me." He uttered a heavy sigh that held a liquid gurgle. "The *skraelings* were waiting there. They took us by surprise."

"And the others with you?"

"All dead," he said woefully. "Every last one of 'em. To a man."

"What about the crew left on the *langskip?*" she asked

huskily, needing to ask, but afraid to be told. "Do you think they will come to our rescue?"

"I fear none were left alive, lady," he replied hoarsely. "The savages swam underwater and boarded the craft. We could hear the sound of battle, could hear their awful screams, but could do naught to help, not tied up the way we were. Then, all of a sudden, the screams stopped. Just real quick-like. And somehow, that was even worse . . . the not knowing what was going on. Then we found out. Them devils came back, and they was carrying bloody scalps with 'em.''

"You said 'we,' John."

"What?" He obviously did not understand.

"You said, We heard the sound of battle."

"Yeah. Me and Malsby. He was still alive then. But one of 'em. A short, squatty savage killed him that first night out. Just walked up to him where he was spread-eagled on the ground and gutted him." He shook his shaggy head. "I wish you was elsewhere, lady, because the end is near and it will be hard."

Brynna felt a shudder pass through her, knowing John was probably right. The savages around them would make sure the end would not be easy.

"What about Patrick and Lacey, lady? What happened to them and the men who went with you? Are they dead, too?"

"I think they may have survived," she replied slowly. "Although I really have no way of knowing. They were engaged in battle when I last saw them."

"If they survived, then perhaps we are left with some hope," John Leverson said.

A stirring near the edge of the crowd interrupted their conversation and Brynna's heart began a slow, heavy beat as she waited, feeling certain the end was near.

As before, the crowd parted to allow one of the *skrae-*

lings to step through. Like most of the men, he was dressed only in breechcloth and moccasins, and a red headband he wore around his forehead. He stopped before a white-haired man whose beaded headband held at his right temple a silver disk with two eagle feathers hanging from it.

Brynna felt the white-haired man must be one of their chiefs, or some other person of importance, by the way the others watched him. His eyes were deep-set and his mouth wide and thin, drawn down at the corners in an expression of severity.

He listened quietly to what the newcomer had to say, his eyes traveling to the bound prisoners often during the conversation.

Although Brynna strained her ears, trying to catch a few words, something, anything that might give her hope, she could hear nothing. Nevertheless, she had no trouble understanding that both she and John, were the subjects under discussion.

When the newly-arrived warrior finished speaking, the chief spoke in the guttural tongue that was familiar, yet spoken too swiftly for Brynna to follow.

Immediately, as if obeying a command, another warrior approached the bound prisoners, drawing his knife from its sheath as he did.

Setting her jaw defiantly, Brynna prayed for courage, refusing to allow the savage to see how frightened she was.

Then John spoke, his voice holding a slight tremble. "Do not allow them to see your fear, lady. These devils would like nothing better than to hear you scream."

"They will be disappointed, then," Brynna said. "For I am prepared to face whatever they have in mind for me without giving them that satisfaction."

"They will make you suffer, lady," he growled. "Be prepared for that."

"I know," she said, biting her lip until she tasted the coppery flow of blood. "Yet I must not disgrace my family by crying for mercy. And if God is willing, our lives may end quickly."

She prayed it was so, wanted it with every fiber of her being. And yet she feared the savages would never allow them to go easily.

Fearing the agony they would be forced to endure, she quietly prayed for relief from such an end.

Let us die quickly, she silently prayed, falling back on the catechism she had been taught in her youth. *Sweet Mary, Mother of God, let the end be swift.*

Chapter Thirteen

Father Sun hung low in the western sky, looking down upon Red Fox where he knelt behind the service-berry bush, his narrowed gaze focused on the girl in the clearing below. Although she appeared unharmed from this distance, that state of affairs would obviously soon change, for her captors had bound her to stakes and it was clearly evident they were readying her for torture.

His gaze swept the compound as he mentally counted the desert warriors. Too many, he knew, for one lone warrior to vanquish. Yet he must do something, must try to help her. There was no way he could just walk away and leave her to suffer such a fate.

No! He could not allow her to suffer endless pain. Yet neither could he save her life.

There was only one thing left to do. He must end her life himself!

A vision of her lifeless body rose in his mind and Red Fox swallowed back the bile in his throat. Could he end her life so easily? he wondered. Suppose his aim was off and his arrow did not reach its mark? If that were to happen, then he would only increase her suffering.

You cannot fail, a silent voice cried. *You must loose your arrow. You must take her life without delay.*

Red Fox tasted bile again as he slid his bow from his shoulder and pulled a feathered arrow from his quiver. He seemed to move in a dream world, his actions incredibly slow while he continued to watch the scene below. He saw the warrior tormenting Brynna, watched him slide his knife blade along the girl's delicate cheek.

Feeling a gnawing deep inside, Red Fox fitted the arrow to his bow, then raised himself to his full height, spreading his legs to better steady himself. His arrow must fly true, must bury itself deep within her heart, for there would surely be no second chance allowed him, no time to send a second arrow. The moment his arrow pierced her body, the desert warriors would swarm over him like angry bees after a bear robbing their honey tree.

With his heart thudding heavily in his chest, Red Fox drew back his bowstring, preparing to loose the arrow that would end the precious life that, somehow or another, had come to mean so much to him.

Although fear was uppermost in her mind as Brynna felt the cold blade slide over her cheek, she fought to calm herself. Nothing could save her now. The end of her life was at hand and she must prepare herself for it.

Her gaze never wavered from the half-naked savage who seemed to take such delight in causing her torment as her lips, perhaps from habit, formed the beginning of the rosary.

"Hail, Mary, full of grace . . ." The words came from deep within her being as she prayed for absolution.

She heard John Leverson's harsh rasping voice as he

chimed in, echoing her words the moment she had uttered them as though they were somewhat familiar, only forgotten from lack of use.

". . . Pray for us sinners, now and at the hour of our death," she continued, wishing she could feel the polished beads of her rosary beneath her fingers. And even as she prayed, Brynna waited for the cold blade of the knife to pierce her flesh, to send her lifeblood gushing from her body.

Yet surprisingly, that did not happen. Instead, the savage abruptly left off tormenting her with the crude weapon and stepped to one side.

She watched with horror as he lifted his knife hand and brought it down quickly toward her right wrist, wondering if he was bent on dismembering her limb by limb. But instead of slicing through bone and flesh, the knife sliced through the leather that bound her. Then, amazing though it seemed, the rawhide thongs parted and her right hand was suddenly free.

While she tried to understand the *skraeling*'s reasons for releasing her hand, he bent over and sliced through the leather binding her right foot. Then, repeating his actions, he freed her left hand and foot.

What was happening? she wondered. Why had she been set free?

Hope was born anew, flaring swift and strong within her breast.

Rubbing her raw, chafed wrists, she watched the savage slice through John Leverson's bonds, saw the Englishman crumple to the ground, for his wounds were such that, without anything to hold him upright, he could not stand alone.

"John," she cried out, "Are you all right?" A stupid question, she realized, even as she uttered the words. Of course he was not all right. He had been beaten severely,

his flesh swollen and discolored around his head, his
shoulders and chest seeping blood where his skin had
been pierced by something sharp, either knife blades or
the pointed sticks the old women had used on her own
flesh.

Intent on helping him, Brynna hurried toward him,
stumbling as she went, realizing as she did that her own
legs were not as steady as she had expected.

Immediately, rough hands closed over her, stopping
her from reaching his side, pulling her toward one of the
crude dwellings nearby and shoving her inside. She landed
on the hard dirt floor with enough force to drive the breath
from her body.

Finding herself alone, Brynna immediately turned to
the entrance, wondering if she had been left unguarded.
A quick look outside answered her question. A guard
stood beside the brush hut. Even though she had been
allowed to live, it was evident she was still a prisoner.

Red Fox expelled a sigh of relief as he slowly released
the bowstring and sought cover behind the bush again.
Although he had no idea why Brynna's life had been
spared—or for how long—he knew that for a short time
at least, she would continue to live. He was grateful he
had not had time to loose his arrow. Now, thanks to the
spirits that had seen fit to intervene on her behalf, there
might still be time to set her free.

Something was going on in the village below, he suddenly realized, his gaze searching for the source of the
problem. The women and children scurried around the
village, gathering their possessions together as though
they were intent on departing from the location.

The children called the camp dogs that were kept for

the purpose of hauling their belongings. Their departure, Red Fox knew, would be swift. Unlike his own clan, who made its homes from buffalo hides, the desert clan would not carry their homes with them. Instead, new brush huts would be erected once they reached another campsite. But, Red Fox vowed, by the time they reached it, wherever their destination might be, they would no longer have Brynna with them.

Somehow, in some way, he would free her before they had traveled far.

Or else he would die trying.

Patrick Douglass was hotter than he had ever been in his life. His tongue felt thick in his mouth, dry from lack of water, yet he knew he must not drink yet. It was necessary to conserve the water that was left since they were traveling through harsh, dry land where vegetation was sparse, where there was not even enough moisture to grow more than stunted trees of some unknown variety.

He had never before journeyed through such desolate land, and he hoped, when they left this land, never to do so again. There was little game to be found. A few rabbits had crossed their path, but mostly there was nothing but lizards to be seen, like the collared one that soaked up the sun on top of a layered rock of gypsum and sand nearby. As though startled by his presence, the lizard rose up on its hind legs and stared at him. Then, quick as a wink, the creature dropped to all fours again and streaked across the ground, dragging its long tail behind it.

A dust cloud in the distance caught his attention and Patrick reined up his mount, wondering if the dust was raised by the strange hump-backed beasts they had encountered in the past, or whether Lacey was returning.

He had no need to wonder long. Soon it became obvious the dust was raised by horse and rider. It could be none other than Lacey.

Patrick was aware of the coiled tension in Lacey's body as he reined up beside him.

"*Skraelings* ahead," Lacey growled, removing his hat and wiping away the sweat dripping down his forehead. "Damn! I never knew it could be so hot."

"How far?" Patrick questioned.

"Maybe ten miles," Lacey replied.

"How many?"

"Must be at least three score of them. Headed this way, too. Armed to the teeth with their crude weapons." His tone held contempt. "Guess they must have spotted me."

"And the lady Brynna?" Patrick asked the question that was uppermost in his mind. "Do they have her?"

"Not with them," the scout replied. "But they have her right enough. I saw her in their village."

"You are sure it was her?"

"Yeah," Lacey said shortly. "No other female in this land would sport a head of hair like hers. It was her, all right."

"And she was alive," Patrick muttered, his heart gladdened by the news. "We have found her in time."

"Just barely," Lacey said, his voice rasping harshly.

"What do you mean?"

"They got her staked out in the middle of their village. And she was not their only captive . . ." He shifted his gaze, staring back the way he had come. "The news is bad, Patrick."

"Out with it!" Patrick ordered. Nothing could be worse than his lady's capture—except to hear they had come too late to save her.

"They had another captive there."

"Another one? Who?"

"Hard to tell. But he was one of our own."

"Then the boat was attacked."

"Must have been," Lacey agreed. "And all our crewmen may be dead, except for the one with Lady Brynna. At least we came in time to save them."

Patrick felt surprise at the scout's words. "We have not yet arrived."

"Nevertheless, whatever they had planned for the captives has been delayed, because they know we are coming. They must. One of their warriors—possibly a guard—went among them and almost immediately they began scurrying around like ants. It was obvious they were disturbed by something, probably the news the man brought."

"And the captives?" Patrick questioned sharply, fear born anew as he realized their presence might endanger Brynna and the hapless crewman. "What happened to the lady and her companion?"

"They were untied and dragged into separate huts, some kind of dwellings that looked like they were made out of brush and sticks. The *skraelings* must be nomads. I noticed a guard was set to watch the huts where the captives were taken. I stayed there only long enough to determine our lady was in no imminent danger before I came back to warn you of their attack."

"You say there are four score?" Patrick asked. "We cannot overcome such odds." He fought against the fear and frustration such knowledge brought. "Even our greater strength and weapons cannot help us against that many. But there might be another way to help Lady Brynna."

"How?"

"We could flee them."

"Flee?" Lacey asked sharply. "How could our running away help her?"

"They would be sure to think we feared them, that they had us on the run."

"And of course that would not be so." The words were spoken dryly.

"No. It would not," Patrick said forcefully. "I would stand and fight to the death right here, were it not for the sake of our lady. Instead, we must appear fearful of their might. We must lead them away from the village where Lady Brynna is being held. Then, when they are far enough away so that they cannot quickly return, we will circle around them and with our mounts to carry us swifter than the *skraelings* could ever hope to travel afoot, we shall ride to their village and free our lady."

"Yes," Lacey said slowly. "It is a good plan. But it depends entirely on the *skraelings* following us. They might not do so."

"They will," Patrick said, with more confidence than he actually felt. "Especially if we take pains to stay close to them. If we go no farther than the eye can see they might be afraid we will turn and fight at any given moment. They would not dare return to their village until we are dead."

"You might be right," Lacey agreed. "It just might work. It certainly beats hand to hand combat where we would most certainly come out losers in such a battle."

With their plans made, they waited only until they saw the war-painted savages, then they put their plan into action, each hoping it would work, each hoping soon they would free the lady who had come to mean so much to both of them.

*   *   *

The western sky was streaked with crimson and pink, left there by the setting sun, but Brynna had no time to admire the sunset. It took all her efforts to keep herself upright as she stumbled along beside John who must, of necessity, hurry in order to keep the noose the *skraelings* had placed around his neck from tightening.

Although Brynna would liked to have helped John, each time she tried, each move she made toward him was immediately countered with a sharp rap on the head. The blow was delivered with a club, wielded by the old woman who had obviously been designated to guard them. Most of the able-bodied men had left them. Now there were only women, children, and old men, probably left behind because of their inability to fight.

Where had the *skraeling* warriors gone? she wondered fleetingly, but really spared little time on the thought. She was too concerned with escape. Since the men were gone, surely she and John would find the opportunity to run away.

But even as the thought occurred, she realized John was not strong enough to go anywhere. He was too badly injured.

As though he guessed her frustration, he met her eyes and she could read within them how fully he had accepted his own impending death.

"My own fate is sealed, my lady," he muttered. "I have accepted that, and so must you. If you find a chance to escape, you must not allow it to pass."

"I cannot accept that, John," she said fiercely. "I will not leave without you."

"Then you will surely die," he replied. "For I cannot survive much longer."

"Do not speak so," she said sharply. "You are not so badly wounded."

"My injuries are such you cannot see them," he said, grimacing with pain. "Even now I can feel the blood spreading from within. Nothing can save me now. But you need feel no sorrow. I would embrace death knowing that you were free."

"You may be wrong about your injuries," she said. "We will escape . . . and we will find someone to help you."

He shook his head in denial. "There is no help for me, my lady. None in this godforsaken land knows enough about medicine. Even in our own land there would be naught to do." He heaved a long sigh. "No. I am surely doomed. I only pray I may live long enough to see you go free."

Brynna felt moisture welling into her eyes and blinked back the tears of pity for the doomed man, knowing he would not want to see them fall. Even though she had accepted his words for truth, she could not verbally agree. Instead, she said, "Do not be so quick to embrace death, John. You must fight to survive."

"Death will not find me easy to claim," he replied. "But it will take me nevertheless. And it will not be so unexpected. I had a feeling when I began this journey that I would never return to my homeland. Now, I know I was right."

"No talk!" the old woman ordered in that harsh guttural language of the *skraelings*. The words had been spoken so often to her now that Brynna had no trouble understanding their meaning.

Brynna and John exchanged a meaningful look, each falling silent, fearful of the blows that would follow the command if it was not immediately obeyed.

The shadows had lengthened when she realized the trees were no longer scraggly and stunted. Instead, they were taller, growing closer together.

Looking about, Brynna wondered fleetingly if the trees would grant her enough cover to ensure escape.

A sudden movement near the edge of a thick growth of pines caught her eye and she narrowed her gaze, studying the area intently.

Was that a face she saw? Before she could be sure, it was gone again. But Brynna's heart knew. Even if her eyes deceived her, somehow she knew that Red Fox was near at hand.

Pretending to stumble, Brynna fell to her knees. As John moved to help her to her feet, she took the opportunity to whisper. "Help is near. Someone has come to rescue us."

He asked no questions, only nodded his head to show he understood. "An opportunity must be made," he replied, quickly dodging the blow the old woman aimed at his head, having obviously decided he was lingering too long beside the red-haired woman. "I will create a disturbance, my lady. While they are distracted, you must flee."

"You must come, too," she whispered desperately.

"No." He barely spoke the word before he was struck a hard blow across his shoulders. He stumbled and fell to his knees. Pain filled his eyes as he looked up at her. "Can you not see that I am already dying?" he asked. "Allow me to do this one thing before I meet my maker."

Realizing he was right, that he would not survive, and knowing that if she stayed, she would die with him, Brynna knew she must do as he asked.

A smile crossed John Leverson's face when he realized she had acceded to his wishes. Seeming to find strength in her acceptance, he gave a howl as fierce as any uttered by the *skraelings*, turned on the old woman and struck her with his closed fist.

Immediately, the crowd converged on him, hitting him with clubs and fists, kicking him with their feet, some even gathering up stones to club him with.

Tears streamed from Brynna's eyes as she watched him fall beneath the blows. But, mindful that his death should not be wasted, Brynna spun on her heels and raced away, leaving the savages and poor dear John behind.

Chapter Fourteen

Brynna's boots thudded over uneven ground as she raced toward the thick grove of pines. She heard a loud shriek and knew her flight must have been discovered.

Could she outrun her pursuers? she wondered.

Her question was answered when she felt the impact of a body striking hers. She fell beneath its weight.

She should have known escape was impossible, she thought with a sense of fatality in that timeless moment before she struck the ground. The jolt was enough to drive the breath from her body and she lay there stunned, pinned beneath the weight of the brave who had caught her. Although he was young, in his early teens, she was aware of the danger he presented. She could see it in his flat black eyes, knew that he would kill her, given half the chance.

"Release the woman!"

The young brave, taken completely by surprise, jerked his head upward, his gaze focusing on the man who had ordered her release.

Red Fox!

Brynna's heart gave a spasmodic jerk when she saw him. He had come! The man who had rescued her before was again at hand in her time of need.

His expression gave nothing away as he spared a quick look at Brynna. And even though that look had been brief, she knew he had seen the bruises on her flesh—the abrasions and cuts that had barely scabbed over—before returning his attention to the brave whose body still pinned her to the ground.

"If you wish to continue this life, then leave while you can," Red Fox told the young savage in a harsh, menacing voice.

Slowly, cautiously, the brave pushed himself away from Brynna, his wary gaze never once leaving the man who towered over them, his muscles tensed, his body coiled and waiting, his legs spread in a fighting stance.

Brynna knew if she had been confronted by such a man, she would have heeded his advice and taken flight, but the brave did not. Instead, he crouched low and circled the larger man, preparing to do battle.

She felt mesmerized as she rose unsteadily to her feet, unable to take her eyes from the two men, one large and unyielding, the other slight, yet, she felt, prepared to fight.

Realizing the brave's life would be forfeited, Brynna tried her best to stop what seemed inevitable. "No, Red Fox! You cannot kill him! He is little more than a boy."

Red Fox's gaze did not waver from the young brave. "The choice is his own," he said harshly. "We cannot waste time waiting for him to decide."

The young brave, apparently realizing Red Fox would honor his words—that he could choose life by leaving them alone—began to back away slowly. Even so, his hand never left his knife.

Feeling immense relief that her young attacker had

chosen to live, Brynna released the breath she had been holding. Now there would be no further violence. They could leave without—

John! How could she have forgotten him?

"Red Fox," she said urgently. "We must help—"

She broke off with a cry as the young brave raised his knife and leapt toward Red Fox. The warrior had obviously been expecting such a move, because he spun away, swinging his knife hand around and slicing a deep gash across the brave's stomach.

Howling with pain, the brave dropped his knife and grabbed the wound, his knees crumbling beneath him.

Brynna covered her ears against his cries, turning her eyes away from him, knowing he had given Red Fox no choice, yet still unable to watch him writhing with pain.

Red Fox stepped over the hapless savage and curled hard fingers around her forearm, urging her deeper into the shadowy forest.

"No," she cried out in his language. "My friend needs help." She pointed toward the crowd of people that had already began to unknot.

"Too late," he said, shaking his head. "Where is Shadow? With his help we can easily escape the desert warriors."

"He ran away when the warrior who captured me tried to ride him," she explained, turning away from the sight of the crumpled figure on the ground. Although she knew Red Fox must be right about it being too late for John, she also knew she must be certain. But how?

If they remained where they were any longer, they would surely become captives of the desert clan.

An undulating cry jerked her head around and she saw an old woman pointing in their direction. Her flight had been discovered by others! Sheer black fright swept over her.

Another shout sounded, then another, and one old man began to issue orders. Several of the younger braves took up their lances and ran toward Brynna and Red Fox.

The warrior, impatient to be gone, jerked Brynna farther into the shadows, and as she turned away, she saw an old man raise a lance and send it plunging into the motionless figure on the ground.

"No!" she whimpered, horrified at the sight.

"He could not feel the pain of the lance. Death had already claimed him," Red Fox said, pushing her ahead of him into the cover of the forest. "And if we do not hurry, death will find us, too."

Realizing he was right, she hurried into the forest with Red Fox, telling herself that she owed him a debt of the greatest value. It was a debt she could never hope to repay, for how did one pay for one's own life? What price could be placed on it?

Red Fox urged her along faster, gripping her arm tightly, holding her upright when she stumbled over some unseen obstacle in their flight through the forest that was becoming ever increasingly darker with each moment that passed.

Brynna wondered how long they could keep up the pace he'd set, yet even as she wondered, she knew they must. Even now she could hear the sound of pursuit, knew her captors were still searching for them.

They continued to travel for what seemed like hours, with Red Fox forcing her onward when she would have stopped to rest. And as they fled, her senses came alive.

She was aware of the sharp pine scent, carried by the brisk wind that whipped around them, rifling through her hair, tossing it this way and that, while at the same time flattening her shift against her body.

High above them, a pale quarter moon hung in a velvet black sky sprinkled with thousands of glittering stars.

How could Red Fox see where they were going when there was only the pale light of the moon to guide them? she wondered.

Even as that thought occurred, Red Fox stopped abruptly and released her arm. "Wait here," he said, moving away from her.

"Where are you going?" she asked, afraid.

"You need have no fear," he said. "I will return shortly."

Without another word, he strode forward, stopping a short distance away from her and staring intently down at the ground.

What did he see? Brynna wondered, her feet moving automatically as she went to join him, ignoring his command to remain where she was.

A moment later she understood.

The very earth upon which they stood ended abruptly, dropping away to a wide valley below. Immediately below their position was a wide stone lip that thrust out over a sheer drop.

"We have found a place to rest for the night," Red Fox said.

"Where?" she asked, looking up at him.

"Down below," he told her. "Those who pursue us will not look for us there." His gaze searched the area around them, then narrowed on a place a short distance away. "Come," he said, taking her hand in his and leading her along the ledge. He stopped several times, inspecting the rocky ledge, then, after once such incident, muttered, "Good. There is a way down here." Releasing her hand, he grasped a protruding rock and said, "Follow me carefully, Brynna."

A chill of apprehension went through her when she realized he expected her to climb down the cliff.

She uttered a sharp refusal. "No, Red Fox! I cannot

do it! To attempt such a climb would be foolish! The cliff is too steep. We would be sure to fall.''

''No,'' he said, easing himself farther down the stone face. ''I am used to such climbs. Just follow me closely and you will be in no danger.''

''No!'' she said again, her panic-stricken gaze moving downward, into the shadowy depths of the valley that seemed so far below them.

Her heart began to pound with dread. How could she tell him she feared heights? How could she make him understand her absolute terror?

Seeming to sense her unspoken words, he eased back up the stone face until he stood on the ledge beside her. Taking her hand in his, he said softly, soothingly, ''We must do this, Brynna. Those who pursue us will run us to the ground. We cannot go back and we cannot go forward. Down is the only way. But you need not worry— you will be safe with me.''

''I cannot,'' she said again, her voice high with hysteria. She clung tightly to his hand, taking comfort in the solid feel of it.

''Calm yourself,'' he said, pulling her against his hard chest. ''Take deep breaths and you will feel better.''

Held tightly in the circle of his arms, she began to feel better. When he tilted her head and looked into her eyes, speaking softly, coaxingly, she found herself giving in.

She had no idea what changed her mind. It might have been his words, or it might have been the strength of his arms around her, or perhaps it was only the persuasion of his voice that swayed her.

Whatever the reason, Brynna found herself following him down the stone face of the cliff, her fingers digging into the indentations and rocky protrusions that Red Fox searched for and found until finally, halfway down to the stone ledge, Red Fox finally admitted they could go on farther.

Brynna froze instantly, closing her eyes and squeezing them tightly shut, afraid to move, afraid even to breathe, lest the mere act of inhaling cause her to lose her balance and plunge to the valley below.

"Brynna? Did you hear me? We cannot descend any farther."

"I heard you!" Brynna cried hysterically, her fingers clawing at the stone face. "We must climb up again."

"No," he said roughly. "I told you we could not stay up there."

"Then what?" she demanded shrilly. "What are we supposed to do? Cling to this stone until we lose our grips and fall to our—"

She stopped abruptly, unable to speak her thoughts aloud.

"Control yourself, Brynna," he said softly. "You have no need to fear."

"No need?" Her voice was hysterical, she knew, but she had no control over it. "Damn you! How can you say that? We cannot go down and you say we *must* not go up, yet we cannot stay where we are!"

"Hush!" he reprimanded sharply. "Your screams are interfering with my thoughts."

Interfering with his thoughts? Damn him! It was his fault they were in this predicament! His fault they were stranded here on this stone face. His fault they were—

Not so, a silent voice said. *None of this is his fault. His life would not be in danger now if he had not tried to save yours.*

Shame swept over her. She must speak now. Must apologize for her thoughtless words. Before she could do so, she heard a sharp cracking sound beneath her.

"Red Fox!" she cried, tilting her head to look down at him, feeling immense relief that he was still there. "What happened?"

"A rock broke loose," he said calmly. "It took a chunk of stone with it. I think I can use it to go sideways." Even as he was speaking, he was edging away from her with crablike movements.

"What are you doing?" she asked.

"Wait there!" he said shortly.

"Wait here?" She began to laugh, her voice high-pitched and shaky, uncontrollable.

"Stop that!" he said sharply. "Control yourself." When she continued to laugh, he went on. "I thought you were brave! But I was wrong. You are nothing but a coward."

"How dare you call me a coward!" she said, feeling a surge of anger that overwhelmed her fear. "I am nothing of the kind!"

"Then prove it!" he snarled. "Move down beside me! Follow me along this stone face. Put your feet where my hands were. The hole is big, easy to find. Grip it hard and move down here. Prove that you have enough courage to follow me."

"I can follow wherever you lead!" she gritted, moving her foot down the stone face until her toes were inserted in the hole, then balancing herself so her hand could search for the depression her foot had previously occupied.

When she was finally beside him, she met his dark gaze and wondered at the expression she saw there. Could it possibly be admiration, from the man who had only recently called her a coward?

"Good for you," he said softly. "I knew you could do it."

"Then you knew more than I did," she muttered. "My

heart is still beating like the wings of a trapped butterfly."

"Nevertheless, you overcame your fear enough to join me here."

"And what did that accomplish?" she asked, her fear surging forth again.

"A great deal," he replied. "I believe I have found a safe haven."

"Where?"

Red Fox nodded toward his left, where the stone face curved sharply. He moved that way, then suddenly disappeared from sight.

"Red Fox!" she cried out in panic, fearing he had missed his step and fallen into the precipice.

"I am here," he said, calming her fears. "Here, take my hand and join me." His hand found hers, guiding her forward into a shallow niche, just high enough for her to stand upright.

When she would have sunk to the floor covered with sharp rocks that had fallen from the sandstone arch overhead, he tightened his grip and forced her sideways. A moment later she realized why. The niche deepened, curving inward for more than twenty feet.

"We will be safe here," Red Fox said softly, releasing his grip on her.

Safe? Brynna could hardly believe it, but it appeared to be true, at least for the time being. As the fear that had held her in its grip lessened, she gave way to tears of relief, throwing herself at Red Fox, who opened his arms to receive her.

He held her tightly against him, smoothing his palm over her hair, squeezing her shoulders lightly, uttering soft words of encouragement as she continued to sob until there were no more tears left inside her.

Then, it seemed the most natural thing in the world to lift her head and press her lips against his.

Immediately, he stiffened and his arms contracted around her, pulling her tighter into his embrace.

Leaning her head back, her eyes locked with his, and she felt a shiver run down her spine. There was something about him, something indescribable. Perhaps it was the beauty of his features, seen in the shadowy darkness that softened the scar marring one side of his face. Or perhaps it was the strength of his body, or the wildness she sensed in him.

Whatever it was, it drew her like a magnet. Even more, perhaps, she sensed how great was his need to be loved, and she longed to reach out, to show him that he was loved.

Did she truly love him? The thought shook her to the core.

Yet it was true, she realized. She *did* love him. How it had happened, when it had happened, or why, she had no way of knowing. But it was so.

She stood in the circle of his arms, happy just to be there, glad to exult in the warmth of his flesh against her own.

Her nostrils twitched as she inhaled the purely male scent of him.

Giving in to a sudden urge, she moved closer, tracing the tip of her tongue around his lips, delighting in the slightly salty taste of his flesh, reveling in the knowledge that she was no longer alone, that Red Fox was beside her, holding her close against him.

Red Fox, the warrior who had proved himself a hero, coming to her aid against all odds. She owed him her life. And although she had no way of repaying him, she wanted desperately to show him how she felt.

She placed soft kisses across his jawline, down his

neck, and across his shoulders, taking extreme delight in his suddenly altered breathing.

Looking up at him, she encountered the fathomless blackness of his eyes that watched her with disturbing intentness. His gaze slowly traveled down her face, seeming to study the feminine lines of her cheeks and jaw, then stopping on her lips.

Brynna felt the impact of his gaze, felt as if he had physically touched her soft flesh, and her pulse began to pound, as hard and sure as the drumming of Shadow's hooves when his long legs were reaching for speed.

She had the crazy, almost overwhelming sensation something was pressing her backward and her body bent with the invisible force until she felt the hardness of rock against her back.

A fire kindled deep within her loins, and although she was still a virgin, Brynna felt a deep need to be possessed by the warrior.

Red Fox, as though sensing that need, fumbled with her clothing, pulling at the shift and tugging it over her head. Then, releasing his own clothing, he spread himself over her.

When he entered her, Brynna felt a sharp pang, gone as quickly as it had come. Then she felt him slide inside, filling her with his maleness and moving with a swiftness that took her breath away.

Something ignited in her loins, a flame that leapt and danced, that burned with an intensity that left her feeling breathless, craving something that lay just beyond her reach.

"Oh, Red Fox," she moaned, moving with him in that ageless rhythm that was older than time itself, wanting more of him, needing it with a desperation that bordered on pain.

Suddenly, Red Fox arched his back and cried out, a

shudder running through him. Then, as though unable to support his own weight, he crumpled against her and lay still.

For a moment Brynna lay there, wondering what had happened. Was it over then? If so, why did she feel so empty, so unfulfilled?

Unable to answer those questions, she stared up into the darkness, her heart thundering furiously in her chest, aware that Red Fox had already gone to sleep.

Brynna told herself to relax, but her tense body would not obey. Even so, she forced herself to remain still, unwilling to wake the warrior beside her.

Finally, after what seemed like hours, the tension began to drain away and Brynna fell into a deep, dreamless sleep that lasted until first light.

Opening sleep-dazed eyes, Brynna stared up at the rock ceiling above her, wondering for a moment where she was and how she had come to be there. As memory flooded back, she turned her head and found Red Fox watching her.

"I did not want to wake you, little one," he said softly. "But we can delay no longer. Our enemies will be searching for us, and if we stay, they might discover our hiding place." He reached for her discarded shift and handed it to her. "I have no wish to cover such a beautiful body, but you cannot travel naked."

She felt a blush stain her cheeks and quickly pulled the shift over her body to cover her nakedness. Then, feeling that all the necessary parts were covered, she looked up and met his laughing eyes.

"Do not be ashamed of our coupling," he said softly. "Although it was unexpected, it was more than welcome. Even if my life were forfeited I would not regret the time in your arms. But things of that nature will have to wait until we are safe."

"I know," she said quickly. "But I was so grateful, so relieved, that—"

"Grateful?" he interrupted, his voice suddenly harsh, his eyes becoming hard as the stone surrounding them. "Is that why you came into my arms? Because of your gratitude?"

"No," she said quickly, realizing she had made a grave mistake in her choice of words. "Yes, there was gratitude. But that was not all. I—"

She stopped, unable to continue with him looking at her in such a hostile manner. How could she admit to her love when he gave every appearance of hating her? To do so would only mean humiliation.

She contented herself with a mere, "The reason does not really matter."

"It matters," he said, his voice low and disturbed. "But there is no time to speak of this now. Words will have to wait until we are safe from those who follow us. Straighten your clothing, Brynna. Cover yourself. It is time to leave."

Leaving her feeling like a wanton, he rose to his feet and turned his back on her, striding swiftly across the length of the cave and squeezing his body into a crevice that had gone unnoticed the night before.

Brynna cursed herself for a fool as she pulled her shift over her head and smoothed it down her body. Then she followed Red Fox into the narrow passage he had found, wishing she had stayed her tongue.

But what was done was already past and could not be undone. Now she must live with the results of her actions. She could only hope Patrick and her men found her soon.

Before she confessed her love for the *skraeling* warrior and lowered herself even more in his eyes.

Chapter Fifteen

Red Fox led the way down the narrow fissure he had discovered while Brynna slept. The wound she had dealt him by revealing her reasons for allowing his possession was deep. He told himself he was a fool, that he should have known, should have at least suspected.

But he had not.

Fool! he chastised himself again.

Yes. He was a fool. For only a fool would think she could desire one such as he. Only a fool would think she loved him the way he loved—

No! a silent voice cried, *do not even think such thoughts! You dare not love again!*

Every fiber of his being cried out against loving anyone again, especially a woman like Brynna. She was not one of the People, but an outsider.

If he was foolish enough to give her his heart, she would surely cast it aside, would trample on both his heart and his pride. He could not risk that.

No! He had learned his lesson. He would never allow himself to love again. Never.

And yet, a silent voice cried, *if you do not love her, why do you feel so wounded, so lost, so terribly, achingly alone?*

Red Fox tried to silence the inner voice, assuring himself that he was not alone. How could he be, when he had only to turn his head to see Brynna, hurrying along beside him, as though afraid, if her steps faltered, she might be left behind.

But she didn't need to worry. If her steps slowed, his would as well. And if she fell, then he would pick her up, would carry her if her legs were too weary to travel. He would do whatever was necessary to keep her with him.

Brynna stumbled suddenly, then looked at him as he took her arm to steady her and her blue eyes widened ever so slightly. "Is something wrong, Red Fox?" she asked.

"No," he denied quickly, pulling his lips into a smile, hoping to reassure her.

Although she seemed puzzled, she returned his smile with one of her own, and quickened her steps. "Do you think we are still being followed?" she asked, throwing a hurried glance behind them.

"Not yet," he reassured her. "They will not easily find the way we have gone. By the time they do, Wind Woman's breath will have erased any tracks we might have left behind."

Brynna fell into silence then, making Red Fox wonder at her thoughts. She had not asked where they were going yet, seemed content to follow wherever he led. If only she would remain that way, willing to stay with him without being forced.

Perhaps, he reasoned, there was a way to ensure that

she stayed without coercion. He remembered the way she had clung to him during their joining, the way she had cried out his name in her passion. She had wanted him then, and he knew, if he tried hard enough, that he could make her want him again.

That thought pleased him immensely. He remembered the way she had felt against him, her soft, rounded breasts firmly pressed against his chest, her nipples hard and taught. Just the memory of that moment was enough to ignite a fire in his loins, to cause his manhood to stir restlessly.

No. It would be no hardship to touch her, to caress her, to torment her with his fingers until she could stand no more. Then she would cry out his name again, would plead for his possession.

But it would be different than before, he decided. She had been a virgin then, and he had taken her too quickly, been too eager for her to derive much pleasure from their joining.

How long must he wait for that moment? Red Fox wondered, throwing a quick glance at her, then looking quickly away again, lest she might guess his thoughts from the expression in his eyes.

Red Fox realized he must not rush her, that he must wait, and watch for the right time to teach her the ways of a man and a woman.

But until that time, until he could win her over, until he could make her want to remain with him, he must take her somewhere safe, somewhere they could be alone without outside interference.

But where?

Suddenly, he knew.

He remembered a little valley he had found last summer that nestled high in the mountains. It was a place with warm meadows, with a lake where many fish could be found, where reeds were plentiful for building a lodge until enough hides could be collected.

Game was plentiful in that valley, and edible roots and plants were abundant. It would make the perfect place to take her.

It would be a place where he would have all the time he needed. Time to make her aware of himself as a man. Time to make her love him, to make her forget the existence of any others besides themselves.

Yes, all that would take time, he decided, turning his steps toward the mountain range where the valley was located. But Red Fox had no better use for his time. What better way to use it than to live in that high green valley, with a flame-haired woman to warm his cold blood?

None that he could see.

When Spreading Branches returned to his clan and discovered the fiery-haired captive had escaped, his feelings were mixed.

On the one hand, he was enraged that he had lost her, and on the other hand, he was relieved that she was no longer a prisoner among his people. Had she stayed, she would surely have been put to death.

Even so, at first light, he followed the trail she had left behind, vowing to find her again. But when he did, he would not return to his people. Instead, he would go with her into a distant forest where they would live alone. That was the only way he could be certain she would live.

Spreading Branches wondered about the warrior who had taken her away. Who was he? Certainly not one of her own people. His clansmen seemed to think the warrior was Wolf Clan, but no matter who he was, he could not have the woman.

Spreading Branches realized the other warrior would

not readily give up his prize. Therefore, he would have to die.

The Desert Clan warrior was pulled from his thoughts as the trail ended at the edge of a cliff.

Where had they gone? he wondered. Did they fear capture so much they had leapt to their death?

The thought had no sooner occurred than he dismissed it from his mind. Such an act would be cowardly, and the woman had already proved she had courage.

She was no coward. Neither was she a fool.

No. There was no way she would have jumped from the cliff. There had to be another explanation, and some-how, he would find it.

He continued to search the ground carefully. Even so, he would have missed the sign of her passing had he not stumbled and fallen precariously close to the edge of the precipice. There, he found a print that could belong to none save herself, for no other wore such strange moccasins.

Had she actually gone down the cliff? he wondered.

Leaning carefully over the edge, he studied the sheer stone face. It seemed impossible to scale.

Suddenly he realized that he need not do so. There had to be another way down to the bottom of the valley, and if he could find that way, then he could simply descend and take up the trail below.

Feeling certain the flame-haired woman was almost within his grasp, Spreading Branches began a systematic search for another way down.

Patrick Douglass was at a complete loss. Although both Lacey and he had carefully watched the people of the desert clan, there had been no sign of the lady Brynna among them. Not so John Leverson, however. While fol-lowing the clan's backtrail in hopes of finding the two

captives somewhere along the way, Lacey had found
John's battered body, abandoned by the clan who had no
more use for it since it had become an empty shell.

Lacey had dug a grave and laid John Leverson's body
to rest. Only then did he return to give Patrick the news.

Since that time, Patrick's concern for Brynna's fate had
increased a hundredfold, but he could do nothing except
follow the clan who journeyed toward the desert . . . until
their warriors had returned to the clan. Then, after only
a short time among them, one of the warriors had left the
clan and gone his own way, looking always toward the
ground, as though searching for signs as he went.

Could the savage be searching for Brynna? Patrick
wondered, hope born anew. Could she have escaped? If
she had, then she would have need of their strength when
the *skraeling* warrior found her.

Patrick looked at Lacey and smiled grimly. "I think
we could better serve our lady if we followed the savage
who left the village."

"My thoughts exactly," said Lacey, reining his mount
around. "If we are lucky, the *skraeling* may lead us
directly to her."

The afternoon sun was warm against her arms as Brynna
walked beside the beaver pond, digging camas roots where
she found them, gathering only the camas with blue flow-
ers on their stems, avoiding the other kind—the ones that
sported cream-colored blooms—for Red Fox had warned
her they were known as the flower of death.

The camas tubers were sweet, and when roasted or
boiled, added much to their diet, as did the wild onions
that grew in such abundance.

It was a good valley, she silently told herself, feeling
at peace with the world around her. Although they had

been there only two weeks, they had already built a lodge that kept the wind and rain at bay.

Granted, the lodge cover was woven from the reeds growing near the water, but Brynna did not mind. She found it comfortable, enough for their needs. Not Red Fox, though. He insisted the reed lodge was only meant to be temporary, that they needed the strength and warmth a hide lodge would provide. It was for that reason that he hunted each day at first light, for he was determined to have enough hides before the next full moon.

Brynna had learned much about the warrior since coming to this high mountain valley. He was a compassionate man, mindful of her needs and fears, and yet his ways were so different from her own.

Red Fox refused to allow any part of the animals he killed to be wasted. Because of that, he had taught her how to cure hides, how to dry meat for future use, how to make thread out of sinew, and how to make fine bone sewing needles to fashion clothing for the two of them.

Yet even though he had already taught her so much, and she was proud of her many accomplishments, there was still much to be learned.

How could he remain so patient through it all? she wondered—so understanding, so forgiving of unskilled fingers that forever seemed to blunder?

A smile lifted the corners of her lips as she looked up the valley where timbered hills provided protection against the north wind. It was there they had built the lodge, near a warm spring that, Red Fox said, would provide ice-free water throughout the long winter.

She smiled wider, remembering the words he had used for the season, calling it the long white cold.

Realizing her thoughts were delaying her tasks, Brynna was on the point of digging more tubers when she saw movement near the edge of the forest. She narrowed her eyes on the spot and realized it must be Red Fox, since they were the only two people occupying the valley.

As she watched, he waved a hand and shouted. But he was too distant, too far away for his voice to carry his words to her. Nevertheless, she realized he wanted her to go to him.

Without thought of ignoring him, she hurried up the valley toward Red Fox. She was only halfway there when she saw a large gray wolf loping toward her.

She stopped, watching the animal cautiously until she realized it showed no sign of being unfriendly. Instead, it wagged its tail and bounded swiftly toward her as though she were a welcome sight.

"Wolf," she cried, her heart lifting with gladness as she realized the animal had returned after weeks of wandering among its kind.

Setting her basket aside, Brynna dropped to her knees, holding out her arms in welcome.

Wolf responded eagerly, licking her face and hands, then turning around several times with its tail wagging energetically, before leaping toward her again.

Laughing, she pushed the wolf away and raced with the animal to where Red Fox waited for them.

"Where did you find Wolf?" she asked, grabbing a sapling to keep from falling.

"You have it wrong," he replied, smiling down at her. "Wolf found me."

Reaching out, he uncurled her fingers from the sapling and clasped them in his big hand. "Come with me," he said, leading her into the forest. "I have something I want to show you."

"What is it?" she asked eagerly.

"You will see."

Throwing him a puzzled look, she followed him into the forest, wondering what he was about. They had only gone a short distance when he dropped to his heels and pulled her down beside him. "Stay quiet and watch closely," he commanded. "Then tell me what you see."

Brynna felt a sense of satisfaction as she realized he was bent on giving her another lesson in survival. Intent on not disappointing him, she searched her surroundings carefully, checking each bush around them, lest there be edible berries she had not yet discovered. But there were none.

Okay, she thought. No berries. Perhaps there were edible greens growing nearby. Again, her gaze went over the ground, stopping on each green stalk that might prove edible, each blade of grass. But try as she would, she found nothing recognizable.

"I see nothing," she admitted. "Nothing except grass and weeds and bushes."

"Look higher," he commanded.

Lifting her eyes, she searched the trees, but saw nothing there except pine cones. Could that be what she was meant to see?

"There are pine cones in the trees," she said. "The nuts inside them can be eaten."

"Good," he said, obviously pleased that she had remembered. "But look again, Brynna. There is something else here you have not found."

She looked at the trees again, wondering what he was seeing that she could not. "The bark?" she questioned. "It makes a good tea."

"Yes," he agreed. "But there is something more here, something you have not found."

"Then tell me what it is," she said, unable to keep the exasperation from her voice. "I see nothing else. No birds. No squirrels. Nothing . . . except," she amended, ". . . some bees."

"Yes," he agreed, his dark eyes glinting with humor.

"Exactly. The bees. Have you noticed how many bees there are, Brynna?"

She frowned and looked at the bees again. There were quite a few, all going into one tree, but why did he want her to study the bees? What earthly use were they? She could not eat them! Could she?

Brynna turned wide, startled eyes on the man beside her. "Do you eat bees?" she asked.

"No!" His laughter rang out, loud and clear. "But we do eat what bees make."

"Honey!" she exclaimed, punching him on the shoulder in her excitement. "Of course! Why did I not think of it?" Honey! Sweet, thick honey! "Red Fox! How do we take the honey? We can get it, can we not?" They must, for even now she could taste its sweetness on her tongue.

"Of course we can get it," he said, straightening up and pulling her along with him.

"Then can we do it now?"

"No. Not now. Preparations must be made, unless you want to feel their sting."

"Not hardly."

"Anyway, we have all the work we can handle today. And tomorrow as well." He moved a short distance away, bent over, and picked up a tri-sled made from three saplings lashed together. A large elk lay atop the sled.

"I see you had another successful hunt," Brynna said, measuring the animal with her eyes. "When the hide is added to the others, there may be enough to make the new lodge cover. But what will we do with the meat, Red Fox? We already have more than we can possibly use."

"There is never too much meat, Brynna," he said gravely. "When the long white cold settles over the valley, the elk will go down the mountain to search for food. Then we will need all the meat put aside to last until they return again."

"Is it your plan that we remain here during the winter, then?" she asked, frowning at him.

"Yes. This is our home now, Brynna." He did not look at her, seeming intent on maneuvering the tri-sled through the thick growth of trees. "We came to here to stay. I thought you knew that."

"You mean forever?" she asked, wishing he would look at her.

"It is our home," he repeated firmly.

"Red Fox," she said hesitantly. "I cannot stay here forever."

"Why not?" He met her eyes then, and she found herself caught and held by them.

"I came to your land for a purpose, to find my brother, Eric. I cannot just forget about him. I have to find him, to see how he fares."

"We will speak more on this later," he said, stopping to secure a strap that had managed to work loose on the sled. "Right now, there are more immediate things to occupy our minds." He straightened again and threw her a quick smile. "The elk, for instance. I will teach you how to skin it so you can do that in the future."

"Skin it? But you always do that," she protested, allowing herself to be diverted.

"Only because you might ruin the hide and we need all of them intact to cover our dwelling."

"And what will you do while I am skinning the animals you bring me?"

"Laze in the sun and prepare for the next hunt," he replied, his eyes glinting with humor.

"Not likely!" she said, throwing him a quick glance

from beneath thick lashes. She wondered at his mood. Although he was always kind and patient with her, it was not usual for him to joke with her.

They continued in that vein until they reached the lodge, then, while Red Fox skinned the elk, Brynna built up the fire for the evening meal that she was already busy planning.

She would cook the best parts of the elk, she decided. The liver and heart. Those were the ones Red Fox liked best. The rest of the meat would be set to dry over the racks they had made when they'd first come to the valley.

That night, after their evening meal, Brynna and Red Fox sat beside the fire, each busy with their own thoughts. Brynna's mind had wandered back to her homeland, and she imagined she could see her mother, her fingers busy with her needlework.

Was she faring well? Brynna wondered.

And Fergus, her father, had he once regretted his decision to force his only daughter into a marriage with a man she hated?

Probably not, she decided. She had never known her father to regret any decision he had ever made.

Red Fox, who had been sitting quietly, watching the flames leap and dance in the firepit, turned to her and said, ''You are silent, little one. What deep, dark thoughts occupy your mind?''

''I was thinking of my homeland,'' she replied. ''Of my people. My mother and father and brothers. And I was wondering if I would ever see them again.''

''Would it sadden you greatly if you did not?'' he asked.

''Of course,'' she replied, flicking a quick glance at him. ''What about you, Red Fox? Do you miss your family?''

''I have no family,'' he replied.

''None at all?'' she asked.

"No. None."

"What happened to them?" she asked.

"They were killed when I was very young."

"How?"

"Our village was attacked by enemies. Many of my people were slain before they were driven away."

"I am sorry."

He smiled at her. "Do not trouble yourself, little one. There is no need to feel sorrow on my account."

"It is sad for anyone to be so totally alone," she said softly.

"I am not alone." He took her hand and caressed it softly. "I have you, and I have Wolf. What more could a man ask for?"

Had there been a husky note of longing in his voice? Brynna wondered. Or was it merely her imagination? Was he remembering the night he had taken her maidenhood, and did he want her again? If he did, then why had he not made a move toward her? It was a fact that he had not. Not since the night she had invited his touch. If he truly wanted her, then what was he waiting for?

Should she make the first move? Her heart beat fast with anticipation. "Red Fox," she said softly, looking at him from beneath the dark fringe of her lashes. "Do you want me?"

"Of course," he replied, his eyes dark with some inner emotion.

"Why have you not said so then?" she asked curiously. "You have made no move in my direction since we arrived here."

He cupped her chin in his palm and lifted her face slightly. "Look at me, Brynna," he urged gently.

Lifting her lashes, she obeyed his command, meeting his black eyes, as fathomless as pools of liquid ebony.

"Can you not see the wanting in my eyes? Can you not hear it in the sound of my voice?"

Yes. She could. Now. "Then why do we sleep apart?" she whispered huskily.

"I need to be wanted," he replied. "I *must* be."

"You are," she muttered, feeling a flush rise to her cheeks. Was he so unaware of how she felt? Did he not know she was his to do with as he pleased? She swallowed around the lump in her throat and said thickly, "I could not manage without you, Red Fox."

"Must I say the words?" he asked.

"No." She could not look away from him. "There is no need," she whispered, straightening up. "Not anymore." She held out her hand to him. "Are you ready to retire now?"

"If you are."

"I am ready," she replied, leading the way into their dwelling. And she *was* ready, more than he would ever know.

A moment later, after their clothing had been discarded and she stood naked before him, he eased her down on his sleeping mat, and lay beside her.

His lips were hesitant as they pressed gently against hers and she returned his kiss, sliding her arms around his neck and twining the fingers of one hand through his dark hair while with the other, she caressed the muscles of his back.

Her whole body was tense with anticipation as his hands began to roam freely over her body, touching, caressing, intimately exploring the secret places. She felt hot and cold at the same time and an odd tingling began in the pit of her stomach. Her heart began to thunder madly and she gave herself over to the wonderful sensations his hands were evoking. Her whole being was alive, for the dormant sexuality of her body had been awakened and her body ached for his possession.

His lips blazed a trail of fire down her neck, while his hands continued to search her body, to seek out the most secret pleasure points. Instinctively, her body arched toward him as his mouth found her breast.

Waves of ecstasy swept over her and the world spun, careening around her. A tremor began deep inside, heating the soft, womanly core of her, and her blood boiled in her veins.

As his tongue began to caress her swollen nipples, she cried out, "No more, Red Fox! Take me now!"

He immediately slid over her, pressing her back against the mat, and she felt him slide within the core of her, felt his heat swell within.

He moved then, slowly at first, then faster and faster, and with each inward stroke he made, she thrust upward, meeting him over and over again, feeling passion rising in her like the hottest flame.

The pleasure she was receiving clouded her brain until she could not think anymore, could do nothing but react as she hurtled ever upward, beyond the point of no return.

Her breath came in harsh moans, rising higher and higher until it became a keening wail that she could not control.

Then she was there, soaring at the peak of delight, shattering into a million stars, exploding in pure, undiluted pleasure beyond description or belief.

And when it was over, their bodies still moist from their lovemaking, she nestled close against him and promised herself that, whatever happened, they would be together always.

Chapter Sixteen

After determining that several of the Vikings had gone ashore before the attack which had left part of the crew dead, Garrick Nordstrom felt encouraged about his sister's fate. Perhaps, he told himself, Brynna had left the *langskip* before it was attacked.

Although he wasted no time following the faint trail the Vikings had left behind, as the days passed with no sign of any other humans save themselves, he began to despair.

It was at one such time, several days into their journey across land thick with tangled growth, that Garrick reined his mount up beside a river that was swollen from recent rains.

Realizing the current was too strong for them to cross at that point without danger to both man and beast, he gave orders to pitch camp.

After they had partaken of the evening meal, Garrick sought solitude, his thoughts on the last time he had seen his sister, shortly after her aborted attempt to escape from a loveless marriage. She had pleaded with him then to speak to their father on her behalf, to persuade him against the marriage he was so set on. But he had refused her request, telling her that she obviously needed a firm hand to keep her out of trouble.

The results of that conversation had been disastrous. Garrick felt certain he was directly responsible for Brynna's flight. Had he not refused to help her, there would have been no reason for her to leave Norway.

But he *had* refused her. And as a direct result, she had taken one of the jarl's longboats and begun the long journey across the ocean, intent on reaching their brother, Eric, seeking the help that Garrick had refused to provide.

Garrick was still silently castigating himself when the sound of approaching footsteps alerted him to another presence, and he turned to see who was coming.

Nama, ever alert to the changing expressions on her husband's face, realized he must be blaming himself for whatever had happened to his sister. It was for that reason she sought him out, taking the path beside the river as he had done.

She found him around the first bend, leaning against the trunk of a cottonwood tree, staring across the muddy river water with that same sad, yet angry look he had worn ever since finding the *langskip* dead in the water.

"Do not torment yourself so, my love," she said softly, reaching for his hand. "There is so much to be thankful for. You must not dwell on what cannot be changed."

His eyes met hers and the sadness she saw reflected there tore at her heart. "At the moment I fail to find anything that warrants my thanks," he replied, his voice grating harshly on her ears. "Not when my sister is missing. Either dead, or certainly wishing she was."

"No, Garrick!" Nama protested. "You must not think like that! Brynna is not dead! Her body was not on the longboat. Do not give up on her, my love. Her soul is still among the living. I am certain of that."

"I guess I am, too," he said, clenching his hands into fists. "But it brings me no relief, Nama."

"Why, Garrick? If Brynna still lives, there is hope of rescuing her."

He pinned her with a hard gaze. "Then you think as I do, that she was captured." It was not a question, merely a statement of fact.

"She might have been," Nama muttered, looking away from him. "There was evidence captives were taken. We must face the fact that Brynna may be among them."

"I have faced it, and I cannot bear to imagine what those savages might be doing to her."

"She will survive," Nama said, wrapping her arms around his waist and pressing her head against his chest. "Never doubt that, Garrick. Brynna is, and always will be, a survivor. If she is a captive, she will do whatever she must to stay alive."

He shuddered, and when Nama looked up at him again, she realized her words had not eased his pain.

"What will they do to her, Nama?" he rasped.

She swallowed hard, knowing she must make things as easy for him as possible without telling an outright lie. "It depends on her, Garrick."

"What do you mean?"

"She is a beautiful woman. One any warrior would wish to possess."

"Yes," he agreed, his gaze never wavering from hers, and yet Nama had a feeling he was not really seeing her, that, instead, his gaze had turned inward, and it was Brynna that filled his mind's eye.

Realizing he was waiting for her to continue, she said,

"If the warriors who took Brynna feel no animosity toward her, then she will become a prized possession, one her owner would treasure highly. He would probably be kind to her so that her beauty would remain. If he is, then she will probably have slaves to wait on her, women who will see to her needs."

"And if that is not the case?" he questioned. "If her *skraeling* captors *do* bear her animosity? What then, Nama? What will be her fate?"

"It is hard to say," she hedged. "Many things could happen."

"Do the desert clan torture their enemies?" he asked grimly.

"Yes," she muttered, remembering her own fear of that clan. "Sometimes."

He sucked in a sharp breath and narrowed his eyes on her face. "Are they likely to kill Brynna?"

Would they? she wondered. She did not think so. Even if Brynna had killed several of their band, it was more likely that she would be allowed to live, to serve the family of those who had died at her hands, to be forever tormented by them until her body could no longer take the punishment they administered.

But she could not tell Garrick that. Instead, she merely said, "No. Not likely." Forcing a lighter note into her voice, she added, "Your sister's outlook on life, her joy at merely being alive, will make her fare well with any people."

"Why do I have trouble believing you, Nama?" he asked. "Why do I feel you are not telling me everything, that you are holding something back?"

"Because you are worried about your sister, Garrick. And no matter what I say, nothing is going to ease your mind. Not until your eyes behold your sister again and you see for yourself that she has come through this ordeal without any real harm."

"You know this is all my fault, Nama."

"No!" she protested. "None of it is your doing."

"Yes, it is," he contradicted. "Brynna would not have been here seeking Eric had I offered my support. Instead, I did nothing."

"You did," Nama cried, unable to allow him to continue berating himself. "You told me you spoke to your father about his plans for her."

"Yes. I spoke to him. And when he insisted the betrothal stand, I salved my conscience by telling myself that Brynna was headstrong and needed a firm hand to guide her."

"All of it true, my love," Nama said sadly. "Your sister *is* headstrong, and the man she weds must, of necessity, be strong . . . and loving." And patient, she mentally added. Brynna deserved a kind man, one who'd give her the kind of love Garrick had given Nama. Perhaps if she did survive, Brynna would eventually find such a love.

Nama prayed it would be so.

The midmorning sun streamed through the entrance of the newly erected hide lodge as Brynna hurried to complete her tasks.

There was little to do in the way of cleaning, since the lodge was sparsely furnished, containing only a few clay pots, several baskets, and their sleeping mat.

Brynna smiled wryly as she looked at the earthen pots. One of them was finely made, obviously constructed by a skilled craftsman, while the others were made by her own incapable hands.

Never mind, she consoled herself. The pots she made

might not look as good as those fashioned by Red Fox, but they were good enough to serve their needs. And the warrior certainly had no time to make other pots, since he spent most of his waking hours either hunting or working the hides of the animals he had slain.

She glanced at the bundle of beautifully cured rabbit skins, worked by the warrior's own hands, that she had stacked in the corner until she had enough time to sew them together for winter clothing. Then, her gaze dwelt on the beautiful quill case—Red Fox's latest gift to her— lying atop the rabbit skins. He had presented the box to her only last night, telling her it was meant to hold her bone needles.

It was for that reason, because he had made her such a fine gift, that she decided to make him a special meal. She would make honeycakes, she decided, using the honey he had taken from the bees, and she would dig more of the sweet camas tubers. They were his favorite of all the root vegetables.

But first, Brynna decided, she would finish the basket she was weaving out of willow fronds gathered the day before near the marshy area at the upper end of the valley.

After seating herself beside the firepit, she picked up the basket and frowned down at it. Something was wrong with the shape. One side was nicely turned, while the other looked as though she had stepped on it.

Turning it over in her hands, Brynna studied the tightly-woven strands, trying to figure out what she had done wrong. But try as she would, she could not identify the problem. She was still worrying the matter over in her mind when she heard something outside.

Surely it was too early for Red Fox to be returning from his hunt.

Before she could rise, the warrior pushed aside the entrance flap and stepped inside.

"Red Fox," she exclaimed, leaping quickly to her feet and sliding her arms around his neck. "You were not gone very long. Did you have any luck?"

"It was not luck that allowed me to return with meat for my woman," he growled, bending to place a quick kiss on her lips. "It was my skill alone that sent the arrow into the heart of my quarry."

"What did you shoot?" she asked, her tastebuds already quickening as she thought of fresh roasted meat. "An elk?" If he had killed an elk they would not need to use any of the dried meat they had put by for a while.

"No. Not an elk."

"What then?" she asked eagerly. "A turkey?" Although a turkey was smaller, it could be made to last for several days. And the feathers could be used for decoration.

"Not a turkey, either," he said, his mouth quirking at the edge as though he were trying to control a smile.

She knew he was teasing her, yet she could not control her eagerness, nor her disappointment that they would not have turkey. "A duck?" she asked hopefully. A duck was almost as big as a turkey and the meat was very much the same.

"No. Not a duck, either."

She stared at him in exasperation. "What is it, then? And where is it?" She tried to push past him so that she might see for herself what he had brought, but he wrapped his arms around her and hugged her to him.

"No," he said dryly. "I will not allow you to see. You must guess. Tell me what I have brought you."

"I cannot," she said, pushing against him, trying to free herself from his arms. "If it is not a deer, nor a turkey or duck, then I suppose it must be a rabbit." A rabbit was small, would allow them no more than two meals. She would have to use the meat sparingly, perhaps might even make stew out of the less tender portions, then there would be broth to drink. And, she consoled herself, they would have the skin to add to the others. "A rabbit will suit me fine," she finally said, speaking her thoughts aloud.

"But I have not brought you a rabbit, my love," Red Fox said, his dark eyes glinting with humor. "No, it is something else entirely. Something you saw yesterday . . . on the ledge near the upper end of the valley."

Brynna frowned, trying to remember what she had seen when they had walked together shortly before sundown. She had been sated after their recent lovemaking, relaxed and happy they were together. They had laughed a lot and he had teased her, accusing her of being lazy, even going so far as to liken her to a lizard watching them from a nearby ledge.

A sudden thought struck her. "A lizard?" she asked hesitantly, eying him with dismay. "You have brought a lizard for our meal?" For the life of her, she could think of nothing good about lizard meat.

"Do you think one lizard would provide enough meat for the two of us?" he questioned lazily.

She swallowed hard, wondering if he expected her to clean the lizard. Then, realizing he was waiting for her answer. "You may have my portion, Red Fox," she said, as though bestowing a great honor upon him. "I am not the least bit hungry."

He threw back his head and gave a hearty laugh, squeezing her hard against him. "Before you give your portion away, my love, you should first look at my kill."

Mystified, she followed him outside the lodge. Her eyes widened as she saw the animal spread out on a large rock. "A deer! That is as good as an elk." She turned accusing eyes on him. "And I thought you were trying to make me eat lizard."

The smile faded from his eyes. "One day it may be necessary, love. Life is uncertain and there may come a time when game is scarce. Anyway, lizard meat is quite tasty, much valued by some people."

"If it becomes necessary, then of course, I will eat lizard," she assured him. "But today it is not necessary, for you have brought me a deer. And the hide . . ." She smoothed her hand over the soft brown hide. ". . . There is enough hide here to make you a winter coat."

"Must I make it myself, or will you sew it for me?" he teased.

"My fingers may not be as skilled as yours yet," she said ruefully, "but with practice they will improve. Until then, you will have to make do with my less than adequate work."

"I am not complaining," he said, his expression becoming serious suddenly. "I know the life you led before coming to my land was much different than the one you lead now."

"Neither am I complaining, Red Fox. In time my hands will become accustomed to such chores and you need not be ashamed of me."

"I could never be ashamed of you, Brynna. Never have I seen a woman so beautiful, so courageous—"

"Beauty and courage do not make fine meals, nor do they create beautiful baskets," she said, thinking of the lopsided basket lying discarded on the floor of the lodge. "It takes practice for those things. And I will practice," she promised. "I will continue making baskets and pots until their beauty equals any made by your hands. And I will sew—never mind that I keep pricking my fingers— until the garments and moccasins these hands create are things of beauty. And I will—"

"Shut up," he commanded, pulling her into his embrace. "Before I kiss you into silence."

Brynna smiled at him and opened her mouth again, not the least bit opposed to his brand of punishment. As she had hoped, his mouth closed over hers with such demand that everything else was driven completely from her mind.

Wind Woman raked cold fingers across Nampeyo's exposed flesh, howling around him, threatening to push him from his high perch, a triangular slab of stone high above the cliff city.

Although he had been standing there for hours and his flesh was pimpled from the cold, Nampeyo would not allow himself to shiver, nor to react in any other manner. Instead, he stood stoic, continually beseeching the Cloud Spirits to prevent the whirling wind's return, thereby eliminating further devastation to their crops.

Time passed and the cold seemed a living thing, but Nampeyo pushed it away when it knocked at the door of his mind, refusing to allow it entry. He continued to stand there, long into the night, calling out to the spirits, pleading, cajoling, asking them for help until, finally, when first light broke over the land, he saw an eagle circle above him.

Nampeyo realized then that his prayers had been heard, for the eagle in flight was surely a sign sent to him by Cloud Man so the shaman would know his prayers had been heard . . . and answered.

Shaking himself, Nampeyo tried to loosen stiff muscles, and he was on the point of turning away from the deep gorge when he saw the whirling clouds. At first he thought the whirling wind had returned, then he realized it was too thick, milky white.

He narrowed his eyes on the whirling clouds, wondering what it meant. Then, slowly, the clouds dissolved and became a river so wide that he was unable to see its shores, and out of the river came a girl.

Nama.

She rode astride a strange-looking creature that was dark as midnight, making straight toward Nampeyo. And in her hands she held a golden globe.

Smiling at Nampeyo as though in greeting, she held the globe toward him. When he reached out to take it from her, Nama laughed and tossed the globe out of reach.

Suddenly, a raven came to rest on her shoulder and watched Nampeyo with cold, round eyes. "Why do you not catch the sun?" the raven asked the shaman.

"No man may capture the sun," Nampeyo replied. "You know that as well as I."

"You could have caught that one," Raven cackled. "If you had but tried. But now it is too late."

"Why is it too late?" Nampeyo inquired.

"See?" Raven pointed with one clawed foot. "Wolf has beat you to it. He has the sun in his jaws."

Nampeyo turned and saw the raven was right. A large gray wolf had indeed captured the golden globe in his wide jaws.

Feeling a terrible sense of sadness because he had waited too late, Nampeyo watched the wolf trot away with the globe in its mouth.

As quickly as it had come, the vision dissolved, leaving Nampeyo to wonder what it meant.

Chapter Seventeen

Lame Duck trudged slowly along behind the women and children of his clan, thinking of how dry his mouth was, and how it would be night before he could quench his thirst.

Why had he been the unlucky one selected? he wondered bitterly. Black Raven had not yet taken his turn at guarding the women and children and old ones. He should have been the one to stay behind and Lame Duck should be in his place—among the warriors who walked ahead of the clan.

His was a useless task anyway, Lame Duck knew. The Monster Men would not attack. Why should they? Even Monster Men could not hope to win a battle fought with as many warriors as the desert clan numbered.

Yes. His was a useless task. But he would bow to the elders' judgment, would stay where he was and keep his eyes open for those who would not come. When he was relieved of that task, though, he would not join the warriors who walked ahead of the clan. Instead, he would go off on his own, would search for his friend, Spreading Branches, who should have been back long ago.

Suddenly realizing that he was falling behind, Lame Duck hurried to catch up with the stragglers, knowing he must stay close by to protect them . . . just in case the others were right about the Monster Men.

The western sky was awash with long streaks of color that heralded the setting sun as Brynna, seated on a rock outside the lodge she shared with Red Fox, worked the last of the deer brains into the hide she had just finished scraping.

Feeling a deep sense of accomplishment, Brynna spared a brief glance at the sunset. Beautiful, she thought, silently admiring the bright crimson and purple and lavender and pink colors.

Brynna realized suddenly the sunset reminded her of the bright array of silken gowns she had possessed in Norway, gowns made especially for her and fashioned from those same vibrant colors.

What a useless life she had led, Brynna thought. Nothing was required of her there. She had only to keep herself looking beautiful and present herself whenever she was summoned, wearing one of those bright, silken gowns that had been made to enhance her beauty.

Yes, she had been nothing there except a thing to be admired. Not so here, though. Here, Brynna knew she was needed, knew that she contributed much to their daily lives. Yet she felt no reason to complain. She was well rewarded for the effort she expended.

Brynna had never known such happiness as she had found since coming to this high mountain valley. That happiness was caused in part by the life she lived, but mostly by the fact that she was with the man she loved.

She breathed deeply and the breeze blowing across the valley brought the pungent scent of pine to tease her nostrils.

The wind gusted, blowing a loose tendril of hair across her face, and she shoved it back, tucking it behind her ear. As she did, she caught sight of her hands and frowned down at them.

They were rough, red, and chafed, marred by harsh work, by constant cleaning and scrubbing. In Norway, her hands had been soft and smooth, kept that way by oils and creams, and the useless life she led.

But Brynna did not regret the change. Instead, she took pride in her hands, for they mirrored her many accomplishments.

The long scratch on her right hand had been obtained while gathering service-berries at the upper end of the valley.

The dark splotches on her right thumb and forefinger were a reminder of the time she had tried to rescue their meal from the flames when the stick she had skewered the rabbit on had caught fire and burned.

Her lips twitched when she thought of that night. Red Fox had been angry and scolded her severely. Not because she had burned the meat, but because she had burned her flesh.

Red Fox had never spoken words of love, but Brynna felt that he must love her. Surely actions spoke louder than words anyway, she told herself.

Although Brynna felt a deep regret that she would never again see her family, her mother and brothers, she knew there was no choice. She would not, could not, leave the man she loved, for having been loved by Red Fox, Brynna could not conceive a life without him.

Red Fox.

Where was he?

It was almost dusk and he was usually home long before now.

Realizing that she had not even started the evening meal, Brynna put away her scraping tools and went into the lodge to prepare the vegetables. She would wait about the rest of the meal until Red Fox arrived, for he had yet to return home without some kind of meat.

Where was he, anyway? she wondered again. What could be taking him so long?

Crossing to the entrance, she looked up the valley, searching for some sign of him. Nothing.

Brynna returned to her vegetables, scraping the camas roots, then cleaning several wild onions. When she had finished, she dropped them into a clay pot, then covered them with water to keep them fresh. Then she left the lodge and searched the valley again, hoping to see her man coming home.

Still nothing. No movement whatsoever to reveal the presence of any other living being save herself.

Her anxiety increased. Each passing moment of his continued absence seemed like hours. What could have happened? she wondered. Where was he? Why had he not returned? Could he be hurt, in danger?

That possibility caused her heart to thump with dread. She could not bear to lose him, could not face life without him.

Another thought suddenly knocked at the door of her mind. If he did not return, she could not survive. Not here alone, in this wilderness.

Oh, Red Fox, she silently cried. *So much of my life depends on you. Where are you? Why have you not returned?*

Anxiety lay heavy on Brynna's shoulders, weighting it down as though it were a mantle of stone.

The hour is so late, she thought. Soon it will be dark.

She was beside herself with worry, so distraught, that when she heard a snap in the shadowy forest, her heart gave a sudden jerk of fear.

Hardly daring to breathe, she listened intently.

Snap! There it was again.

"Red Fox?" she whispered, "is that you?"

Snap! Again the sound came, and again, she called out, "Red Fox? Are you there?"

Brynna strained her ears, hoping to hear the sound of his voice, reassuring her that he had indeed returned. But silence prevailed.

"Red Fox, if that is you, please say something."

No answer.

Snap! The sound was closer this time, as though something were creeping slowly toward her.

The hair at the base of her neck lifted and her goosebumps rose on her flesh. Brynna felt as though eyes were watching her and gave a sudden shiver as icy fingers trailed down her spine.

Fearful of what lurked in the shadows, whether imagined danger or real, she backed slowly away from the woods, moving closer to the lodge, knowing it would afford safety from whatever danger should threaten.

She was on the verge of lifting the entrance flap when she saw movement out of the corner of her eye. Turning quickly, she saw Wolf limping into the clearing, holding his right paw off the ground as though it were injured.

"Wolf?" she called, breathing a sigh of relief. "Are you hurt, Wolf?" She moved closer, all thought of danger gone, erased by her anxiety for the wolf.

He sunk down on his belly and gazed at her with yellow eyes, waiting quietly, as though he knew she would come to his aid.

Striding quickly to his side, she knelt to examine his paw and found a thorn embedded in the pad.

"Easy now," she muttered softly, grasping the end of the thorn and pulling steadily on it. Although the animal whimpered once, it remained still, obviously aware that she was trying to help.

"There!" she said, pulling the thorn out and holding it so the animal could see. "It will bother you no more." She swept her hand over the wolf's neck, ruffling its fur while murmuring sympathetic words. She was on the point of rising when she chanced to look at her hand and saw a streak of red smeared across her palm.

Blood.

Frowning at it, she examined the wolf's paw again. There was no blood there. Carefully, she ruffled the animal's fur, running her fingers through it until she found the torn flesh that slowly seeped blood.

"What happened, boy?" she asked, meeting the wolf's yellow gaze. "How did you tear your skin? Were you in a fight?"

A sudden thought struck her. Had the wolf been with Red Fox when it was injured? Even the thought sent a chill of fear through her. "Wolf," she said urgently, cupping the wolf's muzzle and looking intently into its eyes. "Where is Red Fox? Have you seen him, Wolf? Is Red Fox in trouble? What happened to you, boy? Where is Red Fox?" The last was an agonizing cry. "Take me to him, Wolf! Find Red Fox for me!"

As though it understood her words, the wolf rose to its feet and started back into the forest, stopping once to look over its shoulder as though checking to see if she was following.

Brynna felt encouraged by the wolf's actions. The animal must know where to find Red Fox, and, Brynna decided, wherever the wolf went, she would be right behind.

Easier said than done, she soon realized, for the wolf

always chose the easiest path, crawling beneath bushes that she must, of necessity, circle around.

They went deeper into the forest, and while they traveled, dusk became night, and the way became harder for Brynna.

Suddenly, an undulating howl sounded in the distance, and Wolf lifted his head and echoed the call that was immediately taken up by others of his kind.

As the howls continued, echoing over and over again, Wolf turned continually to look back at Brynna. She sensed a hesitation about Wolf, as he ran forward a few paces, then turned back to look at her, before going on again.

"Wolf," she called, realizing he was getting too far ahead of her. "Wait, Wolf. Wait for me."

Suddenly, the wolf lifted his head and uttered a long, mournful howl, then, leaping forward, the animal disappeared into the forest.

"Wolf," she cried, fear streaking through her. "Come back, Wolf!"

She hurried forward, calling out the animal's name, over and over again, hoping to see the shape of him returning.

But he did not.

Brynna continued to search, moving steadily forward, with nothing but the pale moon to light her way, until she realized that she was lost . . . hopelessly, completely.

Stumbling over an unseen log, she sank to her knees and gave way to tears of self-pity.

Finally, when she could cry no more, she sat up and took stock of her situation.

It was true that Wolf had left her alone in the forest. It was also true that she was lost. But if she took control of the situation, searched the night sky for stars to guide her, then she could find her way back home.

Uttering a heavy sigh, she strode forward again, moving carefully this time, lest she stumble and fall again. Only moments had passed when she broke out of the forest into a clearing.

"Yip, yip, uuurrrooow!" the howl came from the thick grove of trees on the other side of the clearing.

"Wolf?" Brynna called, narrowing her eyes on the thick growth of pines, hoping to see the animal loping toward her. "Is that you, Wolf?"

Suddenly, she saw the animal, silhouetted in the moonlight, slinking from the dense forest and moving slowly toward her.

"Where were you, Wolf?" she cried, fear giving away to anger. "Why did you leave me like that?" She moved closer to the wolf, needing the comfort of another living creature with her.

Suddenly, she stopped short, her gaze narrowing on the animal. There was something about Wolf, something about the way the animal lowered its head, the way it came so slowly, so intently, as though she might present some kind of danger to it.

"Wolf?" Her voice was hesitant now, her heart thudding wildly in her breast. "Is that you, Wolf?"

Chapter Eighteen

As the shadows lengthened and Sky Man donned his darkest cloak, Red Fox remained crouched behind an elderberry bush, watching the narrow stream where game usually watered.

He had been there for hours, watching, hoping, but so far, in vain.

What was wrong? he wondered. Had something driven the animals from the mountain? Perhaps they knew something that he was yet unaware of and for that reason had sought lower ground.

He looked again at the sky. The moon could easily be seen, and so could the stars. No sign there of clouds to predict a coming storm.

So why had the animals left?

It made no sense.

Only yesterday, he had seen a large herd of elk, and yet today there was no sign of them. And where were the other animals that usually occupied the valley?

There were usually squirrels to be seen, rabbits and beaver, yet even they were conspicuously absent.

And the birds . . . although he could hear the beat of their wings as they flitted through the branches, their song no longer filled the forest.

What had come over the woodland creatures?

Surely they were not frightened of one lone warrior.

No. There must be some other explanation. Perhaps some danger that Red Fox was yet unaware of had entered the valley.

That thought sent him to his feet, his heart beating out a rapid tatoo. Brynna was alone in the lodge and it was late. If danger lurked in the forest, then she could be at risk. Besides, she would be worrying about his absence by now, since he never stayed out this late.

Another quick glance at the sky told him he had already delayed much longer than he should have. He could do nothing more tonight, but come first light, he would search the forest carefully. If the game animals had really left the mountain, then he must accept that fact and hunt the lower slopes for them.

Eager to see Brynna again, he made long strides that carried him swiftly through the forest. He was disappointed that he carried no game across his shoulder, but even so, they would not go hungry. Nor would they need to take food from their winter store. Brynna was sure to have some root vegetables cooking, having already realized the lateness of the hour and the demands of his empty stomach.

The thought of his supper . . . and his woman, caused his stride to lengthen even more. Soon he entered a small glade where the trees had thinned out. He hurried across it.

Red Fox would have missed the sign had he not brushed

against the aspen with his bare arm. The deep gouges he felt in the trunk of the tree brought him to a sudden halt.

He looked closer at the marks. An icy chill slithered down his spine and the puckered skin of his scar began to tingle as he stared at the deep vertical scratches gouged into the tree.

Red Fox had no need to search at his feet for the flaky white strips of bark that would be littering the ground.

No. He knew they were there, knew as well the meaning behind the clawed tree.

A bear had invaded the forest and it was not just passing through the valley. By clawing the bark and rubbing its back on the fresh gouges, it had plainly marked its territory.

Memories of another bear flooded his mind and his heart began to beat furiously. He must go home without delay, must warn Brynna. They would have to gather their belongings together, and they would have to flee this place, just as quickly as possible!

Even as the thought came, he cast it aside. That was the coward's way, to flee his home, the place where he had known such happiness, and leave it to his enemy. He was no coward. Never again would he believe so, for had he not fought for his woman and won?

Yes.

Not once, but twice.

And he would fight again, if he must. He would hunt the beast down with the coming of first light, and this time, when the battle was over, he would be the victor.

His lips pulled into a thin smile. A bear hide would make a nice gift for his woman, would keep her warm when the long cold settled over the land.

Perhaps, he decided, the bear's invasion was not really such a bad thing, after all. When the bear had been slain, the animals would surely return and game would again be plentiful on the mountain.

With a lighter heart, Red Fox set off at a lope, eager to reach home . . . and his woman. But he would not speak tonight of his plans. Were he to do so, then Brynna would be sure to worry. Instead, he would present her with an accomplished fact. The bear's hide.

He would need her help, though, he determined. After the bear was dead. The animal must be incredibly large, because the scratches on the tree had been high, placed where a smaller bear could not have reached.

Red Fox's smile widened at that thought. The larger the bear, the more meat it possessed. And if it was an old one, there should be plenty of fat on its body.

His thoughts whirled furiously as he continued to make plans even as his ground-eating pace brought him closer to his woman and the supper he knew would be kept warming beside the fire.

Finally, he broke through the forest into the clearing where they had built their lodge. Immediately, he skidded to a halt.

Something was wrong.

No smoke came from the smoke hole.

There was no sound from within, and the place had an empty feel about it.

Fear stabbed into him. Had the bear already been there? Had it already destroyed everything he loved?

No! his mind cried. *It cannot be so!*

Slowly he approached the hut, fearful of what he would see. Would her body be inside, mangled, chewed?

No! Again, his mind denied that possibility.

Gritting his teeth, he forced himself to push aside the entrance flap, forced himself to enter.

Empty.

He sighed with relief. There was no mangled body, no

torn and bleeding form that waited for him. His imagination had been working overtime. Brynna was safe.

But where?

His gaze swept the interior of the hut, found the pot of vegetables peeled and covered with water, waiting for his return.

But where was the fire?

Red Fox bent over the firepit and found it cold, burned out. He looked around again, searching for some sign, something to tell him where Brynna had gone.

Water, he thought. Perhaps they were out of water and Brynna went to the spring to fetch some.

His gaze settled on the clay jug used for that purpose. Since it was still there, that could not have been her purpose in leaving. They only had one jug and two pots. And they were all here, none of them missing.

Becoming even more puzzled . . . and with worry knocking at the door of his mind . . . the warrior stepped outside again. And saw Wolf.

"Wolf?" Brynna heard her voice waver fearfully as she slowly backed away from the animal that continued to stalk her.

A low growl sounded in the animal's throat and she realized suddenly what she had already begun to suspect. The animal stalking her was not Wolf. Instead, it was a wild creature, untamed and savage, and ready, it would appear, to make her his next meal.

Fear made her legs wobble, threatening to buckle her knees, but she could not allow that to happen, she knew. Not if she were to survive this night.

"Go away!" she cried, trying in vain, to keep her voice from trembling. "Get away from here! Leave me alone!"

The large gray wolf that so resembled the one that had

led her here paid no attention to her words. Instead, it continued to stalk her, moving closer with each passing moment.

Suddenly, a shape to her left caught her attention and she flicked a quick glance in that direction, hoping it was Wolf, racing to her rescue.

But again she hoped in vain. The yellowish brown wolf she saw was unfamiliar to her eyes. So was the smaller gray one that followed close behind.

"Mary, Mother of God!" she whispered. "Please help me out of this. Send Red Fox to me."

Her breath rasped harshly as she searched for a haven of safety, somewhere the wolves could not reach her.

Her gaze fell on a stand of aspens. If she could reach them before the wolves realized her intentions—

No sooner had the thought occurred than she was racing toward the nearest one. Brynna saw the wolves sprint toward her and knew they could move fast, but she could no longer hear them, not when her fast-beating heart drowned out every other sound.

Nearly there, nearly there, nearly there, her heart pounded out the message.

Another few yards would do it, she thought. All she had to do was reach her arm up and grip the lowest branch and swing—

God, no! her mind cried, when she saw the wolf slink out of the stand of aspens.

Realizing that way was blocked, as well as the way behind her, she turned to her left, running as hard as she could, unaware that her flight led her straight toward a cliff that dropped away to a valley several hundred feet below.

* * *

"Wolf!" Red Fox called, striding swiftly to the animal. "Where have you been, boy?" He knelt beside the wolf and looked into its yellow eyes. "Have you seen Brynna?"

At the sound of Brynna's name, the animal turned its head and looked into the forest as though expecting to see the girl behind him.

"Brynna," the warrior repeated. "Where is she? Where is Brynna?"

The wolf whimpered and moved restlessly.

"Where is she, Wolf?" Red Fox asked again. "Where is Brynna? Take me to her!"

Wolf became still, the animal's yellow gaze holding its master's for a long, seemingly endless, moment. Then, the gray wolf turned away from Red Fox and loped toward the forest, stopping for a moment to look back across its shoulder as though to assure itself the warrior was following.

Hoping Wolf was leading him to, and not away from, his woman, Red Fox followed the animal into the forest, loping along behind him, feeling the need to find her as quickly as possible.

That feeling only intensified when Red Fox heard the yipping howls that meant a wolf pack had cornered their prey. And, when Red Fox realized Wolf was following the sound of the wolf pack, new fear was born within the warrior's soul.

Could Brynna possibly be the prey the wolves had run to ground?

Brynna had no idea the chasm was anywhere around until she was already upon it. Her momentum almost carried her over the edge before she could stop, but stop she did . . . barely two feet from the rim that dropped away suddenly, to a vast valley located more than three hundred feet below her.

Quickly, Brynna spun around, putting the open space behind her, aware that the immediate danger came from the wolves.

Amazing though it seemed, when she stopped, the wolves stopped as well, dropping to their bellies and watching her with hungry eyes.

Why had they stopped? she wondered. Did they think she could harm them in some way, or were they merely playing with her, knowing she was at their mercy?

Yes, that must be the reason, she realized. The wolves knew she was trapped and savored that knowledge. Perhaps they wanted to feel her fear, to gloat over it, to feed it until it grew and grew, until that same fear drove her out of her mind. Then they would—

Stop it! an inner voice warned. *Have you no courage left?*

What good is courage when faced with a pack of savage wolves? she silently countered.

But even as the thought came, Brynna was instantly ashamed. It was obvious her time on earth had run out. Now, the least she could do was face death with courage.

"Come on," she shouted, trying to keep the fear from her voice. "What are you waiting for? If you want me, then come and get me!"

The nearest wolf jerked at the sound of her voice and shifted uneasily as though unsure about the being who yelled so loudly. The beast looked back at the pack, then back to her again.

Having apparently satisfied itself that she was bluffing, the beast uttered a low growl and stalked closer, its eyes never wavering from the girl who could do nothing but wait for death to claim her.

Do nothing? Brynna looked down into the chasm. *That was not entirely true*. She could choose the way her life would end.

Brynna stepped closer to the edge.

Red Fox raced through the forest, only a step or two behind Wolf, feeling certain he had heard a human voice crying out in the distance.

It had to be Brynna, he told himself. *It could be no other*. It must be her, for they were the only human occupants of this high valley.

A measure of relief found its way through the dark clouds of fear, because Red Fox knew that if Brynna were still able to cry out, to release her fear in a scream, then she had not yet departed the land of the living.

Nevertheless, he knew he must hurry. She was obviously in great danger. And Red Fox was almost certain that danger came from the wolves he had heard.

He had guessed right, he realized, when he broke through the forest into a clearing, because there, in the distance, silhouetted by the pale moonlight, stood Brynna. While nearby, barely twenty feet distant, were four large wolves.

"Brynna," he shouted, sending his voice ahead of him, hoping to drive the wolves away from her. "I am coming, Brynna. Hold on!"

Instead of sending the wolves in flight, they leapt toward her.

With his heart in his throat, Red Fox saw them rush forward, and in that same instant, Brynna disappeared.

Realizing the wolves had brought the girl down beneath them, realizing as well that her death would be a painful one, Red Fox howled with rage and flung himself among them, drawing his knife from its sheath and slashing at the wolves furiously, barely aware that Wolf had joined the fray until the last savage beast had been driven away.

Only then did Red Fox allow himself to look at the body of the girl who had stolen his heart.

But Brynna was not there.

Chapter Nineteen

Brynna had jumped back as the wolves charged, flinging herself over the cliff, knowing death on the canyon floor would be instantaneous, and preferable to being eaten alive by savage wolves.

As she fell through empty space, Brynna felt a deep sense of regret, caused in part by the knowledge that when she died, Red Fox would be left alone.

Squeezing her eyes shut tight, she spoke swiftly, preparing to meet her maker. "Holy Mary, if thou wilt, hear thy supplicant. I put myself under the shelter of thy shield. When falling on the slippery—*ummphh!*"

Brynna's voice broke off abruptly as something reached out and grabbed her, stopping her downward plunge to the gorge below.

The Holy Mother? Brynna wondered fleetingly. Had *She* physically interceded on Brynna's behalf?

Nonsense, an inner voice cried. But, Brynna reasoned, if the Holy Mother had not saved her from death, then who had?

Twisting her head on the slender stem of her neck, Brynna saw her savior.

It was nothing more than a gnarled, twisted tree with branches reaching toward the sky as though in supplication, and it grew where no tree should be, its roots embedded in a mound of dirt blown into a niche by wind, and nourished by rain and sun.

It was a miracle, Brynna realized with awe. The tree was a gift sent from heaven.

Gazing up the stone face of the cliff, Brynna was almost overcome by fear. Why had she been saved in such a manner? She could never climb that stone face. Never mind that she had accomplished that feat once before. She had not been alone then. Red Fox had helped her through that ordeal. This time, she was completely alone.

Use your wits, a silent voice said. *Maybe you can climb down.* A quick look down dispelled that idea and sent a shudder of fear through her, for the moon cast its pale light over the valley that appeared so very far below.

It seemed her life had been spared, but only momentarily.

That realization was affirmed when Brynna attempted to move and the branch holding her gave a loud creak and dropped several inches.

Brynna froze, afraid to move, yet knowing she must at least attempt to save herself.

Red Fox thought the wolves must have taken Brynna's body with them until he realized he was standing near the edge of a chasm. Realizing she must have gone over, he felt despair wash over him. He had seen that chasm before, knew the depth of the valley below, knew as well there was no way Brynna could have survived such a fall.

Nevertheless, he moved to peer into its depths and his

breath caught harshly when he saw her, caught on the limbs of a tree, perhaps fifty feet below.

"Brynna!" he shouted. "Are you hurt?"

"Red Fox?" the voice was trembly, questioning. "Is it really you?"

"Yes," he replied loudly. "Are you hurt, Brynna?" he asked again.

"No! Not yet! Have the wolves gone away?"

"Yes. Is that tree stable?"

"No!" He heard the hysteria in her voice. "Red Fox. The limb shifted when I moved."

"Then keep still," he shouted anxiously.

"Can you help me?"

"Yes!" he called, wanting desperately to reassure her. "Do not worry, little one! Just hold on until I find something to pull you out with."

Easier said than done, Red Fox realized, for he had no rope with him, nothing to throw down to her. And the stone face of the cliff was much too steep to climb.

Aware of her precarious position, he raced toward the forest where he had seen some vines growing. If he could find one long enough, and stout enough, then perhaps he could pull her up the cliff.

Even though Brynna's situation was perilous, she had felt immense relief the moment she'd seen Red Fox. Until then she had feared he was dead. But he was not. And he had come for her.

Brynna lay among the branches for what seemed an incredibly long time, afraid to move or even breathe deeply, lest even a slight movement rend the tree out by its roots and send her plunging to her death below.

"Brynna?"

Red Fox's voice was faint, seeming to come from a

great distance. Then, she saw him peering over the cliff at her and she heaved a great sigh of relief. Even if he found no way to save her, at least she would see him once again, would hear his dear voice one last time.

"I am here, Red Fox," she called, then stifled a hysterical giggle. *Where else would I be?* she asked herself. *Still here, hanging in the branches of this damn tree where he last saw me, frightened out of my wits, afraid to move lest that movement be my last.*

"Catch this," Red Fox shouted, dropping something dark over the side of the cliff.

Swoosh! Brynna felt the air displaced around her, just before something lashed against her cheek. It was long and slender.

"Do you have it?"

"N-no!" she shouted, her voice quivering. "W-what is it, Red Fox?"

"A vine! Can you hold on while I pull you up?"

Could she? Brynna knew she damn well must hold on to it. She had no other choice if she wanted to live.

"Yes," she shouted, realizing she had not answered the warrior.

Reaching out, she wrapped her fingers around the vine. And, as she moved, so did the limb that held her.

Creak! Damn! It was going to break!

"I have it, Red Fox," she screamed. "Hurry! Pull me up before the limb breaks!"

Cra-a-ck! The limb broke beneath her weight and Brynna felt herself falling, then stopped abruptly as the vine caught and held, leaving her swinging around.

Brynna clung desperately as Red Fox pulled on the vine, knowing that should she lose her grip all would be lost and her life forfeited. Her palms were slick with sweat as the vine, along with Brynna, moved slowly upward.

Could she hold on long enough to reach the top?

She must, Brynna knew, for the alternative was death.

Red Fox's muscle strained to pull the vine holding the woman who had come to mean so much to him up the cliff. He was vaguely aware that Wolf had joined him at the chasm, but he paid the animal no mind. His every thought was centered on the girl whose life was literally hanging by one slender vine.

He could not see how near—or how far away—Brynna was, for he must of necessity lean away from the cliff to get more leverage. But finally, to Red Fox's immense relief, he saw one slender hand reach the edge of the cliff.

Realizing she was almost in his grasp, he braced himself and reached out to her, leaning over just enough to wrap his fingers around her wrist. Then, with it tight within his grasp, he leaned back and pulled her onto the grass.

Reaching out, Red Fox enfolded her into his arms, holding her trembling body tight against his own, silently giving thanks to the Great Creator for allowing her to live, knowing that, had she died, there would have been nothing left in this world for him.

Held tight within his embrace, Brynna lifted her head and looked at him with tearful eyes.

"Are you all right?" she whispered, her gaze sweeping over his features, pausing here and there as though to assure herself he was not injured.

"Yes," he replied. "I am fine. It is you that—"

He never finished what he was saying because she suddenly pulled away from him and stared at him with blazing eyes. "Fine!" she snapped. "You are not injured? Not dead?"

He looked at her, puzzled. "Of course not," he replied.

"As you can see, I am here. Not dead, but quite alive. Not even injured."

"Well, that is good!" she snarled, shoving him as hard as she could. "Just dandy! Then we are all fine! Me! You! And Wolf!" Spying Wolf nearby, she snatched up a rock and threw it at him, barely missing the hapless animal. "Get away from me, you mangy cur! Get out of my sight! I never want to see you again!"

"Brynna, what is—"

"Nor you!" she cried, rounding on him again. "You can leave, too!" She struck him a hard blow on his chest, then repeated it, striking him again, then again and again and again.

Shocked at her loss of control, he pulled her into his arms and mashed her against his chest, suffering the blows she continued to inflict, but now on his shoulders and head and back. When she finally became still, he smoothed her hair down, gentling her as he would have gentled a wild animal.

"Now can you tell me what is wrong?" he asked gently.

"I thought you were dead," she whispered, her tears staining his bare chest. "I thought I would never see you again."

"But I am here," he said, swallowing around the knot lodging in his throat. "Wounded," he added ruefully, "but still here, and ashamed."

"Wounded?" she questioned, lifting her head to look at him again. "You said—"

"The wounds were inflicted by your own hands, my love," he said. "But they are nothing to the wounds your words have given me."

"Where were you?" she whispered.

"Hunting." He looked deeply into her eyes. "I had no thought of worrying you, Brynna. Only to bring you meat. But I could not even do that."

"Never do that again," she said. "I would rather do without than worry that way again." She gave a little sob. "I thought you must be dead."

"And you searched for me? That is why you left the lodge?"

"Yes. I followed Wolf, and he left me when we heard the other wolves howling." She shuddered. "I thought sure I was going to die." She looked around her. "Where are they, anyway?"

"I drove them away, with the help of Wolf."

"Why did he leave me?" She glared at the hapless animal.

"Who can say? At least he came for me."

"That is no excuse for him."

The wolf slunk toward her and she eyed it sternly. "You are not forgiven," she said angrily. "You almost got me killed."

"Or saved your life," Red Fox said, feeling sorry for his old friend. "Wolf could not have driven them away alone. Perhaps he came to me for help."

"Or maybe he is a coward," she said.

"Wolf is no coward!" he said sharply. "Do not even accuse him of being so!" His voice softened. "Come home, love. It is long past time for our meal."

That night they made passionate love, each realizing how very near they had come to losing the other. And when it was over, they lay awake, making plans for the future. But Red Fox had not told her about the bear. That fact he kept to himself. She had worried enough this day. Perhaps by the time she knew of the bear's presence, the beast would already be dead.

Spreading Branches stood on a rocky outcrop, staring into the valley below. He had found what he was searching for. Finally. Although there was no sign of a dwelling in the little valley, he could see smoke drifting slowly skyward.

They were there, all right, he told himself. And soon, the man who had taken what belonged to Spreading Branches would be dead. The girl would soon be his again, he vowed, and this time he would keep her; even though it meant he must live apart from his clan, for they surely would not accept her among them, he would do so, for owning her had become of the utmost importance to him.

And nothing on this earth would keep him from making her his again.

Nothing.

Patrick dismounted and, taking the reins in his hand, began the long trek up the mountain, wondering even as he did why he bothered. It had been so long since they had seen Brynna that he feared she was dead. At least, he told himself, if that were so, then she was beyond pain. That thought brought him a small measure of relief.

His mount balked at the climb, but Patrick pulled on the reins, forcing the animal up the slope. The animal could not be blamed, he reasoned, for the climb was hard, the loose rocks and shale forever sliding beneath foot and hoof.

Lifting his gaze, Patrick spied Lacey on the mountain top. As usual, the man had been scouting ahead. Patrick frowned, wondering when Lacey would admit there was no longer a trail to follow. Even as that thought occurred, he saw smoke drifting skyward and his heart jerked with sudden hope.

Had they found Brynna?

Alive?

Chapter Twenty

Brynna woke to a sensuous feeling of warmth and uttered a deep sigh of contentment as she snuggled closer to the source of heat. She felt safe and secure, snug as a butterfly in a cocoon.

When she felt something swell against her buttocks, she realized Red Fox was awake and turned toward him, finding him staring at her with passionate eyes.

"Good morning, little one." His breath felt warm against her face, stirring the silky tendrils of hair around her ears, causing goosebumps to pimple her flesh and her stomach muscles to contract, quivering.

She shivered with pure joy, sliding her arms around his neck and burying her fingers in his dark hair, feeling a hunger so desperate that she wanted to bury herself in his flesh.

"Do you want me to prepare your meal?" she asked, her voice teasing, knowing very well food was the last thing on his mind.

He groaned, seizing her face between his hands and

pressing feverish kisses on her face, her lips, her eyelids. "Food is the last thing on my mind," he admitted huskily, when he finally drew back to look at her. "I am afraid, though," he added regretfully, "things of that nature must wait. I meant to be in the forest at first light. If I do not leave soon, the deer and elk will already have been to their watering hole."

"We have enough meat in our stores," she coaxed, kissing the dimple on his chin. "Stay with me today, Red Fox. *Please.*"

"I cannot," he said ruefully. "My mind tells me I must leave, even though my body cries out for me to stay."

"Can you not wait awhile?" she whispered, opening her mouth and placing small kisses across his chest in a shameless manner. "It is so warm here." She nipped at his flat male nipple and felt him jerk. "And so cozy." She laved the other nipple with her tongue. "And so pleasant." She traced circles down to his navel, feeling him swell beneath her and finding great pleasure in that fact. "And so warm," she said again, before attacking his navel with the tip of her tongue. "And so wet."

He was breathing heavily now, his breath rasping harshly into the silence. His manhood was ready and throbbing, but she would not stop yet. Not until she knew he would not leave her, breathless with longing.

"And so cozy," she said again, unable to think of other words, moving downward with each sentence. "And so . . . so . . ."

His manhood was so close, so big and throbbing, and she reached for it with her hand, caught it, and held the silky smoothness of him, flicked out her tongue, tasted his flesh, and felt him jerk and utter a curse and pull her upright and fling her on her back and fit himself between her legs and shove inward, into a wet moistness that enclosed him, felt his engorged member straining against her, moving with a rhythm that was as old as time itself, known to every man in the world, instinctive, immediate, and urgent.

His mouth pressed heated kisses across her face as they moved together, heating together, flaming together, stoking a fire that burned higher and higher until it exploded into a million fragments and sent them hurtling into oblivion together.

Afterward, he rolled onto his side, sated, exhausted, holding her perspiration-dampened form tightly clasped against him until her trembling had stilled.

They lay together then, their breathing slow and even, their bodies spent, until they were almost asleep again.

It was a state of affairs that Red Fox would not willingly have changed, had he not heard Wolf's undulating howl. He knew he must go to the animal, because he had recognized that call. Wolf used it only when the need was urgent.

He caressed Brynna's thigh one last time and kissed her cheek softly; then, reluctantly, he put her away from him.

"Stay there, love," he told her. "You need not arise yet."

Since their recent lovemaking had made Brynna sleepy, languorous, she snuggled deeper into the sleeping furs. "I have no desire to move," she murmured.

Then, suddenly remembering her fears of the night before, her eyes popped open and she sat up, uncaring of the furs that slid away, leaving her bare to the waist.

"Red Fox!" she said sharply.

"Yes?" He asked, caught in the act of donning his buckskins.

"You will not stay out so late again?"

"No," he replied gently. "You need not worry, little one. I will be back long before nightfall."

"Promise?" she asked.

"I promise," he said, leaning over to kiss her gently. "You need not worry, little one. I will be safe."

Moments later he was gone.

Indecision weighed heavy on Patrick as he watched the lodge from his hiding place among the pine trees. They had been there since early morning, and now the sun was high overhead.

Hearing a slight movement nearby, he turned to see Lacey approaching. "Find anything?" Patrick inquired.

"Only two sets of tracks," Lacey replied grimly. "One of them much larger than the other. The smaller print most likely was made by a woman or a child."

"Brynna has a small foot."

"Yes. But she wore boots, and the prints I found were made by those soft shoes made out of hide the *skraelings* wear."

Patrick's jaw tightened grimly. "She may have discarded the boots by now for some reason or other." He stared hard at the lodge, wishing he could penetrate it with his gaze, feeling certain that if he could do so, he would see the woman they had searched so long for. "I am most certain she's in there, Lacey," he said harshly. "I feel it in my gut."

"My gut just feels hungry," Lacey growled. "It's been a long time between meals."

Patrick threw the other man a heated glance. How could Lacey think of food when they were so near their goal?

Suddenly, the hide flap covering the entrance to the lodge moved. Was the wind responsible? Patrick wondered, narrowing his gaze on the flap. His question was answered suddenly as the flap lifted and a woman stepped outside.

Disappointment struck Patrick a hard blow. Although the lodge was shaded by a tall, pine tree, he could see the woman wore a hide dress and her hair was plaited in one long braid that hung down her back.

"A *skraeling* woman," he muttered, throwing a quick look at Lacey. "Are you sure there is only one woman living there?"

"If there is another one, she stays inside and never comes out," Lacey said crossly, obviously feeling some disappointment that he had not been wrong in his identification of the tracks.

"We need some way of making certain," Patrick growled. "I need to be sure before we leave here."

"Maybe we could—" Lacey broke off suddenly, then, "My God," he breathed. "It *is* her!"

Patrick spun around, his gaze sweeping the area, focusing on the woman they had been watching before, the woman who had stepped into the sunlight as she gathered several sticks of wood from the pile near the lodge, the woman whose hair resembled fire as she hurried toward the lodge again.

"Brynna," Patrick muttered, his spirits soaring like an eagle on the wind.

He rose to his feet, intent on letting her know of their presence, but Lacey caught his arm, stopping him cold.

"Wait," Lacey urged. "Look there!" He pointed toward the edge of the forest, on the other side of the clearing.

Patrick's blood ran cold as he saw the *skraeling* warrior approaching the lodge. Pure black rage swept over the Irishman as he realized the savage must be the man who had captured Brynna.

What horrible things she must have suffered at the *skraeling*'s hands, Patrick thought. But the savage would not go unpunished. He would never touch Brynna again.

Realizing he must slay the savage before he reached the lodge, Patrick lifted his sword and raced toward him.

The *skraeling* saw him and turned to flee, but Patrick would not allow it.

Uttering a battle cry, Patrick chased the *skraeling* into the forest, his longer strides closing the distance between them with comparative ease.

The *skraeling*, obviously realizing he could not outrun the man who pursued him, turned to face his opponent at the last minute, drawing his crude knife to defend himself.

Terror gleamed in the savage's eyes as he saw the raised sword, already curving on its downward path. The huge blade struck the top of his head, cleaving off his face as it split his skull wide open.

Hearing a cry in the distance, Patrick raced back to the clearing where he saw Brynna, obviously disturbed by the noise, leaving the lodge.

She hurried toward Lacey, unaware of Patrick until he dropped his sword and hurled himself at her, enfolding her in his massive embrace.

"Brynna, my lady," he said gruffly. "It is you. We finally found you. Are you all right, lass? Are you unharmed? We thought we would never see you again. That you were beyond all help."

"I am well, Patrick," she said, and, amazing though it seemed, she did look well. And she was smiling up at him. "And," she added, "I am very happy."

"Happy?" he growled, frowning down at her. "How can this be, my lady? How could you find happiness in captivity?"

"I am no captive," she said swiftly. "Never think that. I can come and go as I please, Patrick."

"Yet you remain here?"

"Yes. With Red Fox."

"Red Fox?"

"Yes," she replied softly, and Patrick could almost have sworn there were stars in her eyes. "Red Fox is the warrior who saved my life. And the man who has made himself responsible for my future happiness."

"He saved your life?" Patrick's breath rasped harshly and his arms fell away from her. "A *skraeling* warrior saved your life?"

"Yes. None of us ever thought such a thing would happen, did we? Even though we knew Garrick and Eric both found love in this wild, beautiful land, we never once thought it would happen to me." Suddenly, as though noticing something was amiss, her green eyes widened. "Patrick!" she questioned. "Why are you staring at me like that? Is something wrong?"

"Oh, lass," he muttered, reaching out to squeeze her upper arms gently. "Please forgive me. I did not know."

"Know what?" she asked, the light slowly fading from her eyes. "Forgive you for what, Patrick?" Her voice rose on the last word. "What have you done?"

It seemed an eternity before Patrick spoke again. Even then, he did not answer Brynna's question. Instead, he said, "I thought he was holding you prisoner, my lady."

Brynna knew the horror she felt must be reflected in her eyes, and she actually felt the color leaving her face. Her mouth worked, but words refused to come, yet she must force them, for she had to know . . . must know what had occurred.

Sucking cold air into her lungs, she forced words around the lump clogging her throat. "You saw Red Fox?" she whispered. "What did you do, Patrick?" Silence pressed around her, making it almost impossible to breathe, but she must go on. "Where is he? Where is Red Fox?" Her voice rose higher and higher until she was almost screaming at him.

"Oh, lass. I am so sorry," Patrick muttered, his face tight with pain, seeming unable to utter the words that would explain why he looked at her as though she had lost the most precious thing in life.

"No," she whispered, her heart skittering over the word. "No. It cannot be true!" Somehow, she forced her legs to work and pushed his hands away from her arms and circled around him, but immediately, his right arm snaked out, his fingers snagging her left wrist.

"Release me!" she cried. "I have to go to him."

"No, lassie," Patrick growled, shaking his shaggy head, attempting to draw her into his arms. "I cannot allow you to see. It is a terrible sight to behold."

Terrible sight to behold, to behold, behold! The words echoed in her mind, over and over again.

God! What had he done? She stared at him, horror stricken, feeling the rush of bile in her throat. What had this man she called friend done?

"I have to know." Her voice seemed to belong to someone else, and she began to shake with undiluted fear. "I have to see his face again."

"Lass, I am sorry," Patrick said, his voice both soft and grim. "I cannot allow it. The man . . . Red Fox . . . well, he has no face left." He pulled her against his chest, holding her tightly as though to give her the strength to accept what he was saying, but she could not. The horror of what he had done took the strength from her knees.

"No," she denied. The thought of Red Fox with his face cut away was almost more than Brynna could bear.

"It is true, lassie," Patrick said harshly. "His face is gone, taken away by my own sword."

Brynna collapsed as grief washed over her like waves upon the sand. Never mind that she was the daughter of a jarl, taught since early childhood to hide her feelings from the world. That meant nothing to her now. Her world was shattered. It lay in a thousand pieces at the feet of the man who was trying to pull her into his embrace.

"No, no, no, no, no!" she screamed, flailing out with both fists, striking Patrick over and over again, taking a small pleasure from the sound of her blows striking against his flesh. "Leave me alone!" she shouted, "Take your hands away! Away, away, away!" She refused to have him touching her, would not allow it, could not allow it!

A hard knot tightened Patrick's gut as he captured Brynna's flailing fists in his hands. He realized he should not have told her the way the warrior had died. His death would have been hard enough for her to bear, but, idiot that he was, he had to give her details.

Realizing she could not stand alone, he pushed her toward Lacey who stood silently watching them. "Take her, Lacey," he said grimly. "She must not be allowed to see him."

"You can do more for her," Lacey growled. "I never had no hand with the ladies."

"Take her, I said!" Patrick roared. "Can you not see that she wants nothing more to do with me? It was my sword that killed her man!" He pushed her into Lacey's arms and strode quickly to the place where he had left the dead man. He would bury him where he lay, Patrick decided. And he would dig the hole deep. It was the least he could do for Brynna.

At least, that way, the wolves could not get at the remains.

Patrick would not allow himself to think, as, with the

sword that slew the *skraeling*, the Irishman now dug the grave that would hold the empty flesh.

And when he had finished the grisly task, he went to fetch the horses from the hiding place where they had been left tethered, realizing they must make haste to leave this place behind . . . for Brynna's sake.

Hopefully, when they left the mountain behind, Brynna's pain would ease. And one day, perhaps, she might even forgive what he had done.

He prayed God that it would be so.

Lame Duck watched the burial of his friend, Spreading Branches, from his hiding place in the forest. He had arrived just in time to see his friend slain by the Monster Man. One part of him wanted to race out and confront the man who had killed his friend, but another part, the thinking part of him, had objected to such a foolish act.

Having listened to the thinking part of himself, feeling it was the only way he would stay alive, Lame Duck had hidden himself away to watch so that he might tell his people all that he had seen.

The clan elders had been right when they said one warrior could not stand against the Monster Men. One warrior could not hope to win a battle against them. Nor could two warriors. If there were many of these Monster Men, even a whole clan could not stand against them.

But their numbers were few, Lame Duck decided. So far, he had only seen two. And that was all the others had seen, too.

But there might be others that they had not seen. If there were, then better to take them two at a time. When he returned to his clan, he would make that suggestion to the others.

He thought they would listen to his words, for had he

not proved his courage by staying to watch when they were so near?

Yes, he decided. He *had* proved himself brave. And others would soon know that if he made it back alive.

Chapter Twenty-One

Only half aware of what she was doing, Brynna began the task of gathering up the things needed for the long journey ahead. She picked up her boots and the shift that she had only recently mended. Although the hide garments she wore were more suited to the lifestyle she had been leading, they were things of the past, better left behind. As were the camas roots she had dug only yesterday. The squirrels and chipmunks were welcome to them, and to the pine nuts and manzanita berries that were piled in an earthenware bowl, ready to be pounded into mush.

She cared nothing about food, felt as though she would never again be able to swallow another morsel. But she would take the quill case filled with bone needles that Red Fox had made for her.

Clutching her garments and the quill case against her chest, she turned to Lacey, who stood waiting quietly beside her. "I have nothing else to take with me," she said quietly. "We can leave here as soon as I have changed my garments."

"Will you be all right in here alone?" he asked, the tone of his voice revealing his anxiety.

She gave an abrupt nod. "I have no intention of taking my own life, Lacey," she said calmly. "I am not that strong."

His gaze narrowed as he studied her for a long moment. Then, seeming to have satisfied himself that she would do nothing foolish, he left the lodge.

Slowly, Brynna stripped off her hide clothing and donned the garments she had worn before coming to the mountain. When she finished dressing, she looked around the lodge where she had known such happiness.

There were the baskets they had made. One perfectly formed, the others fashioned by her own inept hands. And stacked neatly beside them were the earthen pots and bowls.

Brynna's gaze dwelt on the one perfect bowl surrounded by the others of lesser quality that she had made. Red Fox had never laughed at her efforts, she remembered, feeling a burning sensation in her dry eyes. Instead, he had always found something good about what she had done.

The nails of her clenched fingers dug into her palms as her gaze swept over the raised sleeping mat made from pine needles and cattails and covered with the hides that Red Fox had brought her.

Was their bed still warm from the heat of their bodies?

Finding herself unable to resist, Brynna bent over and ran her palms over the soft hide bed.

It felt cool to the touch and she realized their bed had grown cold now. Just like Red Fox. Cold and dead.

A sob caught in her throat. *Oh, Red Fox,* her heart wept. *Why did it have to happen?*

Brynna still found it hard to believe. Red Fox had been

so happy, so vigorously alive when she had last seen him. How could his life be over so quickly?

But it must be so, she knew, because Patrick would not have claimed to have slain him had it not been true.

"If only I could have seen him!"

The terrible finality of death entered her consciousness and filled it with agony.

Unable to remain standing, she sank down on the sleeping mat and rocked herself back and forth, trying to come to terms with her grief.

"Are you ready, lass?" Lacey's worried voice came from just outside the entrance. "Come out now. Patrick should be just about done with his chore."

Chore? He should be done with his chore? Brynna wanted to scream, to rail at the man. Is that all Red Fox's burial meant to them? Nothing more than a chore to be done?

The grief she had been trying to hold off moved in on her and she experienced a frightening, choking sensation which brought with it a feeling of near hysteria. Unable to hold back the tears, she allowed them to spill over and slide down her cheeks, but she uttered no sound.

She heard the hide flap lift, was aware that Lacey had entered, but she would not look at him. Instead, she kept her eyes squeezed tight, wanting to shut the world away from her, wanting to be left alone with her grief.

"If only I could have seen him!" she cried, opening her eyes to look at the man who stood helplessly by.

"Better that you did not see, lass," Lacey muttered. "It would not have been a pleasant sight to remember."

"Why did Patrick kill him?" she cried, squeezing her balled fists against her chest, trying to ease the knot of pain that resided there. "He should have spoken to him first!"

"You cannot blame Patrick," Lacey grated.

"Then who else can I blame?" she cried, rocking herself back and forth. "It was Patrick Douglass who killed Red Fox! It was his hand that wielded the sword. He said—" She choked as she uttered the words, barely able to finish. "—Said that he cut his face off. Why did he kill him in that manner? If he had to kill him, then why could he not have done it different? It was unnecessary to mutilate him in such a manner!"

"If Patrick could undo what he has done, then he would gladly do so," Lacey said grimly. "But he cannot. The deed is done, lass. The *skraeling* cannot be given back his life. Your duty is to the living now. You must consider how Patrick is feeling."

"Why should I care how he feels?" she spat, her green eyes flashing. "It was him that—"

"Say no more, lass!" he gritted. "The deed is done. Patrick Douglass only acted as any many would have in the same circumstances." His voice lowered, became softer. "He feels bad enough already, lass. Do not make him more miserable than he already is." He patted her shoulder awkwardly. "No man could ever care for you more than does Patrick Douglass. He would never deliberately cause you pain. You must try to forgive him, lass. For your own sake as well as his."

Had Brynna been herself, she might have been surprised at Lacey, for he was a man of few words, never uttering more than were needed to get his point across.

But Brynna was not herself. Even so, she knew deep in her heart that Lacey was right. Patrick Douglass would never intentionally do anything to cause her pain. Even so, he had killed the man she loved. She would never be able to see his dear face again. Oh God, how could she face life without him? Endless days of aloneness and missing him stretched out before her.

How then, she wondered achingly, could she be expected to forgive Patrick for slaying the man she loved more than life itself?

She could not, she realized. But Patrick was aware of her feelings. She need not verbalize them again. And perhaps, by keeping silent, she could ease—if only slightly—the pain in her heart.

Even so, Brynna knew she could never forget what Patrick had done. As long as she lived, she would know. Because of Patrick Douglass, her love lay dead, forever lost to her now.

Perhaps one day, she might be able to forgive Patrick. But if that day ever came, it would be a long time in coming.

Red Fox noticed Sky Man was wearing his bluest cloak as he set out on his search for the bear. Wind Woman's breath was brisk, whipping through his dark hair as his long buckskin-clad legs ate up the distance.

He passed a couple of squirrels who chattered at him, taking exception to being disturbed. The flutter of wings sent his gaze darting upward. A large black raven swooped overhead, then dropped to a tree limb a few feet ahead and perched there, staring at Red Fox with round, beady eyes.

Despite the heat of the day, a chill slithered down his spine, for the raven was considered the prophet of doom.

Trying to shake off his apprehension, Red Fox continued on his way, and, although he searched diligently for the bear, he had found no sign of its lair by the time Father Sun reached the center of the sky.

But Red Fox did find something else, something that slammed into his gut with the force of a rock thrown by a powerful hand.

Hoofprints.

Not split hooves, like those found on elk or deer, but hooves that were whole, hooves that were unlike any he had ever seen before . . . until the Vikings had come to this land.

Kneeling beside the tracks which overlapped, he studied them intently, hoping he was mistaken.

But he was not, he realized. The tracks could only have been made by the four-legged beasts ridden by Brynna and the men who had traveled with her.

Horses.

Two sets of tracks meant two horses had come up the mountain.

Were there two riders as well?

Granted, one set of hoofprints might belong to Brynna's horse, Shadow, but the other set could not be accounted for.

Alarm washed over Red Fox as he realized the trail left by the horses led across the mountain toward the forest where he and Brynna had built their lodge. That knowledge alone was enough to make Red Fox forget the bear he had been searching for and set off toward home at a dead run.

Worry streaked his brow and his head thumped with dread as he hurried through the forest that separated him from the woman he loved. He must reach Brynna before something terrible happened, for he was almost certain the horses were not riderless. And he would not allow himself even to contemplate what would happen if whoever rode the animals found Brynna alone.

Red Fox covered his backtrail quickly, his long legs carrying him easily over fallen logs and other debris in his determination to reach Brynna.

When he came to the shallow creek he had previously crossed, Red Fox gave no thought to slowing his pace.

Instead, he leaped from one rock to another in his anxious flight. He was near the middle of the stream when the mishap occurred. He stepped on a rock that was slick with lichen.

Feeling his moccasins slip, Red Fox flailed out with both arms, trying to regain his balance, but in vain. Instead of righting himself, he found himself falling.

Thud!

Pain streaked through Red Fox's head as it struck a large, wedge-shaped rock.

His vision doubled when, mindful of the need to hurry, Red Fox scrambled quickly to his feet again.

Soaked from the icy water, Red Fox paid little attention to the warm wetness trickling down his forehead until his vision became blurred, tinged with a pale pink color.

Wiping away the wetness, he stared curiously at the blood on his hand.

Although he realized he must have cut his head when he fell, Red Fox's pace did not falter. The wound was obviously a superficial one and would grow no worse left unattended.

He raced onward, hurrying to reach the lodge where Brynna waited.

Barely an hour had passed before he burst through the forest into the clearing and sprinted toward the lodge.

"Brynna," he shouted, his voice rasping harshly in his throat. "Brynna. I am here, Brynna. I have returned."

His heart, thudding loudly in his chest, was the only sound he heard.

Stumbling forward, his footsteps quickened, then faltered, like his furiously beating heart. He wanted desperately to reach the lodge, yet he was afraid of what he would find when he looked inside.

"Brynna," he called again. "Come out, Brynna. I have returned."

A squirrel darted into his path and Red Fox altered his course to keep from crushing it. Sitting back on its haunches, the creature scolded harshly for long moments, then turned and dashed away, seeking refuge in the verdant foliage high above the ground.

Feeling a wave of dizziness, Red Fox found himself fighting to stay on his feet. His vision was refocusing, becoming narrower and narrower, consumed by gray mist that pushed inward in ever-increasing waves until he was aware of nothing save what lay directly in his path.

The gray mist turned pink, then darkened, forming a red haze around his eyes, making Red Fox wonder if his head wound was still bleeding.

He spared no time considering that possibility for it mattered little to him. His only concern at that moment was the lodge he approached . . . slowly now, his footsteps faltering as he searched the dwelling for some sign of life.

But try as he would, he could find none!

All was silent around him.

The birds . . . the woodland creatures . . . even Wind Woman had stilled her breath, as though she too waited, for what he would find . . .

Brynna, his heart cried, although he no longer spoke her name aloud. For what good would it have done? He knew now with a certainty that she would not respond. How could she, when she must have departed long ago, leaving the lodge quite empty?

As empty as his life would most certainly be . . . once again.

Chapter Twenty-Two

Although it took most of the day to descend the mountain, Patrick knew they dared not make camp so close to the place where they had last seen the *skraelings* who had captured Brynna. Instead, they continued to travel in a northerly direction until long after there was nothing to light their way except the pale light cast by the moon.

He would not have stopped then if he had not seen Brynna swaying in the saddle and realized she could go no farther. Even then, though, he searched for a place that would offer them the most cover, finding it at last where a river had cut a path through the mountains eons before. Now it was only a shallow creek, banked on both sides by steep cliffs.

Pulling back on his reins, Patrick dismounted. "Let me help you, my lady," he said, reaching for Brynna, afraid her legs would not support her.

"I need no help," Brynna said tonelessly, sliding from

her mount and forcing her trembling knees to lock in place.

Patrick turned away, feeling stricken and realizing he should have known she would respond in such a manner. He was the last person she would seek help from.

Since it was late, there was no thought of cooking a meal. Instead, they unrolled their blankets and spread them beside the fire, then assuaged their hunger with dried meat and water. At least, the men did. Food seemed of little interest to Brynna, Patrick noted. She sat across the fire from him, appearing drained, listless. But what else had he expected? He wondered. She had just lost the man she loved. It would take awhile, but perhaps in time, her loss would not seem so great.

At least he hoped so.

Brynna was aware of Patrick's eyes on her, of the worry in his expression, but she could do nothing to help him. *You could if you wanted,* an inner voice cried. *Just speak to him, allow him to know he is forgiven.*

No! her mind protested. *I will not! I do not forgive him, nor will I ever do so!*

A movement nearby jerked her from her inner thoughts and she looked up to see Lacey holding her jewel-encrusted sword toward her. "Look, lassie," he said softly. "You must have lost in it your flight."

"Thank you," Brynna said huskily, taking the sword and rubbing her fingers over the jeweled handle. "I thought I would never see it again."

She felt a slight regret as Lacey turned away, but knew she could never summon the smile he seemed to need. How could she, when every fiber of her being cried out with the pain of losing the man she loved?

Yip, yip, urroooo. Yip, yip, urroooo. The undulating

call sounded through the canyon. Was it Wolf? she wondered. Was the animal mourning its master's death?

Yip, yip, urroooo. Yip, yip, urroooo. The call came again, the one voice taken up by others, sounding through the canyon, then reverberating off the rock walls over and over again, echoing the pain of her own heart.

It was still sounding when she finally lay herself down and sought rest for her weary body.

Two days later they reached the edge of desert country where miles and miles of harsh, arid land stretched out before them. The men debated the advisability of crossing, but could find no way around it. If they were to reach the mesa, they must cross the desert.

The party of two horses and three riders traveled on.

It was on the third day, as the sun sank low in the west, that they found Shadow standing in the dubious shade of a gnarled juniper growing beside a shallow waterhole.

Brynna's joy at having her mount again was tempered by her grief at having lost the man she loved. At least, she told herself, regaining her mount meant that she would no longer have to ride double with Lacey, having refused from the beginning to ride on the same mount as Patrick.

Another day passed before they saw the mountains rising in the distance. Brynna studied the long range of mountains, resembling nothing more than a blue haze seen from this distance, wondering if the mesa they sought would be found there.

Suddenly, Lacey, having taken the lead as usual, reined up his mount and shouted, ''Hold up back there!''

Curious, Brynna watched the scout dismount and drop to his belly and press his ear against the ground. He stayed there for a long moment, obviously listening to something his companions could not hear.

Upon regaining his feet, he joined his companions.

Nodding at Patrick as though confirming some secret the two men shared, the scout met Brynna's eyes. "Looks like we run out of time, lass."

"What do you mean?" she queried.

"I hear hoofbeats. Not heavy enough to be those creatures with humps on their backs. Sounds more like horses being ridden hard. I might be wrong, though. Could be something else, some animals we have yet to see. But to be on the safe side, we'd better look for cover."

"You are sure it could not be buffalo?"

"Buffalo?"

"That is the name of the creatures with humped backs," she explained.

"Yes. I am sure those creatures are not following us," Lacey said gruffly. "The beasts that follow have been coming along too fast to be those beasts—the buffalo—you speak of. They need grass for grazing. There was plenty to be found elsewhere, but none in this direction."

"What should we do?" Brynna asked, turning to Patrick, seeking his advice for the first time since leaving the lodge. "It might be my father's men."

"If it is, then we will fight, my lady," he said grimly.

"Do you think we have a chance to reach the mountains?"

Patrick looked at the other man. "How far off would you say they are, Lacey?"

"Two hours behind us," came the prompt reply.

"Well," Patrick said, clearing his throat as though finding it hard to speak. "Forewarned means we have time to prepare for them. Mayhap if we ride hard, we can make those mountains ahead of them." He narrowed his eyes on a distant gap in the mountains. "If we can, then best we choose the battleground before they catch up. At least, that way, the advantage will be ours. We certainly need all the help we can muster."

"And more," Lacey growled.

"How many horses you think they have?" Patrick asked.

And riders, Brynna mentally added, waiting silently for the answer.

"Maybe half a dozen," was the reply.

"Then we are two against six," Patrick muttered. "All of them guaranteed to be fighting men."

"Three against six," Brynna corrected quietly.

"Nay, lass," Patrick said. "You cannot be expected to go against your own kin, even if you were a man. Which you are not."

"But I am skilled with a sword, Patrick. If the rest of you fight, then so do I."

"There will be time enough to worry about it later," Lacey said grimly. "Now we must ride swiftly, lest the enemy catch us in the open. If we reach the mountain pass, we may just have a chance."

Who were the men who followed them? Brynna wondered, as they rode hard toward the mountains. And could she bring herself to fight against her own kinsmen? She found the idea distasteful, but if the lives of her men were at stake, then she could do little else.

When they arrived in the foothills of the mountains, she could see the dust of many riders following them and knew that Lacey was right! a fight was inevitable.

Reining up behind the shelter of a large boulder, Patrick shouted, "Take cover, lass."

"No," Brynna cried, drawing the jeweled sword from its scabbard and turning to face the riders who thundered toward them.

Lacey took the forward position on the right and Patrick moved to the left, both men hoping to take the brunt of the attack.

Brynna waited with bated breath to see the rider's faces,

wondering if she would know any of the men whose lives she would most certainly take in order to save theirs.

As they drew nearer, she realized the winged helmet worn by one of the riders was very much like the one belonging to her brother, Garrick.

Her heart stopped beating for a moment, then raced rapidly as her thoughts whirled with confusion. How could she remain where she was and allow her brother to be killed? She could not, she realized. Although they had had their differences in the past, Brynna had never doubted her love for him.

That realization caused her to throw down her sword, to race toward the riders, her tousled hair flaming beneath the noonday sun.

Spreading her arms wide, she called out his name. "Garrick!"

"Come back, lass," Patrick roared. "Take cover before you come to harm!"

"Garrick!" she shouted again, waving her arms to attract his attention. "Stop! Come no closer!"

Instead of obeying, Garrick raced onward, reining his mount up in a cloud of dust on a few feet away from her and sliding to the ground. Then, sweeping her into his arms, he hugged her to him.

"By Thor, you are safe! You are safe, little sister!"

"Your men, Garrick!" she cried, pushing against his embrace. "Tell them to leave mine alone!"

"Your men?" He drew away and she saw the fury that darkened his brow, erasing the tenderness that had been there only moments before. "I will see those men drawn and quartered for what they have done."

"You can try," roared Patrick, brandishing his sword. "But you will never accomplish it. I will die where I stand."

"No!" Brynna cried, fury flashing in her eyes. Snatching up her own sword, she faced her brother. "I will run the man through who dares to lay a hand on my men. If not for them I would have been dead long ago."

Garrick's body was tense as he eyed the two men who moved to stand behind his sister. They were poised, ready to fight if they were challenged.

Although his expression remained hard, he slowly relaxed. "All right, we will leave it for now," he grated harshly. "But do not think I will forget what has been done. There will come a day of reckoning when all debts must be paid."

"Should that day ever come, then Patrick and Lacey are the ones who will collect," Brynna said grimly. "For I am forever in their debt."

A truce was agreed upon, although it was reluctant on Garrick's part, for he felt certain his sister's honor was in question. Having decided no battle would be fought this day, Brynna allowed herself to relax.

As her gaze roved the riders, looking for familiar faces among them, she realized one was a female.

"Nama," she exclaimed, hurrying toward the girl who was dismounting. "You have come, too?"

"I have come, too," Nama agreed. "I would not allow Garrick to come without me. Wherever he leads, I will follow."

Whether it was Nama's words or the love shining in her ebony eyes when she looked at her husband that proved Brynna's undoing, she did not know. She only knew that the stark impact of her loss suddenly penetrated her entire being, and to her everlasting shame, Brynna threw her arms around the other girl and gave way to tears.

* * *

Red Fox's injuries healed slowly, but not so his heart. Even so, as the days slowly passed, the hurt he felt at Brynna's betrayal began to numb, until finally he could think about her without feeling a stab of pain in the region of his heart.

Instead, he began to feel numb. Eventually, though, even the numbness gave way to bitterness, to a feeling of unworthiness.

It was a feeling the warrior knew well, for it was the same one he had known when Sweet Willow had rejected him.

Brynna had said his scar did not bother her, had denied that it was ugly, had told him it was a reminder of his courage, of the strength it took to survive such a ferocious attack.

But she had lied!

Red Fox was finally able to face that fact.

Brynna had lied to him, must have done so, else why would she have fled the moment she had the chance? How could he have trusted her so? Would he never learn the falseness of a woman's heart?

He balled up his fist and slammed it into his cupped palm with enough force to make Wolf, his only companion, slink toward the entrance as though suspecting Red Fox would soon loose his fury upon whatever happen to fall beneath his gaze.

"You might as well go, too," Red Fox snarled, gazing bitterly at the animal. "Leave me alone! Why should you stay when others will not?"

Instead of leaving, Wolf whimpered and crept on its belly to the warrior's side. With watchful gaze, the wolf nudged Red Fox's hand, then licked his fingers. The action broke the ice around the warrior's heart.

When he spoke again, Red Fox's voice held both sorrow

and regret. "I am sorry, old friend. I deserve to be left alone." He rubbed the animal behind the ear. "But you will not desert me, will you? Even when abuse is heaped on your head, you stay beside me."

The animal whimpered low in its throat as though it shared the warrior's great pain. And perhaps it did, for Brynna had been kind to the wolf and the animal surely felt her loss as well.

"I am no fit companion for such as you, Wolf. I spend my days wallowing in self-pity because another woman has rejected me instead of placing the abuse where it belongs. On her own head."

Uncurling his long legs, Red Fox crossed the lodge and pushed aside the entrance flap. He stared up the mountain slope, hoping to see her there.

But of course, she was not there. Brynna was gone from him, and Red Fox had not the slightest doubt about her destination. She would be traveling to the great mesa where her brother Eric lived.

His lips twisted bitterly. Had she already forgotten the man she had left behind?

The beginnings of an idea slowly formed. What would Brynna do if he suddenly appeared on the mesa, if he took her, forcibly, from her brother and carried her off to his own village?

Just the very thought was enough to ease his pain, to fire his blood again. Brynna, with her flame-bright hair, would create quite a stir among his people. He, Red Fox, the man scorned by Sweet Willow, would be the envy of all the other warriors.

Wolf whimpered softly, disturbed by something. When Red Fox met the animal's yellow gaze, he realized he was the cause of the animal's unease, and wondered why it should be so.

But he gave it little thought, for he could not spare the time. There were things of more import to occupy his mind.

Dismissing the animal completely, Red Fox entered the lodge and began to prepare for the long journey that lay ahead.

Chapter Twenty-Three

Nampeyo walked in a dream, and although he realized he was dreaming, he had no wish to wake up. In his dream he saw a swirling cloud, the same one he had seen once before in a vision. He watched the cloud closely, wondering if Nama would appear to him again.

Yes! There she was! Coming out of the milky white river astride the same four-legged beast she had ridden before. But this time she was not alone. Riding behind her, on a beast very much like her own, was a man of huge proportions, with fiery hair that leapt wildly around his head. Nampeyo could almost smell the flames, could almost feel the heat emanating from the man's head.

Nampeyo shrank back from the sight of the man; his first impulse was to flee, but his legs would not carry him away because at the moment, Nama turned toward the shaman and extended her arms toward him. Only then did Nampeyo see the golden globe in her hands.

The shaman's eyes were riveted to the glowing sphere. He wanted it desperately. He reached for it, but Nama laughed, tossing the globe into the sky as she had done before in the vision.

Nampeyo thought his heart would break as he watched the globe soar on high, watched it make an arc, then disappear from view.

A cackle of laughter jerked his eyes back to Nama and the fiery-haired stranger. But the sound had not been uttered by either of them. Instead, it had come from the raven perched on Nama's right shoulder . . . the raven that watched him with round ebony eyes.

"Why do you not catch the sun?" the raven asked.

Nampeyo pressed his lips tight so that he would not answer the raven's stupid question. But, to his utter astonishment, he found himself saying, "No man may capture the sun."

Raven cackled again, and its beady eyes seemed knowing as it sneered. "You could have caught that one, but as usual, you waited too long."

"Why do you keep saying that?" Nampeyo asked. "Why do you think I could have caught it?"

"Because Eagle did," Raven cackled. "See?"

Slowly, Nampeyo tilted his head back to look where Raven pointed with one clawed foot at the sky. He saw an eagle soaring with wings spread wide. In its talons it clutched the golden globe that Nama had thrown into the air.

As Nampeyo watched, the eagle swooped lower and lower, until it was only a few feet above the shaman's head. Hope was born anew as Nampeyo realized he could take the ball now if he wished. All he had to do was leap for it.

But while he remained undecided, a warrior, clad in the fashion of the wolf clan, threw a spear and pierced the eagle's heart.

With a scream that sent terror through Nampeyo's heart, the great bird dropped the golden globe and plummeted to the ground, and the wolf clan warrior opened his hands and caught the falling globe. It was then the shaman realized that once again, he had waited too long.

His heart lay heavy in his chest when Nampeyo woke with a start. What did the dream mean? he wondered. What was its purpose? Try as he would, he could not answer that question.

He stepped outside his sleeping room and looked across the canyon to the small cave where Shala lived with her husband and baby daughter. The man in his dreams bore a striking resemblance to Eric.

Had Nampeyo been given a warning of some kind? The raven had referred to the golden globe as the sun. Why?

If it was really the sun, then how could Nama have carried it in her hands? How could she offer it to her shaman as though it were a gift?

What did it all mean? he wondered again. Try as he would, Nampeyo could find no answer to his questions.

He decided he would have to consider the dream carefully, for he felt the message it contained was important, not only to himself, but to every member of the Eagle Clan.

Worry creased his brow as he recalled the eagle in flight. The eagle was the clan's sacred bird. In the dream it had been slain. Nampeyo still remembered the horror of that moment.

Perhaps there was no need to worry, though. The vision of Nama might only mean she was returning to the clan at last. The joy he felt at that thought was tempered by the fear of the strangers who might accompany her on her journey to the mesa.

But he must consider the dream carefully, Nampeyo decided. After all, it had come to him first in a vision and might be a warning.

Uttering a long sigh, Nampeyo pushed himself upright, forcing his crooked leg to lock in place, then left his bedchamber and limped toward the ladder protruding from a hole in the courtyard.

Although it was late, he must not delay in his efforts to understand the dream. He would descend the ladder, would isolate himself in the kiva, and then he would consult the spirits.

Perhaps, if they were so inclined, they would interpret the dream that Nampeyo, in his stupidity, could not comprehend.

Grasping the ladder tightly, Nampeyo lowered himself into the darkness below.

They had been traveling over rough, rugged country, where shrubs were sparse and cactus was in plentiful supply, for almost two weeks when Nama suddenly reined up her mount and pointed toward a mountain that could only be seen as a distant blue haze.

"There it is," she cried, and the excitement she felt could be heard in her voice. "Look, Garrick! See my home?" Everyone stared at the mesa that rose high into the sky. "See!" Nama continued. "Do you see it? That is the place of my birth. Home of the Eagle Clan. The place where my mother, Ona, lives." She expelled a huge sigh. "It will be good to be home again."

"It will be good to see my brother again, too," Brynna murmured, her gaze fastened on the huge mesa that resembled an inverted bowl, rising thousands of feet into the sky.

He was there. Her most beloved brother, Eric, was there on that mesa. She smiled as she wondered what he would do when he saw them. He would, quite naturally, be surprised, for there was no way he could have known they would come.

If only Red Fox could have shared this moment with her!

At the thought of Red Fox, moisture filled her eyes, and she blinked rapidly to dry them. She refused to allow such weakness, had no time for useless emotions like self-pity. It was a fact that loved ones died, and those left behind must go on with their lives.

But when would the pain ease? her heart cried. How long would she wish she had died with him? God, how long?

Suddenly realizing she was looking at the mesa through misty eyes, Brynna blinked rapidly again, and swallowed around the lump in her throat. She must not think of what was past, must think instead of the joy of being reunited with her dearest brother, Eric.

The past was dead now, gone forever, and she was determined to keep matters of the heart secret. That task should be made easier since there were only two others— beside herself—who knew of what had occurred. And neither man, Patrick or Lacey, would speak of her love, nor of what had happened on that mountain. She was sure of that fact, because she had come to know both men well during their long voyage.

Brynna felt certain both men could be trusted, and for that she would be eternally grateful. She could not speak of her loss. Not now. Perhaps never.

But I will never forget you, Red Fox, she silently vowed. *And I will always cherish the time we had together.*

Shadow moved forward, jolting Brynna from her memories. Squaring her shoulders, Brynna lifted her chin and rode toward the mesa where, she was sure, her brother Eric waited.

Nama felt puzzled as she watched Brynna square her shoulders and jut her chin forward as though facing an unwelcome task. The sight of the mesa where her brother lived should have brought her more joy, should have taken the shadows from her eyes, but it had not.

What had happened on that long journey to cause such a look? Nama wondered, as she had done so many times in the past few days. Why did Brynna's eyes show such sorrow? Food seemed of no interest to her and she had lost weight. Her skin stretched taut over her cheekbones and there were hollows beneath them. Her blue eyes had lost much of their lustre and most of the time her thoughts seemed to be elsewhere.

She had noted those facts before but had not asked for an explanation. Brynna would speak her feelings if she were of a mind, or she would keep them to herself. It was not in Nama's nature to pry.

But she could not help but worry.

She flicked another quick look at Brynna, wondering at the shift that had been mended in so many places, a fact that was unusual because the girl was usually so careful with her garments.

Brynna looked over at that moment, and, realizing what had captured Nama's attention, a red flush stole up the Viking's cheeks.

Contrite at having been the cause of Brynna's embarrassment, Nama looked quickly away, pretending not to notice the other girl's discomfiture. She told herself she must not pry into what did not concern her, but nevertheless, Nama could not still her uneasy thoughts.

Something dreadful had happened on Brynna's journey here, Nama realized. Something that was so horrible it could not be mentioned.

Nama prayed that her husband would never know. If he discovered his sister had suffered at the hands of the people he called *skraelings,* would it affect his relationship with his wife?

Nama feared it was so, could only pray that he remained ignorant of anything amiss where his sister was concerned.

"Spreading Branches is dead? Are you sure?"

Lame Duck stared at the white-haired man who asked the question, holding his gaze even though he wanted to look away. "I saw it with my own eyes," he said. "The monster man held a giant weapon—a wide blade so sharp that it sliced through Spreading Branches head. I saw Spreading Branches fall to the ground. And I saw the earth turn red with his blood. There could be no mistake. He is dead."

Hearing the mutterings of his people, listening to their fear and outrage, Lame Duck forced himself to go on. "We cannot allow them to go free. We must follow and avenge Spreading Branches."

"It is not your place to decide that," the chief said harshly. "It is for the council to decide what is to be done."

"Allow me to speak to the council," Lame Duck said eagerly. "I can make them understand how necessary it is to rid ourselves of the Monster Men."

The chief's expression was hard when he spoke. "The council of elders are able to make their decision without your help, Lame Duck."

Realizing he had overstepped his bounds, Lame Duck bowed his head and looked at his feet. He silently cursed himself for appearing too eager. He should have told them what had happened and then held his own council about what should or should not be done.

Perhaps, though, they would make the right decision. It should be obvious to all that he was right. The Monster Men could not be allowed to live lest the desert clan always remain in fear of their return.

No. Better off to wipe them out, to rid the earth of their kind.

He just hoped the others would see it his way.

Wind Woman howled around Nama, tearing at her hair and pulling at her with cold fingers, reminding Nama that she had no business returning to the mesa. *Go back! Go back!* Wind Woman howled, but Nama refused to listen. Instead, she clutched the saddle horn tightly with both hands while her mount lurched up the path that had been made long ago by deer and elk.

The journey up the mountain seemed endless, yet it also seemed too quickly over. Nama realized that soon she would learn whether or not her people would accept her return.

The hair at the nape of Nama's neck prickled and she shivered, feeling a sense of being watched. How long, she wondered, would it be before the watchers made themselves known?

They had not done so by the time the travelers reached the top of the mesa, but Nama knew they were there—the sentries—watching every move the intruders made.

Having seen no sign of habitation, Garrick took the lead and rode along another path where the grass had been trampled by both man and beast. Soon, as Nama had known they would, they neared the fields where rows and rows of corn could be seen.

Garrick reined in his mount and looked them over. "The crops do well," he said, with grudging admiration. "I am surprised."

"Why?" Nama asked, looking at him quickly. "I told you my people were farmers."

"Yes," he agreed. "I know you did. But the mesa seems so dry." His eyes swept over the dry bushes, the stunted, gnarled junipers that grew near the fields, and when he looked at her again, she could see he was puzzled. "How do they come by enough water? The rest of the vegetation—the trees and bushes around the fields—looks starved for water. As though it rarely rains here."

"You are right," she said. "Rain has been scarce in the last few years. But my people have learned to catch the water and hold it until it is needed."

"You irrigate the fields?" His eyebrows lifted and he smiled at her. "Perhaps we were more wrong in our estimation of your people than we realized."

Her lips quirked in a half-smile. "Then you are ready to admit that perhaps we are not so backward as you once thought?"

"Yes." He smiled widely at her. "But why have we not seen any of your people, Nama?"

"They will show themselves when they are ready," she said, her expression becoming serious.

"They know we are here?"

"Of course. They knew before we started up the mountain."

"Perhaps we should do something to let them know we are not their enemy," Garrick said.

"Anyone who comes on the mesa is considered an enemy," Nama told him. "But I am hoping they will recognize me and give me a chance to explain our presence among them."

The words had hardly left her mouth when, without

warning, they were surrounded by a score of half-naked savages.

Nampeyo heaved a tired sigh, settled down on the courtyard wall, and stretched out his crippled legs where the heat from the afternoon sun would reach them. Almost immediately he felt an easing of the pain that had become his constant companion.

If only he could stay there, he told himself. But he could not. The clan had but one shaman, and he had so many duties that—

"Shaman!"

The voice interrupted Nampeyo's thoughts and he turned to see Shateh hurrying toward him.

"Strangers have come to the mesa, Shaman," Shateh said, his breath coming fast and short, as though he had been running. "Already they approach our city. What must be done?"

Instead of feeling alarmed, Nampeyo felt a calm acceptance of the news. The time had come. What had already been foretold would now occur. "Describe the strangers to me," he ordered. "Is their hair the color of a raven's wing, or does it shine like the face of Father Sun?"

"It is not dark like raven," Shateh said, obviously puzzled that Nampeyo should ask. "But how could you know such a thing?"

"A shaman knows many things," Nampeyo said obliquely. "You should not have to be told that, Shateh. I have been shown these strangers many times, both in dreams and in visions. They are Vikings, like Shala's man, Eric. And they have traveled across the big salt water to come to our land. Do they travel alone?" Nampeyo waited for the answer, hoping the man would speak of another, of the one who—in his dreams—had accompanied the Vikings to the mesa.

"They number as many as both my hands," Shateh replied.

She must not be with them, Nampeyo thought sadly. If she had been, then surely Shateh would have mentioned her presence.

"What should we do?" Shateh asked again.

"Go to Eric," Nampeyo replied. "He will know what to do. Tell him . . . tell him that his shaman has need of him."

Nampeyo watched the man hurry to obey.

Chapter Twenty-Four

A chill slithered down Brynna's spine as she stared at the *skraelings* who surrounded them. Contrary to her expectations, they looked decidedly unfriendly, some with their spears held at ready, others with their bowstrings notched with flint-tipped arrows.

Her hand crept toward the jeweled handle of her sword. "Speak to them, Nama," Brynna urged, realizing the other girl's words would carry more weight than those of a stranger. "Tell them we come in peace, that we mean them no harm. Be quick about it, lest they decide to kill us where we stand."

Nama's face bore a worried frown as she eyed the warriors one by one. "None of these warriors is known to me," she said. "They must be from the Dove Clan, who occupy the north side of the mesa." She gripped the saddle horn, preparing to dismount.

Garrick uttered a quick protest. "No, Nama! Remain astride your mount."

"The warriors would feel less threatened if I faced

them on the ground," Nama said. "You must remember, they have never before seen animals such as these."

"Nevertheless, you will remain mounted," he said grimly. "Your horse gives you an advantage over them."

Realizing her husband was perfectly capable of taking her on his horse with him if she refused to obey his command, Nama settled back in the saddle again. Indeed, she had no real desire to find herself afoot if a battle should occur.

Raising her right hand, she held it palm outward and, in a raised voice, spoke in the language of her people. "Listen to me, warriors of the Dove Clan!"

Although the *skraelings* had been muttering among themselves, they fell silent at the sound of her voice, and as one, their attention focused on the woman who had the look of the people, yet wore strange garments the likes of which they had never before seen.

One fellow, obviously bolder than the rest, stepped forward, having apparently appointed himself spokesman for the group. "Who are you, woman?" he called loudly.

"I am Nama, woman of the Eagle Clan, and I have returned home after a long stay with my husband's people. Who dares to interrupt this woman's journey with raised weapons?"

Several of the men muttered among themselves, but the man who had appointed himself spokesman uttered a sharp reproval. "I am Running Wolf," he replied. "And although you claim to be a woman of the People, how do we know it is so? The warriors with you carry weapons that are strange to our eyes. You, as well as they, ride astride animals we have never seen before. If it is true that you come in peace, then tell your warriors to throw down their weapons. Tell them to leave the beasts they ride and stand before us as men. Only then will we believe your words.''

Nama related Running Wolf's words to the others, then added her own thoughts. ''I think we should comply with his demands, Garrick. It is a way to show them we have only good intentions.''

''Thor's teeth!'' Garrick exploded. ''Are you daft, woman?''

''Quietly, Garrick,'' she urged, throwing an uneasy glance at Running Wolf, who had taken a quick step backward. ''Speak calmly, husband. There is no need to alarm them further.''

''He is a fool to think we will throw down our weapons and face them afoot, leaving ourselves completely defenseless,'' Garrick growled in a low voice.

''He is no fool, either, Garrick,'' she said. ''Neither will he pull back his warriors and allow us to continue our journey.''

It seemed they were stopped cold. They could not proceed, and they could not turn back.

The afternoon breeze blew softly against Eric Nordstrom's face as he sat on a pile of furs playing with his chubby ten-month-old daughter, Juanama. ''She looks exactly like you, my love,'' he said, flicking a glance at the woman who watched them with a satisfied smile. Behind him a ray of sunshine splintered through the cave entrance, setting his golden hair on fire.

''It is a pity she has my hair,'' Shala told him, ''but at least she has your grass-green eyes. It is her eyes that would brand you a liar if you ever tried to deny your daughter.''

''I would never even try,'' he laughed, bouncing the little girl on his knee.

Gurgling with delight, the baby reached out with chubby fingers and tangled them through her father's golden beard, giving it a sharp tug.

"Ouch!" Eric protested, pretending pain. "No, no. You must *not* pull Daddy's beard."

"Only our daughter would dare do such a thing," Shala laughed. "None other would have the courage to pull the great Viking's beard."

"Do you dare mock me, woman?" Eric growled, setting his tiny daughter on the bearskin rug in order to curl his fingers around his wife's neck in a most threatening manner.

The little girl watched him smother kisses across her mother's face and shoulders, seeming to take delight in their loveplay for awhile. But, as babies often do, she soon lost interest in her parents and crawled toward the cave entrance.

"Eric," Shala protested, her voice shaking with laughter as her husband began to nibble on her left earlobe. "Stop it this minute!" Cutting her eyes toward their daughter, who was only a few feet from the sunshine streaming in the cave, Shala's voice became alarmed. "Eric! The baby! Stop her!"

Instantly, he put his wife aside and reached out a long arm to capture the squirming infant. Holding her before him, he growled, "You know better than that. You cannot go out alone! It is too dangerous for you out there. You might fall off the cliff."

The baby's face screwed up and, with a loud burst of noise, she objected to her treatment, screaming at the top of her lungs, large tears rolling down her cheeks.

"You scared her, Eric," Shala cried, taking the baby from his arms and cuddling her against her breast. "Shhhhhh, little one," she soothed. "Your father is not angry with you, only frightened of what could happen.

He did not mean to scold." The look she gave her husband was disapproving in the extreme. "You must remember to be gentle with her, Eric. She frightens easily."

"Better for her to be frightened than fall to her death," he answered grimly. "She has to learn to stay in the cave, where it is safe."

"I know," Shala said. "But there is a way to teach her without frightening her to death. You should—"

"Shala! Eric!"

The voice interrupted Shala's scolding. Eric, eager to escape what was fast becoming an argument, hurried across the cave to welcome their visitor.

"Shateh," he said, one golden brow arching in surprise. Then, suddenly remembering his manners, spoke in the custom of the People. "I bid you welcome, Shateh. My wife also bids you welcome. Come into our dwelling and sit with us for a while."

"Would that I could," Shateh replied quickly, making Eric aware his visit was not a social one. "Today I have come at the request of my shaman."

"Nampeyo?" Eric's brow arched higher. "What does the shaman want from me?"

"He bids you come to him," Shateh replied, his gaze turning toward the cliff city across the canyon as though he expected to see something there that was disturbing. "It is a matter of great urgency, so you must hurry."

Wondering what could possibly be so urgent, Eric turned toward his wife, who stood watching quietly. "It seems I must go see the shaman," he said gruffly. "But unless the matter requires immediate attention, I will soon return. Perhaps . . . ." He arched one golden brow. ". . . Perhaps the little one will be asleep at that time?" It was more a request than a question.

Shala's lips quirked at the corners and her ebony eyes twinkled merrily, obviously guessing the way his thoughts had turned. "Who knows," she said, shrugging her shoulders. "She will sleep when she will."

He laughed heartily, leaned over, and kissed her on one tanned cheek, then followed Shateh up the steep slope that led to the mountain top.

Although his legs were long and his stride swift, there was much distance to be covered before Eric reached the cliff above the city. Almost an hour had passed before he descended the steps cut into the stone face. Moments later he strode toward Nampeyo, who sat quietly on the courtyard wall, his legs stretched toward the sun.

Eric frowned when he saw the shaman, for he knew Nampeyo well enough to realize he was troubled about something.

"Greetings, Nampeyo," Eric said. "How are your legs feeling today?"

"Aching, as usual," Nampeyo replied. "But that is not the reason I sent for you."

"I knew that, of course," Eric replied, studying his friend's troubled expression. "Nevertheless, the answer was important to me."

Nampeyo nodded his dark head. "You have proved yourself a friend many times over, Eric. That is why I sent for you. Rest yourself beside me while we speak together."

Although Eric had no need to rest, he seated himself beside the shaman. "I see you are greatly troubled, old friend. What can I do to ease your mind?"

"Perhaps nothing," Nampeyo replied. "Strangers have come to the mesa," he went on, meeting the golden-haired Viking's eyes. "I am told they are men with hair very much like your own."

Eric's eyes darkened to the color of moss. "Blond hair?" he breathed softly, almost afraid to say the words aloud lest the mere utterance would cause the newcomers to disappear. "Vikings?"

"Are Vikings the only men with your hair color?" Nampeyo asked, uneasily.

"No," Eric replied, the light in his eyes slowly disappearing. "They could be from many places other than Norway."

"Why would they come here?"

"I have no idea, but of course, I will go to them and discover their reason." Eric knew if the strangers were not his brothers, searching for him, then everyone who occupied the mesa could very well be in danger.

"They might be dangerous," Nampeyo pointed out.

"Yes," Eric replied. "But if they are, then we must know immediately." His thoughts flew across the canyons to his woman and child, waiting for him in their home, and he felt an urgency to speak with the intruders, to learn why they had come to the mesa. And if they proved to be enemies, then he would find a way to make them leave.

"There is no time to think this out, old friend," he told Nampeyo. "Runners must be sent out. One to summon Shala and the babe, so they can seek shelter here in the cliff city. Then dispatch other runners to the fields to call the men home. Send word to everyone who is not here, telling them they must return with great speed. Then, when everyone is secure in the city, set warriors to guard the steps with orders to kill anyone who tries to descend the cliffs."

"And what about you, Eric?" Nampeyo asked. "What are you planning to do while everyone is hurrying to take shelter?"

"I will go on the mesa to meet those who travel, uninvited, to our land. If they are my people, then no harm will befall me."

"And if they are not?"

"Then only one man need die," Eric said grimly, rising to his feet. "Send the runners out without delay, Nampeyo. And make sure Shala and the babe are here."

"Consider it done, Eric," Nampeyo said, clasping his friend's hand in a hard grip. "May the spirits be with you."

"And with all of you," Eric growled, his eyes spanning the distance to the small cave across the canyon where his wife and babe were. "And, Nampeyo, if I do not return, look after my family for me."

"Consider it done," Nampeyo agreed.

Without another word, Eric left the cliff city and hurried toward what might very well prove to be his death.

Brynna's heart beat with a rapid tattoo as she realized the *skraelings* were slowly closing the circle around them. Nama's words were obviously having no effect on them.

"What should we do?" cried Brynna.

"We can only wait," Nama advised. "Do not provoke them into attacking. They are naturally suspicious of any stranger who comes to the mesa. The Dove Clan, like my own, has many enemies."

"It seems we are included among those enemies," growled Patrick, who reined his mount beside Brynna, obviously hoping to shield her from the savage warriors.

"All people are enemies until proved different," Nama said, watching warily as the warriors drew closer. Raising her voice, she called, "You are making a mistake, Running Wolf. Tell the others to lower their weapons, lest they make enemies of the Eagle Clan! My people would not take kindly to having one of their own killed by your weapons!"

Her words had no effect on the warriors, who continued

to tighten the circle around them. Brynna gripped the jeweled handle of her sword tightly, knowing that soon, there would be nothing left to do except engage in battle, no matter that their own weapons were stronger than the *skraelings'*, and no matter that the Vikings were men of great strength. The odds of winning against so many warriors were not good. Not good at all.

Impulsively, Brynna dug the toes of her boots into Shadow's flanks, at the same time pulling sharply on the reins. The horse reacted as he had been taught, lunging forward and rearing high, pawing at the air with his sharp hooves.

"Brynna!" roared Patrick. "Get back here!"

Ignoring him, Brynna pulled her sword from its scabbard and swung it in a circle. *Whoosh, whoosh, whoosh* went the blade as it cut cleanly through the air.

Muttering among themselves, the warriors fell back, their attention focused on the fiery-haired woman who rode atop the strange beast with sleek ebony hide as though she'd been born there.

Suddenly, a shout sounded from the large pile of rocks behind the *skraelings* and they immediately fell silent, turning as though to face a new threat.

Brynna turned her head, her gaze sweeping the rocks, and she saw a tall man with golden hair dressed in fringed buckskins. Her eyes widened when she saw the sword in his hand.

"Stay your weapons and name yourselves!" his powerful voice rang out.

The voice was so familiar that Brynna could not stop the words from leaving her mouth even had she tried. "Eric!" she shouted. "Is it you who speaks?"

The man turned toward her, lowering his sword.

"Brynna?" his voice questioned. "Is that really you, Brynna?"

"Who else?" she laughed. "If these are your savages, then call them off and come down to us!"

"Lower your weapons, Running Wolf!" Eric commanded, in the tongue of the People. "These are my friends . . . my people." Almost immediately, the ring of warriors began to draw back, allowing Eric to move through the circle until he stood beside his sister. "I cannot believe it," he said, reverting to their own language. Circling Brynna's waist with his large hands, he pulled her from her steed and whirled her around and around. "How did you get here, little sister?"

"The same way you did, of course," she said, sliding her arms around his neck and hugging him tightly, laughing all the while.

Eric. Dear, beloved Eric, her heart sang. He was with her at last!

She studied every line of his face, expecting to see some change there, but except for appearing happier, there was very little.

"I cannot believe this," he muttered, pulling her head away from his chest to gaze into her eyes. "Who brought you here, anyway?"

"I brought myself," she laughed, her eyes devouring him. "I am no longer a child, Eric. I can take care of myself."

"In a pig's eye!" he grunted, lifting his eyes and setting them on Patrick, who was hovering nearby as though he thought Brynna might come to harm. "Who are you?" he demanded.

"Patrick Douglass!"

"Do I know you? How did you come to bring my sister here?" Eric asked shortly. "Have you no sense, man?"

"You know me!" Patrick growled, answering the questions in the order he had received them. "And I did not exactly bring her. She—"

"*I* brought *him*," Brynna interrupted. "Now, shush your fussing, brother. Have you no greeting for anyone else?"

Eric looked at the other men, his gaze stopping on his brother who had remained quiet, watching the reunion. "Garrick! Is that you?" Eric exclaimed.

"None other," Garrick said, leaping from his mount and gripping his brother's hand. "I think you already know this woman." He beckoned Nama forward.

"Nama!" Eric exclaimed joyfully. "You returned with them, after all!"

"You knew she was with me?" Garrick queried.

"Yes. When I discovered she was still alive and not dead, as Shala had imagined, I searched for her. But by the time I reached the river where I knew I would find the longboat, you were already sailing away."

"Just think of that," Garrick replied. "When I sailed away, I thought you were dead. It was only later that I learned differently." He looked reproachfully at Nama, then returned his gaze to his brother. "And to think that you were only a short distance away. Had I known that, this trip would not have been necessary." He stared into his brother's eyes. "Well, brother. Are you ready to leave this godforsaken land?"

"We will speak of such things later," Eric told him evasively. "At the moment, there are people waiting anxiously in the cliff city. They have no idea if you are friend or foe."

"My mother, Ona?" Nama asked quickly. "Is she well?"

"She is well," Eric said with a smile. "And she will be happy to see her daughter."

"I am anxious to see this city built into a cliff," Garrick said. "Nama has spoken of it so often."

"Have patience," Eric told him. "You will see it soon enough." He set his sister aside and turned to the warriors who stood watching. "These are my people," he told them in the language of the People. "They mean no harm to anyone on the mesa. Go to your homes now and be assured that all is well."

"Is Shala well?" inquired Nama, when Eric turned back to face them.

"Well and happy. And so is our daughter."

"A child?" she asked. "Then the babe was unharmed by her mother's captivity?"

"Yes." His expression darkened for a moment. "We were lucky in that respect. Her name is Juanama. We named her after you."

Nama's eyes misted. "Thank you," she said softly. "I am pleased."

"Shala thought you would be."

"It will be good to see my friend again," Nama said. "What about her mother, Gryla?" She was obviously eager for news of her people. "How is she faring? Is she still Keeper of Memories?"

"Yes," he replied. "She is well. And she is training another for her position in the clan."

"Shala?"

"No. Not Shala." He smiled at Nama. "But Shala is happy with the situation, so you need not worry on her account."

"I understand," Nama said softly, "Shala could not take the position when she will soon be leaving her clan for another land."

Instead of replying, Eric turned his attention to his brother. "Tell me what you think of this wild land, Garrick!"

"How much time do you have?" Garrick asked wryly.

"All the time in the world," Eric replied.

The two men walked together across the mesa, deep in conversation, leaving Brynna to follow behind. Somehow, that fact made her feel ignored, less important to her brother than she had been.

The reunion, although sweet, had not been all she had expected. Perhaps, she decided, she had placed too much importance on finding her brother, believing he would be able to solve all her problems. Instead, her problems seemed to have increased tenfold since she'd come to this new land.

Brynna realized she had placed all her hopes on Eric, had thought he could solve all her problems. But he could not. How could he give her back the love she had lost? No one could raise the dead.

Watching the brothers laugh together, Brynna wondered if she had lost Eric as well. She realized she was being silly, that a man would naturally put his wife before his sister, but it was more than that. After that one joyous moment when Eric had welcomed her, his thoughts had immediately turned away from her, became occupied with other things.

Was Shala to blame? Did the woman he had taken for a wife have all his love now? Was there nothing at all left for his sister, not even one little corner of his heart?

Brynna had thought little about the woman he'd married before coming here. Now she did, and she had to wonder if being married would affect her relationship with her brother. Perhaps not, though. Perhaps it was only this land. Perhaps when they returned to Norway, her brother would be the same as always.

A sudden thought intruded. Eric had seemed evasive when Nama had spoken of leaving the mesa. Was it possible that her brother planned to stay here indefinitely? Even now, when he had the means to leave?

Surely not, Brynna told herself. Surely he would see the sense of returning to Norway.

Wouldn't he?

Chapter Twenty-Five

Red Fox began the long trek down the mountain. It was a trip that proved lonely in the extreme, for when he had gone up the mountain, Brynna had walked beside him. Now he was alone, and he felt that aloneness with every fiber of his being.

He had no trouble following the trail, for the hoof prints of their mounts were deeply embedded in the earth. And, as he had imagined it would, the trail led to the vast desert that separated him from the great mesa where the Eagle Clan lived.

Red Fox had plenty of time to think as he followed them. Plenty of time to wonder if Brynna had gone willingly. It was something he had never before considered. But now that he had, he began to think that perhaps she had been taken from him against her will.

That belief, although it made her situation more desperate, eased the pain that lodged in his heart as he traveled across the desert land where no shelter could be found from Father Sun's gaze, nor from Wind Woman's raw, scorching breath that blew continuously, flinging sand and grit across his face and into his stinging eyes.

The desert was immense, inhospitable, without even one stream where he could find fresh water, making it necessary to break open cactus and suck the moisture out of the pulp in order to keep traveling.

He dug roots where he could find them, then ate them while he walked, stopping only for short periods of time to rest his weary body, but for the most part, plodding endlessly forward, one thought in his mind.

Brynna. He would find her, he promised himself. Nothing . . . neither man nor beast . . . could keep him from the woman who had captured his heart.

The hard planes of his face softened as he thought of Brynna, remembering the way she'd looked the last time he had seen her, naked and replete after their lovemaking, her fiery hair tumbling around her, framing the creamy skin of her face and shoulders.

Brynna, he mourned silently. *Light of my life. How can I live without you?* She had made him come alive again, had chased away the shadows that darkened his mind and heart, had healed the scars Sweet Willow had inflicted with her betrayal.

Aching with the need to hold her, Red Fox loped along the trail left by those who had stolen her away, vowing that he would be with her before another moon passed.

Brynna, having descended the stone face with her heart in her throat, stared in awe at the cliff city that was built beneath a cliff overhang. It was located halfway up the steep stone face where no enemy could reach the occupants from above or below.

The three stories of walls and towers that comprised the cliff city squeezed under the cantilevered sandstone ceiling, reaching back deep into the cave where there were dark places, corners, and niches that sunlight could never hope to touch.

"How ingenious," she exclaimed. "Where do those ladders lead?" she asked Eric, who stood beside her.

"To the kivas," he answered shortly, his gaze searching the crowd that stared curiously at the newcomers. "The kivas are ceremonial pit rooms used by the men. You can see how skillfully they have been cut into the stone floor and covered with timbers so the roof becomes part of the village plaza." Suddenly, his roving gaze fastened on a small, dark woman who stood in the shadows. "Look!" he exclaimed. "There is Shala! Come here, Shala!"

Brynna turned to look at the woman who slowly approached them.

"Shala," Eric said, drawing Brynna forward. "This is my sister, Brynna."

Shala was a beautiful woman who, although a head shorter than Brynna, exuded an odd kind of strength. Her eyes were soft, her expression serene, perhaps because of the babe she carried in her arms.

Brynna smiled at the woman who had stolen her brother's heart. "I am happy to meet you, Shala," Brynna said in the woman's own language. "I have heard much about you from Nama." Her gaze went to the little girl who clung tightly to her mother. "Oh," Brynna exclaimed. "She has green eyes."

Shala nodded, a smile playing at her lips. "A fact that I am eternally grateful for. Her eyes make it impossible for him to deny fathering her."

"I am sure he would never do that," Brynna said, puzzled at the look that passed between her brother and his wife. "Even without the green eyes it would be plain to all who cared to see that she is my brother's child."

"Do you think so?" Shala asked, studying the little girl intently. "Do you really see such a likeness?"

"Yes," Brynna replied. "Has no one commented on it before?"

"No. No one."

"Where did you learn to speak her language, Brynna?" Eric asked, a puzzled frown drawing his eyebrows close. Then, suddenly his expression cleared. "Nama! Of course she would teach you. That is good. Now you will be able to converse with the others. Come along now, Brynna," he added, tugging at her arm. "There will be time enough for the two of you to speak together later. Now you must meet the others."

"Nampeyo!" Eric motioned toward a slender man with waist length hair, pulling his sister toward him. "This is my sister, Brynna," he said formally. "She left Norway to search for me. Brynna, Nampeyo is the clan shaman."

"Tell her she is welcome in our city," Nampeyo told Eric.

"You can tell her yourself, since she speaks your language," Eric said with a grin. "Nama taught her."

"Welcome," Nampeyo said formally, his gaze meeting hers for a brief moment before fastening on the fiery curls that framed her face.

"Thank you," Brynna said, wondering if she should curtsy or something. Although she looked to Eric for help, he had already moved to Garrick's side and begun a conversation.

"You have a beautiful city," she remarked, shifting uneasily. For some reason she felt uncomfortable beneath his intent gaze.

"It is a good place to live," he replied.

He was a good six inches shorter than Brynna, and the cane he carried gave her the impression he might be lame.

Her gaze dropped lower and she saw that one leg was crooked. Had he always been that way? she wondered. Or had he perhaps fallen from the cliff and injured himself?

"You look weary, Brynna."

Brynna turned to see Shala standing behind her. "I am weary," Brynna said. "It has been a long journey today." She could have added that being met with armed warriors had played a large part in her weariness, but she held her tongue.

Even so, Shala seemed to guess her sister-in-law's thoughts. "Being faced with a war party instead of a welcome party must have been unnerving."

"To say the least," Brynna replied.

"Our home is small, but you are welcome in it," Shala said. "It is located there." She pointed across the canyon to a spot halfway up the opposite cliff.

"What about the others?" Brynna asked, feeling she would rather be alone.

"There are many unused rooms in the city," Shala replied. "Nampeyo has given orders they are to be prepared for guests."

"If there is an extra one available and you would not be offended, then I would like to stay here as well," Brynna replied.

"I would not be offended," Shala said. "There is a room prepared near my mother's apartment. Come with me. I will take you there."

Feeling suddenly overcome with weariness, Brynna followed Shala across the courtyard to a room located on the fourth floor. The sleeping mat looked inviting. She looked at it with longing and Shala, obviously guessing the extent of her weariness, left her alone.

Moments later, Brynna was fast asleep.

* * * *

It was late. Everyone slept except Nampeyo, who stood alone in the courtyard, considering everything that had happened that day. He realized that part of his vision had already come true. Nama, his childhood love, had finally returned to the cliff city.

But what of the golden globe the dream had foretold? Nama had offered him no gift, other than the friendship of the Vikings she had brought with her.

Perhaps that was it. Perhaps that was all the vision meant . . . and yet . . . he thought about the Viking girl, Brynna, remembering the way she had looked with her fiery hair floating about her shoulders. When she had smiled at him, the whole world had seemed brighter. Could it be that she represented the golden globe Nama had offered him in the vision?

He thought that might be the answer. Which led to another question: in the vision, the raven had laughed and said he had waited too long, that another had captured the sun.

The wolf?

The warrior?

Which one? How was he to know? He had consulted the spirits but they had remained silent, either unwilling or unable to decipher the vision. Then, in the dream, it had been the wolf who had taken the globe, catching it in his jaws. But in the dream it was the Wolf Clan warrior who had captured her. And that was after he had already slain the eagle.

Nampeyo realized he must decipher the rest of the dream, knew it must be important to his clan, otherwise he would not have been plagued with it in both the dream and the vision.

He only hoped he could comprehend its meaning before it was too late. Because Raven was right: he always seemed to be too late.

* * *

The early morning sunshine knifed through the small opening which served for a window in Brynna's bedchamber, dancing across her eyelids and eliciting a moan that woke her.

Opening sleep-fogged eyes, Brynna looked up at the stone ceiling six feet above her. "Red Fox?" she murmured softly.

When there was no answer, she turned her head and saw that she was alone in the room. It was then the cobwebs flew from her mind and she remembered all that had come before . . . remembered, and wished that she had remained ignorant.

She closed her eyes again, attempting to go back to sleep again, for her dreams had contained her love, breathing and laughing and walking beside her through a verdant green forest filled with every kind of wildflower imaginable. But even though she tried her best, she could not drift into blissful sleep again.

"Brynna? Are you awake yet?"

Brynna recognized Nama's voice, calling from just outside her door. "Yes," she answered. "Just barely, though. Would you like to come in while I dress?"

"No. I shall wait out here. But hurry. There is so much I want to show you."

There was such happiness in Nama's voice that Brynna felt a sudden hatred for the other girl stab through her. Instantly she was ashamed. Nama bore the blame for what had happened to Red Fox. She should not be made to pay the price for his death.

His death.

Yes.

He was dead.

And nothing she could ever do would bring him back.

If thinking of him brought such misery, then better to put him out of her thoughts until she could do otherwise, until she could forget the circumstances of his death and remember only the good times together, the pleasure she had felt by simply giving and receiving love.

"Brynna?" Nama called again. "Did you sleep well last night?"

"Very well," Brynna replied, reaching for her shift and sliding it over her head. "The sleeping mat felt wonderful. And the blanket, Nama ... It is so lovely. How is it made?"

"It is woven from yucca fiber and turkey feathers," Nama said, peeping around the door. "My mother made that particular one. She told me this morning that she had brought it to you." Nama smoothed her hands across the beautiful feathered blanket. "I used to sit and watch her at her weaving. If I practiced forever I would never be able to make such fine blankets."

"I am sure you are wrong," Brynna said. "These blankets would be worth their weight in gold at the markets. We should take some home with us. Do you think your people might be interested in trading with us?"

"My people love trading," Nama laughed.

"We have nothing as fine as these blankets to offer," Brynna said.

"You have many things that would be desirable," Nama assured her. "But there will be time to do things of that nature later. At the moment, the women are waiting for us. We are going berry picking."

"Berry picking?" Brynna's stomach suddenly growled and she laughed. "That would suit my stomach just fine."

The two girls went out to join the other women.

* * *

It was several nights later, after visiting Brynna, that Shala found herself unable to sleep. Each time she tried, a memory of Brynna's sad eyes surfaced in her mind.

"Eric?"

"Hmmmm?"

Although Shala realized Eric was half asleep, she knew she would be unable to rest until her curiosity was satisfied. "Eric," she said again. "Why has Brynna never married?"

"Brynna is too young for marriage," he replied, stifling a wide yawn.

"Has she never thought of marriage before?"

"A marriage was planned," he said gruffly. "That is the reason she left Norway. She wanted me to put a stop to it."

"I see," Shala said thoughtfully. "Is that why she looks so sad? Because she was being forced into a marriage she did not want?"

If that was the case, then Shala could sympathize with her sister-in-law, having been in that same situation herself only two summers ago.

Shu, who had been clan shaman at the time, had tried to force her to marry him. By refusing to obey his will, Shala had become an outcast from her clan. It was only when Shu fell from the cliff to his death that she had been able to return. For although Nampeyo was Shu's son, he held different views than had his father, and had wasted no time in restoring her to her clan.

Lucky for me, Shala silently told herself. *Or else I would still be an outcast.*

"Brynna looks sad?" Eric questioned, pulling her from her thoughts. "I had not noticed. Are you sure about that, Shala?"

"Yes," she replied. "I am surprised you had not noticed."

"I guess I am inclined to take things as they appear."

"Her feelings do not show on the surface, but it is easy to look beyond and see the pain that lies within."

"She has no reason to be sad," Eric muttered, seeming to take offense at the news. "I would never allow her to be wed against her will. Even if I must go against my father's wishes."

"But you are not planning to return to Norway," Shala reminded him. "You have told me so time and time again. How, then, can you help her?"

"Garrick will do it for me," he assured her. "I have already spoken to him on the matter."

"You must speak to her as well," Shala said shortly. "Brynna cannot read your mind."

"I will. Tomorrow. She must be reassured on the matter."

"Speak with her alone, Eric," Shala said quickly. "I have a feeling she will tell you nothing when others are about."

"Of course," he said gruffly. "I intended to do just that. I guess I could take her hunting with me. Brynna always liked to hunt with me." His voice sounded almost wistful, as though he had only just realized how much time had passed.

"Then do that," Shala murmured, snuggling close to him. "Now, forget about your sister and pay attention to me."

He seemed happy enough to do just that.

Chapter Twenty-Six

It was barely first light when Brynna heard someone calling her name from outside her bedchamber. Recognizing the voice of her brother, Eric, and wondering what he could want at this hour, Brynna crawled from her bed and rose to her feet, snatching up the turkey feather blanket to cover her nakedness.

"Is something wrong, Eric?" she asked, having pushed aside the entrance flap and poked her head outside.

"Nothing, little sister," he replied, leaning against the courtyard wall. "That is a beautiful garment of turkey feathers you are wearing this morning."

"Did you wake me just to tease?" she scolded, clutching the blanket tighter, lest it should slip.

"No. Actually, I came to extend an invitation to hunt with me. But since you are so intent on your sleep . . ."

He turned as though he were on the point of leaving, and even though she knew he was only teasing, she called out quickly. "Wait, Eric. It will only take a moment for me to dress."

Eager to accompany him, she snatched up her garments and quickly donned them. After pulling on her boots, she joined Eric in the courtyard.

"Thank you for inviting me," she said quickly. "If you had not done so, I would probably have spent my day berry picking with the women again. Have you brought me a weapon? I have only my sword."

"Shala's bow and arrow are waiting for you on the mesa," he replied. "I thought it would be better left up there since you have the climb ahead of you."

After they were atop the mesa, Brynna allowed herself a moment's rest. She breathed deeply, filling her lungs with the early morning air, finding it sharp, crisp, and cool.

"This early in the morning, the air is much like that of Norway," Eric commented, watching his sister intently. "Do you miss our homeland, Brynna?"

"Miss it?" she asked, feeling puzzled. "No. Why should I?"

"Our parents are there," he said quickly. "Surely you miss them?"

"Sometimes . . . when I have time to think about it, then I miss Mother," she replied. "But it is the way with all living creatures to grow up and leave home, to make other homes for themselves. As you have done, Eric."

"Yes, well." He coughed abruptly. "I am a man, little sister. Not dependent on home and hearth."

"Neither am I," she stated emphatically, wondering exactly where this conversation was leading. "Are we hunting, Eric? Or are we going to stand here all day and talk?"

"We are hunting," he said, with a glint of humor. Bending over, extracted a bow and arrow from beneath a bush. "Shala said you were to keep this."

"She gave it to me?"

"Yes. She has another." He strode quickly toward the woods. "Come along, little sister. Game should be seeking water soon. And we will be at their watering hole waiting, when they do."

It took barely an hour to reach the waterhole and only moments more to find the best place where they could watch and wait for the game that was almost sure to arrive. Although it was their usual practice to wait in silence, Eric seemed inclined to talk.

"I wanted this time alone with you for another reason, Brynna," he said slowly, as though unsure how to proceed.

"Was there any particular reason?" she asked.

"No," he denied. "Just that I have been wondering about you."

"Why?"

"You seem different somehow. Quite unlike the little sister I left behind." His green eyes were intent, as though he was trying to see her innermost thoughts.

"I am different," she replied lightly. "But I am older, too—by almost three years. You were gone a long time." A long time. Much had happened since she had last seen him. She blinked rapidly, realizing her eyes were moist with tears, and she would not allow herself the weakness of tears. "Why did you stay away so long, Eric?"

"It was not my intention to do so, but then things happened. I heard about this new land Lief Erickson had discovered and instead of going home, I came here to explore it. And I met Shala."

"She is a beautiful woman, and the baby is precious. You are lucky to have them."

"Yes." He agreed with a wry smile. "Shala is very beautiful. And I realize how lucky I am. But getting back to your problem—"

Realizing he must have heard the story of why she had left Norway, Brynna said, "Father expects me to wed Angus. But I am not willing to do so."

"Then you must not wed him," Eric assured her. "I am surprised Garrick did not offer his help."

"I went to him for help," she said, "but he refused to intercede for me, claiming for a reason that he thought I needed a firm hand to guide me." She looked away from him. "He said Angus would provide the firm hand."

"Have no fear," he said, tilting her head toward him again, forcing her to meet his eyes. "I will speak to Garrick. You need fear no longer that you will be made to wed Angus." He waited for a long moment as though expecting some reaction from her that she had not shown. Then, "Do you not believe me, Brynna?"

"Of course," she replied. "You have always been a man of your word, Eric. If you say I shall not wed Angus, then I know 'tis true."

"Then why are the shadows still in your eyes, little one? Why is your smile only on your lips?"

Little one.

That was Red Fox's pet name for Brynna, and the use of it broke down her resolve to suffer her pain in silence. To her utter mortification, she broke down and cried.

"Brynna, little sister, what makes you so sad?" Eric asked, pulling her into his arms and patting her shoulder, trying his best to console her.

The unqualified love she heard in his voice was Brynna's undoing. Without another thought, she told him everything that had occurred since she had arrived in this new land. And when she finished speaking, she looked up to see him watching her with a coldness in his eyes that had not been there before.

Hiccuping, she moved away from him and wiped her eyes with the backs of her hands, wondering what part of her story had brought on that reaction from him. He was angry, she could tell, but there was something more in his expression. Disapproval? Of her? If not, then who?

"Does Garrick know about this?" he asked, his voice grating harshly against her ears.

"No. Nobody knows, except for Patrick and Lacey."

"Why has Garrick not been told?"

"B-because I d-did not want—" She stopped, angry at herself for losing control. Taking a deep breath, she went on in a calmer voice. "Garrick could not expect to be told after the way he reacted when I asked him for help before. Besides, I could not speak of it to anyone. Not even Nama, who has become as close to me as a sister. The pain of losing Red—Red F-Fox was—was almost m-more than I could b-bear. Still is more than—than—" Suddenly, her fragile control broke and Brynna began to cry again.

Although Eric patted her shoulder awkwardly, he did not take her in his arms again, and when Brynna was finally able to get herself under control again, she peeked up at him from the fringe of her lashes and saw the grimness in his face.

Eric would have made things all right for her if he were able, she knew. He was angry even now at the thought of his sister's pain, and somehow, that knowledge served to make her own pain easier to bear.

"Come," he said gruffly. "We will delay our hunt until another day. There are things I must do now that are more important." He squeezed her shoulder again, then gave it an awkward pat. "Put your mind at ease, Brynna. I am here now. I will take care of you. You need not concern yourself with what cannot be helped."

With those cryptic words ringing in her ears, Brynna followed him back to the cliff dwellings.

* * *

Brynna would have been astounded, and furious as well, had she overheard the conversation taking place between her two brothers near the corral where the horses were confined. But she did not, remaining instead blissfully unaware of it.

"The *skraeling* captured her?" Garrick asked, a muscle working in his jaw.

"And raped her," Eric replied.

"Damn him to hell!" Garrick roared. "If Patrick had not already slain him, then I would hunt him down and skin him alive."

Eric had expected such a reaction from his brother. It was the reason he had taken him on the mesa before revealing what he had just learned, using the excuse of checking out the rope corral where the horses were confined.

"Better that Patrick did the killing," Eric said, hearing the sour note in his voice. "Because Brynna fancied herself in love with the savage."

"The devil she did!"

"So she says."

"It was probably the only way her mind could deal with what had been done to her," Garrick replied.

"Patrick Douglass has a lot to answer for," Eric stated grimly, just as the man in question left the woods nearby and strode toward the corral.

Obviously overhearing, he altered his course and strode toward them. "Did I hear my name?" he asked.

"You did," Eric said grimly. "We have just learned of what transpired after you left the longboat."

"And what is that?" Patrick asked, his eyes not revealing a thing as they flicked back and forth between the two men.

"You know damn well what it is!" Garrick snarled. "Why did you not tell me that Brynna had been taken captive by the *skraelings?* Why was it left to her to tell us that she had been raped and God knows what else?"

"She said that? Told you she had been raped?" Patrick asked, arching one bushy brow.

"She might just as well have done so. But of course, she put a fancy name on it and called it love. But what else could she have done, under the circumstances? A girl with as much sensitivity as my sister could never live with herself if she were to admit, even to herself, that she had been taken by one of these savages. But that is neither here nor there. You were asked why you did not tell either of us what had happened."

"The answer is quite simple," Patrick said shortly. "It was not up to me to tell others what had happened to her. I knew if the lass wanted anyone else to know, she would tell them herself!"

"You have a lot to answer for," Eric said grimly, his hands clenching into fists, feeling the urge to batter the other man's face.

"How do you figure that?" Patrick asked.

"If you had not aided her in her flight, she would still be safe in Norway."

"And wed to Angus Sigurdson!" Patrick reminded shortly.

"There are worse things than being wed to Angus Sigurdson," Garrick replied.

"Do you agree with your brother?" Patrick asked, his gaze on Eric.

"Yes," Eric said grimly. "I *do* agree. Brynna could have died from her treatment at the hands of that savage. At least with Angus Sigurdson, she would live a protected life."

"And a miserable one," Patrick said shortly. "And to

think she came all this way, believing you would help her. You! Her precious brother, who could do no wrong. Every day of that long journey here, all she could speak of was her brother, Eric, and how he would take care of everything. How he would keep her from wedding a man she did not want." His lips curled scornfully. "She might just as well have stayed home, for all the good you will do her."

"Enough!" Eric shouted. "If I had my sword I would run you through."

"You could try," Patrick said grimly. "But you might just be surprised."

"Some kind of problem here?" A voice asked from behind them.

Eric's lips curled with contempt. He might have known Lacey would be somewhere nearby. The two men, Lacey and Patrick, were as alike as two peas in a pod.

"No problem," Patrick replied. "The brothers have only just found out what our lady meant to keep secret. They hold me to blame for helping her leave Norway."

"Then I insist they blame me, too," Lacey said, his lips curling slightly in a smile that was not reflected in his eyes. "Because it's a fact that I did every bit as much as you to help the lassie escape that potbellied fool."

"We are well aware of that," Garrick snarled. "And I have a good notion to leave you here in this land when I leave."

"Maybe that would suit me well enough!" Lacey replied grimly.

"Is something wrong?"

Eric and the other men spun around to find Brynna watching them from a distance. Thor's Teeth! He might just as well have had this confrontation in the middle of the city, with all its occupants looking on. He waited for either Patrick Douglass or Lacey to enlighten his sister.

"What is the trouble here?" she demanded, her blue gaze flicking from one to the other of them.

"Nothing, lass," Patrick replied with a wry smile. "We were just having a little discussion. But I think we have finished it already." His gaze swept over the two brothers. "If either of you disagrees with me, then feel free to look me up later."

With that, he strode away at a ground-eating pace with Lacey following close on his heels, leaving Eric to give whatever explanation he could to his sister.

Chapter Twenty-Seven

Red Fox crouched low as he ran, making his way through the thick growth of bushes, careful not to brush against anything that might cause a sound, knowing sentries would be posted by the Eagle Clan atop the mesa.

If he was lucky, they would be unable to distinguish him from the bushes unless they chanced to look straight at him while he was moving. He hoped in that manner to reach the cover of the rocks that had tumbled from the mesa to lay in a jumbled heap on the valley floor.

A flicker of movement to his right sent his hand plunging toward the knife sheathed at his waist. His fingers wrapped around the handle, gripped hard as he spun to face the unknown . . .

. . . A furry brown rabbit with quivering nose and large, round eyes.

Chiding himself for being so easily spooked, yet knowing as well that it was the best way to ensure survival, Red Fox circled around a fallen rock the height and width of a man and scanned the dry wash that lay directly ahead of him.

Although Red Fox could sense movement there, he knew the fallen boulders beyond would provide an excellent hiding place for his enemies. His gaze probed the area continually, for he dared not relax his guard. The cost for doing so was much too high, for, since the Eagle Clan and the Wolf Clan were enemies, Red Fox felt certain that if he were caught in their territory, he would surely pay with his life.

Seeing nothing among the rocks to cause him concern, Red Fox made a mad dash toward the dry wash, landing with a heavy thud against the bottom. He stayed there for a long moment to allow his heartbeat to slow, then carefully rose and looked over the edge.

Still no movement.

Leaping outward, he covered the distance to the boulders in a heartbeat, then sank behind the nearest one and leaned his back against it, realizing he needed to rest before climbing the mesa.

Brynna.

Brynna.

Brynna.

His heart beat out her name. She was close now, so very, very, close. He could almost feel her touch against his cheek, almost hear the whisper of her small feet as they ran across the grass toward him, could almost—

Alarm crawled its way up his spine as Red Fox realized he was actually hearing the whisper of racing feet. He spun quickly on his heels.

Just in time. A warrior, young and agile, leapt forward, knife hand raised, ready to strike at the enemy who dared invade his territory.

With a wild cry, Red Fox leapt to his feet and kicked

out, striking his opponent's knife hand just below the wrist. The warrior grunted with pain and his knife spun away, landing with a loud *clunk* among the rocks.

Whirling around, Red Fox delivered another kick; the blow landed on his opponent's stomach and the man fell to his knees.

As Red Fox leapt toward him, his knife hand raising for the kill, the other warrior scrambled for the knife he had lost. His fingers found it and wrapped around the weapon and he leapt to his feet again, at the same time spinning toward Red Fox, raising his hand and bringing it down in a blow that would have cut through flesh and bone had it landed on his target.

But it did not.

Red Fox had already thrown himself aside, and while his opponent was still trying to find him, the warrior from the Wolf Clan lunged forward again and with a single downward stroke of his blade, quickly killed the warrior from the Eagle Clan.

The more Brynna learned about the cliff dwellers, the more she became fascinated by them and their lives. They were extraordinary people, gracious and dignified, always willing to lend a hand where it was needed, and eager to learn anything she might be able to teach them. There were many occasions when she wished she had paid more attention to her mother's teachings.

Late one evening, several days after she had found the men conversing angrily on the mesa—a matter that was never explained to her satisfaction—Brynna sat in the courtyard weaving a basket and watching the children at play.

"Brynna?"

Hearing her name, Brynna looked up to see Nama approaching with two other women much older than herself.

When she realized the newcomers were Nama's mother, Ona, and Gryla, the Keeper of Memories, Brynna laid her basket aside and stood up to greet them, affording them the respect they deserved.

"Come sit with me," Brynna said formally.

After the women were seated and the proper greetings were exchanged, Nama said, "We have a request to make of you."

Brynna smiled at her. "Just tell me what you wish and if it is possible, consider that wish granted."

"Our Keeper of Memories wishes to know more about your people," Nama said softly. "She came to me for help, but I find I have no answers for many of her questions."

Brynna smiled at Gryla and included Ona in that smile. "I feel privileged that you came to me. Feel free to ask whatever you wish."

"Thank you," Gryla said, returning Brynna's smile. "Have you been told of our way of knowing what occurred in the past?"

"Yes," Brynna acknowledged. "I am told the past is held in your mind alone. And I must admit, that concerns me."

"How so?" Gryla asked.

"Suppose something unexpected happened to you. Would the past be dead? Or is there another who would be able to carry your knowledge to your descendants?"

"If I were to depart from the world of the living today, most of my knowledge would go with me," Gryla said gravely. "The matter concerns me greatly because many things in our past have already been lost to us. There have been other Keepers of Memories who left this world before their time without first training another to replace them.''

''Why do you not train your replacement from childhood?'' Brynna asked.

''It is the way of things,'' Ona interrupted quickly, casting a quick look at Gryla, as though wondering if the woman might have taken the question as criticism. ''And Gryla had already begun training her replacement long ago, but things happen—'' She broke off and shrugged as though unable to continue.

''Yes,'' Gryla said, seeming not the least put out that Ona had answered for her. ''Each Keeper of Memories— myself included—selects a new Keeper of Memories from the beginning of her rule and teaches that girl from early childhood the things she must know, but as Ona has already said, sometimes things happen that are unforeseen. Things we cannot control . . .'' She threw a questioning look at Nama who apparently did not notice. ''. . . Things that prevent those we have chosen from continuing their education.''

''Are you allowed to say who you have chosen?'' Brynna asked.

''Yes. Everyone knows.'' Her lips tightened and her eyes glittered darkly. ''Everyone, from the shaman to the smallest child, knows the identity of the next Keeper of Memories. None are left in doubt.''

''How do you go about selecting someone to hold that position?''

''It is quite simple. If the Keeper of Memories has a daughter, then she is always the one chosen to replace her mother.''

''So Shala is the one who will hold your position when you can no longer fill it?''

''No.'' There was bitterness in Gryla's voice now. ''Shala was unable to fill the position, so another was selected in her place."

"Why could Shala not take your place?" Brynna asked, wondering about the bitterness the other woman felt. "Was it because of my brother?"

For a moment there was quiet, then Nama said, "Brynna knows what occurred, Gryla."

The woman frowned at her. "You told a stranger of my daughter's shame?"

"Shame! There was no shame involved!" Nama denied quickly. "There could be no shame! Anyone of the women, had they been blessed with Shala's courage, would have reacted in the same way . . . there were none of us who would willing have become the wife of a man like Shu."

"Nama is right," Brynna said, realizing what was bothering the other woman. "Shala is not to be held in shame for refusing to marry a man she had no desire for." She lifted her chin proudly. "Have you not been told that is the reason I left my home in Norway? I too, refused to marry a man who was being forced on me! To avoid marriage with him, I ran away and began the search for my brother. That is how I come to be here."

Gryla's eyes widened. "Your shaman wanted to join with you, too?"

Brynna laughed. "We have no shaman. It was my father who wished the marriage. He wanted the possessions such a marriage would bring to him."

Gryla nodded wisely. "So it was with me. Our fathers might have felt differently, though, if they were the ones who were forced to join with one they did not wish."

Again, Brynna laughed. Then she sobered. "Since Shu is no longer shaman, could Shala not be considered for your position?"

"Yes. She could. It is by her own request that she is no longer being taught the past."

"Because of my brother Eric?"

"No. Because of the girl who was chosen in her stead. Shala said it would not be right to take the position from her once it had been promised."

"How like Shala," Brynna said, "My brother selected his bride wisely, Gryla. Your daughter is not only beautiful outside where all can see. There is a greater beauty kept hidden inside as well."

Gryla nodded, accepting the compliment as though it were her due. Which it was, Brynna knew, for Gryla was the woman who had given birth to her daughter. Had it not been for the Keeper of Memories, Shala would not exist.

Remembering the reason the women had approached her, Brynna said, "Ask your questions of me, Gryla, and I will answer to the best of my knowledge. Then I would like to tell you about another way of remembering your past, another way that will not depend on the knowledge of one person."

"I would be interested in this way," Gryla admitted. "Perhaps we should speak of it first."

"Among my people, we use written words. Words that are formed by letters written down on—" Realizing they would not understand about paper, she substituted another word. "—bark. Or something else that is portable. That can be carried for long distances. I was fortunate enough to learn those words. If I could teach the written word to you, then you could have something more substantial than memories to record your past." Her gaze swept the ground, searching for something to demonstrate with, and stopped on a slender stick one of the children had been playing with.

Gripping it between her fingers, she looked out over the canyon and saw an eagle soaring on the wind currents.

Eagerly, she bent over and used a sharp stick to write a sentence on the ground. "Look," she said, "Those scratches I made have a meaning."

"I see no picture there," Gryla said. "Only scratches like the turkeys make."

"That is because this is only a word picture," Brynna said.

Realizing the women were still confused, Brynna explained. "Each of these marks represents a word." She told them each meaning then said, "Put them all together like that and they read, 'The eagle is flying.'"

"Why do you not draw an eagle flying? That is the way we would do it."

"Because this way is better. You are limited to what you can say using picture words. This way, you could say so many more things." Realizing she had not used a very good example, she rubbed out "flying" and scratched the word "sad." "Now," she said, "It reads, 'the eagle is sad.'" Handing Gryla the pointed stick, she said, "You draw a picture that means the same thing."

"Sad?" Gryla murmured, staring at the words drawn in the dirt. "There is no way to show a sad eagle."

Nampeyo, who had been listening to the discussion from nearby, moved closer and peered at the words drawn into the ground. "Anyone would know the meaning of the marks you have made?" he asked with interest.

"Anyone who learned how to read them," she replied.

"Could you demonstrate this?" he asked.

"Yes. I guess so," Brynna replied, looking around the courtyard for someone to help her. Although a crowd had begun to gather, obviously eager to learn what was going on, neither her brothers nor her men were in sight. "One of my own people could read what I have written," she explained, "but since they are not here, then it will be necessary to wait."

Nampeyo was obviously unwilling to wait, for he beckoned one of the men to him. "Shateh," he said. "Go to the golden men and tell one of them to come to me."

Brynna had not expected such excitement over the words written on the ground. The crowd gathered closer, having been told what was happening, eager to see the miraculous words that told of a sad eagle.

Soon, Patrick approached them, a look of utter confusion on his face. "Is something wrong, Brynna?" he asked anxiously, his gaze skittering from her to the crowd that pressed close. "Shateh came to me, gibbering in that language of theirs, and the only thing I could understand was your name."

"Nothing is wrong, Patrick," she said, smiling to reassure him. "I am just demonstrating the art of the written word to them." She pointed to the markings she had made. "Please read that for me."

He looked down at the scratches and a red flush crept up his neck. "I am sorry to disappoint you, my lady," he said ruefully. "But I am afraid that I never learned how to read."

"He cannot decipher the marks?" Nampeyo asked, obviously disappointed.

"Apparently not," Brynna said wryly. "But my brothers could. They learned to read and write at an early age." She looked around, but neither man was there. Only Lacey, who had come to see what was going on.

"I can read it for them, my lady," Lacey said, sauntering up to them.

"You?"

"Yes." He smiled wryly. "Believe it or not, I was sent to school." He looked down at the ground, pointing to each word in turn. "It says, 'The eagle is sad.'"

Although Lacey could not translate the words into those of the people, Nampeyo realized by Nama's expression that he had correctly deciphered the marks.

"Do another," Nampeyo said eagerly. "But this time send the man away so he will not know what words are being set down." When Lacey was well out of hearing, Nampeyo bent closer to Brynna. "Set down this," he ordered. "Nampeyo wishes his legs were not crippled."

Brynna felt a curious tightness in her throat and realized it was sympathy for the young shaman. But, realizing that he would not welcome her pity, she gave no sign of her feelings, concentrating instead on scratching out the words that he had requested of her. When she finished, she lifted her head and called, "Lacey. We are ready for you!"

He strode quickly toward them, then frowned down at the words written on the ground. Finally, he looked up at her. "I have never seen that first word, my lady." There was a collective sigh from the audience as Nama quickly translated for them. The crowd began to turn away, but stopped as Lacey continued, "But since the other words read, 'Wishes his legs were not crippled,' then I guess the first word must be 'Nampeyo.'"

When Nama had translated for her people, the crowd began to murmur softly, seeming awed that anyone could find a meaning in the scratches on the ground.

Nampeyo was not yet satisfied, though. He looked at the scratches that meant words again. "Write something else," he ordered. "You!" He looked up at Lacey. "You, go away until we call you."

Brynna translated Nampeyo's words for Lacey, who grinned widely, obviously enjoying himself. "Go," Brynna ordered, pointing to the edge of the cliff city.

Lacey quickly obeyed, going even farther than she had ordered, seeming as eager as a young boy would have been had he been asked to demonstrate his ability.

Brynna turned back to Nampeyo who was frowning down at the ground again. "Write . . ." Nampeyo broke off, obviously trying hard to think of something that could not easily be described with pictures. "Write, 'The cliff city keeps us safe from our enemies. Here, we are warmed by Father Sun and sheltered by Mother Earth. Our people have lived long and prospered here and we will never be driven out by our enemies.'" He looked up at Brynna. "Is there enough room for all that?" he asked anxiously.

"It takes little room for words," she said with a smile, her hands already working the stick, carving the letters into the space between them.

Soon it was ready and Lacey was again called to read what had been written. After he had done so, Nampeyo looked at Gryla, Keeper of Memories. "This is good, Gryla," he said. "We must learn this way of recording our past and our present. Of stating our hopes for the future. Do you not agree?"

"I am in complete agreement," she replied, looking at Brynna. "A thing such as this would have many uses."

"Yes," Brynna replied. "Messages can be put down on small pieces of bark using charcoal to write with. Then they could be carried for long distances."

"Could you teach me this?" Nampeyo asked.

"I can teach you and any others who care to learn," Brynna replied.

"Many at once?" Nampeyo asked, his eyes flashing darkly. "If I am to send messages, then others must know the written word in order to decipher them."

"Yes," she said, smiling at him. "That is so. And I can teach many at once. Yourself included, if you are so inclined."

"I *am* so inclined," he said gravely. "When will the teaching begin?"

"Tomorrow?" she asked.

"Yes," he said eagerly. "Tomorrow is good." He rose slowly to his feet and rubbed his legs as though they pained him greatly. "It is good you have come, Brynna," he told her. "I think you have been sent to us by the helping spirits."

She laughed heartily. "Before tomorrow is over, you may be cursing me heartily."

"I would never do that," he said hastily. "Never in this life would I curse any human being. To do so would doom them to wander forever in eternity."

"I was only speaking in jest," she explained.

"A curse is nothing to jest about," he said. "You are a friend, Brynna. And will always be treated with great respect. And this clan will count itself lucky to have you among them."

Feeling as though she had made many new friends, Brynna retired to her sleeping apartment and went to bed.

Perhaps, she thought, she might have some use in this life after all.

Chapter Twenty-Eight

Halfway up the steep slope leading to the mesa, Red Fox realized he was being followed. There was something puzzling about the pursuer, though. He moved with such carelessness, giving away his presence in so many ways, that it almost seemed deliberate. But why? Could he want Red Fox to know he was approaching?

Unthinkable.

But if he intended to keep his approach silent, why did he walk on fallen branches and leaves that could easily have been avoided?

Yes. It was puzzling, Red Fox decided. What kind of hunter would be so careless and allow its quarry to know it was being hunted? Not one of the Eagle Clan warriors.

But then, perhaps the noise *was* deliberate. Perhaps the hunter *wanted* his quarry to hear him! Perhaps it was all part of some plan.

The corners of Red Fox's lips lifted slightly. Did whoever followed think he was foolish? Did the hunter think Red Fox would not guess what he planned? Warriors from all over, including those from the Wolf Clan, hunted pheasant in that same manner. Several warriors would show themselves and beat the bushes to drive the quail from their hiding places, and when the birds took flight, the warriors who had remained in hiding would loose their arrows after the hapless birds. In that way, many could be slain at once.

They forgot one thing, though, Red Fox silently told himself. *I am no quail. They cannot fool me so easily.*

Taking refuge behind a mountain rosebush, large enough to have hidden two men, Red Fox dropped to the ground and lay motionless, his knife in his hand.

His tanned flesh and buckskin blended well with the shadows, and he knew he had every chance of surprising whoever followed him.

Crack, snap, pop! The sound was conspicuously loud as the hunter came closer, and Red Fox knew he had to be right. The noise was deliberately made so that he could hear the hunter approach. He was closer now . . . so close that Red Fox could actually hear him treading across the heavy mat of juniper needles that Red Fox himself had so recently circled around.

The hunter who, unbeknownst to him, had become the quarry came into sight. Although darkness covered the land, the full moon outlined the newcomer well enough that Red Fox felt a mild surprise at the man's height, which appeared very near his own.

Red Fox had been told the Eagle Clan were smaller people. It was a fact that Shala and Nama were both small, but the sentry who had attacked Red Fox had only been half a head shorter than himself.

Suddenly, as though sensing something not quite right ahead, the hunter stopped short of the bush and held something out before him, something that was long and slender, much like a snake, yet unlike a snake, it was motionless.

The newcomer's eyes searched the way ahead, passing over the rose bush that effectively hid Red Fox. "I know someone is there," he called out. "Come out of hiding. We have no quarrel with each other. I am here on peaceful business."

Peaceful business? Did the man think Red Fox was a fool? Did he think Red Fox would allow himself to be seen and—

Suddenly the man turned and Red Fox realized he carried a heavy pack on his back. Immediately, Red Fox looked at the long, thin object again and recognized it for what it was! a trader's staff.

The man spoke the truth, Red Fox realized, feeling utterly foolish. He was a trader, friend to all, enemy to none.

Although Red Fox felt ridiculous hiding from such a man, circumstances deemed he remain wary. Not of the trader, but of any who might chance upon them, for unlike the trader, he was in enemy territory.

He considered staying where he was, allowing the trader to think he had already departed, therefore going on his way.

Yet even as the thought occurred, Red Fox realized he could not, for the trader was obviously headed for the Eagle Clan with his wares, and if he happened to mention running across a man who refused to stand and be recognized, it would surely alert them to his presence among them. On the other hand—

Slowly, an idea began to take form in Red Fox's mind. Perhaps he could use the trader to his own advantage.

With that in mind, Red Fox rose from his hiding place behind the bush and slid his knife in its sheathe. "I did not recognize you for a trader," he explained, stepping toward the other man. "I thought you might have killing me in mind."

The trader studied him for a long moment. "You are a stranger, not of the Eagle Clan," he said. "Yet you are in their land."

Although it was a statement, Red Fox realized it was also a question and answered accordingly. "Yes. And you guessed right. I am not of the Eagle Clan. I am Red Fox, from the Wolf Clan."

The trader sighed. "I was afraid of that." He lowered his pack to the ground. "My name is Black Crow and I have not eaten since early morn, Red Fox. You are welcome to share my meal." He squatted on his heels and dug through his pack, extracting two pieces of dried meat. "Here," he said, passing one to the warrior who was still standing. "Sit with me for a while and we will work together for a solution to this problem."

"Problem?" Red Fox inquired, biting into the jerked meat. "I see no problem. You are a trader, and I have no quarrel with traders."

"Neither have I a quarrel with you," Black Crow said. "Yet, still there remains a problem."

"How so?" Red Fox inquired, pretending surprise.

"How can I continue on my way, knowing you are encroaching upon enemy lands?" He eyed Red Fox shrewdly. "Exactly what does a warrior from the Wolf Clan seek in the lands of the Anasazi?"

Red Fox decided to answer honestly. "I seek my woman. She came here looking for her brother."

"Your woman is one of the Eagle Clan?"

"No," Red Fox replied. "She is not of that clan, but another, one you have probably never heard of."

Black Crow's lips twisted wryly. "Then she must come

from far away, for I have traveled this land from shore to shore."

"She has come from far away," Red Fox replied. "And her clan does not live in this land, but across the big salt water."

The trader's eyes narrowed. "Tell me more," he said. "I have heard of another clan, have had occasion to meet one of its warriors when I was here last year."

"The Viking, Eric," Red Fox guessed. "He is Brynna's brother."

"Brynna is your woman?" Black Crow asked gravely. At Red Fox's nod, the trader said, "You intrigue me, Red Fox. Tell me how you met her. And more to the point, how she came to be your woman."

And so Red Fox did. They talked long into the night, with Red Fox telling the trader most of what had happened in the last moon.

He spoke of Brynna at length, of the way she looked with firelight on her hair, and how at first she was frightened of his appearance, but how time and patience changed her feelings.

"Perhaps she was never afraid of your scar," Black Crow said. "Did she say she was?"

"No. But she drew away from me."

"A natural reaction, since you were a stranger to her."

"I might have thought the same thing, had not Sweet Willow reacted in the same manner when she saw my scarred face," Red Fox said bitterly, unaware that he was revealing more of himself than he'd intended until the trader spoke again.

"Who is Sweet Willow?"

"She was my betrothed until this happened." Red Fox motioned toward his face. "Then she asked to be released from the marriage because she could no longer stand the sight of me."

"Then she did not care for you," Black Crow said, his eyes dark with sympathy. "Had she done so, she would have been glad you'd survived the bear's attack and would not have worried so much about your appearance. You would do better to put such a woman from your mind."

"I have already done so," Red Fox said. "But you can see why I must find Brynna and take her back with me."

"And if has no wish to go with you?" Black Crow asked. "Would you take her anyway?"

Red Fox took longer to answer this time, searching his mind for an honest answer. "It is hard to think of facing life without her, but neither do I want an unwilling woman. If she does not wish to leave with me, then she may remain with her brothers."

"You seem truthful, Red Fox," the trader said. "But to escort you into the cliff city could cause trouble not only for myself, but for other traders as well. I must think long about your request. And I am weary from my travels. Perhaps we should make camp here and continue this discussion at early light. Then I will consider your words and make my decision."

Red Fox had no alternative except to wait until morning. Black Crow's help could mean the difference between life and death.

The warrior did not allow himself to consider other alternatives, because there were none. Either Black Crow helped him, or he would have to wait for another time, because he could not bring himself to slay the trader.

Not even to find Brynna.

Or could he?

Shateh was worried. To-kee, the sentry Shateh had been sent to replace, was not where he should have been. And although Shateh looked high and low for the man, thinking he might have been attacked by one of their enemies or even by a wild beast, Shateh could find no sign of the other man.

However, his efforts did not go completely unrewarded. While he stood on a rocky promontory searching the steep slope leading to the mesa, his sweeping gaze found two men who should not have been there.

Narrowing his vision, he saw the bulging pack carried by one of the men and realized it was the trader who came once each year to the mesa.

But who was the man who accompanied the trader? Shateh wondered.

Like the trader, the stranger was a tall man, so there was no mistaking him for To-kee, who was of a height equal to Shateh's, probably two heads shorter than the two men approaching.

Worried about To-kee, yet realizing his duty at the moment was to report what he had seen, Shateh hurried back to the cliff city to impart the news of the sentry's disappearance and the arrival of the trader and his companion.

It started out to be a morning just like any other. The air was cool and crisp, fragrant with the pungent smell of juniper and pines.

Several women, Brynna and Nama among them, had climbed to the mesa that morning before the sun had time to burn away the mist covering the valley to fill their baskets with service-berries. It was their intention to pick the last of them before the bears discovered they were ready and stripped the bushes.

"The trader is coming!" A voice rang out.

"The trader is coming?" murmured Nama, turning toward the man who had shouted the news. "Is it really time?"

"The trader?" Brynna asked. "Is that the man you told me about? The one who comes once a year to trade his wares?"

"Yes." Nama's face beamed. "I hope it is Black Crow who comes. He spent some time with me during the last season of long heat. He taught me many things then. If he had not come, I might not have survived."

"Then I must see this trader," Brynna said. "I would like to thank him for what he did. By helping you, he gave me a sister."

"There he is!" the voice was barely above a whisper and came from somewhere behind Brynna. "Look! It is the trader! Black Crow has come!"

As Brynna turned to look at the man who generated so much excitement among the women, she heard a babble of voices, all using that same hushed tone, as though afraid of being heard.

"Who is the man with him?"

"Another trader, perhaps?"

"He carries no staff. If he were a trader, he would carry a staff."

Brynna's curious gaze fell on the two men some distance from them. Her heart gave a startled jerk when she realized they both wore buckskin shirts and trousers. She had seen no others wearing shirts made of buckskin except her brother and Red Fox. Most of the men who occupied this land chose to leave their upper bodies naked.

They were both tall, and the only one she could see clearly carried a bulging pack on his back. Brynna judged him to be the one they called Black Crow. She could see little of the other man, for the pack the trader carried effectively hid his companion from her view.

Feeling a need to see the stranger, Brynna moved sideways, hoping to get a better view.

There! She could almost see him. Just a little more to the left and she could—

Suddenly, one of the younger women, apparently having the same idea as Brynna, moved in front of her.

Biting back a curse, and stifling at the urge to push the girl out of the way, Brynna stepped farther to the left, and again found her line of vision blocked as the girl moved with her.

Damn! Brynna swore inwardly. She must see him. Must look at his face! The urge to identify him was almost stifling in its intensity.

But why? she wondered. What was there about him that forced her to keep trying? Was it because he seemed familiar somehow? Of course, he could not be. Yet there was something . . .

Foolish girl! an inner voice chided. *You cannot know him. You have no knowledge of any man save those who are already on this mesa.*

"I must see," she whispered. "I must know."

"What?" Nama asked from beside her. "What did you say, Brynna? I did not hear you."

"Nothing," Brynna replied, watching the two men disappear over the edge of the cliff without her ever having seen the stranger's face. She turned toward the other girl. "I would like to attend the trading. Perhaps I have something of value the trader would be interested in."

Nama laughed. "The trader would be interested in anything you have—even the buttons from your shift." She reached for another berry to add to her filled basket. "If we hurry, we can be in the city again before it gets too crowded."

Dismayed at the wait, yet unwilling to appear lazy by leaving ahead of the others, Brynna turned her attention to gathering service-berries.

All the while, the women spoke of the trader and the wonderful things he had brought in his pack when he had come before.

"Do you think the trader brought some of those brightly colored birds, like he did last time?" asked Teeka. "I would like one of those. He said it came from a faraway land in the south."

"Perhaps," replied Ona. "But I am interested in the seashells he brings from the shores of the big salt water. I have a turkey feather blanket ready to trade for some of them."

And so the talk continued, going around the circle of women as they commented on other times the trader had come to them and the things he had brought. But Brynna barely heard their words. All she could think about was the tall man who accompanied the trader and the need—the compulsion—she felt to see him.

Brynna had a good view of the cliff above the city, and she was aware of the people that arrived by the scores, each interested in seeing what the trader had brought in his bulging pack, for the goods he brought from the other clans were highly desired by the members of the Eagle Clan.

Finally, they were done, the last berry having been picked and added to her basket, and now, for some odd reason, Brynna felt reluctant to leave. For that reason, she was the last to descend the stone steps cut into the steep cliff.

She could hear the babble of many voices as she reached the edge of the city built beneath the cliff overhang.

Brynna sidled closer to the knot of people, craning her neck as she did, hoping for a glimpse of the man who so excited a people who were generally sober. And, more important to her, the man who accompanied the trader.

Suddenly she saw him. And although he was facing away from her, Brynna's her heart gave a sudden jerk, then stopped beating altogether.

He carried himself like Red Fox, but it could not be him! Could it?

Her heart began a slow, uneven thud as she stared at the man who looked so familiar, so much like her love.

It is Red Fox, an inner voice cried. *It can be no other.*

But he is dead, her mind reasoned. He cannot be here.

You did not see him dead, the silent voice said, niggling at the edge of her mind.

No, she silently admitted. But Patrick told me he was dead, that he had slain him.

What if he lied?

He would not lie! He would not tell me such a horrible thing were it not so!

She waited breathlessly for the man to turn, to look around at her, unable to shake the feeling that she was looking at Red Fox.

Suddenly, as though feeling her gaze, his head turned and she saw his features, his dear, beloved scarred face.

"My God," she whispered. "It is him. Red Fox!" She started forward, would have run joyfully to him, had not a sudden memory held her limbs frozen.

The Wolf Clan and the Eagle Clan are enemies. The words he had spoken rang in her mind. *I cannot go there. They would never allow me to leave their lands alive.*

She could not reveal his identity.

Even as that thought was born, Red Fox, who had been searching the crowd of people, saw her. Their eyes locked, and Brynna found herself flinching from his gaze. His expression was hard, his eyes clawing at her.

Red Fox, she silently cried, *why do you look at me that way?*

Brynna's knees trembled, threatening to buckle beneath her, but she forced them to move, to carry her away from his look.

Retreating into the deepest shadows cast by the cliff overhang, Brynna told herself she must have time to think, to consider the consequences of his presence.

Why had he come? she wondered again. And why did he look at her as though he hated her?

Even as she worried the matter in her mind, her heart sang happily. Red Fox is alive, alive, alive.

But why is he here? she worried.

Red Fox is alive, alive, alive, her foolish heart sang. What difference does it make why he ventured into enemy territory? The only thing that matters is that he lives.

Be still, she told her foolish heart, pacing the darkened area behind the cliff city. *I must know the reason he came here. These people must not be harmed by the Wolf Clan.*

Realizing she would learn nothing if she remained in hiding, Brynna spun on her heels and came up against a solid wall of flesh.

Chapter Twenty-Nine

Black Crow was uneasy, but his expression held no hint of the concern he felt. Although he was kept busy by those wanting to trade with him, he had seen Red Fox sidle away from the crowd that surrounded them and stride toward the shadows where the woman with golden hair had gone.

Would the warrior honor the vow he had made? Black Crow wondered. He must do so.

Red Fox had sworn by everything he held dear that he would do no harm here, that he only wished to speak to the woman. The warrior from the Wolf Clan had sworn that if she refused to leave with him, he would abide by that decision.

But could Red Fox be trusted to keep his word? Black Crow wondered again. If Red Fox's intentions were not good . . . if he caused hurt to any of the cliff dwellers, then the man who had brought him here would be held accountable. And that man was himself . . . Black Crow.

The penalty for bringing an enemy might not be death,

since he was a trader, but his association with these people would surely come to an end, and the turkey feather blankets so desired by other clans would no longer be available to him.

That thought was uppermost in Black Crow's mind when he heard a disturbance near the edge of the cliff city. He looked around and located the source of the noise. It was a warrior who, having descended the ladder in utmost haste, hurried across the courtyard toward them. The expression on the newcomer's face told the trader that the news they were soon to hear would not be welcome.

"Nampeyo," the man exclaimed, stopping beside his shaman who sat in the courtyard. "To-kee has finally been found. His body was found hidden among the rocks near the bottom of the mesa!"

"His body, Shateh?" Nampeyo inquired, struggling to his feet.

"Yes," Shateh replied. "He has been slain."

"Slain!" Nampeyo repeated harshly. "Are you sure he was slain?"

"Yes," Shateh said again. "I am certain, Shaman. No beast could place him the way he was found, covered with rocks. His body would still be there . . . undiscovered, had Lothi—who was among the searchers—not been in that very same spot yesterday. Anyone else would have thought the rock pile was natural, so carefully had To-kee been covered."

"Who would have done such a thing?" Nampeyo demanded harshly, his gaze circling the crowd of people as though searching for the slayer.

"Who but an enemy of the People?" Shateh asked.

"An enemy?" Nampeyo rasped. "You think an enemy is here, among us?"

All eyes turned to the trader.

"Black Crow," Nampeyo growled. "You have heard

Shateh's words. One of our sentries has been found dead. What do you know about it?''

"I?" The trader stood and spread his arms wide. "Nampeyo, why do you ask me? I have no knowledge of this matter. I am but a trader, a man who has no enemies."

"What of the stranger you brought among us," a nearby voice asked.

"Yes, the stranger," said another.

"The stranger." The voice came from another direction.

"What about him?"

"Yes. Ask him about the stranger."

"The stranger. The stranger. Ask about the stranger." The demand was repeated over and over again as other voices took up the question, muttering among themselves.

"You brought a stranger with you," Nampeyo said. "He is dressed in the manner of the Wolf Clan, yet you claim he is a friend who travels with you. Is that true?"

"He is a friend," Black Crow said, considering his reply carefully. "Yet that friendship is of short duration. I know little about him. Only that he swore to me that he did not come here as an enemy."

"And you believed him?"

"I had no reason to doubt his words," Black Crow replied. "If he has deceived me . . . if he is responsible for the death of your sentry, then I am sorry. But I cannot be held accountable for his treachery. My only fault lies in believing his words."

Nampeyo studied the trader for a long moment, then said, "I believe your words, Black Crow. I know you would not intentionally damage our relationship. But you were very foolish to believe him. What reason did he give for coming here?"

"He said his woman was here among you. That he only wanted to speak to her."

"His woman? There is no woman from the Wolf Clan here among us."

"She is not a woman of his clan," Black Crow explained. "Red Fox said she had hair of fire and eyes the color of summer. He claimed the woman was the sister of Eric the Viking."

It was at that moment that Shala, who had heard of the trader's arrival and had hurried to the cliff city thinking to trade some goods, happened upon them. Just in time to hear her husband's name spoken.

"What is happening here?" she asked, looking at the serious expressions on the faces of the men. "You spoke my husband's name. What had happened to him?"

"Nothing," Nampeyo quickly assured her. "I have not seen Eric. The hunters have not yet returned."

"Then what is going on?"

"A body has been discovered, slain," Nampeyo replied. "And we have a warrior from the Wolf Clan among us." He told her what the trader had said.

"The Wolf Clan warrior is looking for Brynna?" Shala inquired, her eyes dark and thoughtful.

"It must be Brynna," Nampeyo said. "The warrior said she was the sister of Eric the Viking."

"Then it must be so," she replied, her gaze searching the crowd. "Where is Brynna?"

No one seemed to know the answer to that question, nor did they know the whereabouts of the warrior from the Wolf Clan.

With her heart pounding like a rabbit that had barely escaped the claws of an eagle, Brynna was afraid to look at the man she had bumped into, fearing the results of that action. Instead, she looked at the fringed leggings that hugged powerful legs. Then she sucked in a sharp breath. There was only one man—to her knowledge—who wore such leggings.

It was Red Fox.

Her eyes were wide and staring as she looked up into his face, then her heart gave a leap of joy. There was no mistake: it was him. Red Fox. Standing before her, looming large and fierce, his face dark and enraged.

Brynna had never before seen him looking so fierce, so absolutely frightening, and yet her heart rejoined in that sight.

"R-Red Fox!" she squeaked, swallowing around the lump that had formed in her throat.

"You appear surprised to see me," he said, keeping his voice low, and the force of his anger held her mute. "Have you nothing to say to your beloved?" he asked scornfully. "Perhaps you cannot speak because you have no words to describe your betrayal."

"I-I n-never b-betrayed you," she stuttered, silently cursing her trembling voice. "Wh-why do you accuse me of such a thing?"

"You lie!" he hissed, gripping her shoulders with fingers of steel while the violent pulsing of a muscle in his jaw betrayed the depth of his fury. "You left me, Brynna! Without a word of explanation, you left!" His fingers dug into her shoulders and she flinched against the pain. "You made me think you cared about me, made me believe you were content, but the first chance that came, you ran away. What do you call that, if not betrayal?"

"I only w-went b-because I thought you were d-dead!" she cried, her teeth shaking with reaction. "You must b-believe that, Red Fox. I thought you were d-dead!"

"Why should you think that?" he grated harshly. "I went hunting. You knew that. I was only gone for a short time, and when I returned, your men had already been there and you were gone."

"I know," she said softly. "But my men came and one of them, Patrick, told me he had killed you."

"And you believed him?" His voice was calmer now, his eyes less cold. "You never once thought he might be lying to you?"

"Why should he lie?" she asked, her eyes devouring his beloved face. "It makes no sense. Patrick *never* lied to me before. He had no reason."

"I am proof of his lie," Red Fox replied. "Do you not see me standing here before you?"

"Yes," she cried, sliding her arms around his neck and pressing herself against him. "I see you! You are really here. Oh, God, Red Fox. I can hardly believe it. I thought you were lost to me forever!"

"And I thought I had lost you," he replied, his arms enfolding her. Laying his head atop hers, he muttered, "I thought I would never hold you again like this, Brynna. I thought I would be forever alone and the thought made me want to die."

Brynna's heart was too full for words. But there was something she needed to say. "Red Fox, am I the only reason you came here?"

"It was reason enough."

"But you are risking your life by coming here like this!"

He nodded his dark head. "Yes," he agreed. "I know. And we must leave immediately. Before they discover the body of their sentry."

"Oh, God!" she whispered, her face draining of color. "You killed one of them? A sentry?"

"Yes." The words said it all. They both knew how disastrous the results of such an act could be. Yet still they were unprepared when two men rounded the corner of the building and stopped short at the sight of them.

"We found him!" one of them yelled. "It is the enemy warrior."

Before they could gather their wits, several other men joined the first two.

Red Fox reacted swiftly then, shoving Brynna aside and turning to meet the attack. But the warriors were too many for one man; he fell beneath a hail of blows.

"No," Brynna cried, struggling to her feet and leaping toward the battle. "Leave him alone!"

Someone grabbed her arms from behind and held her captive, and she could do nothing to stop the beating that was taking place.

"Stop them!" she sobbed. "They will kill him."

"It is only right, since he has slain one of our people," said Nampeyo, who had arrived at the scene. "He must pay for To-kee's life with his own."

"No! You cannot do that!" Brynna cried. "Nampeyo, he was attacked by the sentry! He only defended himself. You cannot take his life for that."

"You must not fight this, Brynna," said Shala, who appeared from the shadows. "The law of the People demands an eye for an eye."

"Shala," Brynna cried desperately. "You must stop this madness. You must help Red Fox."

"I cannot, Brynna," Shala said sadly. "Neither can you. You can only accept what cannot be changed."

The warriors of the Eagle Clan, obviously tired of beating an unconscious man, drew back from Red Fox's limp body.

"Please, Nampeyo. Allow me to go to him," Brynna pleaded. "Just for a moment."

"No," he said, eyeing her sternly. "You are to keep away from him, Brynna. He is an enemy of the People and cannot be trusted."

Brynna could not look away from Red Fox, lying crumpled and unconscious on the cavern floor. Was he still breathing? she wondered. She struggled to free her arms, but her struggles were useless against those who held her.

"Take the enemy warrior out of my sight," Nampeyo ordered. "See that he cannot escape the fate that awaits him."

Two of the Eagle Clan warriors grabbed Red Fox's arms and dragged him away.

"Where are they taking him?" Brynna asked, unable to tear her eyes away from her lover's battered body. He resembled nothing more than a rag doll that had been badly used, then casually tossed aside.

"No matter," the shaman said tonelessly. "You will not be seeing him again."

"I will never forgive you for this," Brynna said, her gaze lashing him with cold fury.

"I know," he replied, and his voice sounded almost sad. "But I do only what I must, Brynna. I am a servant of the People. Nothing more, nothing less." His gaze went past her, to the two men whose hands held her captive. "Keep her here long enough for the Wolf Clan warrior to be imprisoned. Then release her."

Without another word, he walked away from her, leaving her alone with her captors.

Chapter Thirty

Patrick stared at Brynna with mixture of surprise and dismay, unable to believe what she was telling him. "But, my lady," he protested. "I *did* kill him. At least," he amended, "I killed a man, a *skraeling* warrior. And, since he was headed for the lodge where you were, I naturally assumed he was the man you spoke of."

"Well, he was not!" she said coldly. "And because I believed you . . . because I thought him dead, I left the mountains and rode away from him. It was the reason he followed me here . . . the reason his life is now forfeited. You must help me free him, Patrick! They took my sword and left me weaponless, apparently afraid of what I would do if it were in my hand."

"Calm down, lassie."

"How can I calm down when the man I love was beaten senseless before my eyes? He may very well already be d-dead." She heard her voice break and tried to instill some calm into it. "You owe me, Patrick. And I am here to demand payment for that debt."

"You have no need to do that, lassie," Patrick said. "My allegiance is yours. You have but to command and I will obey. Where did they take him?"

"I have no idea. But perhaps Nama can tell us."

"Not Shala?" he asked gently, sensing something in her voice.

"She was there when he was taken. She refused to help him." Her voice was cold, unforgiving.

"What could she have done?" he asked quietly.

"She could at least have pled his case," Brynna said. "But she did nothing. I thought she was my friend, but she did nothing."

Patrick sighed and patted her head awkwardly. "Try to discover where they have taken him," he said gruffly. "I will find Lacey and enlist his aid, but two against so many . . ." His voice trailed away as though he had said it all.

"There are three of us," Brynna reminded. "And Eric and Garrick are five. And Garrick's four men make nine. A number to be reckoned with."

"Do not count heavily on your brother's help, lassie," Patrick advised.

"What do you mean?" she asked. "They surely would not refuse me!"

"The hunters will be returning soon," Patrick replied. "Then we will see."

But Patrick had no need to wait. He already knew what the Nordstrom brothers would have to say on the subject.

Red Fox groaned and opened his eyes, staring up into the blackness that surrounded him. Was it night? he wondered. Or was he just confined in a place where only shadows dwelt?

Realizing how dry his mouth was, he licked his swollen lips and found the coppery taste of blood.

He lifted a hand and felt his face, knowing it must be bruised, probably battered beyond all recognition.

How many warriors had there been? he wondered.

At the time there seemed to be scores and scores of them, piling on him, using their fists and feet to their best advantage.

Had they broken his bones?

He flexed his arms and legs. Although his limbs were sore, they still worked, so his bones must be intact.

Where was he, anyway?

Pushing himself to his knees, he swept his hands over the floor and found a small hole in the middle that made him think of a sipapu. He moved to his left and made a wider sweep, finding the raised portion that ran around the circular room.

Yes. It was true. They had thrown him into a kiva and had pulled the entry ladder up.

He looked up again and was able to make out a narrow sliver of light that he had missed before. A crack in the covering.

Red Fox knew then where he was, for they would not have allowed him to stay in the cliff city. They must have taken him to the abandoned pueblo on top of the mesa to be kept there until the hour of his death.

He wondered what time it was, then decided it could be no later than noon, for he could not have been unconscious long.

Much had transpired during those morning hours, he realized. He had traveled to the place that before now he had only heard of. He had seen the fabled cliff city with his own eyes.

But most important of all, he had found Brynna. He

had discovered that rather than run away from him, she had been coerced into leaving, had believed him to be dead.

Brynna, his heart cried out. *Why have I been allowed to find you, only to lose you once again?*

Brynna. How could he ever have suspected her of betrayal? She was everything that was good and decent, would never pretend to something she was not feeling.

Oh, Great Creator! How could he depart from this world and leave her behind to mourn his passing?

No! He could not! He must not! There had to be a way out! There must be something he could do to escape the fate the Eagle Clan had in store for him.

He would not let go of life so easily. Not now. Not since he had finally found something worth living for.

But what could he do?

The questions hammered at him over and over again, demanding answers that he could not give.

Finally, unable to cope with the restless energy those questions engendered, Red Fox pushed himself upright and began to pace the circle of his lonely cell . . . the prison that had once served as a holy place.

Brynna, frustrated because her brothers had not yet returned from the hunt, set out—accompanied by Patrick Douglass—to find them.

It was mid-afternoon when she found them, bent over a recently killed deer, arguing jovially over whose arrow had slain the animal.

They appeared so normal, so untouched by the horror that was almost smothering Brynna. How could that be? she wondered. Had they not felt the tension that vibrated around them, changing the very air they breathed?

Apparently not, she decided. That meant she must break the news to them.

A lump formed in Brynna's throat. She loved both of them dearly and had no doubt that she was loved in return. They would never let her down in her time of need.

Eric saw her first, standing silently amid a thick stand of junipers, watching them quietly, unable to say a word, now that she had found them.

"Look, Garrick!" Eric exclaimed. "Our little sister has come to settle the argument. What do you think, Brynna?" he asked, arching a golden brow. "If two arrows marked alike penetrate one heart, who can rightfully claim the—?" He broke off suddenly, the smile leaving his face. "Brynna? Has something happened?"

Although Brynna had meant to be strong and remain calm while making her request, the concern reflected in his expression circumvented that resolve, and like a child, she dissolved into tears, running into her beloved brother's arms.

"Here, now," he chided, smoothing a hand over her golden curls that were so like his own. "What has happened to cause such sorrow, little sister?" Suddenly he stiffened, gripping her shoulders and pushing her away so he could look into her face again. "Not Shala," he muttered. "It cannot be. The babe? Brynna? Is she all right?" His voice was harsh and he shook her hard, demanding an answer. "Brynna, has something happened to Shala or the babe?"

"N-no," she stuttered, feeling dismay that he would immediately believe such a thing. "Th-they are unharmed, b-but—b-but I—I—R-Red F-Fox—They . . . he came and they t-took—" Her voice broke and she dissolved into tears again.

"There, there, little one. It cannot be so bad," he consoled her. He looked past her to where Patrick Douglass stood helplessly watching. "What is all this, Douglass?" he demanded harshly. "What has happened to upset Brynna like this?"

Patrick met his eyes grimly. "The *skraeling* warrior is alive. He came here looking for the lassie. Nampeyo ordered him taken prisoner."

Eric's bushy brows met in a heavy frown, and it was obvious that he still did not understand. "Who is Red Fox?" he asked shortly. "And why should Brynna be so upset that he is alive?"

"The lass is not upset because he is alive," Patrick growled. "The thing that bothers her is his being a prisoner. And the fact that, unless someone puts a stop to it, he will soon be dead."

"Thor's teeth, man! You are not explaining matters sufficiently. I see no reason why Brynna would be so emotionally involved with the fate of a *skraeling* warrior!" He patted her shoulder awkwardly. "You must see that we cannot involve ourselves in these matters, Brynna. If this . . ." He seemed to search his memory for the name, then said, "If Red Fox has been judged unworthy to live, then we must abide by that decision." He squeezed her shoulders encouragingly. "You can stay with us until the thing is over. Shala would be glad to have you."

She pulled away from him and stared, aghast. "You think that will make a difference? That I will not mourn if I am not there to see him die?"

"Brynna," he chided gently. "You must see that we cannot interfere with things of this nature!"

"You would damn well interfere if Shala were the one losing her life!" Brynna said bitterly.

"Of course," he replied, frowning heavily at her. "But that is different. Shala is my wife."

"And Red Fox is my husband!" she declared.

"What nonsense!" he growled impatiently. "You have no—" He broke off and looked over her head at Patrick, saw the other man nod his head as though guessing Eric's thoughts.

A change came over Eric in that moment. It was as though he had been struck by lightning. His body arched, seemed to vibrate with tension and his hands clenched so tight that his knuckles showed white.

"He is not dead?" he demanded, his voice harsh and grating, carrying a more than a hint of violence.

"I told you that he was not. Not yet anyway. But, Eric . . ." She stared up at him through tear-wet eyes. ". . . Do you not understand how urgent this is? Nampeyo plans to take his life."

"Good," Eric snarled. "It saves me the trouble."

An aching center of cold settled high in her chest and she made a fist of her right hand, pressing it against the pain, "Eric!" She whispered, flinching away from him. "You cannot mean that. You would not leave him to die!"

"I do mean it, Brynna! The filthy savage deserves no less. He raped you!"

"He did not!" she cried, staring at him with rising horror. "How can you say that? I would be dead now if not for him. I told you what happened." She looked at Garrick, who had remained silent throughout the exchange. "Garrick? Do you believe—" Brynna broke off, unable to continue. But there was no need, for Garrick's expression was dark and thunderous, very much like his brother's.

"I thought I could count on my brothers," she said tightly, turning away from them. The cold lump that had formed in her chest began to crawl toward her stomach, turning to ice as it spread outward toward her extremities, causing goosepimples to break out on her flesh.

"Brynna," Eric said, snaring her wrist with his strong

fingers. "Stop and think for a moment. You cannot love such a man. Your mind has fooled you, tried to make your encounter with that savage more acceptable. Nevertheless, the results of that savagery remain the same."

"What results?" she asked faintly, her mind trying to unravel his cryptic words, hoping they would prove she had misunderstood him.

"If Angus Sigurdson knew what that savage had done to you, then even he would not take you for his bride."

Brynna yanked her arm free from her brother's grip, unable to believe the words Eric had uttered. He was showing her a side of his nature she had never before seen, would never have believed existed, even had she been told differently.

"You believe it is fine for you to wed one of the *skraelings,*" she said, bitterly. "But not your sister. Do you know how that sounds, Eric? Deep down, you are ashamed of your own wife! Are you ashamed of your child as well?"

"Thor's teeth, woman," he roared, his expression thunderous. "I am not ashamed! Shala could stand beside me anywhere and I would be more than proud to proclaim her my wife!"

"Then how is my situation different?" she demanded furiously.

"Can you not see?" he asked, his voice softening ever so slightly. "Shala is a woman of great beauty. She could hold her own anywhere, in any land. But the men here are different, little sister. The *skraeling* warriors would stand out like a sore thumb at home. You could never hold up your head and proudly introduce him to our parents." His fingers gripped her shoulders and dug into her flesh. "Do not blame me for not interfering with these people. I am only thinking of your welfare. You must not throw your life away on a savage. Your beauty is such that you would grace any throne."

"And whose throne would you set me on?" Brynna asked sarcastically. "What king do you have picked out for me to marry, Eric?" Her eyes flashed darkly. "You are a fool, Eric! Little better than our father! And to think I came to you for help!"

Whirling around, she stalked away from her brother. She would never forgive him if Red Fox died. Never. As long as she lived.

"Do not take it so hard, lassie," Patrick said, as they hurried back toward the cliff city. "I had a feeling your brothers would react that way."

"Then you should have told me," she snapped, throwing him a hard glare.

"Would you have listened?" he asked mildly, seeming not the least bit put out by her anger.

She expelled a long sigh. "No. I would not have. I would have insisted on seeking help from them." She looked up at him. "Patrick? Do you feel the same way?"

"What way, lassie?"

"Like I am tarnished now."

"Never!" he said harshly. "And if he was anyone except your brother, then Eric Nordstrom would have felt the edge of my blade for daring to speak such words."

"Thank you, Patrick," she said.

"You have no need of thanking me for speaking the truth, my lady."

"Do you mind if I do it anyway?" she asked.

"No. Not if it makes you happy."

"Where is Lacey?" she asked.

"I have no idea. But if you like, I will find him."

''Please do,'' she said. ''I am going to Nampeyo to make some demands. If I am lucky, I will be busy until nightfall. You must speak to Lacey and determine if he is willing to help us free Red Fox.''

Patrick nodded his head. ''Take heart, my lady,'' he said gruffly. ''We will find a way out of this bloody mess somehow.''

They parted near the edge of the mesa and Brynna watched Patrick stride across the mesa at a ground-eating pace, in search of the one other man they might be able to depend on for help.

After Patrick had disappeared from sight, Brynna descended the stone steps to the cliff city and made her way across the courtyard where Nampeyo sat, as though waiting for her return.

She faced him with flashing eyes and rigid expression. ''Nampeyo. I demand to be allowed to visit Red Fox.''

''I cannot allow it,'' he said gravely.

''You will allow it or there will be no more lessons,'' she said grimly. ''Do you intend to deny your people the right to learn by refusing a request that would be harmless?''

Brynna felt no guilt for putting a price on her teaching. She would use any means at her disposal to see the man she loved.

His look was thoughtful. ''You will resume the lessons if you are allowed to speak to him?''

Hope was born anew until she realized what he had said. ''No. Not to speak to him. I must be allowed to be with him. And alone.''

''I cannot allow that, Brynna. Your life would surely be in danger.''

''He will not harm me,'' Brynna said shortly. ''Nor will he harm anyone else.''

"How can you say that, when you know he killed one of our sentries?"

"You know why he did that, Nampeyo. The man attacked him and he defended himself, as anyone would have done."

"He need not have killed To-kee. He could have overpowered him easily enough, for To-kee was not much of a fighter, even when he was a young man."

Realizing time was passing while they argued, Brynna set her jaw at a stubborn angle and said, "You cannot dissuade me, Nampeyo. I demand that you allow me to see Red Fox. You owe me that much." She had not meant to put it on those terms, but she would use any means at her disposal to see the man she loved.

"Very well," he conceded. "But only for a few minutes."

"No!" Brynna said, grim with determination. "I must be allowed to remain with him longer."

His eyes darkened as though she had angered him, but he showed no other emotion. "You will take the few minutes, or nothing at all."

Realizing from his expression that if she was in danger of losing even those precious moments, Brynna hurried to agree. "I will take them."

Nampeyo turned away from her, beckoning to a man who lingered nearby. "Lothi! Take the Viking woman to see the prisoner."

The Viking woman. Not Brynna. It seemed their friendship was near an end. Brynna had no intention of allowing it to bother her, though, for she had accomplished her goal.

She knew, though, that the battle was yet to be won, but consoled herself with the thought that whatever happened in the future, she would have had these few moments alone with Red Fox.

Cold comfort though, she silently admitted, if she could not devise a way to save his life.

Red Fox had no idea how long he had been confined when he heard wood scraping against wood and the cover to his prison was thrown back. He squinted against the bright light that suddenly invaded the darkness of his tomb, stepping back in the shadows to relieve the burning in his eyes.

Wood scraped against wood again and he realized a ladder was being lowered into the kiva.

Red Fox tensed, wondering if he could overpower his guard and escape. Perhaps if he—

"Red Fox," a woman's voice whispered, interrupting his thoughts. "Are you there, Red Fox?"

At the same instant he recognized Brynna's voice, Red Fox realized she could not see him in the deep shadows. "I am here, little one," he said gruffly, stepping into the light that filtered through the top. "Have you come here alone?"

Instead of answering his question, she threw herself at him, twining her arms around his neck and pressing her body close against his. "Are you all right?" she whispered, burying her tear-wet face in his neck.

In some part of Red Fox's mind, he was aware of the ladder being pulled up, aware of the cover being replaced on the opening, leaving them in darkness again. "I am fine now that you are here, little one," he replied huskily. "I am just surprised they allowed you to come."

"Nampeyo owes me a favor," she said by way of explanation. "I demanded payment." She scattered kisses across his bruised face. "Oh, Red Fox," she whispered shakily. "What are we going to do? We cannot allow this to happen."

"Perhaps your brothers——"

"No!" she said, her voice harsh with pain. "I have already appealed to them and they refused me. I will never forgive them for that!" She burrowed her face in his neck again. "But do not despair, my love. I will not lose you again. Not now. Not ever."

"Brynna," he said, swallowing hard, knowing that he must remain calm, that he must find a way to ease her pain, to help her go on without him. "Listen to me, my love. If fate has decreed that I should die, then there is nothing we can do. Nothing. But you must not mourn for me. You must go on without me. You are young. You have your whole life ahead of you. Look toward the future, my love. Put the past behind you."

"I could never forget you!" she cried, dissolving in tears. "How could you expect me to?"

"I do not expect it, love. I want you to remember me always and to carry the knowledge of our love in your heart forever." His heart was a heavy knot of pain as he searched for the right words. "Brynna, look at me." He tilted her chin toward him, but the shadows were too thick for him to see her eyes. "I do love you," he whispered. "I have loved you more than life itself since the first day we met. Always remember that. And have courage, dear one. For you must be strong enough to accept what cannot be changed."

"No!" Brynna raged. "You are giving up, Red Fox. You cannot do that! All is not yet lost. There is a way out of this, and we will find it somehow."

Perhaps, Red Fox considered, it would be less painful for her if she were allowed to hope. "Yes," he agreed, even while he knew there was no way out. "There is a way, and we will find it. But if we do not——"

"Stop!" she said, covering his lips with her own in a kiss of such infinite sweetness that it took his breath away.

"Do not say the words again, for I refuse to listen to them."

"Little one," he said shakily. "You must listen. If fate decrees that you live without me, then you must find a way to do so in peace. You are a prize among women, Brynna. A woman who could have any man she chose. Do not live your life alone, little one. You have so much joy, so much love in your heart. Give that love to someone else. Find another man and—"

"Stop it!" she cried harshly. "I will not find another! You will not be allowed to die!"

"Brynna—" His voice broke off as the cover to his prison was lifted again and the ladder was dropped into the hole.

"Woman, it is time for you to leave!" the sentry called down.

Brynna's arms tightened around his neck. "Oh, God, Red Fox! I want to stay here with you," she whispered, "I want it desperately. But I cannot."

"I know," he said sorrowfully.

"No. You do not know. I *would* insist on staying, yet I must leave and join my men. Together we will form a plan to free you."

"Do not place so much importance on accomplishing such a deed, little one."

"It *is* of the utmost importance!" she said, trying to control the wobble in her voice. "You will be free, Red Fox. Somehow, in some way, you will be free. I will never allow them to take your life!"

He could not answer, could not utter the words of agreement again when he knew them for a lie.

"Woman!" the sentry called again. "Come out now!"

"I will come to you later," Brynna said, covering his lips with her own in a heartrending kiss. "Wait for me, Red Fox."

"I have nothing else to do with my time," he said wryly. "But, Brynna—"

"Do not say it again!" she snapped, her chin jerking outward. "You will be free, Red Fox! You will!"

Without another word, she mounted the ladder and climbed up into the sunshine again.

When she stepped free of the ladder, she stayed there, watching from that bright circle of light while the guard pulled the ladder up, then reached for the cover that would seal the prisoner in his darkness again.

As the cover grated across the wooden roof, the circle of light grew smaller and smaller until it was only a dim memory in Red Fox's mind, and he was left again in the darkness of his lonely cell.

Chapter Thirty-One

Lame Duck was worried.

It showed in the way his gaze continually skittered between the warrior standing guard near the abandoned city to the wooded area some distance beyond.

An almost silent, slithering sound jerked Lame Duck around and he saw Big Elk slide beneath the flowering bush where he was hiding.

"Fool!" Lame Duck whispered, keeping his voice so low there was no way the sound could penetrate beyond the confines of their hiding place. "Do you want the guard to realize we are here?"

"Howling Wolf sent me," Big Elk replied. "He is uneasy about finding a sentry placed near an abandoned city that should require no guard."

Lame Duck nodded, understanding Howling Wolf's feelings, for the guard was the source of his own unease.

Up to this point, things had gone better than expected. Only one guard had been killed so far, and they had lost Black Rain, one of their best warriors. It was still a mystery how a warrior as young and strong as Black Rain could have been killed by the Eagle Clan warrior, who was an older man and should have been easily overcome by one as strong as Black Rain.

Yes. It was puzzling, but there was little time to consider that fact. There were too many other things to occupy his mind. Anyway, the old warrior had been hidden from eyes that would surely seek him out, covered well with rocks so that none might see and sound the alarm.

Neither would they find Black Rain, whose body had been taken into the desert and handed over to the women to prepare it for burial.

Snap! The sound sent an icy chill slithering down Lame Duck's back. With fingers tightly clutching his knife, he swung around to face the danger . . . and met Big Elk's apologetic gaze.

The man was a clumsy oaf! he told himself, unable to move silently if his life depended on it. Which it did. Lame Duck's as well.

Lame Duck's gaze flew back to the guard, fearing he had heard the noise, but the sentry stood where he had been, appearing completely unalarmed.

"Go back to Howling Wolf," Lame Duck ordered, wanting nothing more at the moment than to rid himself of the other warrior before he managed to reveal their hiding place to the enemy. "Tell him I will wait and watch. If this place is being guarded, then another sentry will be sent to replace this one. Perhaps when he does, the two sentries will speak together about their reasons for guarding this place."

"That may take a long time," Big Elk objected.

"It will take however long it takes," Lame Duck said sharply. "Have you a better way to determine their reasons?"

"Perhaps their reasons have nothing to do with us," Big Elk muttered. "Why do we not plan our attack?"

"And how would you do that?" Lame Duck asked sarcastically. "Their city is easily defended. One warrior could hold ours at bay."

"We could leave the city for last and attack the men in the fields," Big Elk suggested.

"The men in the fields keep their weapons nearby," Lame Duck replied. "Some of them would be sure to get away and warn the others and our losses would be heavy. We must find a way to bring all the warriors to us . . . here on the mesa where they cannot easily escape when they are surprised by our warriors." His gaze focused on the guard again. "And the way to accomplish that just might be here . . . at this abandoned city they are guarding so well."

"I must have something to tell Howling Wolf," Big Elk said. "He will expect reasons. Why do you think we need to wait here and discover why they are guarding the city?"

"Have you not figured it out yet, Big Elk? The sentry is not here to guard the city that has been abandoned. Instead, he is guarding whatever . . . or *whoever* is in the abandoned kiva."

"You think they have a prisoner there?"

"Yes. And if it is the Wolf Clan warrior who came before us, then the People of the Eagle Clan will soon gather here to see their enemy leave the land of the living."

Big Elk's dark eyes flickered. "So that is the reason we wait."

"Yes. Their attention will be focused on the Wolf Clan warrior and none of them ever suspect intruders might be among them."

"What about the Monster Men?" Big Elk inquired. "Do you think they will come, too?"

"It makes no difference. Even the Monster Men cannot stand before our might. After all, there were only two of them and we number many more than we are able to count. No. When they are gathered here to watch the death of the warrior from the Wolf Clan, even the Monster Men cannot stop us from overpowering them. And all that we see here will be ours. The hunting grounds, the fertile fields ripe with corn and beans and squash, and the entire city. Starvation will be a thing of the past and our people will prosper and grow healthy and strong."

"Yes," Big Elk said eagerly. "Then it will be as Howling Wolf has said. With many strong, healthy warriors, we will conquer other people, killing the warriors and making the women and children our own. Yes. It is a good dream. One that Standing Wolf had as well . . . before he was killed in that last battle with these people." He remained silent for a long moment, then, "I will return and give Howling Wolf your words. And he will understand the reason behind your actions."

Lame Duck watched the other warrior crawl away, carefully avoiding the seeking eyes of the sentry who stood guard over the kiva. His conversation with Big Elk had brought to mind that other battle with these people. One of the Monster Men had fought ferociously beside the warriors of the Eagle Clan then, and Lame Duck had no wish to encounter another of them, much less two.

But hopefully, that would not be necessary, for after much discussion, they had decided to leave their quarrel with the Monster Men for later. For now they would concentrate all their efforts on taking over the mesa and everything it contained.

Nampeyo was worried as he watched Brynna and her two men from across the courtyard. They had been in that same position, huddled close together, intent on their conversation, for some time.

What were they planning? he wondered. Had they found a way to free the prisoner?

Even as that thought occurred, Nampeyo quickly dismissed it. They had sense enough to know they could not fight the whole clan. But it would be devastating if they tried, because many of Nampeyo's people would surely be killed before they could slay such powerful men.

And Brynna—what about her? Would she join the fight as well? Probably, he thought, answering his own question, for had not Eric told Nampeyo that his sister was skilled with a sword and could fight with the best of men?

Nampeyo found that easy to believe, for the Viking girl had more courage than any woman he had ever known. It showed in her eyes, in the way she walked beside a man instead of behind. A woman like Brynna would never stand by and watch the man she loved die without at least making an attempt to save him.

Was this what his dream had foretold? he wondered. Did Brynna represent the golden ball that Nama had offered to her shaman? It must be true, for Brynna had brought sunshine into his life again; her presence had chased away the darkness that had enshrouded his heart since he had lost Nama.

Yes. Brynna must be that golden globe Raven had called the sun. His people would benefit greatly from her presence among them, for she had promised to teach them the secret of the written word. But would that promise be kept, now that the warrior from the Wolf Clan had arrived, intent on stealing her away from them?

Nampeyo could never allow such a thing to happen. She could not leave the clan now. Too much depended on her. Yet how could he keep her, if she had no wish to stay? Brynna claimed to love the warrior from the Wolf

Clan, and if that was true, she would never forgive them if they killed their prisoner.

"What should I do?" Nampeyo whispered. "Spirit world, you must advise me so that I may act wisely when the time comes."

Nampeyo looked over the canyon and saw an eagle soaring, wings outspread to catch the air currents.

He watched the eagle at great length but saw nothing out of the ordinary, nothing that could be interpreted as a sign from their sacred bird. Nevertheless, Nampeyo knew a great upheaval was about to occur in the lives of the Eagle Clan, knew as well that he would be unable to stop it from happening.

The sun was only an orange glow in the western sky when Eric arrived home carrying a haunch of deer meat across his shoulders, having shared the kill with those who were needful.

Shala had been anxiously waiting for his arrival, and she was obviously upset. "Eric," she cried. "Something terrible has happened!"

"If you speak of the *skraeling* warrior who raped Brynna, then I agree," he said harshly. "It is a terrible thing that he remains alive. But I understand that Nampeyo intends to remedy that soon!"

Shala stared at him in astonishment. "Eric! How can you say such a thing? Have you no pity at all in your heart?"

"Not for him," he replied grimly. "Why should I?" He tossed the deer haunch down on a large slab of rock kept in front of the cave for preparing the meat he brought home. "Look what I brought for our meal," he said, hoping to end the conversation.

"What about your sister's pain?" Shala persisted. "If

you do not care about Red Fox, at least think of Brynna. She loves him dearly. She—"

"Shala!" he interrupted harshly. "Stop it! I wish to hear no more about that man."

Heaving a frustrated sigh, she searched his expression, obviously hoping to see something that was not there. "I suppose you spoke to Brynna this way when she came to you for help."

"I certainly did my best to discourage her—if that is what you mean." He looked at her curiously. "He killed one of your own people, Shala. I heard it was To-kee. Are you not the least bit angry about that?"

"Anger has no place in this," she said shortly, her dark eyes flashing. "The man is Red Fox, Eric. He is the warrior who helped me when I was taken captive in the north lands."

"He helped you?" Eric questioned. "Shala! Red Fox was the one who captured you. Had he not done so, you would have needed no help."

"True," she admitted. "But he could do no less than take me captive, Eric. He was not alone. And he was a stranger in a strange land. Anyway, he was not the one responsible for my capture. That was Bull Elk, and he is dead, slain by my own hand."

"And because of that, you were doomed to die," Eric said.

"Yes," she agreed. "His people condemned me to death for the slaying of Bull Elk. It is the same thing that has happened here, Eric. Do you not see that? I was defending myself against Bull Elk, and I killed him. Red Fox was doing the same thing when he killed To-kee."

"I cannot believe you are speaking this way," he said harshly. "And I must say, I am displeased with you, the way you are acting."

She laughed, but it was not a happy sound. "Brynna

was displeased with me, too," she said. "For when she came to me for help, I refused her."

"And that is exactly what you should have done!"

"No," she said regretfully. "I acted without thought. Someone needs to help her free Red Fox."

"I will not help the man who raped my little sister," he said gruffly. "Now, put it out of your mind and fix my meal." He entered the cave and reached for the baby who sat playing with a ball fashioned from deer hide, hoping that would put an end to the conversation. "How are you, little one?" he asked gently, lifting the chubby little girl into his arms.

The babe's lips pulled into a smile, and he noticed for the first time how much the little girl resembled Brynna at that age.

Brynna.

Eric remembered the look in her eyes when he had refused to help her. There had been hurt, yes. But there had been something else as well. Was it betrayal? Did she really look on his refusal as a betrayal?

He tried to put the memory from him, remembering instead how she had been as child. He had played with her every moment he had to spare. Had marveled over her smooth, satiny skin, her wide blue eyes and fiery curls. Oftimes he had cuddled her against him as he did his own little daughter and breathed in the sweet baby scent of her and vowed that he would always look after her, that he would never let her down.

See how you keep your promises, an inner voice chided. *Brynna has asked nothing from you all these years. And when she finally does, she is met with a refusal.*

"Damn!" he exclaimed, and to his utter astonishment, little Juanama screwed her eyes shut tight and began to wail.

"What have you done?" Shala asked sharply, snatching the babe from him. "Why is she crying?"

"I have no idea," he said in consternation. "She just started crying."

"It was your expression," Shala muttered. "You are angry because something has happened that you have no control over, and our babe sensed that anger."

"Angry over something I have no control over?" he questioned slowly. Could it be true? he wondered. "I suppose my love for my sister *has* been controlling, Shala. But I never meant it to be. I only wanted what was best for her."

"Perhaps Brynna has sense enough to know what is best for her!" Shala snapped angrily, but it was an anger that could not be retained. "Eric," she said softly. "Do you believe you have control over your love for me? That you could end it anytime you chose?"

"No. Of course not, Shala."

"Then how can you expect Brynna to be any different? She cannot control who she loves! Do you not see that? Loving is a thing that just happens. Some people never find the love that we have together, Eric. But I think Brynna is one of the lucky ones. Will she consider herself lucky, though, if the man she loves is put to death? You know she would not. And you will lose your sister forever if such an event occurs."

Eric was afraid his wife was right. But what in hell was he supposed to do about it? Damn it! The man from the Wolf Clan was an enemy to her people. He would be betraying them if he allowed the prisoner to go free. No! He could never do a thing like that.

Could he?

* * *

The sun painted the sky with gold and red, tipping the pine trees growing on the valley floor with a bright burst of color. But the beauty of her surroundings went unnoticed by Brynna. All her thoughts were focused at the moment on devising a plan that would free the man she loved.

"There is only one man left there to guard Red Fox," she told Patrick and Lacey, who squatted on their heels beside her. "One man should be easy enough to overcome. After all . . ." She uttered an unsteady laugh, ". . . His resistance will be nothing, considering the Norsemen we have already conquered to journey to this land."

"I am sure you are right, lassie," Patrick agreed. "*If* there is still only one guard there. Which is questionable." His gaze swept across the courtyard and stopped on Nampeyo, who sat in his usual place on the short wall, stretching his crippled legs toward what little sunshine was left to them. "Have you noticed the way that shaman of theirs has been eyeing us ever since we started this conversation? There has been plenty of time for him to set more guards to watch over the prisoner."

"I am fairly certain he did just that," Lacey muttered. "I been watching him real close and a little while ago he motioned toward that man of his—Loki, I think you called him—and they talked some together for a long while. Afterwards, Loki went away . . . crossed the courtyard . . . and climbed those chiseled steps up to the mesa."

Brynna allowed her gaze to drift casually toward Nampeyo, and as their eyes met, his jerked quickly away. "Yes. He might have done exactly that," she admitted. "I certainly would if I were in his place. Or else I would move Red Fox to another place." The last was only an afterthought, but it was enough to set her heart racing. "Damn! That must not happen! Lacey! Go on the mesa to the abandoned city. If they are trying to move Red

Fox, then follow them to their destination. We must not allow them to hide Red Fox from us.''

"Consider it done, lassie," Lacey said, rising as he spoke. Then he was striding quickly away from them, soon disappearing from sight.

Brynna's gaze went to Nampeyo again. As before, he avoided her eyes. Yes, she decided—he was definitely planning something. But what?

Patrick put his hand on her forearm and squeezed it gently. "Have no fear, lassie," he said soothingly. "Between the three of us, we can free that man of yours. Neither Lacey nor myself will ever let you down. You need have no fear about that."

"I know," she said, summoning up a smile. "And I hope you know how much I appreciate that fact. Patrick . . ." Brynna paused, wondering how he would react to what she was about to say.

"Yes, lassie?" he prompted.

"Patrick, I wonder if you realize how this will affect your life . . . yours and Lacey's." When he remained silent, she continued. "If you help me with this thing, my brothers may refuse to take you back to England. You may have to spend the rest of your life here."

"You need not worry yourself on my account, lassie," Patrick said. "I knew there was that chance before I ever signed on with you. And it was a risk that I was eager to take. What need have I to return to England, anyway? There is no one waiting for me there. No parents, no brothers or sisters. No family to speak of at all."

"You have one now," Brynna said softly. "You have become as dear to me as my own brothers, Patrick. Indeed, you have been far more dependable, more faithful than my own brothers. I have come to depend on you in so many ways since our first meeting! It is hard to envision a life where you are not somewhere nearby."

For the merest instant, something flickered in the depths of his eyes, then was just as quickly gone. "Nothing would make me happier than to give my life in your service, my lady."

"You will make some lucky woman a good husband, Patrick Douglass. It is a wonder that some woman has not snatched you up before now."

"No wonder," he said gruffly. "Guess I never settled down long enough to find a wife. Had I done so, then I would likely have stayed out of trouble." He smiled widely at her. "Now, about this plan of yours . . . it just might work. Unless Nampeyo has ordered a little surprise for us." He looked thoughtfully across the canyon where Eric and Shala lived. "Have you no doubts in your mind about leaving your brothers behind?"

"No. Not even one. Red Fox means more to me than family, Patrick. I never thought it could happen, but he is the most important thing in my life. If I cannot have him, then life has no meaning for me."

"I thought that was the way of it, my lady. And I will do everything in my power to see you have him," Patrick said grimly.

"I could ask for no more from anyone," Brynna said. "Together, we will free him, or lose our lives in the attempt."

"Do not speak of dying," Patrick growled, "lest your words make it happen."

She looked at Nampeyo again. "I pray we meet with no resistance, for I would rather accomplish his rescue without meeting resistance. I would not like causing these people injury."

"I fear there is no other way, though," Patrick said grimly. "They will not allow the prisoner to be taken from them without a fight."

Brynna was to remember his words later.

* * *

They waited until the quarter moon hung high in the ebony sky. Then, with no light to guide them except that which was cast down by the glittering stars surrounding the pale slice of moon, Brynna and Patrick set out into the darkness.

As they ascended the steps leading to the mesa top, a cool breeze lifted a lock of Brynna's golden hair, blowing it across her face, and she pushed it away impatiently.

Fear and excitement hummed through her veins as her wary gaze swept the stone face of the cliff she wondered if there would only be one guard to overcome. She felt no real alarm, though, for Lacey had not returned to them. She took that to mean there would be no interference from the warriors of the Eagle Clan.

Upon reaching the mesa, Brynna insisted she take the lead, saying she was more familiar with the path leading to the abandoned city. Although Patrick allowed that, he stayed close beside her lest they be surprised by those who wished to stop them.

Brynna's wary gaze was searching as they wound their way through junipers and bushes that blocked their way.

Finding nothing to alarm them, they crossed the mesa until they reached the abandoned city. The dwellings seemed eerie in the dim light of the quarter moon. The old stone wall looked firmly rooted as though having grown with the trees, a natural part of the forest itself. Tangled vines smothered most of the rough stone, filling the cracks with organic life.

Brynna shivered, caught by a breeze skimming across the mesa. The place seemed deserted, the darkened doorways appeared to be blank eyes glaring at them, warning them to leave while they were still able.

Where was the guard? Brynna wondered.

She narrowed her eyes as a shadow shifted within a shadow, but her sharpened focus detected no further movement.

Then she saw the guard, standing beneath a tree whose twisted branches loomed over him. Brynna realized by the way the sentry held himself that the man was uneasy.

Why? she wondered. Did the darkness affect him in the same manner that it was affecting her? Did he imagine the tree had taken on a life of its own, that its branches were reaching down like gnarled tentacles for him?

Brynna hoped it was so, for a nervous guard would be eager to leave such a place behind.

She tightened her fingers around the knife that Patrick had given her, wishing she had her sword in her hand, silently cursing Nampeyo for depriving her of her weapon, while hoping she would not be called upon to use it.

Thud, thud, thud. The sound stopped Brynna cold. Someone was coming. From the sound of it, more than one person, too.

Patrick put a warning hand on her forearm and pointed toward the forest. Brynna narrowed her eyes, trying to focus them where the shadows were thickest. But try as she would, she could not penetrate the darkness . . . until suddenly, two figures separated from the shadows and approached the sentry.

The newcomers spoke to the guard, words that were indistinguishable to Brynna's ears, although she tried her best to hear.

Why had the two men come? Brynna wondered.

She had not expected them, had thought to find the guard alone, or else, backed up by at least a score of warriors.

Should they alter their plan in any way? How could they, when Lacey was hidden somewhere in that enshrouding blackness? There was no way to advise him of a change of plans.

No, she decided, there was nothing else to do except go on as they had planned.

The two newcomers chose that moment to leave, and with Patrick at her side, Brynna crept forward again, intent on silencing the guard before he was able to utter a sound that might give them away.

Chapter Thirty-Two

Red Fox sat in the darkness of the kiva, wondering about the man who now shared his prison. Although it was too dark to make out his features, his size alone told Red Fox the man was not a member of the Eagle Clan. It was more likely he was one of Brynna's men.

Did that mean that her plan to free him had gone awry? he wondered. If so, then where was Brynna?

The thought that she might have been harmed in some way caused a new stab of pain in that growing knot that had become permanently lodged in his chest.

Yip, yip, uurrooooo! Yip, yip, uurrooooo!

Recognizing the howl as Wolf's, Red Fox pushed himself to his feet, barely resisting the urge to answer the call. He must not reveal his presence to the animal because Wolf would surely come, and in doing so, would probably be slain by the warrior who stood guard.

No. He must keep silent and hope the animal would rejoin its own kind. The wolf would mourn its master for a while, but in time, Red Fox would become only a distant memory.

Feeling the urge to lash out at something, Red Fox doubled up his fist and struck the kiva wall as hard as he could.

"Wh—who is here?" a thick voice asked.

Red Fox spun on his heels and tried to penetrate the darkness with his gaze. Apparently his companion had regained his senses. "I am Red Fox," he identified himself in the Norse language. "Who are you?"

"They call me Lacey," was the reply. "I find it name enough. I suppose the devils knocked me over the head and threw me in the hole with you?"

Red Fox could hear movement and guessed his companion was searching the darkness with his hands, intent on finding out more about his circumstances. "I have never before heard a kiva referred to as a hole," Red Fox replied. "But yes. You are here with me. I have no knowledge, though, of how you came to lose your senses."

Shuffle, scrape, shuffle. Shuffle, scrape, shuffle. The sound was moving away from Red Fox, and he imagined the man called Lacey holding his hand against the earthen wall as he traversed the circle. "Lost my senses?" Lacey grunted. "Now, that's a funny way to look at it. I guess you are right, though. An unconscious man does not retain his senses." Thud! "Damn it," Lacey cursed. "There must be a hole in the floor. It nearly unbalanced me when my foot went in."

"It is the sipapu," Red Fox explained.

"A sipa—what?"

"A sipapu. It represents the hole that leads to the third world. This was once a holy place, used by the shaman and elders of the Eagle Clan."

"You can tell me more about that third world if we

manage to get out of this mess," Lacey grunted, his voice sounding nearer all the time as he continued around the circle.

Red Fox gritted his teeth fighting for control. He had no interest in teaching this man about their religion. "Were you alone up there?" he asked, trying to keep the urgency from his voice.

"No man could have been more alone," Lacey said wryly. "Or so I thought. Somebody else had to be there to give me that knock on the head."

"You speak too many words without saying anything," Red Fox declared harshly, and wondered why that should cause the other man to laugh. "I am seeking news of Brynna. What has happened to her?"

"Dunno," came the reply. "But she would laugh her head off if she heard you say that. The lassie has often accused me of being too scarce with my words."

"Perhaps the blow to your head loosened your tongue," Red Fox growled. "But you have yet to say what I wish to hear."

"The lass was fine the last time I saw her," Lacey said gravely. "But apparently Nampeyo got wind of what she was about and had someone waiting for me when I showed up here." He laughed abruptly, but it was not a pleasant sound. "Guess I should have been watching closer. Still hard to figure how they surprised me like that."

"A warrior can move as silently as a snake," Red Fox replied.

"And strike as swiftly, too," Lacey growled. "I fear the lassie will come soon and walk into a trap."

"Brynna is coming alone?"

"Patrick will be with her."

"But not her brothers."

"You've got it right, mate. Not her brothers."

"She must be warned, Lacey," Red Fox said. "Perhaps

if you stand on my shoulders, you could shove the lid out of the way."

"We could try," Lacey replied.

Squatting on his heels, Red Fox waited for the other man to straddle his neck, then, using the wall for support, the warrior slowly slid up the wall. When he had extended himself to his full height, he waited for Lacey to stand on his shoulders.

Moments later, while fighting to balance himself, he heard the sound of wood scraping against wood. Then a sliver of pale light filtered into the kiva.

They were going to do it! Yes! A moment more and there would be enough room for Lacey to pull himself out of this dark prison and he would—

A loud cry sounded, then Lacey seemed to lose his balance and plunge to the earthen floor, striking Red Fox heavily as he went.

Thud! Scrape! The sound of Lacey's body striking the floor blended with that of wood grating against wood. Then the sliver of light was gone, leaving them in total darkness again.

Red Fox was dazed, and his knees refused to hold him. He slumped to the earthen floor beside Lacey. He wondered bleakly if the other man was badly injured, knew he should check to see, but somehow he could not bring himself to move again.

They had been so near their goal, so near to regaining the freedom they sought. But it had all been in vain. Now they were back where they had started, imprisoned in a world without light.

And without hope.

Eric tossed and turned, unable to fall asleep, even though he had courted it for hours.

Why did he have this terrible sense of foreboding? he wondered. He had already regretted his earlier decision, had decided that he owed it to Brynna to speak to Nampeyo. And he would. At first light. He would go to the cliff city and seek out the shaman. Hopefully, between them they could find a way—other than death—that would satisfy the people of the Eagle Clan.

Perhaps, Eric considered, the widow of To-kee might be comforted if she had his assurance that her future would be provided for.

Yes. Eric would see to her future himself. He would make himself the provider for To-kee's widow. He doubted though that she would judge that compensation. Her husband had been taken from her and she would not easily be placated. Eric could not blame her either. Nothing could compensate him for the loss of Shala.

Nothing.

Even so, Brynna would know that he had tried his best to save her warrior.

Feeling better at having made that decision, Eric expelled a long sigh, turned over and snuggled closer against the warmth of his wife. His tense muscles slowly relaxed and he felt himself sinking into the arms of Morpheus. In that moment before he fell asleep, he heard a voice hailing him from outside.

"Eric! Wake up, Eric!"

Recognizing the voice of his brother, Eric quickly rolled off the sleeping mat and snatched up his trousers, sliding his right foot into one leg. He had acted automatically, for he had no doubt in his mind that he would need his clothing. There had to be trouble afoot, or Garrick would not have used that tone of voice.

"Eric?" Shala asked sleepily. "What is wrong?"

"Go back to sleep," he said gently. "It is only Garrick who has come to see me."

Striding across the cave, he pushed aside the deer hide
that protected his small family from the cold night air
and stepped outside. ''What is wrong, Garrick!'' he asked
quickly, taking the two extra steps needed to stand beside
his brother, who was looking across the canyon at the
cliff city. ''Is it the Wolf Clan warrior? Surely Nampeyo
is not bent on carrying out the prisoner's sentence this
late at night?''

Even as he asked the question, Eric realized that Nampeyo would probably do exactly that. For if the deed were
already accomplished, if the sentence imposed on the
prisoner had already been carried out, there would be
nothing anyone could do about it. Not even the Vikings,
with their combined strengths. For it was a fact that
nobody could raise the dead.

''I fear so,'' Garrick said. ''Most of the warriors have
left the city. And they did it very quietly ... I doubt
they told any of the women what they were about. What
troubles me even more is that Brynna and her men are
nowhere to be found.''

''Brynna, gone?'' Eric exclaimed. ''Thor's teeth! If
Nampeyo or any others dare to lay a hand on her, then
I will see them—''

''Nampeyo would never hurt Brynna.'' Shala's voice
startled them both, spinning them around to face her. She
stood just outside the entrance, watching the two of them
anxiously.

''How can you know that?'' Eric asked.

''A woman knows these things,'' she said calmly.

''Even so, if all the warriors have left the city without
telling anyone where they were going, it is because they
know we would not approve. Since Brynna and her men
are gone too, it is very likely they are having a confrontation ... or soon will.'' He reached around Shala and

picked up his sword that was leaning against the cavern wall. "Go back inside, Shala," he said grimly. "Stay there with our daughter until I return."

"What are you going to do?"

"I am going to help my sister."

Silently, Shala entered the cavern.

Eric felt surprised that she had obeyed him without first uttering some kind of objection, yet at the same time he was relieved, knowing he had no time to waste arguing with her.

He followed his brother up the steps carved into the cliff, and when they reached the mesa, a figure stepped from the shadows, armed with a spear. It was Nama.

"What are you doing here?" Garrick growled. "I told you to stay home."

"I go with my husband," she said calmly.

"No! Obey me, woman. Return to the city and stay there with your mother. I have no time to worry about you."

"I go with my husband," she repeated. "This matter is of great concern to me."

"And me," said a voice near the cliff.

Eric spun around to see Shala standing near the edge of the cliff and he could tell by the bulge on her back that she had donned the backpack he had designed for their daughter. "Have you lost your senses, woman?" he roared. "Go home!"

"No."

"You cannot mean to take our daughter into battle!" he snarled. "I will not allow it."

"There will be no battle," she replied.

"You cannot stop it!"

"I am going, Eric. You are wasting time that could be put to better use."

"Thor's teeth!" he exclaimed. "You are the most stubborn woman I have ever known in my life! How can you even think of taking our babe into danger?"

"There will be no danger with her there," she said calmly. "It is the only way. We cannot fight so many warriors and hope to win. Our only chance is to stand together and show them our determination to save the enemy warrior."

"It is crazy enough that it just might work," Garrick said slowly. "You know how they are about children, Eric. Seeing Shala and her baby there might be enough to stop the fight. If we could speak together calmly, we just might find a way to work things out."

"Come along then," Eric said grimly. "Give me the babe, Shala. I have more strength so I will carry her until we are near the abandoned city. I have a feeling that we might already be too late."

It was a feeling that the others seemed to share, and each one prayed in their own way that they would reach the abandoned city in time to stop the battle that was about to erupt.

Chapter Thirty-Three

Lame Duck's mouth was dry and his legs were becoming numb from lack of movement. He was considering working his way back to where the other warriors were waiting to quench his thirst when a soft, slithering sound alerted him to another presence.

"Lame Duck," Big Elk whispered hoarsely, "Howling Wolf sent me with a message."

Lame Duck stifled a groan of exasperation. The other warrior's voice sounded unnaturally loud in the stillness that surrounded them. How could the sentry standing guard over the kiva continue to remain ignorant of their presence?

"Give me the message," Lame Duck said shortly. "Then return to the others, lest your noise alert the Eagle Clan warrior."

Having been firmly reprimanded, Big Elk lowered his voice slightly. "Soon it will not matter how loud we speak," he said cryptically, then went on to explain. "Only moments ago, Small Wind reported a large group of warriors that appeared to be coming this way. Howling Wolf said you must report to him the moment they leave the shelter of the forest."

Coming here? Why would they come under cover of darkness? Could they have somehow discovered the presence of their enemies? He was unaware he had voiced the thought aloud until Big Elk spoke.

"Small Wind said the Eagle Clan warriors remain unaware of our presence among them."

"How can he know that?"

"He said he watched them closely. They made no attempt at silence. If they knew we were anywhere around, they would approach stealthily, hoping to take us unawares."

Lame Duck knew he was right, and yet he was bothered by the news of the approaching enemy. "Is it Howling Wolf's intention to wage a battle this night?"

"Yes."

"Some of our warriors may lose their lives," Lame Duck said.

"Yes," Big Elk agreed uneasily.

The silence loomed between them like a heavy mist because both knew that if they should lose their lives during the night, they could be doomed forever. Without Father Sun to light their way, their souls might become lost in the eternal void that lay between the land of the living and the Great Beyond.

Expelling a shuddering sigh, Lame Duck muttered, "You have delivered your message, Big Elk. Return now to Howling Wolf."

Although Lame Duck's ears heard the slithering sounds Big Elk made as he departed, his attention was focused on the shadowy figure standing near the abandoned kiva. If they had been overheard, there would surely have been some kind of change in the guard's stance. But there was none, nothing to indicate the sentry knew he was being watched.

Good. Lame Duck told himself. *The guard remains unaware of our presence.* Yes. It was good. As long as the guard remained ignorant of his enemies, his fellow warriors would have no reason to seek safety in the cliff city.

A smile tugged at the corners of Lame Duck's mouth. The long wait was almost over now. As soon as the men of the Eagle Clan were in the clearing, he would alert his companions and they would act quickly and surround their enemies. Then the outcome would be victory. Victory for the desert clan, for the enemy, having been surprised in the clearing, would be dealt with quickly. And these lands and everything that remained on them would belong to the People of the desert clan.

Crack! The sound startled them, freezing Brynna into immobility, and halting Patrick's progress toward the sentry guarding the kiva.

Brynna's stomach clenched tight and her heart fluttered like the wings of a trapped butterfly as her searching gaze swept around the clearing, pausing on the shadowy figure that limped from the cover of the thick growth of junipers.

Nampeyo!

"Go back, woman!" he said, his voice revealing no emotion whatsoever. "Take your man with you and return to the cliff city, for I will not allow you to free the warrior from the Wolf Clan."

"It is you who should go back, Nampeyo!" Brynna said angrily. "You can do nothing here. You certainly cannot stop us."

"Perhaps I cannot," Nampeyo replied evenly. "But my warriors can."

The shaman had barely finished speaking when several shadowy figures separated from the deeper shadows beneath the heavily wooded juniper thicket. It was then that Brynna realized he was not alone.

Nevertheless, she refused to be intimidated. Although there were only two of them in the clearing, she felt certain Lacey was somewhere nearby and he could be counted on for help if Nampeyo forced the issue.

"I count five warriors, Nampeyo," she said sternly, hoping to unnerve him. "It will take more than that to overcome my men."

"I see only one man," Nampeyo replied. "Do you have others?"

"You know I do," she said, realizing her voice held a trace of sarcasm. "But Lacey will not reveal his presence unless he deems it necessary. And, Nampeyo . . ." She made her words threatening. "You may not like the way he chooses to reveal himself."

"Your man will not be coming to your aid," Nampeyo spoke in an odd, yet gentle tone.

"How can you know that?" she asked sharply.

"He was taken captive long before Father Sun sought his rest for the night." He allowed her a moment to think about what he had said, then, "Lay down your weapons and no harm will come to you. Return to the city and we will forget this ever happened."

Forget it ever happened? Leave Red Fox confined in the kiva, waiting for the end? Abandon her love to such a fate?

Never!

Brynna would rather die where she stood.

It was impossible to steady her erratic pulse, but surprisingly, her voice remained calm, unwavering when she spoke again. "We came here to free Red Fox, Nampeyo. And I refuse to leave without him."

The tension between them increased with frightening intensity. Yet when he spoke again, his voice was almost sympathetic. "I cannot allow you to free him, Brynna. Surely you must see that."

"You cannot stop us!" she snapped, feeling like a volcano on the verge of erupting.

"I think we can." A wave of his hand brought more warriors from the darkness and Brynna realized that every warrior in the clan must have come to stop them. "You cannot win a battle with us," Nampeyo said.

"You will have to kill us where we stand," Brynna said, clutching her knife with fingers that had suddenly grown numb. "There is no other way, for we are determined not to leave without Red Fox."

"Then you will die, Brynna," he said, and she imagined she heard a deep sadness in his voice. "Surely you see how futile such an act would be. Go back to the cliff city while there is still time. Forget you ever met the Wolf Clan warrior."

"No. I will not."

"Then prepare to die."

A thrill of frightened anticipation touched Brynna's spine. "Patrick," she cried. "To my back!"

Brynna need not have spoken, for the words had barely been uttered when she felt Patrick's back against her own. They spread their legs, bracing themselves to face the attack that would end many lives.

Nampeyo raised his hand, readying himself to give the signal that would send his warriors racing toward them. Before he could give the signal, however, a powerful voice boomed out.

"Hold!"

Hope was born anew as Brynna, and every man there, turned to look at the speaker. But even before she saw him, she knew it was her brother Eric.

Her heart gave a joyful leap as Brynna realized that despite everything he had said before, her brother had relented, for it was obvious he was there to help her.

Another figure stepped from the shadows, looming as large as Patrick himself.

Garrick.

His appearance came as no surprise to Brynna.

She knew her brothers well. They were so very much alike. If Eric had relented, then it followed that Garrick would do so, as well.

Since Brynna's attention wavered between the warriors of the Eagle Clan and her brothers, she had no knowledge of the two women until Nampeyo spoke again.

"Shala! Have you lost your senses, woman?" Nampeyo demanded. "You place your babe in grave danger by bringing her here."

The babe? Brynna thought. Shala had actually brought her baby with her?

"What danger?" Shala demanded, striding forward almost casually. "Do the brave warriors of my clan make war on babies now?"

"This does not concern the babe," Nampeyo said harshly. "Our quarrel is with Red Fox."

"His quarrel is my quarrel," Brynna said shortly.

"And the lady Brynna's quarrel is mine!" roared Patrick, swinging his sword in a huge circle.

Whoosh, whoosh, whoosh, the blade sounded, as it went around and around. If it was Patrick's plan to intimidate the warriors, then he certainly accomplished that. They drew back, muttering uneasily among themselves as the blade sliced cleanly through the air.

That backward movement most likely saved many lives, for it was at that moment that many arrows were loosed toward the warriors. Although some of the deadly missiles found their mark, many others missed and fell harmlessly to the ground.

"Shala! See to the babe!" Eric roared, obviously realizing they were being attacked from a source other than her own people.

"Aaiiiiieee!"

At the sound of the first war cry, Brynna was galvanized into action. She made a wild dash toward Shala and the babe, lashing out at any man who got in her way, her knife blade connecting with flesh in several instances.

"Run, Shala, run!" Brynna screamed, striking out at a man who seemed to rise from the ground ahead of her.

"Uunngghhh!" he grunted, leaping away from the reach of her blade.

"Take the babe and run, Shala!" Brynna shouted. "Hurry!"

"Look to yourself!" Shala cried. "Free your man while you can!"

Brynna saw another man racing toward her and faltered momentarily, wondering if he was friend or foe. But only for a moment. The pale moonlight silhouetted the blade of the knife he lifted, then brought down swiftly.

Quickly, Brynna spun out of his reach. The hapless warrior, deprived of his victim, was momentarily unbalanced. She used that moment to lash out, sending her own blade deep into the flesh of his upper back.

Without a word, his knees buckled and he fell to the ground, lying there in a crumpled heap.

Praying to God that Shala would reach safety with her babe, Brynna leapt toward the unguarded kiva and curled her fingers under the edge of the slab of wood that covered the opening.

Scrape, slide, scrape . . .

The sound of wood grating against the roof was covered

by other sounds . . . those of men fighting, of fists thudding against flesh, and the anguished cry of those who had been mortally wounded.

Brynna tried to ignore those sounds, tired hard to concentrate instead on moving the opening to Red Fox's prison.

She gave a grunt of exertion as she expended every ounce of strength she possessed, then the cover moved to disclose the yawning mouth of the kiva.

"Red Fox," she cried, holding raw emotion in check as she snatched at the wooden ladder laying within easy reach. "Are you down there, Red Fox?"

"I am here," came the reply. "What is happening up there, Brynna?"

Instead of trying to explain, she concentrated on dropping the ladder into the kiva. "Hurry," she said urgently. "We must leave while we can."

The words had barely left her mouth when Red Fox's head appeared. He leapt from the ladder and embraced her. Despite her fears for their safety, she felt a burning joy at being held in his arms again.

"*Aaaiiieee!*" came another cry.

Possibly it was that cry that made Red Fox release her. Or it may have been Lacey's voice coming from behind them.

"Look to yourselves," he growled. "All hell is busting loose around us."

Suddenly, Patrick was there beside them. "Go to the horses, Brynna!" he commanded swiftly. "Take your man and ride away from here while you are able."

"I cannot leave, Patrick!" Brynna said quickly. "I would not abandon the rest of you."

"We can take care of ourselves," Patrick replied harshly. "Hurry, lass. Go while you are able."

"No! I cannot—"

"Take her!" Patrick roared, shoving her at Red Fox. "Get her out of here! The horses are corralled behind the abandoned city. Take them and go!"

Red Fox needed no further urging. He scooped Brynna into his arms and hurried away from the fighting.

"Put me down," she commanded. "I cannot leave the others!"

"Do not fight me now, Brynna," he said harshly. "I will not be denied this. You must be sent to safety."

"I will not fight you," she said calmly. "But we can make better time if you are not encumbered by my weight."

Realizing that she was no longer fighting him, he set her own feet and they raced to the corral. Even from there, they could hear the sound of battle continuing.

Although every fiber of Brynna's being urged her to return, to stand beside her brothers and fight, she realized that if she did so, then Red Fox would return with her. And when the fighting was over, when they had won the battle, as they surely would, then her love would again be imprisoned, his life forfeit.

No! Patrick was right. She must leave with Red Fox, and she must do it now!

Shadow nickered softly when he recognized his mistress. Taking a bridle from a nearby pole, Brynna slipped it over the stallion's head and fastened the straps.

Then she turned to face Red Fox. "Would it do any good if I asked you to go without me?"

"No. I will not rest until I know you are safe."

"I thought as much," she said. "Are you ready to leave?"

His dark gaze roved over her features as though he were trying to memorize them. Brynna felt blood coursing through her veins like an awakened river. Then, suddenly, he pulled her roughly, almost violently, to him. His mouth covered hers hungrily, his lips hard and searching. She returned his kiss with reckless abandon, even while her mind told her they must not delay their escape.

Brynna felt a sense of extreme loss when he suddenly broke the kiss. Then, while she was still trying to regain her senses, he lifted her to the stallion's back and put the reins in her hand.

She was waiting for him to mount behind her when a loud smacking sound broke the silence. Instantly, Shadow's muscles bunched and he leapt forward, racing away into the darkness as though suspecting the hounds of hell might be chasing him.

Brynna, knowing she would be unable to stop the animal's panic-stricken flight through the darkness, turned her head to search for Red Fox, who was surely following on another mount.

But he was not. Instead, he remained motionless, obviously watching her leave.

Why? she wondered. There were other horses remaining. Red Fox was horseman enough to ride any one of them. Why then did he not do so?

The answer came swiftly.

He had never intended to leave with her. She should have known. A man like Red Fox could never run away and leave others to fight his battle.

And she would never be able to stop Shadow's fear-ridden flight in time to be of any use to them. That was a fact that Red Fox had obviously been counting on.

Damn him! If she didn't love him so much, she would hate him for what he had done.

Chapter Thirty-Four

Brynna fought for control as Shadow raced headlong cross the mesa, frightened not only by the anguished ries of the mortally wounded, but by the coppery scent f blood as well.

Red Fox, Red Fox, Red Fox. The blood pulsing wildly hrough her veins seemed to pound out his name.

Oh, God! she cried inwardly. Why did he go back? Vhy?

Her eyes welled with tears and she blinked furiously t them, knowing that she dared not allow herself that veakness. She must regain control of her mount, must eturn to the site of the battle!

Tree branches lashed at her, scraping the flesh of her rms and face, but she ignored them, compressing her nouth hard and pulling steadily on Shadow's reins, trying o force the animal to stop.

Brynna felt the stallion tiring, his gait beginning to low, until finally, he stopped and shuddered, his head rooping low.

"Oh, Shadow," she whispered, leaning over to run he hand over the perspiring animal. "Why did you carry u so far away?"

Brynna realized she dared not ride the stallion in hi condition. Yet she must return to the abandoned city.

Sliding from her mount's back, she left him standin there and ran back the way she'd come. She would no allow herself to think what she would find when sh arrived.

It was the half-light before dawn when she reached th abandoned city again. At the edge of the clearing sh paused to catch her breath, taking in the bloody scene.

Her gaze skittered among the bodies that littered th ground, searching for one familiar face among them.

"Brynna!"

She looked up to see Patrick striding toward her.

"Is it over then?" she asked shakily.

"Yes. It is over."

"And ..." She swallowed hard, fearing to ask th question, yet knowing that she must know. ". . . Red Fox Is he—"

"He lives," Patrick said, his gaze sympathetic. "Bu Nampeyo insists on taking him prisoner again. He sai nothing Red Fox did here changes the fact that he kille a member of their clan."

She had expected as much. "Where is Red Fox?" sh asked quickly.

"There!" He pointed to a small group of people.

Brynna recognized Red Fox, held captive by two Eagl Clan warriors, and circled by Nampeyo, Eric, Shala— who still carried the babe—Garrick, Nama, and Lacey And they all seemed to be involved in an argument o some kind.

Striding toward them, determined to gain Red Fox' freedom some way or another, Brynna passed severa enemy warriors who sat on the ground, bound hand and foot. They seemed to be quarreling among themselves.

"We had no chance against them, Lame Duck!" one of them told the warrior next to him. "You said they had only a few young warriors! That most of them were too old to fight. I saw no old men. Only the young and strong. And the Monster Men! You never said there would be so many of them! We had no chance at all!"

"Do not be so quick to place the blame for our defeat," the man called Lame Duck snarled. "It appeared their men were old! You saw the old man we killed! If there were younger men available, then why was that man used for a guard?"

Brynna paused, turning to look at the two men. They had killed a guard? An old man? When?

Remembering that Red Fox had spoken of the strength of the young guard he had killed, she felt a sudden, burning need to question them.

"What is it, Brynna?" Patrick asked from beside her.

"Those men . . . I must question them."

Although he looked at her curiously, he asked no questions. Instead, he waited quietly beside her, posing a threat to the warriors if they had a mind to refuse her.

"You!" She pointed to Lame Duck. "You said you killed one of the Eagle Clan guards. Where?"

He ignored her, clamping his lips tightly together, his expression unyielding.

"Patrick," she said, having no compunction about using him to intimidate the enemy warrior. "He refuses to answer me."

Leaning over, Patrick grabbed Lame Duck's hair and forced his head back. His very stance was threat enough, without the dangerous glitter in his eyes.

Although Lame Duck's expression remained unruffled, he gave a short laugh. "I have no need to keep silent," he said calmly. "My life is already forfeited for the enemy warriors I have slain this night. I cannot lose it again for killing one old guard."

"When did you slay him?" she asked harshly.

"Two nights past. The night the warrior from the Wolf Clan killed one of us."

Hardly daring to believe what she was hearing, Brynna asked. "What did you do with the guard?"

"We covered him with rocks so that none would be aware of his death before we were ready to attack."

Her eyes shone with triumph as Brynna hurried over to Nampeyo and related what the enemy warrior had told her. The man was brought before the shaman and made to repeat his story.

For a long moment afterward, there was silence, then Nampeyo spoke. "Even though you had no hand in slaying To-kee, you would have done so without a second thought."

Red Fox remained silent, his eyes locked with Brynna's as they waited for the shaman to decide his fate.

"I have no wish to allow you freedom," Nampeyo said finally. "But it seems I have no choice if I am to retain a good relationship with the Vikings. For that reason alone you may go."

"You are doing the right thing," Eric assured the shaman. "Brynna would never forgive any of us if anything happened to the Wolf Clan warrior."

"I know," Nampeyo replied. "But I could not allow that to sway my decision." He looked at the two men holding Red Fox captive. "Release him," he said. "Allow him to leave the mesa in peace."

They did so, although reluctantly.

Instantly Brynna flew at Red Fox, who opened his arms to welcome her into his embrace. Unmindful of the onlookers, Brynna raised herself on tiptoe and covered his lips with her own in a long, passionate kiss. When it was over, she turned to face her brothers.

"I take it you are going with him," Eric said gently.

"You take it right," she said, her eyes meeting his. She felt only a slight regret at leaving her brothers behind, feeling sure their paths would cross at some time in the future. "I cannot envision life without Red Fox. I imagine it is the same with you and Shala."

"Yes. It is," Eric agreed.

There was deep regret in her brothers' eyes as they watched their sister leave the mesa. But they were not the only ones who regretted her departure, she knew, for she had sensed that same regret in Nampeyo's eyes . . . and something else. There had been sadness there as well.

Brynna walked away without a twinge of regret that day. Nor was she plagued by regret later, as the days passed and they continued their northward journey.

Prairies gave way to mountains, then became prairies, time and time again. Until one day, when the sky was a cloudless blue, they reached the top of a mountain and looked down on a high, sheltered valley that was lush with verdant growth.

A ribbon of silver wound through the middle of the valley and Brynna realized it was a river. She turned to Red Fox then and saw from his expression that this was the place they would call home.

An errant sunbeam found its way through the smoke-hole of the lodge and played across Brynna's eyelids, waking her from a pleasant sleep. She snuggled closer to Red Fox, resting her cheek against his shoulder, thinking of how much she loved him, and how close she had come to losing him that night on the mesa.

Although it had been over a month since the battle had

occurred, the events of that night were burned into her memory. She had come so close to losing her love . . . so damn close.

"Brynna, are you awake?"

"*Mmmm-hummm,*" she murmured.

She felt his hand raking through the masses of tangled hair, then he moved her so that she lay facing him.

Sliding her arms around his neck, Brynna reveled in the feel of his hands exploring the hollows of her back. They lay there for a moment, each drawing pleasure from the feel of the other.

Then, suddenly, she felt his body stirring to life against her own and she felt delighted that even though they had made passionate love the night before, he could want her again this morning.

"I suppose we should get up," he said wryly.

"Yes. We really should," she whispered huskily, stretching until she could reach his mouth.

"I really need to hunt today."

"I know," she muttered hoarsely, her lips moving softly against his.

"You know you are detaining me," he groaned.

"Yes. I know."

"You also know there is no fresh meat for our evening meal," he continued, his teeth nipping softly at her ear-lobe.

"Yes. I know," she said again.

"And you do not care?" he groaned, his arms tightening around her.

"What do you think?" she asked huskily, drawing back slightly to examine his features. His face was flushed and his breathing had become ragged, but the pained expression in his eyes was somehow encouraging.

Her gaze focused hungrily on his mouth again and she

pressed her soft lips against his, then deliberately hardened the kiss, feeling an immediate reaction in his lower body.

Becoming even bolder, the tip of her tongue streaked out, tracing the outline of his mouth, then dipping quickly inside.

It was obviously more than Red Fox could take, for he pressed hot, feverish kisses all over her face.

Eagerly, she tried to capture his mouth again, but he would not allow it. Instead, he continued to evade her lips, kissing her ears, her neck, her nose, and her eyelids.

His teeth fastened on her earlobe again, and she could see that he was bent on tormenting her just as she had tormented him.

"Stop it," she breathed, trying again to capture his lips.

But again he eluded her, sliding lower on the sleeping mat and fastening his mouth over one rosy nipple. He began to lave it with his tongue while his calloused fingers worked their magic on the other nipple.

Brynna's pulses were going wild, her breath coming in harsh gasps. She wanted him now, wanted him desperately. But he was not ready to accommodate her yet. He continued to lave her nipple with his tongue while his other hand slid slowly down her body, searing her with its heat, as his mouth continued to tease her, to torment.

Suddenly his hand stopped and she realized he had reached the center of her desire. Her breath halted, waiting . . . waiting . . .

One finger suddenly plunged into her moistness, drawing a gasp of pleasure from her. A moment later the finger was joined by another, and together, they stroked and probed the hotness between her legs, igniting a fire, stoking it into flames that burned higher and higher, making her a quivering mass that pleaded for relief.

Unable to control herself, her hips began to undulate, moving suggestively as the ache in her body grew and grew, becoming almost unbearable.

"Now, Red Fox," she urged. "Take me now!"

Immediately, Red Fox slid up her body and spread himself over her. His maleness probed for entrance and found no resistance, for she was more than ready to receive him.

Unable to help herself, Brynna writhed beneath him, her finger clutching him tightly, urging him onward as he plunged deeper and deeper, faster and faster.

She moaned loudly, surrendering completely to the ecstasy he was creating, urging him ever onward. And as the tension mounted, driving her into a complete frenzy, she cried out.

Then the final explosion came. She heard a voice wailing as her emotions splintered her into a thousand pieces and scattered them throughout the universe. One part of her mind knew that it was her own voice she heard screaming, but the rest of her mind could not reason. It could only feel the rhapsody as she gained her release in a convulsive climax.

They lay there together then, each replete in the aftermath of their love. Finally, Red Fox released her and rolled away, reaching for his buckskin trousers.

"Are you still intent on your hunt?" she asked wryly.

He sighed deeply and smoothed her hair back from her face. "I would like nothing better than to lay here and hold you in my arms, little one. But I must not give in to such laziness."

"Why?" she pouted.

"Because the long cold season is not far away and we have yet to put aside enough food to last us until the season of new spring grass," he replied.

Regretfully, Brynna watched him don his trousers.

"Would you allow me to come, too?" she asked, reaching for her own garments.

"If you wish." He gave her a long look. "Are you worried about being left alone, Brynna?"

"No," she denied. "But I so very nearly lost you, Red Fox. I will never forget how I felt when I thought you were dead." Her eyes misted over.

"Stop that," he said gently, taking her face in his hands and looking deep into her eyes. "The past is done with. We are together now. And we shall never be parted again."

"Promise me?" she asked.

"You have my promise," he whispered, kissing her passionately. "I worry about losing you, too. That time was bad for both of us. But it will never happen again. No one will find this high mountain valley of ours."

"You are sure?"

"I am sure," he said. "We are safe enough here. And so will our children be."

"And our children's children," she said.

"And their children," he went on.

She laughed gaily. "Perhaps one day we might return to the mesa and see my brothers again."

He smiled at her. "If it is your wish, then we shall certainly do so."

She smiled softly up at him, silently thanking God for allowing her to find this man. She had made a good choice in her husband. She reached out and took his hand. And together they left the lodge and went out into their high mountain valley.